BEGUILING BIRTHRIGHT

Book Six of The Extraordinaries

MELISSA MCSHANE

Night Harbor Publishing

Night Harbor Publishing

www.nightharborpublishing.com

Cover design by 100 Covers https://100covers.com

For Sherwood,
with profound thanks

CONTENTS

CHAPTER 1

IN WHICH JENNET DEFIES
HER DESTINY, WITH
PREDICTABLE RESULTS

A damp, drizzling haze blanketed the town of Soissons, bringing with it a chill that seeped with the wet into everything Jennet wore. It had been an unusually rainy spring, according to the talkative shop owner whose wares she had browsed less than an hour ago, rainy and cold and grey as the mists that rose off the Aisne River. Thus far, June, while warmer, was shaping up to be just as wet, and the shopkeeper had dire predictions for the crops. Jennet had not experienced a French spring before, but she had not seen the sun for three days and could not argue with the shopkeeper's assertion.

She trudged along the road, avoiding puddles; her boots were new, and she intended to keep them intact for as long as possible. Contemplating the leather, she could not help comparing them to the terrible footwear provided by the Army at the beginning of the campaigns in Spain and Portugal. Those had practically fallen apart before she had taken ten steps on Portuguese soil, and for months she had tied the soles and uppers to her feet with string for what little protection that had given.

Now that the war was almost over and it no longer mattered, the Army had come through with new uniforms and new boots. As the new boots were little better quality than the first, Jennet had dipped into her substantial savings to purchase the ones she now wore and did not regret the expense. They were heavy and kept most of the rain out. The uniform jacket, too, was sturdy and warm and handsome, and her new trousers were no longer more patch than fabric. Now she looked like a soldier, and not like a scarecrow.

Aside from a scrawny brindled dog that pawed listlessly through a heap of refuse across the way, she was the only living thing on the street. She felt as if she might be the only living thing in Soissons, with its tall brick or stone houses made dreary by the rain and gloom. At just after four o'clock in the afternoon, as her precious silver pocket watch told her was the time, the sky was dark enough to pass for twilight, but no lamps nor candles burned in the windows. And yet it did not resemble the many, many Spanish villages she had seen destroyed by French troops, the ones where houses had been turned to so much rubble and beautiful churches gutted.

Ahead, the cathedral of Soissons stretched its towers heavenward, its warm yellow stone a bright contrast to its grey surroundings. Jennet turned her steps in that direction. Though religion meant little to her, the reassuringly solid edifices raised in its name drew her to marvel at their beauty. She knew many of them had been built to the glory of Man, not of God, but that did not diminish their appeal.

Shouting, and the screams of high-pitched voices, stopped her in the middle of the road, and moments later a pack of children raced past, crossing the street in front of her and disappearing down a narrow street to her left. She watched them go, idly remembering running with her brothers and the MacPherson children who lived in the house next to theirs when she was young. Then she registered the real fear in the voice of the child at the head of the pack, the sharp excitement of the other voices, and, curious, she crossed to the head of the street.

The narrow passage was a blind alley, strewn with refuse and terminating in a brick wall. The pack had its prey cornered. A boy, smaller than the others, had come up against the wall and was scrabbling at it, trying to climb. He slipped and slid back to sprawl at its base. The other children, seven in all, stood in a half-circle, blocking the boy's exit. Jennet watched the boy stand and put his back to the wall. His torn clothes trembled with his heaving breaths, and even at a distance Jennet could see his hands shake.

The pack shifted, but did not pounce. The boy's visible terror shook Jennet, though she was no Discerner, capable of feeling the emotions of another as if they were her own. She did not need to feel his fear to recognize a child in despair, nor feel the anticipatory glee of the pack at running their prey to ground to know the boy was in danger.

Jennet assessed the situation. This was no game; the pack intended to beat the boy and do it in the most humiliating way possible. She might shout, or find a stick and administer a beating herself, but she was not a large person and that might simply turn those other children's anger on her—and some of those "children" were nearly adult sized. She might throw rocks, or make the pack believe she was one of many, but deception only worked so long as one could back it up with convincing force.

But Jennet had another option.

The children were all grimy, not just the one they pursued; they had untidy hair and clothes grey with long wear. Beneath the surface, on a level only Jennet could perceive when she exerted herself, they were also each a tangle of feeling, something she was aware of the way she might follow the track of an ant across her sleeve. She noted excitement and malice and even fear, which told Jennet the prey was in greater danger than she had at first imagined. It was the kind of fear that accompanies the knowledge one intends to do evil.

The pack shifted again, two of its members stepping forward. Their prey cringed back, foolishly pleading with them. Jennet knew enough of bullies to know they thrived on their prey's fear. On the other hand, their joy in tormenting the boy would be their downfall. Anger and excitement, malice and fear—those were things Jennet could work with.

She had never tried to explain to another how her talent worked; why explain a thing that could get her killed if its existence were known? She had never even tried to explain it to herself, ferreting out the mechanism by which she Coerced others by altering their emotions. She knew only that in becoming aware of what a person felt, she could manipulate that tangle of feeling into whatever shape she chose, and each shape corresponded to some new emotion. It was not a matter of experiencing another's emotions; she simply knew in her bones the truth of what she did.

Anger was but a short step to passion, and passion carefully tended and shaped turned into happiness, and happiness could be made to ebb into contentment. Turned outward on another, it became kindness. Jennet made her targets' emotions flow smoothly and so rapidly she was barely aware of the intervening stages. She knew they were not conscious of

3

being altered at all. Why no one ever realized they were being Coerced, she did not know, but in all her years of experience using her talent, she had come to learn that when it came to their emotions, people were capable of justifying almost anything into an answer that made sense.

Her targets' backs were to her, so she did not have the pleasure of watching their faces change as their feelings did. Instead, she watched their prey, whom she had not Coerced. His fear faded to uncertainty, his narrow face and thin eyebrows drawing in on themselves in an expression that said he could not understand what was happening. Then one of Jennet's targets stepped forward, his hand outstretched. The prey cringed back. The erstwhile bully said something. Jennet could not make out words, but the tone of voice was friendly, even coaxing.

The prey stood up straighter. Then he rushed past the pack, shoving his way through though no one tried to stop him. The one who'd spoken before said, in French, "Then we will see you later, friend!" in a cheerful tone, and he and the others turned to follow their former prey, but slowly, joking and pushing each other desultorily. Their laughter now had a merry edge to it.

Jennet stepped aside to let the children pass. None of them paid her any heed, but she smiled at them in a friendly way, her heart light. Surely that must count in her favor. She had prevented a beating today—might have saved a life, given how many there were in the pack and how ugly their mood had been. Coercion need not result in evil. True, they had no choice in that friendly feeling, but it would lead them to better behavior. And she might not be damned, after all.

The rain fell more heavily now, and Jennet ran, dodging puddles, until she came to the arch of the great cathedral. She would wait the rain out and then return to camp. Huddling into the arch's shelter, she removed her shako and shook water out of her dark curls, wiping her hands on her trousers, though she suspected she was merely spreading water around. She was still too content to care.

She tilted her head back to look up at the vaulted roof of the entrance, or whatever it was called in a cathedral. Many narrow, peaked arches of stone gave the sheltering roof a ribbed appearance, as if those arches had once formed a graceful colonnade that some Mover had compressed with the power of his mind to suit his fancy. Jennet's company had been camped outside Soissons for almost a week, and despite her occasional forays into the town, she had never dared go farther than the cathedral's arched doorway. Some of that was discomfort at giving even tacit approval to the existence of Papistry, some of it was a feeling that she should not intrude on someone else's faith, and some of it was fear that her talent might somehow be visible to whatever priest lurked within the cathedral.

She rubbed her hands together and tucked them under her arms. The rain fell harder now, musical in its varied tones: the harsh, snapping sound of rain hitting the stone of the cathedral; the duller *thunk* as drops pelted the hard-packed earth; the lighter *splish* of water against water where the rain made the puddles grow. Jennet drew back farther into the arch. She had the sudden mad feeling that the rain was looking for her, that it intended to sweep her away to be drowned. The thought crossed her mind that perhaps she deserved that fate, and impatiently she quashed it. She would not give in to despair again.

The door opened behind her, startling her into whipping around to face the black-clad woman who now stood in the dark opening. A dark, close-fitting coif shaped like a helmet shrouded her face, giving her a rather sinister appearance, but she smiled kindly. She did not seem surprised to see Jennet there. "You should come inside, young man," she said in French. "You are likely to be carried away by the deluge."

The words echoed her own recent thoughts so closely Jennet replied, in the same language, "I am an English soldier, and not fit for your hospitality."

The woman smiled more broadly. "All God's children are welcome," she said. "Please. I will not be comfortable knowing you are out here drowning."

Jennet hesitated a moment longer, then followed the woman inside.

The cathedral's interior was dimly lit by candles on many-branched stands placed throughout the vast room. Pillars of grey stone held up the roof, and Jennet gaped in awe at the many stained glass windows looking down on the empty floor and the altar. Rain pattered against the glass with a sound like the rushing of a great river. The room would be astonishingly beautiful in full light. In the dimness, it was haunting, but not in a terrifying or disturbing way; Jennet had the sense of a very old place that had seen much in the course of its existence. It was a place that had sheltered countless individuals, and it comforted Jennet, as if those people's awareness lingered, watching over those who lived and worshiped here now.

The smell of hot candle wax mingled with the sweeter smell of incense, faded as it dispersed through the vast open area. The cathedral was more chilly than outdoors, but Jennet imagined if the space were filled with worshippers, it would become warm and ripe with body odors quickly. She felt obscurely relieved at being the only person there as she had not felt in her awareness of being alone outside in the street. Well, the only person except the black-clad woman and two others identical to her who moved about the cathedral, tending the candles.

"You are not of the Roman Catholic faith," Jennet's benefactress said.

Jennet shook her head. "I fear I'm not much for religion." She had been raised in the Presbyterian faith, but that, like every other aspect of her youth, had been left behind in Scotland.

"I would have thought soldiers were in greater need of worship, living hand-in-glove with death as you do." The woman's words did not sound condemnatory, but rather were curious.

"We have those who preach to us when they've the means, but..." Jennet found she could not easily explain the relationship between a soldier and organized religion. So few men of God braved the battlefield, although most of those who did preached stirring sermons that moved even Jennet's life-hardened heart. "It is difficult to make room for God when one may not see the morrow. Either He is there for us, or He is not, and there's naught we may do to change that."

"I see. That seems a very hard way to live."

Jennet shrugged. "It is what we have chosen. For many of us, it is a better choice than what we left behind in England."

"You come close to breaking my heart, child." The woman put a gentle hand on Jennet's arm. "But now Napoleon is gone, what will you do?"

Mention of the erstwhile Emperor's name chilled Jennet's heart as it always did. "He may not be gone forever," she said, "and we must stand ready against the day he returns."

The woman's brow wrinkled. "I have heard he is dead, and good riddance to him," she said. "An Extraordinary Coercer is a foul, evil creature, one who forces others to love him or fear him. Many of those he Coerced are yet under his thrall. Better he die than drag all of France to Hell with him."

A brief icy numbness gripped Jennet's heart, freezing her hands and her face. "He has done evil, true," she managed through numb lips, "but suppose he had done good with his talent instead?"

"Coercion, good?" The woman's astonishment rang out, her words echoing off the distant ceiling. "Impossible. There is no good to be found in compelling another against his will, regardless of the intent. Evil is evil, young man."

Jennet's pleasure in having saved that boy from a beating dissolved, making her heart leaden. The woman's words were so certain, her attitude so resolved, that Jennet could not conjure any response. This was a woman of God, even though Jennet did not share her faith; if anyone knew the truth of good and evil, it was she. Jennet would have wept had she not sworn ten years ago never to cry again.

"I imagine you are right," she said. "But surely he would not be damned if he chose not to use his talent? If he had never Coerced anyone?"

"My brother is a Seer, and in his youth he spoke often of how he could not imagine not using his talent." The woman's expression was hard and unyielding. Jennet could not imagine how she had ever found the woman kind. "Talent may not be destiny, but how could someone possessed of it not use it? I doubt the late Emperor had much choice."

Jennet swallowed. "It may be as you say," she managed, "but I do not believe we are not possessed of free will. Even Napoleon had to choose to Coerce those people."

"Of course we are." The woman's eyes softened, the lines at their corners disappearing. "But we must breathe, must we not? And that is not a thing we choose to do. I believe talent is the same." She patted Jennet's arm. "But you should not worry over such things, not when your existence is so precarious. We are grateful for your strong fighting arm."

"Not all of France believes so," Jennet said. "They would have us English off their soil, not taking their crops and living in their houses. It is why we camp across the river and are not billeted here in Soissons."

"I understand your officers stay in houses here, though."

"Officers, yes. We men must make do with tents." The tents were a luxury Jennet had longed for during the years of the Peninsular campaign, where she had slept blanketed by dew or freezing under light snowfall. "It is not so bad, and you need feel no pity for me."

"I would not insult you so," the woman said. Jennet forced a smile. After all, the woman could have no idea she had already insulted Jennet. Her fear of her talent being obvious was just a fancy, after all; no one could tell from looking that Jennet was, like Napoleon, an Extraordinary Coercer.

The rushing sound had tapered off as they spoke, and now it ceased entirely. Jennet cast one last glance at the windows. The sky outside was a paler grey than before. "I should leave," she said. "Thank you for the shelter."

"God go with you, child," the woman said. Jennet managed not to flinch. It was no more than words, nothing that could harm her, and the woman meant well. How ready she would have been to grant her blessing if she knew Jennet's talent, Jennet could not guess.

The numbness was gone, but her heart remained heavy. She tried to tell herself it was not true, that she was not damned; she rehearsed in memory all she had done to redeem herself in the past ten months. But a handful of words from a stranger shouted down all the rest.

An Extraordinary Coercer is a foul, evil creature.

Evil is evil, regardless of intent.

Better he die than drag all of France to Hell with him.

Jennet stopped at the door without opening it and laid her palm flat against its cool, damp surface. No. She could not permit anyone to tell her there was no hope, not even one of God's servants. If she believed she was damned, she might as well throw herself off the bridge into the river and let her soul pass into God's judgment. And she was not yet prepared to face that ending. Surely God cared about the intent of one's heart? Jennet had sinned, yes, but so had many others, and why should she be damned simply because hers had been sins of Coercion?

She turned and drew in a breath to challenge the woman, and the smell of fire struck her, all those candles burning. Memory enfolded her, taking her back to a dark night in Spain where torches lit the ancient stones and a mob roared around her, bringing pistols and muskets to bear on her. A man, putting himself between her and the deadly hail, saving her life. And a woman, Amaya Salazar, kneeling beside her, saying *You must do something. And if you start here, that is a good place.* Jennet blinked, and the memory faded and was gone.

She could tell her story to the black-clad woman, of everything she had done that had brought her to this point. She could confess her talent to her. But it would not matter. The woman would see only an Extraordinary Coercer with a terrifying talent. She would never believe that Jennet had crossed Spain and France to rejoin the Army and seek atonement in abjuring the evil use of Coercion. And if she would not believe, then there was no point to Jennet's saying anything.

Jennet closed her eyes and prayed silently, just a few words. She had fallen into the habit of picturing her own father when she addressed God and speaking to Him as if she were once more five years old and small enough to curl up in her father's arms, even though such behavior was not at all what she had been taught as a child and was very likely blasphemous. The conceit comforted her as the thought of a distant, omniscient and omnipotent Being did not. *I'll live as best I may,* she now prayed, *and, Papa, forgive my weaknesses.*

She curled her fingers into a fist so her knuckles rested against the door, as if she had knocked for admittance. The wood was rough against her skin, and on a whim she rapped once. The sound echoed through the cathedral, startling Jennet with its loudness. *Knock, and it shall be opened unto you,* she thought, dredging scripture from where Time had buried it in her memory. She could not remember what it meant, but it seemed a good omen, the idea of being granted something simply for the asking. She pulled the door open and stepped outside.

CHAPTER 2

IN WHICH COMRADES-IN-ARMS ARE INTRODUCED, AND TERRIBLE NEWS ARRIVES

Jennet paused for a moment on the step, breathing in the damp air before donning her shako. Men and women had emerged from the nearby houses and shops and stood, like Jennet, blinking at the sudden absence of rain. The remaining overcast likely would not produce more before nightfall, but Jennet found herself longing for a true summer like those she remembered from her childhood, the air fresh and clean and warm, the skies blue as her father's eyes, the wind carrying the scents of hydrangea and marigolds.

She hurried across the bridge nearest camp, not stopping to gaze down at the Aisne as she often did. The river flowed sluggishly at this time of year and was broad enough she was grateful for the bridge. It smelled of cold water and, more faintly, of waste, but not as noxiously as the Thames did where it passed through London. Jennet had been to the great city only once, but the smell was unforgettable.

The Army's tents spread out in orderly rows across the fields north of Soissons, looking from a distance like a flock of drab butterflies settled on the winter-yellow grass. If "flock" was the correct word. Jennet believed there was a better one, if only she could recall it. Her father would have known.

The memory of her father did not trouble her as it once had. Perhaps the war had hardened her to true feeling, or it might be her manner of prayer had made thinking of him a commonplace. Or perhaps it was simply that he and Mother and her brothers had all been dead for many years, and grief's grasp on the heart wore off with time.

The camp was smaller now than it had been more than a week earlier, when her rifle company along with others of the brigade had set up here. Jennet had been vaguely aware of other companies of the 95th and those of their companion light infantry regiments, the 43rd and the 52nd, striking camp and marching away, but she was not much interested in the doings of those who were not immediately part of the 3rd company of the 95th, her own company.

She skirted the place the quartermasters had claimed, where oxen grazed insensible of their eventual fates and wagons loaded with supplies made a bulwark against the sky. Soldiers milling around the various camp-fires ignored her. Even the scent of wood burning warmed her, as did her hurried pace. All was quiet in camp.

She sought out Ensign Townsend, the officer who had given her permission to enter Soissons. She did not at first see him, and hoped he had not returned to his billet in town. The newest General Order, which had been responsible for seeing the rank and file pitching tents in the fields rather than being assigned to French houses, had also decreed that no soldier not an officer was permitted to enter a French village or town without permission from a superior. Rumor abounded that the French were becoming hostile to the English troops who had done so much to defend them against their Emperor's abuses, and Wellington himself had chosen this course of action to counter that hostility. Jennet did not believe it would make much difference, not if the Army's presence alone was enough to anger the citizens, but in the end, it did not matter what she believed.

She ran the ensign to ground near her own tent, by coincidence. Townsend was deep in conversation with Sergeant Hedley and did not look up at her approach. Jennet stopped a few feet away and waited patiently for the conversation to end.

Hedley noticed Jennet first. He cleared his throat and said, "Sir."

"I won't—" Townsend turned to see what Hedley was looking at. The ensign was a plump man no taller than Jennet, with ruddy brown hair cut unfashionably short and small, close-set eyes. He regarded Jennet as if he had forgotten she existed until she popped fully-formed from the earth in front of him. "Yes?"

"You gave me leave to visit the town, sir. We're to report back when we return, so as not to be delinquent." Jennet reminded herself to salute, though in truth the ensign was not a man who inspired loyalty or respect. But as a woman passing for male in the Army, she needed never to draw attention to herself, for fear too-close scrutiny would reveal her deception.

Townsend continued to stare at her until his regard made Jennet uneasy. "Well?" he said.

Jennet recollected herself. She pulled a small package from her jacket and extended it to Townsend. It smelled sharply of tobacco. "Beg pardon, sir, I nearly forgot."

Townsend took it and tucked it away inside his own uniform jacket, which bore marks of being imperfectly laundered. "Might come to believe you'd keep it for yourself, Graeme," he muttered.

"Don't use the stuff myself, sir," Jennet replied promptly. "Just an honest mistake, sir."

"Well, see it doesn't happen again." Townsend turned his back on Jennet, and she hurried away.

She had not understood why Townsend used her to buy his snuff, nor why he did not simply arrange to have a supply brought to him from England by a Bounder, someone capable of traveling instantly from one place to another without passing through the space between. Then she had by happenstance overheard him complaining that the tobacconist in Soissons overcharged him when she did not simply refuse him service, and discovered the old woman disliked the *rosbif* who was never respectful of her.

Since the tobacconist *did* have an arrangement with a local French Bounder to maintain her supply specifically to cater to the British officers, Jennet could not understand why Townsend would make an enemy of the woman. But as Townsend paid Jennet well to be his purchaser, Jennet decided she did not care about the lieutenant's problems.

A handful of soldiers huddled around the campfire near the tents, two of them sitting next to their wives. Jennet dropped into an empty spot, wincing inwardly as the cold, wet ground immediately chilled her posterior and the damp worked its way through her trouser seams. "It is a miserable afternoon, to be sure," she said.

Sadler and Fosse, flanking her, sat forward eagerly. "Ned, give it here," Fosse said. The lanky, narrow-faced man wore a look of avidity, his dark eyes bright like a crow's. The brown ribbon tying his black hair in a queue draggled over his shoulder, and he flicked it away impatiently.

Jennet produced a somewhat larger package from beneath her jacket and handed it over. Fosse swiftly untied the string and unfolded the brown paper wrapping. Spicy fragrance filled the air, the smell of distant lands. Fosse broke off a piece of the brown cake and popped the gingerbread into his mouth, closing his eyes in ecstasy. "Can't believe as there's anyone in this little place does proper cooking," he said.

"It is not their cooking," Jennet said. "The farrier's son is a Bounder, and he makes the trip to Paris once a week. His young lady has quite the sweet tooth, and he did not mind bringing back something extra for a few francs."

"A few francs, and your charming tongue," Sadler teased. He pushed his dirty-blond hair, too short to queue but long enough to look unkempt, back from his face. Jennet's own dark, curly hair was dangerously long and threatened to make her look feminine. She resolved again to find someone to cut it.

"I vow you could convince the birds to fly north for the winter," Sadler continued. "Tell true, Ned, what did you promise the Bounder?" He reached across Jennet and nipped off a piece of gingerbread, jerking his hand away with its prize before Fosse could slap it.

Jennet tried and failed to control a blush. "Naught but coin, and what else have I?"

"Nay, don't tease the lad," Whitteney said from across the fire. His wife, a pretty young Frenchwoman named Marie, leaned her head on Whitteney's shoulder and smiled lazily at Jennet. "It is hardly his fault he is young and looks harmless, and that the officers believe the townsfolk will not feel threatened by him. Ned, you don't mind running our errands, do you?"

"No, not at all," Jennet said. Her heart beat a little too quickly. She knew Sadler, despite his comment, had not guessed any of her secrets. But she had Coerced each of her comrades months ago to feel friendly toward her, her fear of discovery being greater than her self-loathing every time she leaned on her talent, and Whitteney's friendly words filled her with shame and guilt.

She dug in her pockets, added to her jacket by a Frenchwoman who had said Jennet reminded her of her lost son, and set her silver pocket watch on the ground to get at the rest of their contents. More digging produced bars of lye soap, a rolled pair of wool knit stockings, a spool of thread, and three needles pinned to a slip of paper.

The last two items she passed to Marie, who took them with another smile. Jennet remained straight-faced. She liked Whitteney and wished he had not taken up with Marie, whom Jennet suspected of being rather more free with her favors than a married woman should be and who often looked at Jennet as if considering offering her favors to her.

"You are so kind," Marie said in French to Jennet, then in her halting English added, "For true, it is a blessing to have a thing to mend with. The coats, they are too worn."

Whitteney's jacket was as new as Jennet's own, and Jennet could not imagine why Marie would pretend it was in need of repair. Perhaps Marie wished to make herself useful so Whitteney would overlook her flirting.

Whitteney beamed at Marie's fond look, though Jennet did not consider it a genuine one. The man scratched one leg, hiking up his trousers to reveal the thick red-brown hair covering it. Jennet's father had had a book about Greek myths, with colored pictures, and Whitteney reminded her of the dancing fauns with their furry legs, his hair was so thick.

She handed the stockings and one bar of soap to Corwin, on Whitteney's right; he took them in his customary silence. Beard growth permanently shadowed his gruff face regardless of how often he shaved, and when he frowned, he looked close to murdering someone, but Jennet knew his harsh exterior concealed a kind heart. Why he was in the Army, she did not know, but she treasured her own privacy enough not to pry. Corwin nodded his thanks and tucked his new possessions inside his jacket.

"And Ned is hardly harmless," Corporal Josephs said. He extended a flask to Jennet with a smile far friendlier than Marie's. "Never seen such a fair shot with a rifle." His gaze drifted to the white armband Jennet wore that indicated her prowess as a marksman. Josephs' round-cheeked face and permanent smile had fooled many a new rifleman into believing him a soft touch. In truth, the corporal had a quick temper, and those whom he took in dislike soon learned how sharp the edge on his tongue was. To his friends, though, Josephs was the picture of amiability, and Jennet took care to remain among that number.

Jennet accepted the flask and drank, not too deeply. Her father would have said liquor was a mocker of men, but he had never marched thirty miles over bad ground with nothing but that fire in the belly to keep him walking. Even so, Jennet avoided becoming drunk, both because she risked giving away her sex and because she had no idea if Coercion was possible when one was intoxicated. Both of those prospects terrified her. She took another drink and welcomed how the rum warmed her.

Appleton, seated beside Sadler, took the last bar of soap and handed it silently to his wife Veronique. The thin woman never met anyone's eyes, not even her husband's, and Jennet believed her grasp of English was too poor to permit her to follow the conversation they were having. She had never attempted to befriend Veronique, as she had found women were more likely to penetrate her disguise. Although she did not believe the silent Frenchwoman a threat, she had not got as far as she had by taking unnecessary risks.

Appleton, for his part, rarely paid much attention to Veronique. He was tall and as thin as she was, with large, bony hands, and his uniform jacket hung off his lanky body in the way a scarecrow's might. Had Veronique not been obviously with child, Jennet might have suspected them indifferent to one another.

Fosse took another bite of gingerbread before wrapping his parcel up and stowing it in his jacket. "Nay, do not make that face," he told Sadler, who appeared to be on the verge of dramatic tears. "No one believes you are injured."

"We have marched together across Europe and you won't give me even a bite," Sadler said, pretending to great mournfulness. "Ned, tell him to share his bounty."

"You could buy your own," Jennet pointed out.

That roused Whitteney, Fosse, and Josephs to laughter. Sadler's fortunes were always on the wane, and he was well known to be in debt to half a dozen men. Sadler shook his head. "I'll make my fortune someday, see if I don't, and then all of you will come crawling to me for a taste of something better than gingerbread."

"You spend your sixpences as fast as you earn 'em," Whitteney scoffed. "Or are you counting on some grand inheritance, then?"

"Not I. I've no kin to shower me with money." Sadler prodded Jennet's pocket watch with his forefinger. "Not like Ned, carrying this around like he's got a dozen more like it back home."

"It was my father's," Jennet said, gathering it up and stowing it away. "And you know I don't gamble."

"No, more's the pity—at least as far as my lean pockets are concerned." Sadler leaned back on his hands and tilted his face skyward. "But I'll win my fortune back tomorrow, see if I don't."

Josephs groaned. "You know we ain't to play for high stakes."

"Then you can pretend you didn't hear that," Sadler shot back.

"You'll have more luck making your fortune by capturing a French eagle for the bounty," Fosse said. "And as Napoleon is gone for good, there's not an eagle standard to be found for miles, so that ought to tell you your chances of winning at cards."

"Boney isn't dead," Whitteney said, making Marie gasp as dramatically as Sadler ever dreamed of. "He's biding his time, waiting on the right moment, and then—he'll strike!"

"He must be dead to be gone so long," Fosse said. "I heard it from a Frenchwoman that his Coerced troops have started trickling home."

"As if you ever listen to the women you bed," Sadler scoffed. "We're still here, ain't we? And Wellington wouldn't leave us in the field save he thought he'd need of us."

"The 95th is the best of the Light Division," Josephs declared. "We won't go home until it's certain Boney is dead."

"You all sound like a passel of gossiping hens," Appleton said. His narrow face was pinched in disapproval. "Haven't you any care for your dignity?"

"'*Haven't you any care for your dignity?*'" Fosse repeated in a high-pitched, mocking voice. "We none of us have that, not after six years in His Majesty's service, sleeping cold and wet and shivering with Guadiana fever and tracking blood from wearing through our boots—what in all of that sounds like dignity?"

"Have a care, Appleton, you'll make the rest of us look bad," Sadler said, elbowing Appleton sharply in the ribs. "Mayhap you and your dignity should aim for a sergeant's rank and gain the right to tell us what to do."

Appleton snorted derision and stood. "You're all fools, the lot of you," he said, and strode away. Veronique struggled to her feet before anyone could offer to help her up and followed her husband, her head still ducked low so she met no one's eyes.

Whitteney shook his head. "He's got the stick shoved so far up his ass it's a wonder he can still bend."

Corwin, who had been silent throughout the bantering, looked past Jennet. His gruff face stilled. "Look sharp," he murmured. "It's the lieutenant."

Jennet slewed around where she sat. "The lieutenant" meant Lieutenant Falconer. Her heart once again beat faster, and this time she berated herself for her foolishness. But there was no harm in looking, and Falconer was well worth looking at. The tall, slim lieutenant carried himself like a prince, his legs and shoulders shapely yet masculine, his profile perfect in every way. Jennet knew Falconer's beauty was unnatural; the lieutenant was a Shaper, capable of molding his body to the epitome of strength and attractiveness, and likely he had chosen that Shape to gratify his vanity. But her heart refused to listen to logic.

She turned away and took yet another drink of rum. She had thought herself immune to masculine charms, after what had come of the raider attack that had killed her family. Certainly her time in the Army, surrounded by men of all shapes and visages, had not changed her determination never to love a man. She was a fool to be moved by anything so ridiculous as a well-Shaped body, particularly since Falconer had the haughty air of someone who knew how handsome he was. But this was hardly love; she might as well have admired a beautiful statue or painting as to feel anything more for Falconer than the respect due an officer.

Falconer drew near, and Jennet and the others scrambled to their feet. Jennet furtively brushed dirt from her posterior and avoided meeting Falconer's eye. The lieutenant surveyed them all with his habitually arrogant expression. "I seek Ensign Townsend," he said.

Jennet had not seen where the ensign had gone after she gave him his snuff. Sadler, however, said, "He went toward the village, sir."

Falconer nodded. He glanced at the flask in Jennet's hand, and one eyebrow rose. Jennet, unaccountably flustered—it was not as if the soldiers were not permitted drink—refrained from putting her hands behind her back like a naughty child.

But Falconer said only, "Take your comforts where you can. We will be moving out soon."

"Is the captain back, then, sir?" Fosse asked.

"Not ten minutes ago," Falconer said. His lips compressed in a thin line. "Bringing with him the worst news. Napoleon has returned, and in three days he will be at the gates of Paris."

CHAPTER 3

IN WHICH JENNET RECEIVES
AN UNEXPECTED ELEVATION
IN STATUS

The following day, Jennet stood with her fellows in a field near camp, listening to Captain Lord Adair speak. She did not like the captain much; he was a hard man, prone to ordering floggings for the least infraction and claiming such harshness was essential to maintaining the character of the company. Jennet, who could not risk her secret being revealed through a flogging, stayed well out of his way and made herself a model soldier. Even so, she had resorted to Coercion once or twice to prevent punishment, justifying her use of her talent as necessary rather than an indulgence. The justification did not stop her feelings of shame.

"We do not know many details as yet," Adair was saying. "Only that Napoleon landed in the south of France in the first week of May and has made his way northward since then, growing his army as he comes. None have resisted his Coercion, not even those who declared they would defy him until the end. It is rumored Marshal Ney went to meet him with the intent of bringing him to justice, and instead fell back under the former emperor's sway, taking all his thousands of men with him."

"The more fool him," Sadler murmured beside Jennet. "Don't know why even a high-ranking Johnny-crapaud would think he could get within a dozen paces of Boney without falling under his spell."

Jennet silently agreed with him, though she guessed, if Napoleon's talent was as powerful as hers, he could affect a distance much greater than a mere dozen paces.

"As I returned from England, I encountered many fleeing from Napoleon's advance," Adair continued. "King Louis and his court have removed to Ghent rather than become victims. I do not know the exact position of the former emperor's forces, but it is only a matter of days before he attacks Paris—and it is unlikely anyone remains there who can defy him. Excuse me."

The captain stopped speaking and tilted his head back in the attitude of a Speaker receiving a mental communication. Jennet waited patiently with the others, some of whom shifted restlessly. Jennet suspected Adair of enjoying how his mental Speech with other Speakers acted as a form of compulsion on his command, since the soldiers had no choice but to wait for him to finish regardless of what else they might have been doing. It seemed the sort of thing Adair would find satisfying.

Adair lowered his head. "As I was saying," he went on, "Paris will certainly fall to Napoleon's troops. He could not have chosen a more opportune time for an invasion, given that our army is scattered and our allies, for the most part, believed Napoleon dead and have to some degree stood down. But the 95th is ready, as always, to do our duty."

A murmur rose from the crowd. Adair cast a steely eye over the soldiers. "The 3rd will march south, to reinforce the battalion positioned at Troyes. Our mandate is to prevent the French cutting off the Austrian Army from joining our forces. If our army is to make a stand against Napoleon, we will need our allies' assistance. Prepare to march at first light." He nodded once, sharply, and Sergeant Hedley shouted the command to disperse.

Jennet watched Adair turn away to speak to Lieutenant Falconer. For once, she did not admire the lieutenant's form. She wondered what else Adair knew that he had not told them. He would not feel obligated to reveal every detail to the men, and she did not expect that of him, but she was curious nonetheless. They were to march into danger; a certain curiosity was natural, especially when his orders, whatever they were, might result in her own or her fellows' deaths.

Her curiosity about Napoleon, equally natural, was more complicated, tied up as it was with her knowledge that he was the only other Extraordinary Coercer she had ever heard of. Had he not been who he was, she might have wanted to meet him, to learn what he knew of their shared talent. Though it seemed likely a meeting would end in a fight, because Napoleon could not risk her Coercing him. She did not know if she was vulnerable to Coercion, or if her talent made her immune the way a Discerner's did, and the idea of testing herself against the greatest enemy England had ever faced filled her with simultaneous excitement and horror.

Falconer stood with his head tilted down, listening to Adair, who was shorter than he. His brows were slightly furrowed, as if Adair's words concerned him, but in all other respects he appeared as haughty as ever. Townsend, standing next to Falconer, concealed his boredom well, but Jennet was familiar with the restless motions of his hands, twitching in eagerness for a pinch of snuff and a glass of brandy somewhere far from this field.

"Come, Ned, let's be off," Fosse said. He nudged Jennet. "Last night in camp, we should make the most of it." He grinned, leaving her in no doubt as to how he intended to spend his last night.

"And they've issued an extra ration of rum," Sadler said, his grin matching Fosse's. He followed the line of Jennet's gaze. "I thought he'd look different now he's a lord," he added, jerking his thumb in Adair's direction.

Fosse shrugged. "It's not as if it shows on the skin. You've seen Major Drummond, Lord Quincey, and he's as common-looking as muck."

Jennet had to agree that Adair, narrow-faced with pockmarked cheeks and hair thinning at the back, did not look like her idea of a lord. His trip to England had been necessitated by his father the Viscount Adair's death and the need to handle certain matters of business, or so camp gossip ran. Jennet had expected the new viscount to remain longer in England, well away from the hardships of the field. But he had returned looking just as he always did, though his eyes were shadowed with tiredness. Falconer was more her idea of what a lord should look like, though she never spoke her fancy aloud. Her romantic notions embarrassed her, even kept within the privacy of her own head.

At that moment, Falconer glanced away from the captain, and his eyes met Jennet's. Surprised at the unexpected contact, Jennet did not immediately look away. She wished his face were more readable, that he had the affable smile of Fosse or Whitteney, or Sadler's knowing smirk, or even Corwin's perpetual frown. She could never guess, from his expression, what he thought of those around him, and that disturbed her. She had never peeked at his tangle of emotions, as she rarely did so when she did not intend to Coerce someone, and without either of those guides, she could not know if he was a threat to her. She reminded herself that Falconer had no interest in a lowly soldier and swiftly turned away.

Corwin was stoking the campfire when she returned, his craggy face as intent as if he were tending a child. "We've the best meat tonight," he said. "Should be glad of it, as it's the last we'll see of the good beef for many a day."

Jennet was just as happy to turn cooking duty over to Corwin, whose skills at turning even the worst leavings into delicious food were legendary. She had not expected to find such genius among the soldiers, but then, when she had sworn oath to serve as a rifleman, she had not expected her comrades in arms to be anything but the worst dregs of society. True, most of them were illiterate, and some had been thieves and murderers, but many were simply down on their luck, craftsmen whose livelihood had collapsed, young men who were the sole support of their widowed mothers, rough types who knew nothing beyond fighting for their lives.

And so many of them had unexpected character, loyalty to their fellows and generosity where none was demanded. Jennet had wondered often whether her Coercion of the others in her company had been necessary, given how firmly they stood together. But she never dared release them. All it would take would be one man becoming hostile toward her, and then her identity would come under scrutiny, and then... She had no desire to leave the Army, not when it provided such excellent protection. She recognized the irony of that sentiment.

She sat near the fire and drank from her flask, welcoming the little fire in her belly and enjoying the smell of cooked beef that rose from the camp kettle. Corwin had saved out some choice pieces to roast over the flames, sending up more delicious aromas. The prospect of a good meal relaxed muscles sore from a good morning's drill. She loved the feel of the rifle in her hands, the powerful kick as it fired, the pleasure of seeing her shot hit her target. Her father had taught her to shoot when she was young, but experience with a musket had not prepared her for the beauty of a Baker rifle. Her lips still tasted faintly of gunpowder, and there was a trace of it along her right hand she now rubbed off on her trousers. She had rarely felt so content.

Sadler, across from her, accepted a piece of hot roasted beef from Corwin and bit happily into it. "We eat like kings," he mumbled, "better than kings, who must sit in their halls and pretend to pretty manners. There is nothing like eating outdoors for the health of a man."

"Unless it's eating indoors in the company of pretty ladies," Fosse said. He had his own meat in his tin plate and was chewing energetically.

"A lady wouldn't give you the time of day," Whitteney said. He accepted a steaming helping of beef on his own plate and then on Marie's. "And there's naught stopping you from making an honest woman of one of your many light-skirts."

Fosse's eyes widened in mock horror. "And have her following me and wanting things of me? Not I, not for a million pounds." He twiddled the brown ribbon binding his queue and looked surprised when it came untied at his tugging.

Corwin smiled, the faintest quirk of his lips that made him look slightly less villainous. "A million pounds could take reet good care of a wife," he said.

"Not for a million pounds," Fosse repeated, tying the ribbon and flicking his queue over his shoulder. "And I'm going to find me some kind-hearted woman for one last tumble before we march into danger."

"How dangerous will it be, I wonder," Jennet said, half to herself. "We do not know what lies between here and Troyes."

"Mondy will find it out," Sadler said, referring to the company's Bounder. "He's an ass, but he knows his work." He swallowed the last of his beef and held out his tin plate to Corwin, clutching his chest with his other hand and pretending to starvation. Corwin's smile broadened at his antics.

Jennet could not but agree with Sadler's assessment of Ensign Mondy's character. He was as humorless as Appleton and more strict in his obedience to military law even than Adair. In many companies, the Bounder made private trips to and from England on behalf of the soldiers who could pay, even though this stretched the letter of the law. Mondy, however, never Bounded or Skipped except under direct orders. He would not even make exceptions for the other officers, hence Townsend's dependence on Jennet for his snuff.

Just then, Appleton appeared out of the growing dusk, scowling. He thrust his plate toward Corwin—just one plate. Veronique was nowhere to be seen. "Ought to be making your souls right with God, on this night of all nights," he said.

Fosse flicked a clod of earth at Appleton that struck him on the shoulder and bounced off, leaving a faint smudge. "If God wants my soul, He knows where He can find it."

"Blasphemer," Appleton said, but not very forcefully. "Graeme, the lieutenant wants you."

Jennet stopped chewing mid-mouthful. "Me?"

"You," Appleton said. "At his billet in town. And you ought go quickly. I don't know why you all believe you can be disrespectful and not pay the price. God knows what trouble Graeme is in."

Jennet's heart beat painfully hard. She finished chewing, swallowed, and set her plate with her half-finished meal aside.

"Nay, you needn't rush off," Whitteney said. "Finish your meal. The lieutenant can wait."

What little Jennet had eaten sat like a leaden weight in her stomach. "I'm full," she said, standing. "I might as well go."

"Don't listen to Appleton," Sadler said. He cracked the knuckles of his left hand, one by one. "You've naught to fear."

Jennet managed a smile and hurried away.

She kept to a sedate trot, a compromise between the walk she would have preferred and the run Appleton no doubt would have demanded. Campfires dotted the fields among the tents, crowded around with soldiers who ignored her passing. The pickets stopped her, but only briefly; they were accustomed to her frequent trips into Soissons, and a word or two was enough to assure them she had been sent for. She had no idea what Falconer wanted of her, but she could not stop remembering that last, measuring look he had given her. She did not believe she had done anything wrong, but suppose it was some infraction she hadn't even been aware of making?

She reminded herself that Falconer was not cruel or unjust despite his arrogance, and that he was not likely to order her flogged; she could not, in fact, remember him ever having anyone flogged, though she also could not remember what punishments he had ordered instead. There must have been something, for he could not maintain his authority if he permitted insubordination or disobedience.

She knew she was being foolish, but now her mind threw up all manner of possibilities, chief among which was that he had discovered the secret of her sex and intended to dismiss her from the Army. No. No foolishness. Likely this was nothing. *Nothing, nothing, nothing*, she made herself repeat silently in time with her running steps.

The sky had cleared that afternoon, and the setting sun sent a rosy glow over the streets of Soissons. Despite her anxiety, Jennet could not help being struck by the beauty of the town. In full light, it looked like any other French town, old and slightly dilapidated; in the warm orange light of sunset, it looked mysterious and beautiful, every stone softened so the scene looked like a painting and not anything real. To the west, the spires of the cathedral caught the light and glowed like gold. Eastward lay the ruined abbey she had furtively explored once or twice, invisible now, but easy to imagine touched by the same light. She would miss Soissons when she was gone, and an inexplicable disquiet filled her heart, as if liking this town made her no longer English.

Falconer and Townsend both stayed in the same house in Soissons, an old stone structure three stories tall that looked as grim as a prison despite the lanterns warmly lighting its many small windows. It must belong to someone wealthy or important, because a short stone wall divided it from the road, and all the windows were made of tiny glass panes rather than oilcloth. Even so, it was not a welcoming house, and although Jennet scented more rain in the air, she could not help feeling that she and her fellows in their rough tents had a better situation than the officers.

She trotted up the short paved walk to the front door, which was age-hardened oak once painted a deep blue, still marked lightly with the chalk the quartermaster's men had used to show the officers which houses had been chosen for their billets. Time had weathered the door's paint to a paler shade and worn it from the wood in places, giving the door a seedy appearance that suited the dour, oppressive place. Dead plants Jennet did not recognize drooped in planters beside the door. She drew in a deep breath, calming herself, and rapped lightly on the door.

No one answered at first. Jennet cast another glance at the sky, off to the east where more clouds gathered. If rain did come, it would likely be in the early morning. She hoped it would leave off before they had to march in it tomorrow.

The door abruptly creaked open. Jennet assumed a polite, respectful demeanor as a short, burly man with a black moustache and small dark eyes addressed her. "Yes?"

"Sir, Lieutenant Falconer summoned me, is he here?" Jennet said in French.

The man shrugged. "Upstairs, top floor, on the right," he said, stepping back.

Jennet entered and nodded her thanks. The door opened on a narrow hall that appeared to run the entire length of the house, front to back. The plaster of the walls was cracked, the whitewash faded, but Jennet took in the elegantly carved ceiling beams, the doors that fit their frames perfectly, and guessed the family chose to appear less prosperous than they were to prevent the English soldiers from ransacking their house for supplies. She sympathized with them if that were so. Distant memories of screams and fire rose up, and she quashed them reflexively, not giving them room in her mind. English soldiers—*most* English soldiers, she amended—would not tear through civilian houses and put them to the torch, but even the knowledge that she, as a soldier, had bene-fited in the past from the forcible appropriation of food and firewood did not keep her from cheering the Frenchman's efforts on.

The smell of supper, of garlic and hot bread, emanated from behind one of the doors lining the hall. Jennet was still too apprehensive to be tempted by it. The man did not accompany her, nor did he retreat behind a door. She felt his gaze on her as she walked down the dimly lit hall to the stairs at the far end. They had once been stained a dark walnut, but time and use had worn the color from the center of each step, enhancing the appearance of hollows where countless men and women had trodden the stairs. The steps were not wide, and Jennet could easily brush the walls on either side without stretching her arms to their full extent. But the walls were grimy, and whether or not that was intentional, Jennet did not wish to touch them.

She ascended the narrow, steep stairs into near-darkness, leaving the hall lantern behind for an even dimmer light she took for a window letting in the last rays of sunlight. When she reached the first landing, she discov-ered that was true, though the light was barely enough to see her way by.

Forgetting her earlier squeamishness, she ran her fingers along the wall to guide her as she continued to the next floor.

Above, the light was brighter, and she came out of the stairwell to find a lantern glowing on a narrow console table in the short hallway. It cast her shadow behind her, and when she turned to knock on the door to the right, the shadow moved with her like a skeletal puppet without strings. The strange sight caught her attention so when the door opened, she was looking back at the stairs rather than at Falconer and gave a little startled jump at his sudden appearance.

Falconer was in his shirtsleeves and braces, with his uniform jacket hung on a peg on the wall just inside the room. He looked unsurprised to see her, but of course he was expecting her. For the first time, Jennet made herself aware of the tangle of emotions he carried inside him, not intending to Coerce him, but wishing for a hint as to his intentions. To her surprise, she saw nothing to indicate haughtiness. He was instead perfectly calm in a way Jennet rarely saw, calm and intent upon her. She released her awareness and saluted him. "You sent for me, sir?"

"Come in, Graeme." Falconer turned away from the door, not waiting to see if she would obey. Jennet entered and let the door swing shut behind her. The room was small but tidy, with a narrow bed, a small square-topped table, and a ladderback chair whose seat looked in need of re-caning. The table bore the remains of the lieutenant's supper, a cheese rind and crumbs of bread and the smell of roast pork. A glass tinged with red dregs and a bottle half full of wine completed the picture of a French supper, as Jennet imagined it.

Falconer walked to the table and collected the dishes into a neat pile centered on the red and brown earthenware plate. "You speak French, am I correct?" he asked, not turning to face her.

Startled again, Jennet said, "Aye, I do, sir."

"How did you come by such a skill?"

"I, well, my father taught me, sir, when I was young, and then I relearned it here, talking to the people." She knew it was strange, a young man in the ranks having learned French, but there was no helping that. It was not as if it implicated her as female. She did not volunteer that she spoke Spanish as well.

"And you can read and write?"

Jennet dearly wished to know where the lieutenant was going with this line of inquiry. "Aye, sir."

Falconer left off tidying the table and finally turned to face her. "I'm in need of a servant," he said. "My previous man ran off on the road to Soissons, or just after we arrived—we've had deserters here and there ever since Napoleon vanished. I want you to fill the position."

"*Me*, sir?" Surprise made Jennet's voice shrill, and she cleared her throat and said, more normally, "Me? Why me?"

"I watch the men carefully, Graeme." Falconer still sounded calm, as if her fate mattered nothing to him. "You display good sense and proper respect without being servile, you get on well with everyone, you've never been called up on a charge, and Townsend has said you're reliable enough to be sent into town without a worry that you'll cause trouble. And, as it happens, I have need of someone capable of reading and writing who is also fluent in French. Well? Do we have an agreement?"

"Do I have a choice?" Jennet blurted out.

For the first time, she saw Falconer smile, and she cursed the little flutter it started in the pit of her stomach, an excited, warm feeling at being the focus of his attention, beautiful as he was. "I won't force you against your will, Graeme," he said. "But the position comes with an increase in pay, as well as other benefits, and I believe you'll find me an easy taskmaster."

Jennet mentally slapped herself out of the stupor his handsome visage and appealing form had thrown her into. "Yes, sir, if you think I'll suit," she said.

"Indeed," Falconer said. "Then you can begin by returning these to the kitchen, and in the morning I'll expect to see you here so I can show you where my baggage is stowed. You'll have the care of my things, but I don't expect you to dress me. You'll also leave the line of march to guard the wagon train."

"Begging your pardon, sir, but isn't that unnecessary? That is, I understood the wagon train to have guards already." Jennet had almost no understanding of what officers' servants did, but she was certain waiting on Falconer's person was separate from guarding the wagons.

"If we are marching into danger, the wagon train will require more soldiers. Did you wish to argue further?" Falconer arched an eyebrow, giving him a rather sardonic expression. Jennet shook her head.

"Very well. Tomorrow I'll no doubt have other instructions for you." He gestured at the stack of dishes. Jennet gathered them up, leaving only the glass and wine bottle, which Falconer had not set with the others.

"In the morning, then, Graeme," Falconer said. He opened the door for her and closed it with a faint click when she was in the hall.

Jennet stood for a moment, blinking in surprise. Had that actually happened? Of all her imaginings, being Falconer's servant was not one of them. And yet...yes, her hands were full of his dishes, she was to report back in the morning. It was all true.

A momentary fear struck her heart. Staying out of the way of her fellow rank-and-filers so as to protect her secret was not difficult; soldiers were, by and large, extremely self-absorbed and concerned about promoting their own interests. But close proximity to an officer, one whose attention would necessarily be on her—that could be dangerous. And the idea of Coercing Falconer made Jennet uncomfortable in a way she could not explain.

She wondered, now, if she had been wrong about his character. Arrogance was one of the emotions most visible, as it was also one easiest to manipulate, and she had seen none of it in Falconer. Perhaps she had misread his calm, smooth visage, and—she flushed with embarrassment—had drawn the wrong conclusions about the way a man of his appearance might feel about his self-worth. In any case, he bore closer watching, out of curiosity, naturally. And this new position put her in an excellent position to do that.

She shook her head and made her way down the narrow stairs. She would simply have to be careful not to draw attention to herself, that was all. And the extra money would pad her savings nicely. She was frugal, never spending more than she had to, and between her pay and the money she had received in her time in Spain, she had a substantial amount tucked away in the lining of her jacket and hidden in her other possessions. When the war was over—no, she did not actually have a plan for when the war was over, aside from a desire not to depend on others' charity. She deliberately put the idea out of her head. Tonight, she would enjoy the company of her fellows, drink and laugh and let them tease her about her change in status. And tomorrow? Tomorrow they would march to war.

CHAPTER 4

IN WHICH JENNET'S CURIOSITY ABOUT LIEUTENANT FALCONER REMAINS UNSATISFIED

J ennet woke from dreams of Spain, her heart pounding and cold sweat prickling her hairline. The dreams were always the same: musket balls flying in all directions, the bloody body of a man who had put himself between her and danger to save her life even though he hated her, the race to find an Extraordinary Shaper to Heal him. And, finally, fire blossoming everywhere as Alejandro Valencia turned his Extraordinary Scorcher talent on her.

Now she waited in the pre-dawn darkness for her body to remember it was not burning to death, squeezing her eyes shut and controlling her erratic breathing. Nothing in the dream happened as it had done in real life; Valencia had already been dead when Edmund Hanley had taken those shots meant for her. She still did not understand why Hanley had not simply let her die, as she had Coerced him more than once and he justifiably hated her. She had not deserved his sacrifice, she who had Coerced so many people in Valencia's name and for her own sake.

A last fragment of the dream surfaced, herself staring helplessly at Hanley's body riddled with holes and Amaya Salazar's voice saying, *You must do something. And if you start here, that is a good place.* And then she had turned her Coercion on a mob, quelling it, before running to fetch the only Extraordinary Shaper she had ever met to save Hanley's life. She was under no illusions that this act made up for years of sin, but it was that night she had felt, for the first time since manifesting her talent, that salvation might be within her reach.

She wiped sweat from her brow and drew in a deep, slow breath, releasing it as slowly. She remembered then the events of the previous night. Servant to Lieutenant Falconer. She berated herself for the rush of pleasure that suffused her at the thought of being in a position to look at him more often. True, he was beautiful, but that did not make him more worthy as a man or more deserving of consideration. She had little idea what he expected from her as his servant, but she would do her best to fulfil those duties, not because of his looks but because that would bring her better pay and possibly other benefits. She had heard of some officers' servants being given their masters' castoffs, clothing or other personal articles that had to be of better quality than her own, and that was nothing to turn up one's nose at.

She rose and donned her jacket and boots before leaving her tent. It was little more than a length of canvas draped over a slat and a ramrod, weighed down at the sides with stones, but it was decent shelter she was grateful for. Some clever person in the engineers' corps had come up with the design and the materials, and now every soldier was able to carry his own tent on his back. So much better than exerting oneself and one's fellows to build huts from local wood or put up the larger, bulkier tents that had to ride with the baggage train.

Outside, others were rising, and someone from the quartermaster's company moved among them. Jennet accepted a small loaf of bread and a hunk of cheese. There would be no fires this morning. The bread was fresh and unexpectedly delicious, the cheese not too hard, and Jennet ate quickly, conscious that the meals would likely not be so good henceforth.

When she was finished eating, she swiftly packed her gear and folded her tent as small as she could manage. Nearby, Sadler and Fosse were doing the same. She did not see Corwin, but Josephs strode among the soldiers, not speaking, but casting a baleful eye on anyone who moved less quickly than he liked.

Whitteney approached her, his pack already loaded. "So, you're back with the baggage train now," he said, quietly so as not to draw Josephs' attention or that of Sergeant Hedley, whose progress among the men was louder than Josephs' and more strident. "You'll keep an eye on Marie, will you?"

Jennet's fondness for Whitteney warred with her feeling that Marie did not need looking after, at least not the kind Whitteney intended. "If I can," she said. "We're to watch the animals and the road behind, in case of ambush. But I'm sure she'll be fine."

Whitteney clapped a hand on Jennet's shoulder. "Strange that the lieutenant would pick you," he said. "Though a crack shot might not be wasted in the baggage train, not after what happened to the 43rd last October."

Jennet nodded. A few companies of their fellow regiment, the 43rd light infantry, had been surprised by French troops coming upon their rear intent on taking their supplies. The companies had barely fought off the enemy and had taken heavy losses to their equipment and supplies, not to mention the many women who marched behind who were taken or killed. "But I doubt there's any French left between here and Troyes, not if Napoleon came from the south and drew them all to him," she said.

"That's the way to look at it," Sadler said, coming up beside them. "Trust Ned to make the best of a bad situation."

"You call being pulled out of danger to watch over the mules a bad situation?" Whitteney said, raising both eyebrows in surprise.

"Nay, not that. I mean marching into God knows what country." Sadler cast an eye on the heavens, which were cloudless and showed clearly the light of the rising sun, and rotated his back to pop the bones of his spine in a crackling cascade that set Jennet's teeth on edge. "Mondy may scout ahead, but it isn't as if us soldiers hear what he sees. The first we may know of an attack is when the shooting starts."

"No sense borrowing trouble, Sadler." Whitteney clapped Jennet on the shoulder again. "We'll see you tonight, then?"

"Unless the lieutenant has other orders," Jennet said. She shrugged her pack on, shouldered her rifle, and with a nod for the rest of her fellows she headed for the bridge into Soissons.

The sun had not yet fully risen, but the day was already warmer and drier than the weather had been all week, and the people of Soissons were outside taking advantage of it. They stepped wide of Jennet, but turned friendly when she addressed them in their language, and one man even gave her a fresh-baked tart in greeting. She ate as she walked, reaccustoming herself to the weight of her pack and the drag of the rifle on her shoulder. The remnants of her dream had faded, and in the cool morning air she felt almost cheerful.

As she approached the officers' billet, the door opened, and Falconer and then Townsend stepped out, followed by the householder. Falconer said a few words to the man and then shook his hand; coin gleamed as it passed between them. The householder looked marginally less disgruntled than he had the previous night.

Falconer came to meet her at the little gate in the low stone wall fronting the house. "Graeme," he said, sounding calm as always. "Follow me. Townsend?"

Townsend eyed Jennet as if expecting her to do something foolish that would prove she did not deserve her elevation in status. "I must retrieve my jacket from the tailor's," he said, and headed off southward.

Falconer walked in the direction from which Jennet had come without another word. Jennet followed him, keeping up easily despite his longer stride. This time when they passed the townsfolk, the men and women stepped aside without saying anything, merely eyeing Falconer and ignoring Jennet. Falconer ignored them as completely. Jennet dipped into her awareness of his emotions, feeling guilty embarrassment at doing so, and found no hidden fears of being attacked.

She wished she understood how he maintained his demeanor. Sometimes such emotions indicated one who cared nothing for other people, someone who was prone to hurting others because he saw them as things, but Jennet had never seen anything in Falconer's behavior to indicate this. Rather, she believed from her few assessments of his emotions that he might be one of those individuals who had no fear of what others thought of him and had perfect confidence in his ability to meet any challenge that might come his way. It was not an uncommon attitude in extremely attractive people, and one that was, in Jennet's experience, rarely justified.

She knew enough of such people to know his equilibrium might be shattered by something truly unexpected, revealing his inner nature. The idea that she might shake him from his indifference crossed her mind, but she dismissed it as an unworthy, selfish one. There was nothing wrong with who he was, and doing something to prod him into a different emotional state was wrong even if she did not Coerce him.

They crossed the bridge to where the line of march was forming up and past the soldiers to the loose gathering of horses and mules and wagons near the end. Jennet saw Veronique, wrapped in a grey cloak, standing nearby, her gaze fixed on the ground. Despite herself, her sympathy for Veronique roused. It could not be easy, marching with the Army in her condition, and Jennet said impulsively, "Can that woman not ride in a wagon?"

Falconer glanced around until he saw where Jennet's gaze lay. "If she rides, they will all want to ride," he said, but he sounded compassionate rather than indifferent. "It is unfortunate, having so many women in our train, but it cannot be helped."

"You are opposed to women in the Army, sir?" Jennet could not help saying.

His gaze fixed on her. His eyes, Jennet observed, were an ordinary hazel, the only thing about him that was not truly beautiful. As neither hair color nor eye color could be Shaped, that made sense. "This is a hard life," he said, "and harder on those not accustomed to it. In Portugal I saw women and children left to die beside the road because they could not keep up with the march. It is not a memory I care to dwell on. I suggested the women be required to stay behind from this march, but my suggestion was overridden."

"I suppose many of them would follow even if they were forbidden," Jennet said.

Falconer nodded. He was back to being indifferent again. "This is my pack horse, Copper," he said, continuing on to where the horses were gathered in a makeshift paddock. He approached a bay mare, already laden with boxes and bags, and stroked her nose. "My groom, Boyce, will have the care of her on the march, but you will convey my belongings to my tent when we make camp."

Falconer moved on to a different horse, a heavier-built black gelding a hand or two taller than the bay. "This is Suleiman," he said, and his voice changed. For the first time, he sounded human, his words touched with a warmth and friendliness that made Jennet shiver. "He has been my companion all the way from Portugal. Say hello to Graeme, Suleiman."

To her astonishment, Suleiman nodded as if he understood Falconer's words. She laid a hand on the horse's nose and smiled when he whickered at her. "He's beautiful," she said.

"And well he knows it." Falconer smiled fondly at Suleiman like a father taking pride in a precocious child's accomplishment. "This is Boyce, my groom. He will care for the horses' needs in camp. Boyce, Graeme." He gestured to a short, compact man with very fair hair and skin. Boyce nodded at Jennet and then apparently lost interest in her, hoisting Suleiman's saddle onto the horse's back and buckling it in place.

"Now," Falconer said. "I know you are a crack shot, and I intend you to be extra security for the wagon train—you recall what happened to the 43rd. You are to be prepared to defend or attack just as you would if you were in the main body of the company. I expect you to care for my belongings and prepare my meals—no fear, Graeme, I don't expect fine dining," he added as Jennet blanched. She could cook, but not well. She caught Boyce's eye as he glanced her way. He looked skeptical, as if he, too, did not believe she was a good choice for an officer's servant. Still, Jennet could not imagine herself challenging Falconer on any of his demands so far.

"I may also call on you to speak to those we encounter, in hopes of learning more of Napoleon's advance." Falconer sounded grim. "With luck, we will learn nothing."

"How is that luck, sir?"

Falconer gave a little shake of his head. "If Napoleon's advance is faster than we expect, there is a chance anyone we encounter who knows of it may be Coerced. That means we will be fighting those who have no choice in the matter, and that sickens me. The best outcome will be to find no sign of Napoleon, and to reach Troyes and join the rest of the Army with no encounters."

"How likely is that, sir?" Jennet ventured.

His eyes fixed on hers again. "I cannot guess. Napoleon's advance on Paris has been rapid and intent on nothing but his goal. He needs to conquer that city as a rallying point, a symbol of his successful return. However, who is to say he always stays with his army? He has as many Bounders as we, and he might go anywhere and return immediately. Even a Seer might have difficulty predicting his movements."

Jennet could think of nothing to say to this. She had not considered that Napoleon might Bound throughout the country, Coercing those he encountered, but it made sense.

"Don't let the possibility trouble you, Graeme," Falconer said. "We have no control over the enemy, only over our own movements, and the most likely outcome of this march is simply that we will join the forces at

Troyes and prepare for battle." He mounted Suleiman and controlled the horse's first few restless steps. "I will see you this afternoon when we stop for the night. The others will tell you what to do." He nodded in farewell and turned away.

Jennet watched him go, feeling unexpectedly bereft. Even Boyce had not stayed, but was walking toward the quartermaster's wagons with Copper. She shook off the feeling. This was still the Army, and she belonged here regardless of the irregularity of her new position.

"You there! What are you doing?"

The peremptory voice startled Jennet into turning around fast. A tall, gangly young man, surely too tall to be a soldier, but wearing no uniform jacket or insignia of rank, approached her rapidly. "You should be with the soldiers," he said, pointing off toward the line of march.

"I am Lieutenant Falconer's new servant," Jennet said. She felt odd saying the words, as if she had marked herself as belonging to the lieutenant, as much his property as Copper or the burdens the horse carried. "Who are you?"

The gangly man came to a halt some paces away. His astonished expression was comical in its extremity, his eyes wide and his mouth open as if she had confessed to being an Extraordinary Coercer or even Napoleon himself. "You, Lieutenant Falconer's servant?" he exclaimed. "But you're nothing but a common soldier!"

"I assure you it's true," Jennet said, but she was less certain than she sounded. Now that her initial surprise had passed, she was again aware of how little she knew of the requirements of her new role.

"He cannot have been in his right mind," the man muttered, mostly to himself. "What do you know of service?"

That was directed at Jennet, with the slightest emphasis on "you" that cut through her feelings of inadequacy and irritated her into a sharp response. "I know it is polite to introduce oneself," she said, falling back on a formality of language she had not used in over ten years, "and I know the lieutenant is of sounder mind than you. My name is Graeme, and while it is true I am new to the lieutenant's service, I do not believe he would have chosen me if he did not believe I would suit. Now, I ask again, what is your name?"

The astonished look vanished, and the man's eyes narrowed. "My name is Eustis," he said, "and I am the personal servant to my lord Captain Lord Adair. And you will not take that tone with me."

"I apologize," Jennet said, not very contritely. "You can see how, lacking a knowledge of your identity, I might have responded poorly to someone who spoke to me so. I hope we shall get on." Why the man wore neither uniform nor stripes, she could not guess, but she did not wish to be at odds with someone who was in another respect her co-equal.

Eustis frowned, but when he spoke, his voice was calmer. "That will do, Graeme," he said. "I will overlook your rudeness this once, since I am convinced you know little of the requirements of your new station."

"That is true, and I hope you will be generous with your explanations." Jennet did not rate the odds of this very high, but she could pretend to humility if it meant not making a fool of herself in front of Falconer—or worse, making him look the fool because his manservant did not know his duty.

Eustis sniffed haughtily and turned to tend to one of the other horses, laden as Copper had been. He removed a uniform jacket from the bundles and donned it. It had no rank insignia and was tailored to fit him in a way unusual to an ordinary soldier. Jennet again eyed his stature—he must be nearly of a height with Falconer, which put him three inches taller than regulations demanded for a soldier not an officer—but refrained from asking how he had got around the restrictions.

"I have served the cap—my lord for many years," Eustis said, "so I am quite experienced at meeting an officer's demands. You are to prepare the lieutenant's food, yes? You will join me when we stop for the night, and follow my lead. There is a cookpot amongst his supplies, as well as dishes for use in service. I hope you know something of cooking."

Jennet nodded rather than saying anything about her inadequacies. Well, it was Falconer's lookout if he chose a soldier from the ranks as a servant.

Eustis eyed her again. "How odd that he should choose you," he said, but without his earlier rancor. "I trust you will not fail him. We who hold these positions have a duty..."

Jennet stopped listening. She did not need to have the importance of her position impressed on her, and she had already determined to do her best.

From far ahead, the signal sounded to advance. Jennet settled her gear more securely on her own back and waited for the wagon ahead of her to jerk into motion. To one side, the women following the company passed, trudging along in the chill morning air. Veronique still walked with her cloak wrapped around her, but showed no signs of discomfort.

Marie, walking near Veronique, caught Jennet's eye. Her smile widened, and she lowered her lashes coquettishly. Jennet pretended not to notice. It secretly amused her that Marie did not know Jennet was female and that her attentions were wasted on "Ned Graeme," but again for Whitteney's sake, she wished Marie were not so flirtatious.

The wagon ahead shuddered, one mule let out a sound between a groan and a snort, and the ponderous wheels began turning. Excitement stirred within Jennet as it always did upon beginning a journey. Soon enough, the road would become tedious, and Jennet would long for camp, but for now, with the breeze stirring her curls and the sun peeping over the horizon, all was right with the world.

CHAPTER 5

IN WHICH JENNET MAKES A NEW AND EXTRAORDINARY ACQUAINTANCE

The road leading south and west out of Soissons had not dried yet since the early morning's rains, and wet earth clung to Jennet's boots, giving her step a heaviness that would weary her over time. She could not help it; she glanced ahead to where Marie and Veronique and the other women walked. Their shoes could not be as sturdy as her own, and Jennet grudgingly sympathized with their plight.

Immediately ahead, one of the baggage wagons churned up earth into mud, its heavy, waist-high wheels leaving deep tracks that would fill with water at the next rainfall, making the road a nightmare to travel. Jennet hoped they would not return this way until summer's heat dried the road and made it passable again. Then she wondered what she *did* hope. She was not afraid to fight, but she did not love combat, her skill with the rifle aside. And yet battle was likely in her near future. Which meant her hope, like that of any soldier, was to survive.

To distract herself from such melancholy thoughts, she cast her gaze far ahead, past the head of the line. The French countryside was dreary in early summer, the fields either rows of barely-sprouted crops or fallow with tall yellow weeds. Off to one side, spreading, thick-leaved oaks delineated an unseen river. One of the trees, taller than the others, looked furry at this distance, and Jennet squinted to make out hundreds of black birds clinging to the branches. They looked cold, huddled together, despite the warmth of the day.

She walked faster out of habit, but had to slow when she realized her increased speed would have her running into the wagons. Controlling her impatience, she looked far ahead to where the line of marching men spooled out across the bleak landscape. Normally, she would have Corwin or Fosse or Sadler to converse with, provided the pace was not too brisk. Now, with no one to talk to, the pace dragged, one foot after another, on and on into the distance. Sighing, she picked a spot by eye about a quarter-mile ahead and focused on reaching it. That would give her something to look forward to.

No natural sounds disturbed the stillness of the morning, no birds crying, no rushing water from the distant river. There was only the creaking of the wagons' wheels and the sound of the mules' hooves striking the ground, a soft squelching noise echoed by Jennet's own feet. She began to fall into a reverie about warm fires and hot wine and shook her head to rouse herself. True, they were not anywhere that an enemy might surprise them, but that was no excuse for air-dreaming.

They reached Jennet's chosen milestone, a stone nearly big enough to be called a boulder, and Jennet found a new one. Then another. An hour passed, and the bugler sounded the signal for a five-minute rest. Jennet dug a loaf of bread out of her pack and ate a few bites, though she was not terribly hungry. It was always a good idea to take advantage of a rest when one could. A couple of soldiers raced forward from where they had fallen out of the line of march to relieve themselves, rejoining their comrades who had been carrying their packs for them.

When bugle and drum sounded again, she hoisted her pack and walked on, avoiding the mess the wagons made of the road. She made herself watch the farther tree line, which was nearly half a mile away to the west, for sign of ambushers. Alertness, and a certain amount of anticipatory fear, had kept her alive all these years.

A sharp crack echoed across the fields, startling a flock of birds into cawing flight. Jennet whipped around, bringing her rifle into position and scanning her surroundings for the shooter. Then she noticed the wagon just ahead had come to a stop, tilted alarmingly to one side with a wheel fallen flat on the ground beside it. The wagon drivers had climbed down and stood gathered around the damaged wagon, muttering to each other. They did not look up when Jennet approached.

"Axle's snapped clean in two," one of them was saying. "I told them it wouldn't hold, but no one listens to me, I'm just the one knows this beast backwards and forwards."

"Get 'er unloaded," another said. "We'll split the burden between the others."

Jennet hesitated. Unloading wagons was not one of her duties, but she did not like to leave a wagon unguarded, even here with no danger in sight. "Should I go ahead and tell the captain?"

The three men looked startled, as if they had not noticed her listening. "Might ought do that," said the first man. "Don't like falling behind." None of the other wagons had stopped when this one had broken down, and the women and others trailing the line were nearly past.

Jennet nodded and sprinted for the head of the line, one hand on her rifle to keep it from banging against her side.

The officers rode in advance of the men, but not very far ahead, and it took less than a minute for Jennet to find the beautiful black Suleiman. Out of breath, she could not call to Falconer, so she ran to where he would see her and came to a halt, panting. Falconer reined in, a look of concern on his face. "Graeme?"

"Wagon broke down, sir," Jennet gasped. "Axle. They're unloading."

Captain Lord Adair joined Falconer, glaring down at Jennet as if she were responsible for the debacle. "Delays," he growled. "Always delays." Without another word, he tilted his head back in the attitude of a Speaker. Jennet, uncomfortable, shifted her weight and looked away from the captain, feeling that her observation was in some sense a breach of his privacy, though he did not behave as if he felt he was doing something improper.

She looked covertly at Falconer, whose attention was on the captain. One hand gripped Suleiman's reins, while the other stroked the horse's mane. Jennet watched the hand move, her attention riveted on how perfectly shaped and masculine it was, just like the rest of him. What would it be like, she wondered, to have a Shaper's talent? How did he know what Shape to take? Jennet knew nothing of Shaping and could not help but think that it must take a great deal of effort and wisdom to alter one's body without altering it into something that could not survive, or would be easily injured.

"You there. Graeme, is it?" The captain's peremptory voice cut through Jennet's reverie. "Go back to the wagon and tell them not to unload. Someone will join them shortly to repair it. You're to stay with the wagon until it can move again, understood?"

Jennet cast a quick glance at Falconer. He did not look at all disturbed at this appropriation of his servant. "Yes, sir," she replied, and ran back the way she had come. She passed Fosse on the way; he looked at her inquiringly, and she said "Broken axle" as she rushed past.

Several boxes and bundles lay stacked neatly some short distance from the wagon when she returned. "Captain says not to unload," she said. "Someone's coming to repair the wagon."

The three men exchanged glances. They were all burly, heavily-muscled men who might have been triplets, so closely did they resemble one another with their thick black hair that grew heavily over their heads and bristled over their wrists. All that kept the illusion from being complete was their ages; two were older, their black hair threaded with grey, and one might have been Jennet's age. They looked exactly as Jennet imagined quartermaster's men would look.

"Repair the wagon," one of the older men said. It was not a question, but a statement of disbelief. "That axle's not fixing itself, I can tell you that."

"So, must we put everything back?" the younger man said. He removed his flat, wide-brimmed hat and scratched his head with grimy fingernails.

"I'm doing naught until I see this miracle," the third man said. He mopped his forehead with an enormous red handkerchief and tucked the cloth into his shirt. "No point doing the work twice."

They were now the last of the wagons in line. The position made Jennet anxious, as if they were being left behind in enemy territory. The wagon drivers had retreated into a huddle and ignored her. So she watched the company march away and tried not to feel abandoned.

She reminded herself of her duty and scanned the horizon. To the right, the west, was the forest, rising up past the fallow fields of yellow weeds. To the east, beyond the river, the fields were furred green with new growth, though Jennet could not tell what crop grew there. A stone farmhouse complete with outbuildings stood at the fields' far side, and smoke rose from its chimneys. Another river, this one unseen save for the line of trees that marked its course, flowed beyond the fields and the farmhouse. Its line of trees was decorated here and there with the black blotches of birds clinging to their upper limbs.

Something startled one of these flocks, and they winged upward in a confused, chaotic mass before organizing themselves into a glorious sphere that shifted and billowed like a black curtain and then flew away. Jennet watched them go. Birds were like the Army; they had structure and purpose and left no one behind if they could help it. Jennet could not imagine life outside her company.

And yet it seemed she was wrong, because one lone bird remained, grey rather than black and flying in a different direction from the flock. Flying toward Jennet, in fact. Jennet watched it idly. Any moment now, it would realize its mistake and rejoin the group.

But it never did. Instead, it continued on its path toward Jennet, growing larger until she realized it was not a bird, it was a man, flying behind something long and thin. Jennet watched, astonished, as the man approached as swiftly as a bird could fly and eventually alighted near the wagon. He wore a knit cap and a heavy grey twill coat with a fur-lined collar and strange billowing grey trousers tucked into boots of even better make than Jennet's. Enormous leather and glass eyepieces gave him the appearance of a startled insect. Beside him, the long, rounded wooden pole came to rest on the ground.

"I hear you have some trouble," the man said, and to Jennet's astonishment his voice was that of a woman, husky and low but recognizably female. "Lady Ashford, at your service."

The three men, who had been watching Lady Ashford's approach with open-mouthed astonishment, bowed low. "My lady, we didn't expect—" said the man who'd had doubts about the axle being fixed.

"No one ever does," Lady Ashford said cheerfully, removing her goggles. "Unhitch those mules, will you? And you might lead them farther away. Sometimes Moving makes animals skittish."

The wagon drivers hastily did as she asked. Lady Ashford smiled politely at each of them. Her smile wavered as she came to Jennet, and a narrow-eyed look of interest took its place. But she said nothing, merely turned to face the wagon and took up a stance that suggested she was bracing herself for exertion. Then the wagon lifted off the road, so smoothly none of its remaining cargo shifted. Gently, it rotated until the broken axle was nearest her. Still Lady Ashford remained motionless, though Jennet, watching her closely, saw that her stillness was the rigidity of extreme concentration.

The remaining wheel popped free of the axle and drifted to lie flat beside the other. Slowly, the broken halves of the axle slid free of their supports and fell to the ground. The new axle lifted into the air.

"This is the difficult part," Lady Ashford said. Despite her body's rigidity, her voice was calm, her breathing unlabored. "It has to fit just so, and sometimes it does not go in properly the first time."

Jennet held her breath. She would never have said replacing an axle was the stuff of legends, but she felt a great anticipation, as if Lady Ashford were performing some dangerous act. Beside her, the youngest wagon driver had his hat in both hands and was twisting it out of shape.

But Lady Ashford's warning was unnecessary. The axle slipped into its supports as neatly as a pin sliding into cloth. Both wheels followed and were fastened into place. Then the wagon came to rest on the ground, once more facing south.

"There," Lady Ashford said with satisfaction. "Shall I help you load?"

The three wagon drivers gave her identical horrified looks, as if she had suggested something indecent. "Couldn't ask her ladyship to load up, not at all," the oldest man said. "Quick, you lot, we can still catch up."

The three men began heaving boxes into the wagon. Jennet expected Lady Ashford to take to the skies again, but to her surprise, the woman walked to Jennet's side. "Are you their guard, then?"

"I...it is a precaution," Jennet stammered. "For when we are in enemy territory."

"That is sensible," Lady Ashford replied. She took a step closer, and in a low voice that proceeded no farther than Jennet's ears, said, "And what is a woman doing garbed as a soldier?"

The blood drained from Jennet's face. "You are mistaken. I am often taken for female—"

"Because you are female." Lady Ashford's expression was serious, and once more the searching, questioning expression narrowed her eyes. "Never fear, I shan't betray you. I am merely curious."

In the face of that stare, Jennet could not continue dissembling. "It is a protection. I do not wish to be openly female, not when that makes me prey to any man with hostile or lascivious intent. And I am a good soldier and an excellent marksman."

"I understand." Lady Ashford plucked at her trousers. "A woman in the Flight Corps is not always taken seriously, regardless of her talent and skill. But there, it is not possible to conceal one's sex." Then she smiled, dispelling her seriousness. "My protection is to be the best and most competent Extraordinary Mover in the Army."

"And are you?" Jennet spoke without thinking.

The smile deepened, and a dimple showed at the corner of Lady Ashford's mouth. "At the risk of sounding immodest, I am. Well, I am among the five most accomplished. Movers are all highly competitive, you know, and we love pitting ourselves against one another, vying for ranking. So today I am at the top, but tomorrow someone else might best me. It is enough for me."

The idea seemed preposterous, but Jennet knew as little about Moving as she did about Shaping, and it would be impolite to protest that Lady Ashford was having a joke at Jennet's expense. She merely nodded. "I understand the need to prove oneself." She touched the white armband. "If I am a good enough shot, it might protect me against the day my ruse is discovered."

Lady Ashford nodded. "I wish you luck, then, and hope I may see you again someday." She glanced to where the company was nearly out of sight, and her lips curved in another smile, this one mischievous. "What do you say we give them a show?"

Jennet frowned. "I don't understand."

"Climb up, and we will see how quickly we can catch them up." Lady Ashford turned away. Jennet watched her speak to the wagon drivers, none of whom looked happy. But they looked at the receding company as Lady Ashford had done, and apparently that brought them to a decision. Two of them mounted the mules, and the third broke into a run, following the receding company.

Lady Ashford again faced Jennet. Her smile broadened. "Surely you are not afraid? Not you of all people?"

Jennet finally understood what the woman had in mind. Swallowing, she said, "You want me to ride?"

"Unless you prefer to run," Lady Ashford said. "Quick, now, the wagon drivers will outpace us!"

In the face of Lady Ashford's impish smile, Jennet could not refuse. She climbed into the wagon seat and braced herself. The wagon lifted again, and Jennet grabbed the seat reflexively, but Lady Ashford's Moving was as steady as if the wagon had not left the ground at all.

Lady Ashford rose into the sky above Jennet. "It's not much of a distance," she called out, "and we need not hurry, but think how impressive it will be when we come Flying in to join them!"

Jennet gasped as the wagon Moved through the air, picking up speed as Lady Ashford Flew above it until they seemed to match the birds in their flight. Jennet let out a cry of delight she could not suppress. They passed the wagon drivers and their mules, and Jennet let go the seat long enough to wave at them as they looked up in astonishment. Wind buffeted her, tangled her curls and tried to steal her breath, yet she felt nothing but excitement. If she were a Mover, she might never come down to earth.

In practically no time, they reached the end of the line, and Lady Ashford put the wagon down. The wagon drivers appeared a moment later, tumbling off their mounts and hurrying to harness them. Jennet climbed down and grabbed the side of the wagon to steady herself. Her legs wobbled as if she had run herself to exhaustion.

"That was bracing," Lady Ashford said, startling Jennet with her near-silent approach. "I will report in to your captain, so you need not do so. And good luck to you." In another breath, she was in the air and Flying faster than a bird for the head of the line.

Jennet watched her until she swooped down and was lost to sight. She wondered if all Extraordinary Movers were so carefree. What would it be like to have a talent one could take joy in? She doubted Lady Ashford would have been so friendly had she known Jennet's talent.

The horses were hitched, the wagon drivers seated, and with a crack of the reins the wagon moved out. Jennet, sighing, strode to where she could walk beside it. It was unlikely she would have such great entertainment the rest of the way to Troyes.

CHAPTER 6

IN WHICH AN UNEXPECTED
ANIMOSITY IS REVEALED

Two hours after midday, the trumpet blared for a halt. The company had been walking for more than eight hours, since sunrise, and although she was accustomed to a much harder pace than this one, Jennet was weary and ready for a meal. But she no longer had the freedom to care for her own needs first. Suppressing a grimace of dismay, she crossed the camp in search of Copper and, with some effort, unloaded the lieutenant's possessions. Whoever had stowed them had done so with great cunning and care, and Jennet was not sure she would remember how to pack everything up again. She arranged the bags and boxes around her person and set off for the officers' tents and, with luck, Lieutenant Falconer himself.

All military camps were arranged along identical lines, and the officers' tents, erected by the quartermaster's men, were not far from the horse pickets. Jennet found Falconer outside the tents, speaking to the captain near a campfire tended by Eustis. It was an awkwardly-built affair that would smoke more than burn if not trimmed properly. Eustis paid Jennet no attention, but with an ostentatiousness that said he was keenly aware of her presence.

Jennet took her load into Falconer's tent and set down the many bundles. She did not know how he liked his things arranged, and after a moment's consideration, she decided not to make guesses. She did not believe he was the sort to expect her to intuit his desires; better to ask, and let him instruct her.

When she left the tent, the fire had indeed begun to smoke. Jennet hesitated, weighed the disadvantages of making Eustis look a fool against her desire to serve Falconer properly, and knelt next to the fire, carefully shifting logs until it was no longer smothering itself. Eustis glared at her, but said, "That's enough, Graeme, quite enough. Do not extinguish the fire."

Jennet reminded herself she wished to be polite and said, "Do we cook together, then?"

That seemed to offer Eustis the opportunity to redeem himself. "If you are not capable, surely," he said in a way just short of contemptuous. "The officers choose to eat together when the march makes it possible. I will, of course, supervise the meat, and you will fetch bread. Now, hurry on." He jerked his head in the direction of the quartermaster's wagons.

Jennet suppressed a comment about how she had just come from the quartermaster's wagons and might have fetched any amount of bread had she known. She hurried away and was soon the possessor of a couple of loaves of crusty bread, fresh that morning from the ovens of Soissons. They would not eat so well in future.

She knew little of how officers' meals were managed. On the march, a soldier carried his own rations, at least a few days' worth, but this sounded as if the officers were given fresh food every meal. She could not begrudge them; it was difficult to imagine captains or lieutenants hauling food. So undignified.

When she returned to the fire, a pot of water bubbled over the flames, and the smell of hot meat emitted from it. Captain Lord Adair and Ensign Townsend sat on camp stools near the fire, while Lieutenant Falconer stood a short distance away, talking to Lady Ashford. Jennet had not realized the Extraordinary Mover had remained with the company. She wished she had some reason to eavesdrop on their conversation, as Lady Ashford intrigued her, but she had to content herself with searching Falconer's belongings for dishes.

"Lady Ashford will dine with us," Adair said. He had not obviously been watching Jennet, but she knew his words were intended for her. She opened a basket containing fine pewter dishes, cups and plates and utensils. Falconer only had place settings for two, so where was she to find more plates?

"Graeme," Falconer said, startling Jennet, "we will need tea."

"Yes, sir," Jennet said. She looked around, but whoever had fetched water had apparently filled only enough buckets to boil the meat. She took another bucket and walked down toward the river, going upstream to find a spot that did not run foul. When she returned with the full bucket, she discovered there was no room over the fire for a second pot. She hated the thought of complaining to Falconer, who she knew would give her an indifferent look and instructions to figure it out herself. So she hurried back to where Fosse and Sadler had started a fire themselves.

"Ned!" Sadler exclaimed. "Here's himself condescending to sit with us lowlies. Have a seat, Ned." He rose and ostentatiously bowed, low enough to sweep his fingertips across the ground.

Jennet scowled at him in a friendly way. "I'm making tea for the officers."

"And so you are," Fosse said. "There's plenty of room. But tell us what it's like."

"Did I see an Extraordinary Mover go past above?" Sadler added.

Jennet settled in while the kettle boiled and told them of her morning's adventure. Corwin and Whitteney drifted in as she spoke, and at the end, Whitteney said, "Rubbing elbows with nobility, eh? Don't you all know who Lady Ashford is?"

"You know none of us cares about lords and ladies and what they get up to," Sadler scoffed. "But you can tell us anyway, as you're clearly keen on the subject."

"She inherited the earldom a few years back, on her father's death," Whitteney said, loftily ignoring Sadler. "There was a stink about it and no mistake. Her younger brother said as how he should be the new earl, him being a man and all that, but the House of Lords judged a woman who's an Extraordinary can inherit a title in her own right. So she's Countess of Ashford."

"Not that that exempts her from her four years' service," Fosse said. "She's quite the looker, though. Think she'd fancy a strapping young man like myself?"

"You'd need that million pounds you keep going on about," Sadler said, elbowing him. "She's fair above your touch."

Fosse twitched his queue over his shoulder. "Might could change my mind about settling down, with the likes of her."

"What's she like, Ned?" Corwin said in his slow, deep voice. He tossed a twig at the fire, but his eyes were on Jennet.

Jennet could hardly say that Lady Ashford was perceptive enough to have seen through Jennet's disguise. "She has a very free and easy air about her," she said instead. "She seemed almost casual about her talent, as if Moving an entire wagon were nothing but a game. And she said she and the other Extraordinary Movers are very competitive, always vying to see who is best."

Corwin whistled, long and low. "Can't imagine those competitions. See who Flies fastest, maybe? Or can Move the heaviest weight?"

"Extraordinaries get up to all manner of strangenesses," Whitteney said. "I heard as how that Lady Enderleigh, the Extraordinary Scorcher, burned her own husband and no one says nothing to challenge her."

Jennet had seen the power of Lady Enderleigh in Madrid and judged it even greater than Valencia's. She could easily believe the woman could get away with any abuse of her talent. Unexpected anger rose up within her. And yet Lady Enderleigh had high rank and a respected position in society, while Jennet... She made herself stop such imaginings. She had no right to judge others, not after the things she had done, and she certainly had no right to compare herself to another and demand equal treatment, even only in her heart.

The tea kettle let out a strangled whistle, and Jennet wrapped the tail of her jacket around the handle and lifted it from the fire. "I may be back later," she said.

"Hope as you don't have to desert your friends," Whitteney said with a smile.

"If those officers have aught sweet to eat, save us a crumb," Sadler added, clutching his uniform jacket over his heart with a piteous look.

Jennet returned to the officers' campfire and finished making tea. Eustis had laid out dishes from the captain's belongings. He had place settings enough for four people, complete with teacups, and Jennet poured out tea and handed the cups around. She had an absurd flash of memory, of watching her mother serve tea to visitors to the manse, and in that memory one of the guests had accidentally slopped hot, dark tea over the side of her cup, filling her saucer with a puddle. Jennet had been five, or was it six? Young enough not to realize laughing at another's misfortune was wrong. Why that memory remained when so many others from that time had vanished, she had no idea.

She dragged herself back to the present and set the kettle near the coals, where it would remain warm. The officers and Lady Ashford sat conversing casually, with no regard for the servants bustling about nearby. Since they did not lower their voices, Jennet felt not at all guilty about eavesdropping.

"We have another three days' journey ahead of us," the captain was saying. "I will have Mondy scout ahead every morning, but it is unlikely there are any French troops in the area. Most of them will have been drawn to join Napoleon's army near Paris."

"It is a good precaution," Townsend said. "You are wise to take it."

That, to Jennet, sounded like fawning sycophancy, given that there was nothing so remarkable about taking basic measures to protect the company. She kept her face as still as Falconer's so her disgust did not show.

"I am not so certain there are no French troops in a position to threaten us," Falconer said.

He was back to looking haughty again, but Jennet would not be fooled a second time. She assessed each of the four, examining their emotions. Townsend was, as she guessed, engrossed in wanting Adair to approve of him, possibly so he might achieve a promotion, though Jennet knew advancement in Army rank did not work that way; merely liking someone was not grounds for a field promotion. Or he might believe *Adair* was due a promotion, and wanted the captain to take him along as aide-de-camp or some other rank that would take Townsend away from the field. In any case, his toadying disgusted Jennet.

Lady Ashford's emotions were placid, indicating that the line of conversation did not disturb her. She had a cheerfulness about her Jennet liked. Falconer's demeanor again did not match his emotions; this time, however, he was tense, ready for an argument. His ability to maintain a calm if haughty demeanor despite his feelings impressed Jennet even as she wondered at the cause of his frustration.

Oddly, Captain Lord Adair had the same tension about him that Falconer did. Possibly there was bad blood between the two men, and they were accustomed to disagreeing with one another to the point that they anticipated every interaction turning into a fight. Adair also harbored a warmth of feeling whose object Jennet could not discern, as if he remembered someone he loved. She was about to examine the emotion more closely when she realized Eustis had addressed her at least once while she was preoccupied, and she withdrew from her observations.

Eustis had the meat from the pot and was engaged in slicing it, glaring at Jennet and then at the bread she had procured. Jennet came to herself and snatched up a loaf, which she began slicing. Her cuts were not even, and the bread had a ragged appearance, but there was nothing she could do about that save gain experience.

"I apologize for the rough living, Lady Ashford," Captain Lord Adair said, more politely than Jennet had believed him capable of. "We normally camp near enough to a town to take advantage of their hospitality, and eat more genteelly. But with the French becoming hostile to English presence on their soil, we must of necessity eat poorly."

Jennet caught a glimpse of Eustis' face; two pink spots rode high on his cheeks, and he kept his head ducked low so as to conceal his humiliation. Unexpectedly, Jennet sympathized with his desire to impress his master.

"Oh, it is no matter," Lady Ashford said with her customary cheerfulness. "I enjoy eating out-of-doors, and this beef is quite tender. Though I daresay I would prefer being in Paris—though not now, of course, not if Napoleon has captured it."

"I was in Paris recently, on my return from England." Adair patted his lips with a napkin, just as if he were dining in Paris himself. "The city was in an uproar, and there was nearly fighting in the streets between Napoleon's supporters and the royalists. It was quite melancholy, actually, recalling how beautiful the city used to be."

"I am very fond of Paris," Lady Ashford responded. "What of you, Lieutenant Falconer?" Her smile grew warmer, and she leaned toward the lieutenant in a way Jennet found irritating.

"I am not one for large cities," Falconer said, his voice cooling as if she had offered him insult instead. "I have never been to Paris."

Lady Ashford's smile faltered, but she pressed on in the face of his near-hostility. "Then you prefer the quiet of the countryside? I look forward to spending time on my estate when the war is over and my term of service is complete."

"I have always disliked the anonymity of a city." Falconer sounded marginally less arrogant. "I prefer the quiet company of a town. But I believe I can appreciate other people's experiences. Were you in Paris long, captain?"

"I was there only a day, long enough to discover Napoleon's intent," Adair said. "And then I left. I had no desire to become a victim of Coercion."

"Surely Napoleon's talent is not so strong as to enthrall those he cannot see?" Townsend exclaimed. "Would you have been in danger?"

"That is not a fate I wish to risk." Adair's eyes narrowed as he gazed at the fire, seeing some vista far from their camp. "It is unlikely his ability is so great, and I doubt he can Coerce anyone but those closest to him, but better not to take the chance."

Jennet could not argue with the captain's fears. She herself could Coerce people at a great distance, as far as her range of vision, though she could not Coerce anyone she could not see. That did not make her inclined to assume Napoleon's talent was the same. He had exercised it more frequently and for a longer time than she had, and who was to say whether Coercion did or did not become more powerful with use? But not wishing to put oneself in jeopardy—that, she understood.

"Then you were wise not to remain in Paris," Falconer said. He ate as steadily and placidly as if he were in an elegant dining room and not seated on a camp stool, but there was an edge to his words that recalled the tension Jennet had sensed before.

"It would have been foolishness to remain," Adair retorted, as if Falconer had challenged him instead. "I daresay *you* would have tested your luck in remaining."

"Not I." Falconer raised his cup to his lips. "I am certain you made the right decision."

Jennet considered peeking at their emotions again because she did not understand the conversation between the two men, aside from a suspicion that something deeper passed between them. But she disliked doing so when the need was not great. It was too close to actual Coercion. She silently refilled Townsend's cup when he held it out to her.

"We might have made overtures to the citizens of that town a mile west of here," Falconer continued. "We have no guarantees all the French will be hostile."

"You know the General Order as well as I, lieutenant," Adair said.

"I do, and it says nothing forbidding us interacting with the people, so long as we do not molest them." Falconer set his empty plate aside. "Billeting within a town is standard procedure."

"Longing for your comforts, Falconer?" Townsend jeered.

"I was thinking of the men," Falconer said. "The more we can depend on fresh supplies from the villages, the less the burden will be on them."

"I see," Adair said, in a tone that suggested he agreed with Townsend's assessment of Falconer's motives. "I judge it better to stay well away from any potential encounters, especially since we cannot know if anyone we meet has not been Coerced."

"That is overly suspicious thinking," Falconer said. "There may be French soldiers hereabouts, but we are not in country Napoleon could possibly have overtaken personally."

"Are you calling me a fool, lieutenant?" Adair sounded as if he hoped this were the case. Jennet held her breath, hoping he would not recall her presence and dismiss her.

Falconer did not react. "Those were not my words, captain. I suggest merely that too much caution can be as dangerous as too little."

"*I* decide how we are to proceed, not you." The captain thrust out his cup to Jennet to be refilled, but said nothing about how she and Eustis should withdraw. She poured silently. The tension between the two men fascinated her. She had assumed without considering matters that the officers stood on one side of a divide and the soldiers on the other, and that officers sided with one another whenever conflict arose. That Falconer and Adair might not agree with one another, let alone like one another, had never occurred to her.

"Naturally," Falconer said, sounding so indifferent it was impossible not to hear his words as an insult.

The captain shot to his feet. "I beg your pardon, lieutenant, for not being able to provide you living space and sustenance to meet your high standards," he said coldly. "Perhaps you would prefer to return to Soissons?"

Jennet held her breath. *That* was surely beyond the pale. Sending his lieutenant away as the company marched toward battle could be seen as nothing but contempt for Falconer, if not an outright demotion in status. Adair could not break Falconer the way he might, for example, take

Sergeant Hedley's stripes, but he was a lord as well as Falconer's ranking officer, so who knew what power he might have?

Falconer stood, slowly and with great deliberation. "I apologize for inadvertently criticizing you," he said, still as placidly as if this were no more than a mild difference of opinion. "Please excuse me. I must speak to Sergeant Hedley about the disposition of the camp. Graeme, with me."

Jennet hastily put down the kettle and followed Falconer, whose stride was almost too fast for her. Behind her, Townsend let out a nervous titter of a laugh that grated on Jennet, though it was likely not directed at her. She took a few more hopping steps to fall into place at Falconer's left and slightly behind.

The overcast had burned away mid-morning, and the afternoon was pleasant, the sun bright and the air warmer than it had been all week. Even the ground felt springy, not sodden. They walked past the ranks of tents set up in the fields on both sides of the road with the smell of dozens of cookfires filling the air. Jennet nodded quickly at Fosse and Sadler, who were seated at the fire still; they cast a glance at Falconer, and Fosse raised his eyebrows, but then Jennet and the lieutenant were past and Jennet could see no more of her comrades.

"No reason," Falconer said abruptly.

"Beg pardon, sir?" Jennet replied.

He glanced down at her. "That was not meant for you, Graeme. Do not trouble yourself."

"Of course, sir."

Falconer stopped, bringing Jennet to a halt. "I wonder," he mused. "But...no. If I send you to that town, I will certainly be accused of insubordination."

This seemed not to need a response. But Falconer had the look of a man who was not finished speaking. Jennet waited. Finally, Falconer said, "But it is very peculiar."

"What is, sir?"

Falconer looked off eastward. "That we should avoid that town so assiduously. It is not in the regulations. We should at least have sent someone to gather information."

His words made Jennet deeply uncomfortable. Surely Falconer should not criticize Jennet's superior officer in front of her? She shifted her weight, but said nothing.

"And Paris, too." Falconer shook his head, appearing to return to himself. "Forget I said that, Graeme. We will not approach that town." He set off walking again, and Jennet scrambled to keep up.

She waited patiently while Falconer spoke with Sergeant Hedley, not paying attention to the conversation. Falconer's indiscreet words puzzled her. It sounded very much as if he suspected Captain Lord Adair of something, she could not guess what. She did not believe the captain's behavior strange; he might be overly cautious in avoiding that town, but that was not in itself unusual. And leaving Paris before Napoleon overran it was simple good sense. Yet Falconer seemed to believe both these things spoke ill of Adair.

Eventually, Falconer left Hedley to his duties and gestured to Jennet to follow him again. This time, they crossed camp to where the animals were corralled. Suleiman and Copper were pegged out side by side, and Boyce was engaged in grooming Copper when they approached. Falconer stopped to greet Suleiman, and as before Jennet was struck by how his whole demeanor changed when he talked to the horse. After that, he turned to Jennet and said, "You will arrange my things in my tent. Then you'll clean my boots and see to making up my bed. In the morning, you will attend on me before sunrise. Do you have any questions?"

Jennet had many questions, beginning with *which of your things do you want?* and ending with *What bed?* But they were the sort she believed a real servant would not need to ask. "I thought—will you show me how you like your things arranged?" she asked instead.

Falconer petted Copper's broad nose absently. "I will show you presently." He made no move to leave Copper's side. Jennet tried not to fidget, though Falconer's stance was that of a man deep in contemplation of some riddle.

"I wonder," he said, again in that distant, half-audible way. "Why Paris? Why not Bound directly to Soissons?"

Again, Jennet's discomfort increased. She cleared her throat discreetly and shifted her weight, hoping Falconer would take the hint.

Falconer's gaze came to rest on her, and she shivered at being the focus of his attention. He really was too beautiful for words. "Never mind, Graeme," he said. "Come with me. I will show you how I prefer my things disposed."

"I'll do my best, sir," Jennet said.

Falconer smiled, and Jennet shivered again. "I did say you would find me not a harsh taskmaster, did I not? After your duties, you are free to return to your tent—I will not insist upon you waiting on my every whim."

Jennet gave Copper a pat and hurried after Falconer, for once not admiring his tall, shapely form and broad shoulders. He interested her more for the discrepancy between his arrogant demeanor and his calm, confident emotions. Surely someone who looked the way he did could be excused a little arrogance? And yet that did not seem to be his nature at all.

She wondered, too, at his relationship to Adair. If they disliked each other, it was not apparent to the men, or at least no one Jennet knew had ever commented on it. So their animosity would not affect her. But she was curious nonetheless. And why not indulge that curiosity, so long as she must of necessity be in a position to do so? It would give her something to consider during the long days' trek to Troyes.

CHAPTER 7

IN WHICH JENNET MAKES A HORRID DISCOVERY

Jennet woke, as she usually did, in the twilight hours before dawn, before the bugle of reveille. Rather than lie awake reflecting on how pleasant it was to have a tent, she rose and donned boots and jacket immediately. Dew quivered over the ground and the edges of the tent canvas, and the air was cool enough to feel refreshing rather than muggy.

No one else was awake yet, and she took the time to stir the fire from where Corwin had banked it the previous night. Then she jogged through the camp, stopping briefly to say good morning to Suleiman and Copper. The horses moved restlessly as she spoke to them in a low voice. The skies were clear, the sun a faint glow on the horizon, and Jennet guessed it would be a real summer day.

She arrived outside Falconer's tent just as the flap moved and the lieutenant emerged. He was as clean-shaven as ever, and in some dismay Jennet said, "I should have been faster, and you should not have had to fetch shaving water yourself, sir."

Falconer smiled, his eyes lighting with amusement. "No Shaper need ever worry about shaving. We can choose to prevent those hairs from growing." He ran his hand over his smooth chin. "Not something you are concerned about at your age, yes?"

Jennet was accustomed to men commenting on her youthful "male" appearance and did not so much as twitch. "Not I, sir, but my father was as hairy as they come, so I warrant that is in my future."

Falconer shrugged into his uniform coat and began buttoning it. "What family did you leave behind in Scotland, Graeme?"

That struck her a blow as his casual comment about shaving had not. For an instant, she heard screams and musket shots and the crackle of uncontrolled fire. "I...none, sir. My family are all dead, long ago."

"I beg your pardon, Graeme, I did not realize." Falconer fixed her with his steady gaze. "Is that why you joined the Rifles?"

Jennet nodded, swallowing hard against memories. "I had nowhere else to go, and I am a fair shot. It seemed the best choice."

"Yes, you are quite the marksman, I see." Falconer nodded at her armband. "Well. Start the water boiling, Graeme, I like a cup of hot tea to start the day. Can you make porridge?"

"I can, sir."

"Then I suggest you do that. It is Captain Lord Adair's opinion that porridge for breakfast is healthful. I will visit Suleiman." With another nod, Falconer walked away. Jennet watched him for a moment or two before coming to her senses. She picked up the kettle and trudged away to the river.

The sky was a paler blue, and water boiled in two camp kettles, before Eustis appeared. He was yawning, and his uniform jacket was buttoned improperly. Jennet briefly considered not telling him, but decided she did not feel the kind of resentment toward him that would take pleasure in seeing him chastised by Adair for slovenliness. "Mr. Eustis," she said, "I believe your jacket is awry."

Eustis' expression soured. "I don't need your help, Graeme," he said, but his fingers flew to the jacket front, running up and down before discovering the misalignment. He half-turned away and swiftly buttoned the jacket correctly. Jennet worked at pouring oats, a pinch or two at a time, into one of the camp kettles, and said nothing more.

"Taking your time, Graeme?" Eustis said when he turned back to face her. He extended a hand for the sack of oats. "We will be here all day at this rate."

Jennet did not hand it over. "Aye, and they will eat solid lumps of porridge if I hurry," she said. "It will not take so long, sir, and better the officers have something edible, yes?" It had taken her exactly one time pouring all the oats into the pot at once, and eating the resulting solid mess, to teach her the value of patience.

Eustis grunted, but lowered his hand. He turned his attention to the tea kettle, measuring out tea and setting out cups. "I see you're not a complete loss, Graeme," he said, as if his insistence about the porridge had been a test.

"Thank you, sir," Jennet said without a trace of sarcasm. "Have you served the captain long?"

"I came out with him in '09, when the 95th made its first big recruiting push." Eustis for once did not sound hostile. "My father is steward on Lord Adair's country estate."

That explained both Eustis' lack of rank and why he was taller than regulations demanded. "That is a great honor, then."

"I am conscious of what I owe my lord." Eustis poured out a dark, aromatic stream of liquid into one cup. "As you should be conscious of the duty you owe Lieutenant Falconer. He need not have singled you out, so you must always show him respect."

Jennet nodded. She did not need a lecture about gratitude, and she did not believe she owed Falconer servility, but it benefited her to have Eustis as an ally. She continued stirring the pot and gradually adding oats. The hot-water scent turned richer and slightly sweet. Jennet was not fond of porridge, but she had learned not to turn her nose up at any food that was forthcoming. But the officers were unlikely to invite her to eat with them, so it did not matter.

A slight *whoosh* of air drew her attention to where Ensign Mondy abruptly appeared a short distance from the fire. The company's Bounder flexed his hands as if they were cold and stiff. "Tea," he demanded, striding forward. "I am near frozen from Skipping so high."

Eustis poured him a cup, which Mondy cradled in his hands rather than drinking immediately. His pale grey and blue uniform contrasted oddly with Jennet and Eustis' dark green jackets, but it would blend in well against the daytime sky, a precaution against being shot at by the French. If Mondy had Skipped high, he likely wished to take the added precaution of staying well out of range.

Jennet wanted to ask Mondy what he had seen in his Skipping about the countryside, but she knew he would say only, "That is for the officers," and therefore there was no point. It surprised her that Mondy was abroad so early, as she knew Bounders did not usually Skip during times of darkness because they could not see to surveil the ground. But Mondy was nothing if not diligent.

A nearby tent flap moved, and Adair emerged, fully dressed and looking alert, if slightly bleary-eyed. "Mondy," he said. "Your report?"

Mondy glanced at Jennet and Eustis, then back at Adair.

"Never mind the servants," Adair said impatiently. "What news?"

Mondy settled into a respectful parade rest stance. "No French troops within ten miles, sir. There are a number of villages on today's route, but nothing big enough to conceal any strength of the enemy."

"You'll continue to scout ahead as we go." Adair walked over to Eustis and accepted a cup of tea. "Not too far ahead. With Napoleon directing his army again, we must be alert to the possibility of danger, but you should not advance so far you cannot return in a timely fashion."

"I will return shortly, then," Mondy said, and vanished with a faint *pop*.

Adair took a seat on one of the camp stools. "Ah, porridge," he said, inhaling deeply. "I have never regretted beginning the day with such a bracing meal. Take care not to ruin it with hastiness, Graeme."

"No, sir." Jennet gave the pot another stir. It had assumed a gloopy, glutinous texture Jennet did not find appetizing. Fortunately, she was not expected to eat it.

She served up a plateful and handed it to Adair, who ate with every appearance of pleasure. Despite her lack of interest in the porridge, Jennet's stomach rumbled with hunger. She hoped Adair could not hear it, as he might take it as presumptuousness.

She saw Falconer approaching across the weedy, overgrown field and scooped up more porridge for him. He was eating something, she noticed, but it had disappeared by the time he reached the officers' fire. "Thank you, Graeme," he said when he accepted his plate. Jennet controlled a smile. If Falconer had the cleverness to claim some more appetizing morsel elsewhere in camp so that his breakfast need not be solely porridge, she approved.

"You will pack my things, and then you may return for your own breakfast," Falconer said. He ate more daintily than Adair, taking small bites slowly that concealed the fact that he ate very little of what was on his plate. Jennet handed him a cup of hot tea, which he drank with more apparent pleasure.

Falconer's belongings were still arranged tidily enough they seemed the set of a stage play rather than anyone's living quarters. Jennet stowed everything as neatly as she could, hoping she recalled accurately where everything had gone before. There was, in fact, no shaving tackle, though Falconer owned a fine steel mirror. She examined it for a little while, wondering if Falconer used it to guide his Shaping of his body or face. Her own face was still thin from months of marching on poor rations. To her eye, she looked feminine, but that could not be the case or she would have been discovered years ago.

Having folded away Falconer's bedding, she disassembled the clever little cot he slept on and packed the pieces into their bag, which was the size of her own pack but narrower. She had heard some officers carried actual folding iron bed frames—or, more accurately, the baggage train carried them. Falconer's cot was lightweight yet sturdy, and it was easy enough to assemble that Jennet had needed only one demonstration to understand how it worked.

When she emerged from Falconer's tent, it was to the sound of an argument. Falconer and Adair faced one another, plates and cups abandoned on the ground near their feet. Both men stood mere inches apart, their bodies tense with anger. Townsend had joined them, but he stood a short distance away, holding a plate half-full of porridge, his eyes wide. Eustis crouched beside the fire in the attitude of someone who wished he were invisible.

"You are in no position to make demands, lieutenant," Adair shouted.

"It is hardly a demand," Falconer replied, his voice quieter but every bit as intense. "It is practice—"

"*You* were the one who pointed out we are not in territory Napoleon could possibly have captured." Adair's face and throat were red with fury. "There is no reason to send Mondy far afield. I am satisfied with the report he has made."

"Ensign Mondy's capabilities are not the issue." Falconer raised his voice enough to cut across Adair's. "It is standard practice for the company Bounder to scout ahead a minimum of twenty miles, so as to provide intelligence about the ground the company will cover—"

"Twenty miles will take Mondy most of the day, in which time we will have covered half the ground he surveils. I decide how to implement policy, lieutenant, not you. *You* will set the troops packing to move out. Is that understood?"

Falconer looked more furious than Jennet had ever seen him. But he merely said, in a forceful but polite voice, "I understand. Pray, excuse me."

He turned and nearly ran into Jennet. Blushing, Jennet retreated a few steps. "Graeme, with me," Falconer said, as calm as if he and the captain had not nearly come to blows. Jennet hurried to match his pace as he strode away.

They walked in silence for a time. Jennet cast quick, covert glances at Falconer from time to time. He still looked angry, his brow furrowed, his perfect lips pinched so tight they made a thin white line across his face. Jennet could not imagine why he wanted her with him and was afraid to disrupt his meditation with questions.

Finally, Falconer said, "You have not yet breakfasted."

"No, sir. Everything is packed, though."

"Go and get something to eat. The quartermaster's men will load my things onto Copper. Then report to the wagons before the signal to march."

"Yes, sir." Hesitating, Jennet added, "May I ask a question, sir?"

Falconer glanced her way. "Of course."

"Why should Ensign Mondy not scout fully ahead?" It was impertinent, but Jennet had not liked the bad feeling between the officers, and she wished to know what lay behind it. Animosity between her commanders could spill over onto her.

To her surprise, Falconer came to a halt. "Captain Lord Adair would like Ensign Mondy to stay close to the company, in case he is needed to Bound elsewhere. Ensign Mondy's Skipping range is a mere three hundred and fifty feet, which makes him slow at Skipping. If he scouts a full twenty miles in advance of our march, he will not be able to return quickly enough to warn us of trouble."

"Because a Bounder cannot Bound to an outdoor location." Jennet knew little of talents other than her own, but she knew what everyone did about Bounding: the outdoors, full of trees and birds and other things that were constantly moving, could not provide a Bounder with anything solid enough to act as a signature, or focus, for traveling to. In camps, they erected Bounding chambers, but those were not practical on the march.

"Correct." Falconer was not looking at Jennet; his gaze was fixed on some distant point, his eyes unfocused as if he were thinking of something else. "But that twenty miles is our security, Graeme. It protects our company from walking into an ambush. That is why it is standard practice."

"Then, why?" Jennet knew it was none of her business, but she had always known Adair to be committed to following the rules, and this struck her as out of character for him.

Falconer shook his head, again as slowly as if he were in deep contemplation. "I don't know, Graeme. But it disturbs me. I wonder if his anger indicates some other trouble, possibly a personal one." He blinked, shook his head once more, and added, "I don't imagine I have to tell you to say nothing of this to anyone."

"Of course not!"

Jennet's outraged outburst amused Falconer, and she warmed at his smile before sternly telling herself to stop being foolish. "I would never speak of anyone behind his back," she said.

"You are the soul of discretion, Graeme." Falconer continued to smile, but the expression became contemplative again. "Go on, have your breakfast. I hope it is not porridge, for your sake. I have no idea how a man can march all day on a bellyful of oats, as if he were a horse or an ox."

"I'd rather sausage, sir," Jennet said with an answering smile. At his laugh, she hurried away to her tent.

Hers was the only one still standing in the area where they had camped the previous night. The delicious aroma of sausage wafted toward her, and she ran the last few steps only to say with dismay, "But you cannot have eaten all of it?"

Whitteney and Fosse laughed. Fosse produced a battered tin plate upon which lay two fat sausages, greasy and delicious-looking. "We would not treat you so poorly, Ned," Fosse said. "Since you were unlikely to dine with the officers."

Jennet bit into one of the sausages. The salty, meaty taste exploded in her mouth. It was so much superior to porridge she could not help saying, through her mouthful, "The captain believes in the healthful properties of an oat porridge."

The men around the campfire groaned. "Good thing the captain cannot override what we men are allotted by law," Sadler said, "or at any rate by Army regulation."

"I savor every bite now that we have regular, proper rations again," Whitteney said. He put his arm around Marie and hugged her close. "I have more mouths than my own to feed."

Jennet wolfed down the rest of her sausage and started in on the second. Probably Whitteney was correct, and she should eat slowly to appreciate her meal, but she was too hungry for that.

Corwin was engaged in putting out the fire, but he stopped what he was doing to smile at Jennet. "Nay, do not choke, we have no Extraordinary Shaper to save you if you do."

"'Tis not a thing an Extraordinary Shaper can manage," Sadler said. "It would be all Ned's own lookout if he chokes."

Jennet did not reply. Appleton had just come into view, with Veronique trailing him as usual. Veronique's cloak was flung back, revealing her high, round belly. Jennet was too far away to hear what Appleton and Veronique said to one another, but they did not touch or stand close together the way two people in love might. "I hope she is not close to her time," she said under her breath.

"What was that?" Corwin, who was closest to Jennet, turned to follow the line of her gaze. "Nay, she has weeks to go, poor lass."

"How do you know?" Jennet asked.

Corwin shrugged. "My mother was a midwife, and I saw her deliver many a child. But 'tis a wonder Appleton did not arrange for Veronique to stay in Soissons. The march is no place for a woman with child."

The others had stopped talking to listen to Corwin. Fosse said, "Fancy you knowing all that! 'Tis a pity you went for a soldier, and not for a midwife yourself."

"A man-midwife?" Corwin laughed, which he did rarely, and his deep, slow voice boomed out in the morning stillness. "Sure and that's unnatural. And it has been many a year since I helped at my mother's side."

"'Tis like to be a good thing, that, as your face might scare the babes," Sadler joked.

Corwin's laughter faded. For a moment, his face looked positively villainous in its terrible scowl. "I am no one a new mother is like to want nigh," he said. "Nor any of us, killers of men as we are. 'Tis a bad omen over a child. My mother—" He blinked, then turned away. "We ought fall in, 'tis nearly time to march."

Fosse cleared his throat, but said nothing. Sadler for once looked embarrassed. Whitteney took Jennet's empty plate. "Go and put away your tent, Ned."

"Do you still enjoy your new status?" Fosse asked. He clearly wanted to pretend Corwin's moment of raw honesty had not happened.

Jennet considered the argument she had heard and what she had witnessed of Adair's behavior. "Enjoyment is the wrong word," she said. "But it is interesting."

The others laughed awkwardly as she hurried to her tent and packed her things. It had not occurred to her, until Fosse's last words, that becoming Falconer's servant might put a divide between herself and the others. But they were as genial and pleasant as always. Guilt at having Coerced them into friendliness stabbed her heart. *Suppose*, she thought, but fiercely suppressed that silly, sentimental notion. They would not be her friends if they knew who she was.

She reached the wagons a minute before the signal to march sounded. Her silver pocket watch told her it was just gone six o'clock. Once again she observed Veronique, whose expression was still and placid. The woman rested one hand on the lower curve of her belly, but she did not look pained or uncomfortable. Jennet hoped Corwin's assessment of her condition was correct. She could not imagine the difficulties of giving birth in a field or, worse, in the middle of a battle.

The day was much like the previous one, though with the minor diversion of crossing the Marne River just after nine o'clock. They took brief rests every hour, with those who had fallen out of the line of march returning in a hurry to their fellows at those times. Jennet trudged in the wake of the repaired wagon with her mind roaming free, focusing now and then on some distant landmark to give herself something to dispel the boredom.

She watched the skies for Mondy, but never saw him Skip past. Marie continued to cast coquettish glances her way; Veronique continued to fix her gaze on her feet, with her cloak pulled tightly around her. The air was warmer, enough that Jennet could wish to remove her jacket and feel the breeze against her body.

They passed a village at nearly eleven-thirty, though the line of march took the company well to one side of it, too far to see people. Jennet watched thin spirals of pale smoke trail from the chimneys across the blue sky. It had been a long time since she had had a home with a chimney. The realization startled her, not because of how long a time it had been, but that she had considered such a thing at all. It was not as if she missed having a home, not when the Army suited her so well. And yet this was the second time in days she had contemplated what she might do when the war was over. She deliberately dismissed the thought. Time enough for maundering when Napoleon was defeated, if that ever happened.

Like the previous day, the company stopped a few hours after noon. They were, again, nowhere near a village, which struck Jennet as odd. Usually the quartermaster's assistant rode ahead to assess the villages as possible hosts for the company, or at the very least for its officers, and they had passed a likely-looking village only an hour before. But, odd as this was, it was nothing Jennet was responsible for. She wearily walked to where the horses were gathered to find Copper. The horse greeted her with a pleasant whicker and a soft nose pressed against her chest. Copper seemed to enjoy the company of her fellows, at least as far as Jennet could imagine a horse to have such feelings.

Jennet removed Copper's burdens and made a neat pile of Falconer's possessions before turning the horse over to Boyce for grooming and care. She gathered up the load, distributed it evenly around her person, and trudged away to Falconer's tent. As before, the bundles and bags were heavy and slipped often. Jennet stopped to heave the bag containing the cot across her shoulders and marched on, cursing under her breath.

"I did not intend you to be a beast of burden, Graeme," Falconer said. Jennet jumped, made a grab for one of the bags that slid down her back, and dropped two others in her surprise. Falconer picked both of them up. "I think, between the two of us, we can manage," he said, and strode away, leaving Jennet gaping after him. She recollected herself immediately and hurried to catch up.

"Sir, I really can carry it all—you need not—" she stammered.

Falconer did not look her way. "When I was a boy," he said, "my brothers and I used to play at highwaymen. We cajoled our father into permitting us to camp behind the house—a copse grew there, and we had a tent we all three barely fit into. I now believe two of the stable hands kept an eye on us, but at the time we imagined ourselves quite grown-up. We would stage raids on the stables and the kitchens, and eat our fill of bread and cheese and tartlets beside our fire. Then we went away to school, one by one, and when we returned, the joy had gone out of our youthful activities." He shifted his load to ride higher on his shoulder. "Making camp reminds me of those lost days. You would not deprive me of my pleasures, would you, Graeme?"

Jennet gaped. "No, sir. Of course not. But—"

"Do not suppose me too intent on my privilege, soldier," Falconer said, with amusement rather than sternness. "We all still have boyishness in us, even the loftiest general."

Falconer's tent had been set up by the time they reached the officers' fire. The lieutenant set the bags inside the tent flap and gestured to Jennet to hand over the rest of her load. "Fetch water, Graeme, and let's have some tea," he said. "I will handle this."

"But—sir, surely an officer—or is Boyce—"

Falconer waved a hand. "Boyce is caring for the horses. I have nothing else to do at the moment, and I see no reason I should sit idle."

Jennet got a good look at his face finally. He had sounded carefree, but his mouth was drawn down at the corners in an expression of anger. "Is something wrong?" she dared ask.

Falconer's eyes narrowed, as if he were considering something. Finally, he said, "Mondy has not returned from scouting ahead."

Jennet blinked. "But you said, if he were to go the full twenty miles, it would take him some time to return."

Falconer lowered his voice. "Captain Lord Adair chose to send him only ten miles ahead. He should have been back by now." He stepped closer to Jennet as if inviting a confidence. "It may yet be nothing. Pray, do not speak of this to anyone. There is no point rousing concerns until evening."

Jennet nodded. "You can count on my discretion, sir."

Falconer smiled. "I know, Graeme. Now. Kettle. Tea."

Jennet grabbed up a bucket and saluted Falconer with it. "Right away, sir."

She ran across the field to where the trees grew along the riverside. Thick green leaves covered every branch, a welcome sign of summer, and the air smelled clear and fresh and damp. The river, which was only about ten feet across, flowed swiftly, intent on its rendezvous with the Aisne. Jennet made her way carefully down the muddy bank and leaned well out to fill the bucket, trying not to stir up silt that might find its way into it.

Her foot slipped a little as she stood upright, and she flailed to keep her balance, finally grabbing hold of a sapling to steady herself. She crouched, breathing heavily, until she was confident she would not fall into the mud.

Her eye fell on an oddly-shaped shadow between two of the larger willow trees that had been obscured by the undergrowth. It had not been visible until she had crouched and could look beneath the bushes. Her first thought was that it was an abnormally regular and thick branch. Jennet pulled herself upright using the sapling and carefully took two steps toward the shadow, brushing aside the undergrowth.

Then the scene came into focus. Jennet gasped, dropped the bucket, and fell to her knees beside the body. This close, the scent of the blood drenching the man's chest was overpowering. The blood was bright red and smelled and looked fresh. Jennet's gaze took in the man's uniform— pale gray and blue, not green like a rifleman's—and the gash in his throat that had bled so horribly before finally coming to his face.

It was Ensign Mondy.

CHAPTER 8

IN WHICH FALCONER DRAWS A
SHOCKING CONCLUSION

Jennet stuffed a fist into her mouth to keep from crying out. She had seen many dead bodies in the past six years, had made many of them dead herself, but seeing Mondy's body so carelessly abandoned, his eyes open and startled, horrified her in a way she had never thought to feel again.

She scrambled to her feet and backed away through the willow branches. It felt like dropping a curtain to conceal the horrid sight, though now she knew what the shadows actually held, she could not stop seeing the body. Her foot kicked the bucket, and shakily she picked it up. Water sloshed in its bottom. She looked at it uncomprehendingly. Mondy was dead; what did a bucket matter?

In the next moment, she was off and running for the camp. She should report this to the captain, but instinct directed her feet elsewhere.

It took her several minutes to locate Falconer, during which time her mind madly insisted she was taking too long and something would happen to the body because of her slowness. She knew that was foolishness, but the sight of that bloody gash left her unable to think sensibly. Finally, she ran the lieutenant to ground at the makeshift paddock, where he was talking to Suleiman as Boyce carefully checked the horse's shoes. That Falconer spoke to his horse as if it were human struck her as reasonable for once, at least as reasonable as Mondy's death, which was to say, not reasonable at all. But she still was not reasoning clearly.

Falconer's cheerful expression—the one he usually wore when communing with his horse—faded as he took in Jennet's appearance. She had no idea what that appearance was, but surely she looked frightful, her eyes still wide with horror, her clothes disheveled from running. "Come with me, sir," she panted. "You must come immediately."

Falconer, to his credit, did not argue or insist on an explanation. He ran with her, shortening his stride to match hers, to the river. Panic threatened to strike as she searched for her trail and did not at first see it. In the next moment, she saw trampled grasses, and she led the way to the willow tree and the body beneath it.

She held the branches aside, once more feeling as if they were a curtain on some stage play. Falconer came to a halt just inside their shelter, breathing in sharply. Then he knelt near the body and tilted Mondy's head back. "Someone very nearly removed his head," he said, sounding as calm as if he were discoursing on the plants that grew nearby. "The wound is deep. And I daresay, by the look on his face, he was not expecting it. I believe he was attacked from behind."

"Who would do such a thing, sir?" Jennet's hands had stopped shaking, and she had nearly regained her breath.

"Someone he knew, clearly. Someone he did not fear turning his back on." Falconer rubbed his hands off on the short grass that grew by the willow's roots and stood. "This was premeditated. As to the specifics, Mondy was not popular, and he might have had any number of enemies. But one who hated him enough to kill him? I cannot guess who that might be."

"What is to be done, then, sir?"

Falconer held up a hand for silence. He scanned the ground, then took a few careful steps toward the river. "Were these here when you discovered him?" he said, gesturing at the muddy wreck her fumbling had made of the bank.

"Those are my tracks, sir," Jennet said. "I slid on the bank, and scrambled to find footing."

Falconer nodded. He circled Mondy's body, pushing aside the undergrowth to peer at the ground. He stopped near the base of the willow tree and dropped to one knee, touching the ground. "Show me your boot."

Jennet obediently lifted one foot. Falconer shook his head. "The print is too large to be yours, and I have not trod here. Two deep prints, and three shallower ones to the side."

"What does that mean, sir?"

Falconer turned in her direction, but his eyes were remote, staring past her at the river. "It means Ensign Mondy was assaulted by one man, not a gang. One man, who left this spot and headed back toward our camp. The boot prints are not so remarkable as to identify a singular individual, unfortunately. One man who might be anyone in the company..."

His voice dwindled to nothing, and he continued to stare at the river in thought. Jennet, impatient as well as frightened, said, "Sir, what else is there?"

"There was no time," Falconer said, almost to himself. "I believed Mondy to have disappeared two hours ago, but he was obviously killed in this place—the amount of blood on the ground proves it. And yet we stopped for the night not even an hour ago." He blinked, and focused on Jennet. "Go and fetch Captain Lord Adair. Revealing to the men what happened here is his responsibility."

Jennet nodded and ran for the camp.

Adair was having a conversation with the quartermaster when Jennet located him. She waited, breathing heavily from exertion, until he deigned to notice her. "Graeme, yes? What is it?"

Jennet glanced at the quartermaster, who regarded her with a complete lack of interest. "Captain Lord Adair, sir," she said, "it's about Ensign Mondy."

"What about him?" Adair glared at Jennet, his eyes narrowed.

Jennet decided she did not care if Mondy's death should be kept secret. "The ensign is dead, sir."

Adair jerked back in surprise. Beside him, the quartermaster let out a grunt. Adair ignored him. "Show me," he said.

Jennet ran with the captain back to the riverbank to where Falconer waited. She saw the nearest picket watching curiously, and she could not help wondering what he imagined of her running back and forth. He could not possibly guess the truth.

When they were close, Falconer said, "Ensign Mondy has been murdered, sir."

Murder. The word hung in the air like a miasma, something that would not vanish with the wind. Adair said, "Murder, lieutenant?"

Falconer merely beckoned the captain to follow him. Jennet stayed behind. She did not need to see the body again.

Presently, Adair and Falconer emerged. "It might have been bandits," Adair was saying. "Some passerby who attacked Ensign Mondy for the contents of his purse. We should not jump to conclusions."

"I agree, sir, but we can make certain assertions based on the evidence," Falconer said. "The footprints indicate there was one assailant, not a band of thieves. And whoever it was returned in the direction of our camp. I will talk to the picket sentries immediately. I believe the murder was committed as camp was being set up, before the pickets were posted, but if I am wrong, they may have seen our murderer."

"This is a disaster, lieutenant, a true disaster," Adair said. "We have no idea why someone might have wanted Mondy dead? No enemies?"

"I knew very little of Ensign Mondy." Falconer was back to sounding indifferent. "Once I have spoken to the pickets, I will search the area further."

"Good." Adair's gaze fell on Jennet, and she stood up straighter. "Graeme, fetch me some of the quartermaster's men, and have them bring a large piece of canvas. Then you're to help with the meal. There's no reason your regular duties should be shirked."

Jennet nodded and ran for the wagons.

When she had sent the quartermaster's men on their way, she hurried back to the officers' tents. Eustis was there, tending the fire and a steaming pot of boiled meat. "Where have you been?" he demanded. "I had to fetch water myself. That's your job, fetching and carrying. It's beneath me."

"My apologies, Mr. Eustis." Weariness descended on Jennet all at once, not just because of all the running she had done. Explaining the situation to Eustis felt impossible, not to mention that Adair almost certainly did not want her spreading the news about Mondy's death, not even to his personal manservant, until he was in a position to announce it.

She trudged to the quartermaster's wagons for bread, unable to stir herself to greater alacrity. Mondy dead. He was—had been—arrogant and quick to report infractions of military rules, but surely that was not enough to get him killed? Nor would anyone whose request to be Bounded he had refused see that as a reason for murder.

She cut somewhat neater chunks of bread than she had managed the day before and made tea while Eustis tended the meat in silence. At some point, the news would become public, and then Eustis might have much to say. She considered asking him if he had known Mondy, but decided that was too close to giving away the secret.

She saw, some distance away still, Falconer and Adair approaching. The two were deeply involved in conversation that cut off when they were within earshot of the fire. Falconer veered away to enter his tent, while Adair lowered himself onto a stool and accepted the plate of food Eustis prepared for him. Jennet poured out tea, but he waved it away, instead helping himself to the flask he wore at his hip. It was of silver engraved lightly with a swirling letter Jennet thought might be an N.

"You might as well know," he said in his gruff voice. "Ensign Mondy has been murdered."

Eustis gasped and let the long-handled fork with which he turned the meat fall into the pot. "*Murdered,* sir? You don't mean murder. Was it the enemy, sir? Or bandits?"

Adair shook his head and took another drink, not as deep as the first, before putting the flask away. "I mean murdered, Eustis, by someone in this company. We'll get to the bottom of it, but for now I've requested another Bounder to retrieve Mondy's body, to return him to his parents, and then to take over as scout for the 3rd."

Falconer emerged from his tent. He had combed his hair and straightened his jacket, but Jennet was still too shaken to appreciate the sight. He sat beside Adair and settled his plate on his knees. "We cannot afford to stop if the Bounder does not arrive immediately. We may have to bury Mondy for later retrieval."

"I won't leave a man behind, even if he is dead," Adair said. He cut a piece of meat and bit into it ferociously, as if he could dispose of Falconer's objections as readily. "Particularly as his father has great political influence and will not want his only son buried in a foreign land. The Bounder should arrive before nightfall."

Falconer said nothing. Jennet supplied him with a cup of tea, to which he nodded thanks. She knew he was fond of the beverage, but she had never seen him drink quite so avidly before, avidly and without attention to the flavor, something he normally savored. He might appear calm, but he was anything but.

Rapid footsteps preceded the appearance of Ensign Townsend, whose fair face was flushed from running. "Is it true, sir? About Mondy?"

"It is." Adair continued eating in that rapid, almost angry manner.

"What a shock," Townsend said. "I suppose that is why he went missing? What a terrible shock."

"He went missing long before he was killed," Falconer said. He had his eyes on his plate as if it were the most fascinating thing he had ever seen.

Townsend turned his gaze on Adair. "How is that possible?"

"What matters is that the evidence shows he was not killed by a passing French peasant, and the footprints near the body returned this direction." Adair, too, was not looking anywhere but his plate. "Someone in this camp killed him, and I will find out the truth."

"Of course you will, sir," Townsend said. "Graeme, a cup of tea, if you please."

Townsend had never been polite to Jennet before. It was astonishing what a terrible surprise could do for someone's personality. Jennet handed him a cup and then covertly watched him drink it. His eyes were bright and his cheeks continued redder than usual. His reaction struck her as more extreme than the situation warranted, unless he had been better friends with Mondy than she believed, and she was sure that was not the case. She peeked at his emotions, but saw nothing indicating guilt, only astonishment. On the other hand, she had known murderers who felt no guilt over the deaths they caused, so that might mean nothing.

Still pretending her attention was on the tea kettle, she examined his uniform, looking for blood or mud spatter from the riverbank. The uniform was not immaculate—Townsend's never was—but it bore no large, dark stains, nor even small ones. Of course, if Falconer was right and Mondy had been killed from behind, his body would have shielded his murderer from the blood spray from a slit throat. Even so, Jennet did not like to eliminate Townsend as a suspect.

Then she caught herself. She was not responsible for discovering anything. It did not matter what she believed so far as anyone's guilt or innocence went. And yet the fact that someone in her company was capable of murdering one of its own frightened her. Very little frightened her anymore, but this—this horrid, creeping fear that someone she knew might be a murderer—terrified her. Not because she feared she was in danger, but because she had come to consider the 3rd her home, and this came far too close to reminding her what had happened to the last home she had had.

Falconer set his plate on the ground. "With your permission, sir, I will ask the men if any of them saw Mondy this afternoon."

"I suppose it is too late for discretion," Adair grumped. "Very well, lieutenant. Bring me word when you have discovered the assassin."

"I appreciate your faith in me," Falconer said with a totally straight face. Jennet did not need to look at his emotions to know he was dissembling.

Adair clearly knew it, too. "Murderers are stupid and short-sighted, Falconer, and I doubt any of the men are capable of concealing such a deed. Even you must see that."

Falconer saluted, a perfectly correct gesture that made Adair's face redden. But Adair could not challenge Falconer on his insubordination when the lieutenant's behavior was proper. Jennet bowed her head in case her amusement showed on her face. She did not want to anger Adair, and be forced to Coerce him out of his anger.

"Graeme," Falconer said, "you will accompany me."

Startled, Jennet scrambled to her feet. Falconer had already turned away. She set aside the tea kettle and followed him, finding that once again he had slowed his stride to match hers.

"What can I do to help, sir?" she asked.

"In truth, I thought to remove you from the situation before you laughed and drew the captain's wrath." Falconer sounded amused himself. "I apologize for stimulating mirth."

"Oh, I would not laugh at an officer, sir!"

"Then you have better fortitude than I, Graeme." Falconer had chosen a path that took him through the camp and ended near one of the quarter-master's wagons. "What do you see?"

Again, Jennet's surprise left her momentarily speechless. "See, sir? I see the wagons, and the trees. I do not know what more you wish."

"This is the closest the camp comes to the river." Falconer glanced around. "And it is the closest point to where Mondy was killed."

"You believe one of the quartermaster's men might have seen something," Jennet said, enlightened.

"I do. I would like you to watch as I speak with these men. Look at them, at what surrounds them. Sometimes a man gives more away with his reactions than his words."

Jennet could do better than that, but she could not share her talent with the lieutenant, obviously. Even so, she determined to look at the emotions of each man Falconer questioned. She was not as good as a Discerner, whose talent permitted them to know not only whether someone lied, but often what the lie concealed. But guilt was a strong emotion, easily visible and easily identified. If one of these men had murdered Mondy and felt guilt about it, she would know.

She hovered slightly behind Falconer in the hour that followed, letting him draw the attention of those he spoke to while Jennet was a silent, unnoticed companion. Being overlooked reminded her of her months with Alejandro Valencia, where she had also gone unnoticed in the shadow of his charismatic presence. Then, too, she had used her talent on his behalf, but that had been Coercion, and she was determined not to repeat that mistake. Instead, she made note of each tangle of emotion, teasing out what feelings were predominant.

Her attention to their emotions meant Jennet did not notice where they were going, and was surprised when Falconer came to a halt on the far side of the wagons. "Well?" he asked.

"Me, sir?"

"I did ask you to observe. What did you see?"

Though she had looked at the men's emotions for just this reason, now that Falconer had asked her opinion directly, she was nervous, as if he might be able to deduce her talent from her words. Which was ridiculous; no one but Coercers knew how Coercion worked. She drew in a breath. "None of them behaved with guilt the way they might if they were the killer," she said. "Many of them were uncomfortable, but I daresay that was fear of an officer or fear of being unjustly accused."

"That was my conclusion as well." Falconer sighed. "I cannot speak to each man directly, to question him as to his guilt. Even a Discerner could do no more than interrogate the men one at a time. I believe we will need a different approach."

JENNET HOVERED BEHIND FALCONER AGAIN, WISHING HE HAD NOT ordered her to stay. She did not need the other soldiers believing she felt she was somehow special simply because she stood with Falconer as the troops were drawn up for inspection. But when she had tried to sidle away to stand with her comrades, Falconer had said, "Not yet, Graeme," and Jennet had been forced to stay at his side.

She surveyed the soldiers standing in ranks, more or less at attention though none could be accused of insubordination. She caught Fosse's eye; he made a face that indicated the question *What's this about?* She shrugged slightly. There was no way to answer that question with only gestures.

"You all know Ensign Mondy was murdered," Captain Lord Adair said, pitching his voice to carry to the farthest ranks. "He was killed by one of his own. One of you. I am asking anyone who knows anything about this matter to come forward."

Falconer stood with his hands clasped behind his back. Only Jennet could see how tightly his fists were clenched. This had not been the "different approach" he had had in mind. Jennet had been present for the loud argument between the lieutenant and his captain, an argument that had ended with Adair raging at Falconer that he would see him strung up for disobedience. It was not a threat with any real force, given that Falconer would have to do much worse than argue with Adair to warrant hanging, but it had driven home Adair's point: he was the captain, and this was his command.

No one moved. The soldiers did not even glance at one another, though a few of them looked at their feet. Jennet searched their emotions for a sign of guilt. Doing so with such a large group was difficult when one did not intend to Coerce them, but she had enough experience that it was not impossible. She perceived nothing but fear and anger, both of which were worrisome emotions, easily intensified to a fever point. Adair, nearer her, pulsed with rage; Townsend feared the men's reactions. Falconer was, perhaps justifiably, angry, but he held that emotion in check.

"Very well," Adair said. "I see none of you are the kind of men who care about the fate of your fellows. If you are too cowardly to speak publicly, then come to me privately. Dismissed."

The mutterings that arose as the men dispersed worried Jennet further. The captain had made all of them suspicious of everyone else, just as Falconer had predicted in that argument. But Adair seemed not aware of this. He walked away in the direction of his tent without a word to either of the other officers.

Jennet looked at Falconer, who was watching the men. Finally, he said, "Go and get something to eat, Graeme. Then join me at my tent. I require your further services."

Jennet found where her comrades were camped and was stunned to see her own tent already set up. "Who did this?"

"We did, of course." Sadler sat beside the fire, chewing idly on a long piece of dry grass. "But don't get used to it. We're not the servants around here."

"Ignore him, Ned," Fosse said. He handed Jennet a lump of bread, only a little dry. "What's this about Mondy's murder? His lordship can't think any of us done it."

"He does not know who did, and he is—" Jennet took a large bite of bread to keep from criticizing her superior officer. Even if he was a fool, Jennet could not take the chance that someone might hear her call him that and get word back to him.

"Well, it wasn't me," Fosse said. "Why not a stranger? Someone what met Mondy in the woods and killed him for the contents of his purse?"

"No strangers for miles," Corwin said. His deep voice gave added weight to his assertion.

"The lieutenant doesn't know, either." Jennet took another bite and her stomach stopped rumbling. "But he won't let the captain accuse anyone without proof."

"You think as he'd do that?" Whitteney stood and beckoned to Marie, who was talking to another soldier at a fire some distance away. Marie did not at first notice. Whitteney's second wave was more tentative, and the disappointed look on his face made Jennet's heart ache.

"I think we all know what the captain is like," Jennet replied.

No one replied. They all knew. Jennet remembered the floggings when a rash of thefts in the camp three months earlier had resulted in accusations and convictions. She had not been convinced the captain had the right men, but there was nothing she could do.

She and the others ate in silence. Marie eventually returned to their fire and put her arms around Whitteney, who brightened at once. There was no sign of Appleton or Veronique until Jennet was almost finished with her meal, and then Veronique emerged from the tent she shared with her husband and walked to the fire, holding a plate. She said nothing, but Jennet felt an unexpected surge of pity for the woman.

"Give her some supper," she said, and then in French added, "Would you like some bread?"

"Yes, please," Veronique said in her dull, colorless voice. Sadler heaped her plate with meat, and Jennet gave her a chunk of bread.

When Veronique turned to go back to her tent, Jennet said, still in French, "Where is Mr. Appleton, ma'am?"

Veronique shrugged one shoulder. "I never know where he goes. Thank you for the food." She walked away with no other word.

"I don't understand that woman," Fosse said. "D'ye suppose he beats her?"

"He doesn't seem interested in her at all," Jennet said. "Not even enough to beat her."

"She's got a husband, at least," said Whitteney. "That makes her better off than half the women who follow the camp." He smiled at Marie, who smiled back. Jennet could not help but see the woman's smile as false.

She stood and brushed herself off. "I'm to return to the lieutenant. Try not to despair at my absence."

"Ah, we were planning to sell your things, but they ain't worth a shilling," Sadler drawled. Jennet saluted him with a rude gesture and a smile and was off running.

Falconer sat inside his tent, honing his belt knife. It was a beauty of Spanish steel and an ivory-inlaid hilt, and Jennet exclaimed, "That's lovely."

Falconer looked up at her entrance. Then he extended the knife to her. "It was a gift from a Spanish grandee whose house I helped save from *guerrilleros*. Were you in Spain, Graeme?"

Only some of what she could tell him was true. "I came out from England in '09, when the Rifles made their first recruitment push. I was wounded in Spain last year and left for dead, and took several months recovering. By the time I was well, the Army had crossed the Pyrenees into France, and I walked hundreds of miles to rejoin them. But my company had been disbanded because of, well, what we believed was peace, and I was reassigned to the 3rd." She did not say that she had deserted the Army to serve Valencia in Spain; that was not something she would be forgiven.

"That's remarkable dedication." Falconer opened the top of a portable writing desk and removed pen, ink, and paper. "I would like to see your handwriting."

Jennet refrained from saying *My handwriting?* like a fool. Instead, she settled the desk on her knees and arranged the writing supplies. "What shall I write, sir?"

"Anything. Have you nothing committed to memory?" Falconer's smile gave him the look of an amused teacher who had sprung an unexpected examination on his pupil.

"I—" Jennet ducked her head. A fragment of poetry came to mind, and she carefully wrote:

O wad some Power the giftie gie us
To see oursels as ithers see us!
It wad frae monie a blunder free us,
An' foolish notion:
What airs in dress an' gait wad lea'e us,
An' ev'n devotion!

Falconer accepted the paper from her hand and waved it in the air to dry it. He read it, his brow furrowed and his mouth turned down at the corners. Then a smile slowly spread across his face. "Robert Burns," he said. "I might have guessed."

"He was my father's favorite, sir, and I learned it in the Habbie dialect even though we did not speak it." Jennet's face heated with embarrassment. She had not thought what he might make of her choice.

"Well, your handwriting is far better than mine, as I hoped." Falconer set the paper aside. "I need two letters written. I will dictate—though the second will need to be translated into French as well."

Jennet took up the pen again and laid out fresh paper. "Whom should I address the first to, sir?"

"General Omberlis of the War Office." Falconer's smile fell away. "And I must impress upon you the urgent need for confidentiality, Graeme. I believe I can trust you. Don't betray that trust."

Wide-eyed, Jennet nodded. "I would never," she said. "General Omberlis. Is this to do with Mondy's death, sir? But Mondy was not an Extraordinary and could not have been the general's subordinate."

"I know. But I have need of a Discerner, and as there are no Discerners in service with the Army, General Omberlis is the only one who can arrange for one to be sent."

That made no sense. "Why would you need a Discerner, sir?"

Falconer's eyes were intent on her in a way that made her uncomfortable, as if he could see through her uniform to her skin. "Because I believe Captain Lord Adair murdered Ensign Mondy."

CHAPTER 9

IN WHICH FALCONER
REVEALS HIS UNEXPECTED
BUT CONVINCING THEORY

Jennet stared at Falconer uncomprehendingly. "How could—why would Captain Lord Adair kill Ensign Mondy? He is the captain!"

"I don't know," Falconer said. His grim expression made him look even more like a statue carved of marble, beautiful and serious and prepared to deliver the worst news imaginable. "I have no idea what his motives might be. But his behavior has been curious ever since he brought word of Napoleon's advance on Paris. He is normally very stern, but he has crossed the line into hostility more than once on this march. He shows little interest in the men's drilling and marching order where once he made that his primary preoccupation. And then there is the matter of changing standard practice with regard to Mondy's patrol range."

"Sir," Jennet said slowly, "those are not such large changes. After all, he has greater responsibilities at home now that he is Lord Adair as well as a captain. He might simply be distressed at those new burdens. Or perhaps it is thwarted love." She recalled perceiving Adair's emotions the other day and wondering at who the object of his affections was.

"I considered that." Falconer stood and walked to the tent flap, which he lifted slightly to peer outside. Then he returned to sit opposite Jennet. "It is possible he feels the burden of his position, though to my knowledge he has no romantic attachments. But I have served with the captain long enough to recognize his habits. When he feels the strain of his position, he withdraws into himself. He does not lash out at others and he does not get into arguments. And he is in every case conscious of the men under his command. I know you must believe him a tyrant, as he is quick to order punishments, but his decisions are all made carefully and with the intent of improving order within the company. What he did today…" He sighed deeply. "Something is very wrong here."

"That still does not mean he is a murderer." Jennet's reply astonished her. She would never have dared dream of addressing the lieutenant so directly, without acknowledgement of the difference in their stations, before this afternoon. It was as if their shared discovery of Mondy's body had made them allies, on a more equal footing than soldier and officer should be.

"He is the one who told me Ensign Mondy had failed to make his rendezvous," Falconer said. "He was very vocal about the ensign's short-comings and irresponsibility. At the time, I believed his reaction more of the same oddity of behavior I mentioned. In hindsight, I wonder about how very careful he was to draw attention to Mondy's absence."

"You mean," Jennet said, "he intended to make it seem Mondy had simply disappeared. Or deserted."

Falconer shrugged. "The place Mondy was killed was secluded from view of the camp, but not so secluded that *someone* would not have eventually found his body. A roving patrol, if nothing else. But a patrol would have inadvertently destroyed the evidence that pointed us in the direction of the camp."

"And Captain Lord Adair suggested it was bandits," Jennet said. "There would have been no reason to believe otherwise, and that is what we would have searched for."

"Indeed. He must have been desperate, or foolhardy, to kill Mondy so close to camp, and likely he counted on no one looking too closely." Falconer picked up the page upon which Jennet had written the poem and folded it in half, then in half again, on and on until it would fold no more. "But you came upon the body earlier than he anticipated, and brought your discovery to me rather than to him. I drew a different conclusion from the evidence, and the captain could not ignore my suppositions without looking guilty. Instead of investigating sensibly, he chose to address the issue in the way most guaranteed to foment fear and suspicion among the men. Now every man distrusts his neighbor and will be looking for signs of guilt in those he calls friends. It is exactly the course of action a guilty man might take to divert suspicion from himself."

"I see." Falconer's reasoning was sound, and Jennet did not believe it was her attraction to him that inclined her to agree with him. "But what is to be done?"

Falconer's grim expression faded, and he smiled. "I will dictate letters that you will write, and then you will return to your tent until I summon you. If I am correct in my suspicions, we must be careful not to reveal these suspicions to Captain Lord Adair. Once we have a Discerner, I will insist on that person interrogating everyone, beginning with the captain. Then the truth will out."

Jennet nodded. She settled the desk more securely on her lap and readied her pen. "Yes, sir."

Falconer rose and paced the small distance from the tent flap to the rear wall, his hands clasped loosely behind his back. "Direct the letter to Colina House, Lisbon, Portugal. 'To General Omberlis: Sir...'"

Jennet wrote in her neatest handwriting as Falconer dictated. Part of her wondered if his handwriting was really so bad that he needed a scribe. But if that were not true, then he had made this task up to give her work, and why would he do that? For that matter, why would he speak so freely to her about matters that endangered both of them if Adair really were a murderer?

She dipped her pen and resumed writing. On the other hand, she *had* been the one to discover Mondy's body, which made her involved regardless of her feelings on the matter. Possibly Falconer recognized that this made her a ready confidante. There was no mystery save why Falconer needed a confidante at all, and even that made sense: he was likely the only one who suspected Adair, and Jennet knew well how hard it was to keep a secret and what a relief it was to share it, even with one's enemies. And she was far from being Falconer's enemy.

By the time Falconer was finished with his letters, it was nearly sunset, and Jennet was squinting at the pages and hoping she had not smudged anything. The second letter was addressed to the mayor of the nearest town, and its contents confused Jennet. Why would Falconer care about their contacts with other towns and villages? But she dutifully translated it and handed it over before leaving the tent.

She trotted slowly through the camp. The fireside gatherings were quieter tonight, and Jennet avoided looking at anyone closely. From the few people whose emotions she assessed, she could tell Adair's ploy had worked; they were sullen and angry, or frightened and suspicious. Some of them gathered in little knots of three or four men, whispering, while others spoke and laughed too loudly despite feeling, when she looked at their emotions, no amusement or good humor.

Her steps slowed as she neared her own tent and the fire that burned outside it. Fosse, Sadler, and Whitteney sat around the fire, more widely spaced than usual, while Corwin knelt beside the camp kettle, prodding the meat that boiled within. A short distance away, Marie and Veronique were conversing in French, though they were far enough from Jennet she could make out no words. Another conversation was going on in a nearby tent—more accurately, an argument conducted in low but intense voices. Jennet recognized Appleton and Corporal Josephs' voices.

She approached the fire cautiously. Sadler and Fosse looked up at her approach. "Ned," Sadler said. "Not staying with your officer friends?"

"They're not friends," Jennet shot back. "And before you say anything else, I know none of you killed Mondy."

Fosse sat up straighter. "Didn't you hear the captain? It was one of us. How d'ye know it wasn't me, or Corwin, or any of us?"

"I just do." Jennet stared him down. She had never heard the easygoing private sound so angry. "You weren't talking this way earlier. What happened?"

The flap of the nearest tent shot back, and Josephs emerged. He looked calm, but Jennet had seen that expression before, and there was a glint in his eye and a set to his lips that told her Josephs was enraged. He stormed up to Jennet. "What do you know?"

Jennet stood tall, which put her an inch taller than Josephs. "I found Mondy's body," she said. "It was hidden well—whoever killed him wished him not to be found. D'ye think I'm fool enough to tell the world what I'd want never discovered if I'd killed the man?"

"Who knows how a murderer thinks?" Josephs said. "You've been out and about all day, going where you please. I say you should prove you didn't do it."

"Ned couldn't have," Whitteney said, putting himself between Jennet and Josephs. "The lad's naught more than a stick. And Mondy was like any Bounder—strong and tall and able to lift a man twice his size. Whoever killed Mondy was at least that big."

Everyone looked at Corwin, who was still stirring the pot. At five feet and nine inches, he was just within regulation height, but his broad shoulders and hulking form were powerful, and lit by the fire his features were harsher than usual, almost sinister. Corwin ignored them all for a moment longer. Then he stood. "You're all fools," he said in his slow, deep voice. "We none of us have been out of each other's sight since before making camp today. If one of us had gone off alone, the others would have seen. So leave off your accusations, corporal."

Josephs squared up to him. Despite the height difference, he bore himself with a belligerent authority that made him seem Corwin's equal. "I want to know the truth. We're none of us safe so long as there's a killer about."

"We're all killers, or had you forgotten?" Whitteney said. "But none of us murdered Mondy. None of us had reason to. Or time." He put a hand on Josephs' shoulder. "Bill. We can't go on like this or it will tear us apart. Imagine trying to fight Napoleon's troops when we can't trust our mates."

"It's true, corporal," Jennet said. "And the lieutenant—" She couldn't tell them Falconer's suspicions, but she needed to tell them something. Her heart ached to see her home torn apart by mistrust and fear. "The lieutenant will find the murderer. He won't let him go free."

Instantly, they were all staring at her. "Does he know who it is?" Whitteney demanded.

Jennet shook her head. "Not yet," she lied. "But he doesn't want the wrong man punished. He'll do everything he can to discover the truth."

There was silence for a moment. Then Sadler said, "True and it sounds like you're nigh in love with the man," and everyone laughed, and the tension disappeared.

Jennet managed not to blush. Nobody took Sadler seriously, and it wasn't as if any of them believed Ned would be attracted to Falconer at all —it was a joke. But she couldn't help feeling embarrassed, as if Sadler had seen to the heart of her infatuation. Which wasn't infatuation, it was just interest and attraction to Falconer's beauty, and anyone might feel that.

"Aye, in love with a statue," she joked back, which made them laugh harder and come up with increasingly ribald comments. It discomfited Jennet to hear them make fun of Falconer, but their good humor could not hurt him, and she had to admit some of the jokes were quite funny. Even so, she had to refrain from leaping to his defense when the talk grew ever more lewd. He did not need her protection.

⚜

JENNET WOKE A LITTLE LATER THAN USUAL THE FOLLOWING MORNING, startled out of a dream by reveille. She hurried to dress and stood inspection with the others before racing for Falconer's tent. The air was not as cool as it had been the previous morning, and she reached the officers' tents feeling almost uncomfortably warm. There was no one stirring outside, no Eustis preparing porridge. Jennet stirred the fire into life and hurried to fetch water.

There was still no one about when she returned, so she set the water to boil and knelt beside the fire. She wished she dared disturb Falconer, as she was curious to know the fate of the letters. The new Bounder would have arrived the previous night, and he would have carried the letter to General Omberlis. That Bounder might even now be waiting on a Discerner to return with him. The idea filled Jennet with mingled excitement and dread. The possibility of proving Adair a murderer was exciting, but only a Discerner was immune to Coercion, and although Jennet did not intend to Coerce anyone in the Discerner's presence, let alone the Discerner himself, she admitted to some nervousness that he might divine her talent just by looking. It was impossible, but fear was rarely rational.

The water was boiling and the oats beginning to cook when Adair's tent flap opened and the captain emerged. He looked spruce as ever, though his eyes were still shadowed and tired-looking, and he actually smiled at Jennet.

Jennet stared up at him, wishing character might show on the skin. She immediately assessed his emotions, hoping to learn something that would prove he had killed Mondy. His emotions revealed no trace of guilt, which disappointed Jennet, but that might mean he was not remembering Mondy at that moment, nor dwelling on anything else related to the murder. Instead, she noted that same feeling of deep, loving attachment she had seen before, the one Jennet believed meant a love affair. Aside from that, he was at peace, which struck Jennet as odd. Surely the fractures within the company would give him some distress?

"Good morning, Graeme," the captain said. "Ah, porridge. You know the secret of making it."

"Yes, sir. I learned many years ago." She could not say her mother had taught her, for what mother would teach a son kitchen skills? "I'm glad to be of service."

"Indeed. I'll be back shortly." He walked away toward the quartermaster's wagons. Jennet continued dropping pinches of oats into the kettle and stirring slowly.

Eustis came running up, breathing heavily. This time, his jacket was buttoned properly, and his hair was barely disordered from running, so he looked more like an officer's servant than usual. "Graeme. Good initiative." He nodded at the kettle.

"Good morning, Mr. Eustis." Jennet kept a respectful look on her face purely for convenience's sake. Antagonizing Eustis would be pleasant only in the short term.

"Graeme," Falconer said from behind her. "With me. Eustis, carry on with the cooking."

Jennet handed Eustis the sack of oats and rose, brushing off her knees. Falconer, his face as impassive as ever, walked away in the direction opposite the quartermaster's wagons, and Jennet hurried to follow him.

Falconer said nothing until they were well away from the camp. On the camp's western side, a copse of trees barred the way to a farm beyond. Falconer walked until they were both well concealed by the trees. Then he said, "I am more convinced than ever that Captain Lord Adair is the murderer. No Bounder arrived last night."

"I don't understand. Why wouldn't a Bounder arrive?"

Falconer looked around as if he expected eavesdroppers against all reason. "The captain is our only Speaker. I believe he never reported Mondy's death, nor asked for another Bounder to replace him."

His words made Jennet shiver. She did not know why Adair's failure to report chilled her more than the knowledge he was a murderer, but it struck her as more sinister than straightforward murder. "Then we are at his mercy," she said.

"We are," Falconer said. "I have no way of getting this letter to Lisbon, to gain the proof I need of the captain's guilt. And if we continue our march, we will have no idea what lies in our path."

"Then, what is to be done?"

Falconer glanced around again. "We continue, and I will search for concrete evidence that will prove the captain's guilt. This is not over."

Jennet did not like to say that they were at a terrible disadvantage. Falconer almost certainly knew that. "You could send me back," she said. "We are not so far from Soissons. I might return there and speak with Major Dru—I mean, Lord Quincey."

But Falconer was shaking his head. "Major Lord Quincey was to leave Soissons shortly after we did, on his way to Paris. There is no one left in Soissons who can help us." He put a hand on Jennet's shoulder. "For now, you will have to behave as if you know none of this. Captain Lord Adair claimed last night, when the Bounder did not appear, that there is no one the Army can spare to help us for a few days. That is preposterous, but we must act as if we believe it."

"But if someone comes..." Jennet's voice trailed off. Of course no Bounder was coming in a few days. That was more of the captain's lies. "I see. Questioning him might be dangerous."

"Precisely." He squeezed Jennet's shoulder and released her. "This is not anything I ever expected to do in the course of my duties. I would have sworn the captain was loyal unto death."

"You do not know he is not loyal, sir," Jennet said. "If it was a personal matter between him and Ensign Mondy—"

"Then why would he not arrange for another Bounder?" Falconer's eyes were intent on her. "And Captain Lord Adair and Ensign Mondy were not close, not in any way that suggests they had personal matters between them that might result in murder. No, Mondy died not because of who he was, but for what he was capable of. Bounding."

Jennet realized what he was getting at. "You mean, the captain did not want him scouting ahead? Did not want him scouting at all?"

"That is what I believe, yes," Falconer said. "The captain wants us marching blind, and I can think of only one reason—he already knows what awaits us."

A sick feeling started in the pit of Jennet's stomach. "Then you mean he is leading us into a trap. A trap he knows is there."

Falconer nodded once, a curt gesture. "That means Captain Lord Adair is a traitor."

"But that is impossible," Jennet said. "I do not—that is, it is not my place to judge, but I know the captain has fought for years, leading from the front. He despises Napoleon and everything he stands for. I would sooner believe Wellington himself a traitor."

"Nevertheless," Falconer said. He let out a deep sigh. "As I said, Graeme, it is nothing I ever expected to deal with. I believed I would rise through the ranks, never encountering anything more challenging than a difficult decision at court-martial, and here I am contemplating how I will protect this company from its own captain."

"There must be something," Jennet insisted. "It cannot be impossible."

"I will hold to your hopefulness, Graeme." Falconer once more clapped her on the shoulder and then walked back through the trees with Jennet following closely.

Adair was seated by the campfire, eating porridge, when they returned. "Where have you been?" He sounded irritated, and Jennet recalled what Falconer had said the previous day about Adair's behavior when he was distressed or burdened. She made herself small and insignificant behind Falconer. She did not need to draw the captain's antagonism and be forced to Coerce him to protect herself.

"Seeing that the wagons are loaded," Falconer said, sounding indifferent.

"Excellent." Adair returned to eating, dismissing Falconer so thoroughly it was almost an insult.

Falconer did not react. "Off to get your meal, Graeme," he said, and Jennet darted away.

She examined the waking camp as she ran, swiftly assessing those tangles of emotion. There was still far too much sullen fear, but the tension was less than it had been. Jennet hoped the captain would not do anything to aggravate the situation. Though, if he did, that would be more evidence for Falconer's theory—not that more was needed.

She veered wide of the campfire, where her comrades were eating, and hurried into her tent to pack her things. She could only hope Falconer was wrong in his conclusions about Captain Lord Adair's loyalties, because a traitorous commander might be more dangerous to his men than a whole regiment of French soldiers.

CHAPTER 10

IN WHICH CAPTAIN LORD ADAIR'S BEHAVIOR GROWS EVEN MORE SUSPICIOUS

Thanks to the clear sky and the blazing hot sun, the day wore on more punishingly than the previous two. The company's regular rests seemed to come at much longer intervals than one hour. Jennet's awareness that they were marching into unknown country left her on edge, startling at every unfamiliar or unexpected sound. She would find her hand gripping the barrel of her rifle so tightly it left marks on her palm, and she would make herself relax for minutes at a time, but then she would forget about it as she scanned the horizon looking for enemies and discover later that her hand had of its own volition resumed its iron-hard grip.

She wished she were closer to the front of the line of march. Not knowing what they were marching into made her uneasy. If Falconer was right, and the captain was leading them into a trap, she would be unable to fight to defend her fellows from back here. Though if Adair's plan involved permitting the company to be attacked from the rear, Jennet would be essential to protecting the others.

She took a look around, assessing those nearest her. She did not look at their emotions, which was pointless, but at their faces, identifying those she knew and guessing at the capabilities of those she did not. There were unfortunately few soldiers with the baggage train, and she knew none of them to speak to. The wagon drivers, however, all were big and muscular and looked as if they would be able to fight if it became necessary.

And then there were the women. The company was technically permitted only six women "on the strength," meaning officially on the company roster. But somehow there were always far more than that. Adair, otherwise strict, ignored their presence, and the women did their best to keep up. Some of them might be able to shoot, but if not, at the very least they could help the men in combat, reloading weapons or carrying powder and shot.

Jennet examined Veronique, who walked nearby. Veronique, on the other hand, might be a liability in a fight, unless Jennet's understanding of the capabilities of an expectant mother was wrong.

Veronique continued to walk as steadily as ever. Jennet could not imagine how the woman managed her condition when she must walk all day, every day. She remembered what Falconer had said about how if Veronique rode, all the women would want to ride, but she could not imagine any of those women begrudging Veronique that small comfort. Still, it was none of Jennet's lookout, and better she not interfere.

Despite Jennet's worries, nothing befell the company that day, and she eventually walked to the makeshift paddock feeling as if she and not Copper had borne the weight of Falconer's possessions and been relieved of them. She unloaded bags and boxes and arranged her load before going to the officers' tents, hoping to find Falconer there. He was not with the wagons, and he had not been to visit Suleiman, according to Boyce.

She reached the officers' tents to the sound of argument. Captain Lord Adair and Falconer stood facing each other, less than a foot apart, both their bodies rigid with anger and their faces red. Adair, Jennet had seen in a passion before, but Falconer's fury frightened her. Instinctively, she took up their tangles of emotion, hot and wildly angry, but before she could Coerce them into a calmer state, Adair shouted, "And by God I will see you court-martialed if you continue!"

Falconer was breathing heavily. "Who do you imagine will be blamed for taking this company off course and into no one knows what kind of country? We need that Bounder!" But despite his angry words, his emotions were subsiding, as if Adair's threat had calmed rather than inflamed him.

"There are no Bounders available," Adair shot back through gritted teeth. "Do you challenge my word?"

Falconer shook his head. "No. Sir. But if there is no Bounder, we must scout another way. Let us send a few men forward now to get the lay of the land."

"A few men." Adair, too, had calmed down slightly. "That is acceptable. I will choose five and give them their orders."

"You can leave that to me, sir."

Adair eyed him suspiciously. "It is, as you so vocally pointed out, my responsibility. See to questioning the men about Mondy's murder. Now."

Falconer saluted, another one of his perfect crisp gestures that seemed to anger Adair without giving him any way to retaliate. The lieutenant turned, and his eye fell on Jennet. With a nod, he indicated she should follow him.

They walked through the camp as soldiers pitched tents in regular ranks and started campfires burning. Jennet was afraid to speak; Falconer's jaw was still rigid, and his emotions pulsed with anger. Again, she ventured to Coerce him, and again she stopped herself. He would calm himself without her intervention, and she took comfort in knowing there was one person whose emotions she had never altered, as if in leaving Falconer free she had expiated some of her sins.

"How much of that did you hear?" Falconer said in a voice that did not carry farther than the two of them.

Jennet shook her head. "Not much, sir. Enough to know there still is no Bounder, and we must scout the old-fashioned way."

Falconer's lips twitched in a smile that relaxed his features. "The captain resists any suggestion I make with regard to reconnoitering our path. It surprises me that he is willing to send out scouts—though I wish I would be the one to choose them."

"Do you believe Captain Lord Adair will not choose wisely?" His accusation of malfeasance unsettled her. It occurred to her that she had only Falconer's word that the captain was behaving strangely, and suppose it was the lieutenant who was interested in sabotaging the company?

She glanced again at Falconer. She did not believe she was so sentimental as to be swayed by a beautiful face. And when she considered all their previous interactions, she could not bring herself to believe ill of him. After all, she was no one of importance, and if Falconer were intent on causing harm to the company, he would not benefit from having her dubious assistance.

Falconer did not look at her. His gaze was fixed on the quartermaster's wagons, which they now approached. "That will depend on what the captain's intent is. If he truly wishes us not to know what we are marching into, he will choose men whose tracking and scouting skills are minimal. And if he is leading us into an ambush, he will not wish anyone to discover that."

"That is a serious accusation, and it seems so out of character for Captain Lord Adair."

"Which is why I have not made it. Suspicion of odd behavior is not grounds for an accusation of treason. Not to mention that I have no guess as to what would motivate a man like him to throw away years of loyal service." Falconer stopped a few yards from the wagons and turned to face Jennet. "I must question the men or face more charges of insubordination. I do not want you involved."

Jennet protested, "But I was of use—"

"No arguments, Graeme. This line of questioning, however I pursue it, will cause bad feelings toward me, and I have no wish to see any of that spill over onto you. You are to return to your campsite for a meal and wait upon me at sunset." Falconer walked away, leaving Jennet caught mid-objection.

She hurried away to join her fellows. Falconer might be correct in his assertion, though that did not make her like being excluded any more. But she would obey as she was sworn to do.

Obey as she was sworn to do. The idea stopped her unexpectedly in her tracks. There *was* a reason someone's behavior might change, a reason someone might break his sworn oaths. Captain Lord Adair might have been Coerced.

Immediately, Jennet discarded the notion. Who would Adair have encountered who might have Coerced him into betraying his country? No one knew how many Coercers there were in the world, let alone just in France, and it was possible Adair had met one of these on his journey back from England. But no ordinary Coercer would have had any reason to Coerce Adair thus. And Napoleon had not gone close enough to Paris to influence those in the city.

Unless that, too, had been a lie. They had only Adair's word for it that

Napoleon had not entered Paris. If Adair had met Napoleon and been Coerced into following him, everything he had done in the past week made sense.

The excellence and completeness of the theory satisfied Jennet. It was perfect—except for the small problem that she had seen no evidence of Coercion in the captain. Anger, fury, self-satisfaction, and love, but no adoration such as would be necessary to force someone to obey against his will. She had made too many people adore Alejandro Valencia in Spain not to recognize it in others.

Almost Jennet turned around to search for Adair. She had not thought to search for evidence of Coercion before, and perhaps there was something she had overlooked. But she could not justify entering his presence for no reason, and he would certainly wish to know why she was there. She would have to wait until later. She hoped she would not be too late.

When she arrived at the campfire, only Corwin was there. "Fetching bread and water and firewood," he told her when she inquired about the others. "You might could help me pitch tents."

Jennet set to helping with a will. It felt surprisingly good to perform the service for her fellows, something clean and uncomplicated that had nothing to do with Coercion. Corwin had already lit the fire with what little wood they already had. "What's it like, walking behind?" he asked in his slow, measured voice.

"Not much." Her preoccupation that day with Adair's possible Coercion could not be shared, but she added, "It is a pity Veronique must walk. I would find that intolerably uncomfortable."

"'Tis nothing can be helped." Corwin blew lightly on the tiny flames, making them dance merrily. "Mayhap she will stay in Troyes. I don't suppose you know whether we're moving on from there, you being in that officer's pockets?"

"He does not confide in me." Jennet arranged her pack inside her tent and joined Corwin at the little fire.

Many footsteps heralded the approach of Fosse, Sadler, and Whitteney. Fosse and Sadler carried armloads of firewood. "'Tis more than we need," Corwin protested.

"Which is as I told that one," Fosse said with a grimace and a jerk of his head at Sadler. "But he insists he knows best." His brown ribbon had loosened, and he dropped his load and freed the ribbon to retie his queue.

"'Twill be a cold night," Sadler said. "I feel it in my bones. You will all be grateful to me ere long."

Whitteney set down the camp kettle full of water. "You preferred not to do real work, and picking up sticks is as far from real work as anyone gets in the Army."

Sadler turned up his nose with a lofty air. "Only a fool puts in for more work than he must." He stretched, making his neck joints pop.

More footsteps, these of Appleton. He carried an armload of old bread, which he set on the ground near the fire. "I might have expected you all would argue over who does the least work. Don't any of you feel a responsibility?"

Fosse settled on the ground and tilted his head to look up at Appleton. "We've walked as far as you this day, so don't go putting on airs."

Appleton shrugged. He gestured to Veronique, who with Marie had come drifting in from beyond the wagons. "I believe in giving my best to the Army. You should do the same."

Fosse, Sadler, and Whitteney jeered at him. "You think you're superior to us," Sadler said, "but you still march to the same drum."

Appleton ignored him, walking away to meet Veronique. Jennet heaved the kettle over the fire. "Wonder who he used to be," she said.

"Tailor's apprentice, until his master drank away the business," Fosse said promptly. "No one who'd have a right to lord it over us."

Jennet, who had been watching Appleton and Veronique as they stood close together, not touching, lips moving in conversation, now looked past them at a soldier running toward their fire. Curious, she sat up straighter as the young man drew near.

The boy was well out of breath as if he'd run hard. "Which of you is Appleton?" he panted.

Jennet and Corwin both pointed. The boy immediately hurried to Appleton's side. There was a brief conversation, and then Appleton walked away, following the boy. Veronique stood watching him go until he was out of sight. Then she slowly walked to the fire and past it. Jennet could not bear the suspense. "What was that about?" she asked in French.

Veronique paused, but did not face Jennet. "He was to report to the captain. They wish for him to scout ahead." She moved on, ducking to enter her tent and letting the flap fall behind her as decisively as if she had slammed an oak door.

Jennet repeated this to the others, who all looked as mystified as she. "Appleton?" Whitteney said. "I wouldn't have picked him for a scout." He put his arm around Marie and hugged her.

"He's qualified, though," Fosse said.

"No more than any of us," Sadler countered. "Wonder why the captain picked him?"

Jennet wondered this, too. She was a better scout than Appleton, though not as good as either Corwin or Sadler. It seemed Falconer's suspicions were correct, and Adair had chosen at least one man not as good for the task as others.

She laughed and joked with the others until the food was ready, ate her fill, and watched Veronique again accept a plateful of boiled beef and a hunk of bread. As the woman turned to leave, Jennet impulsively said in French, "Won't you join us?"

Veronique looked at her. Her eyes widened fractionally, but that was all the surprise she showed. Jennet wondered for the first time if Veronique were mentally deficient, and that was the reason for her reticence. Then Veronique said, "I do not speak English well. I cannot understand your jokes."

"It doesn't matter," Jennet said. She patted the ground beside her. "You should not eat alone." She found her earlier reticence about befriending Veronique had vanished in the face of the woman's loneliness. Well, Jennet did not know she was lonely, but her emotions were a tangle of sadness, and Jennet sympathized with that.

Veronique hesitated a moment longer, then sat beside Jennet. "I thank you," was all she said before tucking into her meal neatly and quietly.

Jennet did not join in the conversation the others were having. Fosse and Sadler's exchange of verbal sallies had the others in an uproar of laughter and made Jennet unexpectedly content. Elsewhere, Falconer was no doubt inflaming unrest by having to question the men about Mondy's murder, but here, all was peaceful. She hoped the peace would last.

Falconer did not appear to question them. At sunset, Jennet excused herself and crossed the camp to the officers' tents. Falconer was not there, either. She busied herself with tidying his already neat things and then helping Eustis prepare an evening meal and tea. Eustis was either weary from the march or had come to accept her presence, because he said nothing snide or condescending.

The sun had nearly set, and the firelight the only illumination, when Falconer approached. He said nothing, merely held out his hand for the cup of tea Jennet put into it. He drank deeply and indicated she was to refill it. "Mondy's murderer as yet remains undetected," he said to Jennet and Eustis. "Have our scouts returned?"

"Not yet, sir, not as far as I know," Eustis said. He served Falconer his meal, which Falconer ate with an air of distraction, as if he did not taste the meat and bread.

A tent flap rustled, and Captain Lord Adair emerged, startling Jennet, who had not realized the captain was present. Adair looked as if he had been asleep, his hair slightly disordered and his jacket rumpled behind. Jennet glanced swiftly at Falconer, to see his reaction and learn whether this, too, was odd behavior. Falconer looked impassive, though, and said nothing to the captain.

Adair seated himself on his stool. "A fine evening, don't you agree, lieutenant?"

"It is indeed." Falconer speared a last bite of meat and set his plate aside. "I look forward to hearing what our scouts have learned."

"As do I. They should return within the hour."

"It grows dark, and there is no moon, so I hope you are right." Falconer still sounded impassive, not at all accusatory, but Adair's face reddened visibly even in the firelight.

"Do you question my authority?" he said in a low, harsh voice.

"Of course not," Falconer said. "I express the same hope you have."

Adair snorted, but returned his attention to his plate.

Jennet handed Adair a cup of tea, and then retreated to poke at the fire. With no one demanding anything of her, she took up her sense of Adair's emotions and examined them. He was still angry with Falconer, angrier than he appeared, and his emotions were dulled with weariness.

The feeling of love was still there, and Jennet took a closer look. It reminded her of something she could not quite recall. Attachment, that was it. Fondness, or even love, for someone not present, which made it a memory of love rather than the immediate emotion. Jennet was increasingly certain the captain was in love with someone, probably someone he had left behind in England. The emotion of adoration was definitely absent. So was the emotion of guilt, but she had not expected him to give away his secret of having murdered Mondy.

Jennet saw Ensign Townsend approaching and stood to offer him tea. He waved her away, but in a friendly manner. "The first of the scouts has returned," he said. "Here he comes now."

Jennet stayed where she was. There was a chance Adair might order the servants to leave, and she dearly wanted to hear what news the scouts brought. So she made herself small and insignificant and waited.

There were actually two scouts, one Jennet recognized as a corporal named Knaggs, the other unfamiliar to her. The two saluted Adair sharply, and Knaggs said, "I scouted five miles ahead and to the southeast, sir, and found nothing important. There is a town east of here that we will pass in tomorrow's journey."

"Very well. And you?" Adair nodded at the other man.

"Five miles due south," the man said, "with no sign of trouble."

Adair eyed Falconer. "I suppose that's not good enough for you?"

"On the contrary," Falconer said. "Our scouts are extremely competent. Though I suggest we continue to send them ahead as we march."

Adair ignored this. "Get some rest," he told the men, then, when they had again saluted and trotted away, said to Falconer, "I won't exhaust our men just so your fears can be assuaged. There is nothing between us and Troyes."

"That is your prerogative, captain," Falconer said, more impassive than ever. He stood and gestured to Jennet. "Come with me."

Jennet expected to follow him into his tent, but instead Falconer made his way through the camp, slowly in the darkness between fires, to where the horses were tethered. He petted Suleiman's nose absently and said, "I fear there is nothing else I can do, short of..." His voice trailed off, and he glanced around, looking for eavesdroppers. Jennet sympathized with his wish not to have his potentially treasonous words overheard.

"You have done what you can, and that will have to be enough," she said. "Whatever comes in the next day or two, well, we are all strong fighters, and we do not fear a challenge."

Falconer chuckled. "Well said, Graeme. Your example is an inspiration." He sounded as if he meant it, and Jennet blushed and cursed herself for being so moved by him.

"If there's nothing else?" she asked, wishing to get away from him so her feelings would not be so tumultuous.

"Nothing tonight. Get some rest, Graeme. We are within a day and a half's march of Troyes." Falconer clapped her on the shoulder and turned his attention to his horse. Jennet saluted and ran, hoping she did not appear to be fleeing even though she felt she was.

When she was out of sight of the paddock, she slowed her steps. She was a fool to permit herself to entertain such wild fancies. Falconer was an officer, he was a gentleman, and he believed she was male. He would not return her interest even if none of those things were true. She should not let her infatuation lead her into behaviors that might compromise her secret.

She reached her tent and discovered the others had already turned in for the night. That was unusual, as Fosse and Sadler, at least, liked sitting up late swapping stories and drinking. She did not even hear the laughter and other noises from Whitteney's tent that would indicate he and Marie were coupling. Feeling oddly relieved, she ducked inside and removed her jacket and boots. The tension of the day bled out of her the instant she lay down, and she fell asleep listening to the night noises of insects and the wind soughing across the canvas.

She came awake before first light to the sound of someone scratching at her tent flap. Confused, she pushed it aside and poked her head out. Veronique stood there, her body tense, her expression agitated, her cheeks flushed. "Simon is gone," she said.

It took Jennet a moment to remember Simon was Appleton's given name. "What?" she said. "You mean he has gone somewhere?"

Veronique shook her head vehemently. "I mean he is gone," she said. "Simon did not return from scouting ahead."

CHAPTER 11

IN WHICH THE MYSTERY LEADS TO A TERRIBLE CONFRONTATION

J ennet scrambled into her jacket and shoved her feet into her boots. "Did you speak with the officers? Surely they must know if Appleton did not return."

Veronique shook her head. "I do not speak English well enough, and they will not understand me, nor I them. Please, help me."

"Come with me," Jennet said, and took Veronique's hand.

She pulled the woman along after her at a rapid pace until she realized Veronique was out of breath and struggling to keep up. "I apologize," Jennet said, and came to a stop while Veronique recovered. "Tell me, when did you first realize he had not returned?"

"I tried to stay awake. I am not comfortable when he is not near." Veronique's breathing gradually returned to normal. "But it was very dark, and eventually I slept. When I woke, his bedroll was undisturbed. He had not used it."

"Are you certain he did not simply rise before you?"

Veronique again shook her head. "I sleep lightly. I would have known if he had returned." Her face was ashen in the pre-morning light, and her lips trembled, surprising Jennet. She would not have believed the woman could be so distraught about a man she barely seemed to care for.

"Very well," Jennet said, taking her hand again, but gently this time. "We will speak with the officers and they will know more."

She did not know how to gracefully wake Falconer without intruding on his privacy, so she was grateful to see he was awake and seated by the fire, staring into the flames whose light flickered over his face and gave him an unexpectedly sinister appearance. He looked up when Jennet approached. "Graeme? What is this?"

"Sir, this is Veronique Appleton. Her husband Simon Appleton was one of those sent to scout ahead. Veronique says he did not return last night. Have you any news of him?"

Falconer rose swiftly. "I believed all the scouts to have returned. Is she certain?"

"Very, sir." Jennet drew Veronique closer and urged her to sit on Falconer's abandoned stool. Veronique huddled into herself, drawing warmth from the fire, and rubbed a hand absently over her protruding belly.

Falconer did not protest the appropriation of his stool. "Wait here," he told Jennet, and disappeared into Adair's tent. Jennet rubbed her hands together to warm them. The morning was not chilly, but she felt cold nonetheless. An advance scout disappearing could mean nothing good.

She heard voices within the captain's tent, though nothing clear enough to be intelligible. Then Adair emerged, followed by Falconer. The captain was in shirt and braces, though he had donned his boots, and his face was drawn up in a thunderous scowl. "What's this about a scout not returning?" he boomed. "That is nonsense. They all came back before sunset last night."

"I beg your pardon, sir, but Mrs. Appleton is very certain her husband did not," Jennet said. Swiftly she assessed the captain's mood and found him irritable but not angry, not yet, and still possessed of that feeling of love. "Perhaps he explored too far, and was forced to remain behind rather than try to find his way back in the dark? Or—" She glanced at Veronique. "Or he might have been attacked. We do not know if there are bandits in the area."

"The other scouts returned safely. It is unlikely to have been bandits." Adair's scowl was less terrible this time. "Lieutenant Falconer, inquire at the forward picket. If...Appleton, yes? If Appleton did not return last night, he will surely come back soon."

"Yes, sir," Falconer said. "Graeme, I take it Mrs. Appleton speaks little English?"

"That's correct, sir." Jennet quickly translated the captain's words for Veronique. As she expected, they did not cheer Veronique at all. "I request permission to wait here with her for news."

"She might be more at ease in her own tent," Falconer said. For the first time since she had known him, he looked uncomfortable. Jennet suppressed a smile. He would not be the first man discomfited by the presence of an expectant woman.

"I believe she will not be reassured until she knows her husband is well," she said. "Sir?"

"We can give her what aid we can," Adair said. He did not seem taken aback by Jennet's suggestion. "Pray, prepare us a meal, Graeme, and see to her needs."

Jennet had never liked the captain so much as she did just then. She explained to Veronique what the captain had offered, then, when Eustis appeared, hurried away to fetch water.

When she returned, however, her good feelings toward Adair evaporated. He and Falconer again faced one another, and the anger was thick in the air without Jennet needing to use her talent to detect it. Adair was not shouting; his voice was perfectly calm and correct. But his words were anything but placid. "We have *no choice*," he said. "You will ready the men to march out in half an hour."

"You did not wish to leave Mondy behind," Falconer said. His words sounded sharp, as if he had bitten each one off to spit at Adair. "And he was dead and did not care what became of his body, whether we restored him to his family or buried him properly. Now you intend to abandon a living man simply because we have a rendezvous to make."

"You accuse me of callous disregard for my men?" Adair's voice rose slightly, though he still did not shout.

"I do not accuse you of anything. I would like to understand your change in attitude. Surely we are not in such a hurry to reach Troyes that we do not have time to search for Private Appleton?" Falconer's voice remained quiet, if hard-edged, but Jennet saw his hand curl into a fist as if he kept a tight rein on his emotions with that gesture alone.

"I decide what we have time for," Adair said. "You have your orders, lieutenant. Dismissed."

Falconer glared at the captain, who glared back, clearly challenging him to make an issue of the order. Then the lieutenant saluted and stepped away. He passed Jennet with no sign that she should follow. For a moment, she considered following him anyway, but then she remembered Veronique and decided she should not abandon the woman, however curious she might be about Falconer's opinion of that argument.

Adair seated himself beside Veronique. "This must be so distressing for you," he said.

"Beg pardon, sir, but Mrs. Appleton speaks little English," Jennet told him. She examined his emotions once more, but saw neither guilt nor unnatural triumph such as would accompany success at a ploy. She never had seen guilt in his emotions. Doubt struck her, and worry that perhaps she and Falconer had made the wrong assumption about the captain.

"Ah." Adair nodded as sagely as if Jennet had spoken some great wisdom. "Pray, assure her we will continue to care for her."

Jennet relayed this. Veronique glanced at Adair, then at Jennet. "Did he send Simon on that errand?"

"He did." Jennet did not know what to make of Veronique's sharp tone of voice.

"Then he is responsible for his death," Veronique said bitterly. "And I am again alone."

"We do not know that he is dead, Veronique," Jennet responded, putting a hand over Veronique's. "Please, do not despair."

Veronique turned her head away, but her shoulders shook, and a sudden rush of sympathy for her struck Jennet. She did not know what would happen to Veronique if Appleton really were dead. How awful, to be in such a precarious state!

"We will watch out for you," she said impulsively. "You need not fear."

Veronique said nothing. Jennet, feeling helpless, busied herself with preparing the meal. There was nothing more she could do.

Soon enough, the porridge was ready, but Veronique refused a portion. As soon as Jennet finished dishing it out for the officers, Veronique rose and said, "Thank you," to no one in particular and walked back toward the tents. Jennet watched her go. She hoped for Veronique's sake Appleton returned soon.

Falconer came back to the fire a few minutes after Veronique's departure. He politely turned down a dish of porridge and did not resume his seat. "No one has seen Appleton since he left yesterday afternoon," he said.

Adair did not at first reply. He scraped the last of the porridge from his plate and ate it, his eyes unfocused and staring at the fire. "Very well," he finally said. "I can see only one reason for a scout to fail to return. Tell the men to watch for Appleton, and when he is apprehended, he will be tried as a deserter."

"A deserter?" Falconer sounded utterly astonished. "That is not the only possibility."

"There is no other explanation. Appleton must have had this plan in mind for a while, and when the opportunity to scout arose, he took it." Adair stood and wiped his mouth with his handkerchief. "See to it, lieutenant."

"The man has a wife who is in a delicate condition," Falconer retorted. He made no move to walk away. "I doubt he would have abandoned her."

"He would not be the first to wish to be free of an unpleasant obligation." Adair turned to enter his tent.

Falconer took a step toward him and then stopped, both fists clenched. On the other side of the fire, Townsend watched wide-eyed, and Eustis crouched in the act of picking up the captain's dishes. Jennet held her breath. If Falconer attacked Adair, discipline would break down entirely, and Falconer might end up hanging after all. Despite her resolution never to Coerce Falconer, she seized his emotions and prepared to soothe them.

Then the lieutenant drew in a deep breath. "You heard the captain," he said. "Prepare to move out in twenty minutes." He turned and ducked into his own tent.

Jennet could bear it no longer. She followed Falconer unbidden. Within his tent, she found him packing his things. "I should do that, sir," she said.

"I need something to do or I shall run mad," Falconer replied in a low voice that would not carry farther than the tent. He paused in putting his mirror away inside his jacket. "Do you know Private Appleton?"

"I do, sir. Not well."

"Did you take him for a deserter?"

"No, sir." Jennet considered all her interactions with Appleton. "He is not well liked, but he is exact in his obedience to orders and has a strong sense of responsibility to his position. And he would not leave Veronique behind."

"Precisely." Falconer's gaze was intent on her, and it made her tremble with its intensity. "Something else has happened. And now we are marching into God knows what territory, with no Bounder and a captain who..." His voice trailed off.

"But the scouts—"

"Five miles is nothing. It is what lies beyond that mark I fear." He sighed and shook his head. "Finish packing this, and return to your position, Graeme. And if you are at all a praying man, you might ask God's mercy on us this day."

Jennet nodded, though she was not sure how well God ever listened to her unorthodox prayers.

Falconer left, and Jennet hurried to pack his belongings. When she was finished, she ran back through the camp to collect her own things. Veronique was not there, but Sadler said, when Jennet inquired, "She's relieving herself, I believe. What's this about Appleton disappearing?"

Jennet related as much as she dared, leaving out only Falconer's suspicions about the captain. By the time she finished, she had an audience of most of her fellows. Fosse whistled a low, long note. "I wouldn't have pegged Appleton for a deserter."

"Nor I," said Whitteney. "But what else is there? We're the only ones around for miles, right? So if he was attacked—"

"And he's no weakling, even if he is a bit of an ass," Sadler said. "I can't see him being taken unawares."

"The captain said we're to watch for him as we go," Jennet said, "which means the rest of you, as I doubt the baggage train will see anything you do not."

Sadler clapped Jennet on the shoulder. "'Tis no use protesting," he said, "we all know you love being out of harm's way."

Jennet gave him a friendly elbow in the side and wrenched away from him. "You should scream if you meet danger, so I may run to your rescue."

It was more than half an hour before the company moved out, according to Jennet's watch, closer to forty-five minutes and well past sunrise. Jennet wished she could be present to hear what Adair had to say about that. It was not so much that she enjoyed his anger, but she had always found more information to be safer than none, and she disliked having a commanding officer whose moods were so mercurial. Those were the ones most dangerous to her.

She eyed the sky, which was grey with a heavy overcast. To the east, darker grey clouds billowed and roiled as the winds picked up and carried them in her direction. The wind carried the scent of the river to her and ruffled the long, green grasses that had only just begun to yellow under the summer sun.

Movement above caught her eye, a large grey bird all alone against the lighter overcast. Another, longer look told her it was no bird, but a man. Jennet watched eagerly as the Extraordinary Mover swooped down and alit somewhere near the head of the column. Shortly afterward, the bugle sounded a halt to fall out.

Jennet walked to where the soldiers stood, relaxing as soldiers do when given the opportunity. Fosse and Sadler were near the end of the column, and she joined them. "What's amiss?"

Sadler shrugged. "No idea. Looks like that Extraordinary Mover came back." He rotated his shoulder, making it pop, then repeated the motion with his other shoulder.

"How can you tell it is the same woman?" Jennet asked.

"We can't," Fosse said. "But why should there be more than one Extraordinary Mover interested in us?"

"I only care for a stop longer than five minutes," Sadler said, "and never mind the reason."

Jennet had never wished so much to have an excuse to join Falconer. She peered into the distance only to see the Mover leap into the sky again and Fly in their direction. Jennet returned to her position, guessing the company would march out again soon. To her surprise, the Mover slowed and descended to where the baggage train waited. It was Lady Ashford, Jennet realized, and the woman was headed Jennet's way.

"I wished to speak with you again," Lady Ashford said when she was within easy speaking distance. "I hope I do not disturb."

"No," Jennet said, feeling confused, "of course not, but—why me?"

Lady Ashford laughed. "You intrigue me. And I—" Her voice lowered — "I know of no other woman who has chosen this life. Fare you well still?"

"I suppose. At least as well as any."

The countess laughed again. "I make you uncomfortable. That was not my intent. I must scout ahead for your company now, and will leave you, but I hope you believe I mean you no ill will."

"Wait," Jennet said. "*You* are to scout?"

"I was at Troyes when I learned your company had lost its Bounder." The mirth fell away from Lady Ashford's face, leaving her looking serious and extremely competent. "It is fortunate I came when I did, for you have already moved off course. But I will guide you in the right direction, never fear."

"Off course," Jennet said, mostly to herself. "Lady Ashford?"

"Yes?" The woman had taken a few steps to one side, preparatory to launching herself into the air, but now she paused.

"Could you...will you scout ahead in the direction we were going? The wrong direction?"

"I can, but why should I?" Lady Ashford sounded more curious than suspicious.

"It is just that one of our scouts disappeared while he was searching in that direction, and we do not know what is there." Jennet was not sure how much she should say, aside from not implicating Adair—that could have serious repercussions if she and Falconer were wrong—but Lady Ashford's intercession might make a difference.

"How odd." The countess looked over her shoulder toward the head of the line. The country in that direction continued as it had for miles—fields that had never been tilled, lines of trees delineating their edges. "I will look. Do you believe he was waylaid by bandits? Or—I suppose he might have deserted."

"We do not know," Jennet said. "The captain believes he deserted, but his expectant wife is with us."

"That is a mark in his favor, yes. And if there are bandits about, better you not be attacked. Very well. I am much faster than a Bounder and it should take no time at all for me to scout ahead." Lady Ashford adjusted her goggles, nodded in farewell, and shot away into the sky, the wind of her passage ruffling Jennet's curls.

Jennet watched her Fly out of sight as the baggage train resumed its cumbersome, slow march. Now they would know the truth Captain Lord Adair wanted hidden. Jennet hoped it would not be something too dire to face.

The clouds drew ever nearer. Chilled, Jennet rubbed her arms and eyed them speculatively. They were likely to get very wet, very soon. She watched the skies for Lady Ashford, but she did not reappear. After half an hour, Jennet became worried. Surely an Extraordinary Mover could Fly faster than this?

The road they followed passed beside one of the many fields, green with long grasses and darker tangles of weeds. Jennet once more looked to the head of the line. A dip in the road that turned into a slight rise meant the officers on their horses were clearly visible, as were the first score of soldiers behind them. Jennet settled her shako more firmly on her head. Another row of trees lay some fifty feet beyond the line of march.

Then the crack of a musket shattered the still summer air, followed by another, and another. The horses at the head of the line reared up, and Jennet heard faintly their cries of terror. The bugle sounded an alert. The sharp formation of the double line of soldiers dissolved as men scattered and dove for cover. And out of the trees marched a long, long line of French soldiers in blue and red, no longer pausing to shoot but advancing inexorably toward the surprised British forces.

Jennet swore and ran toward the nearest wagon, dodging fleeing horses frightened by the gunfire. "Stop, stop!" she screamed at the driver. "We are under attack! Stop moving!" But the wagon was already coming to a halt, warned by the bugle, and the wagon drivers were jumping down to use the wagons as cover. Seeing them preparing for battle, Jennet dashed forward to join her fellows, holding her rifle steady with one hand so it would not bang against her side and leg.

She fell to her knees beside another soldier and brought her rifle around to load it. "Did you see what happened?" she demanded.

The man was Corwin, and he had already loaded his rifle and now took aim from where he lay in the grass. A crack, a puff of smoke, and Corwin whipped the gun around to reload. "No," he said. "Only heard the shooting. You?"

"I was too far behind," Jennet said. "Where is Lady Ashford?"

"Gone, I supposed," Corwin said. "I saw her Fly off and believed she returned to Troyes."

But she had not. She had scouted ahead at Jennet's request, and something had befallen her. Which meant her death was Jennet's fault.

Jennet's hands automatically fell into the rhythm of loading the rifle. No. If Lady Ashford were dead, it was the fault of the one who killed her, not Jennet. She well knew at whose door evil should be laid. And if she believed that, she could not take on more guilt than actually belonged to her. She felt guilty nonetheless.

She had fired her rifle so many times over the years she no longer paid attention to the steps. Her lips were bitter with powder from biting the top off the cartridge; she had primed the pan with a trickle of gunpowder and poured the rest down the barrel without noticing. She crammed the ball in its patch of leather down the barrel, and with a twist of her wrist freed the ramrod from beneath the barrel. She let her hands guide the metal rod in ramming everything home as she scanned the battlefield, then replaced the ramrod and brought the rifle to the ready.

She lined up the rifle's sights and took aim at a French soldier. Her shot took him right in the center of his chest, and he fell as bright red blood spread across his gaudy uniform. The shot had been at the extreme of her range, though, and as she began reloading she heard Corwin shoot again and curse. "Too far," he said.

"We must move up," Jennet replied, and the two of them ran in a scuttling, crouching dash across the rough ground as musket fire exploded all around them. The French must be trying to demoralize them, Jennet realized, because musket fire was notoriously inaccurate except at close range, and the French were still at least two hundred yards from where she and Corwin lay.

A drop of rain struck Jennet's cheek, then two more, and then it became a light sprinkling that pattered over Jennet's shoulders. More shapes rushed from both sides to fall beside her and Corwin. "It is an ambush," Sadler said, serious for once. "An ambush. How could we not have known?"

"More shooting, less talking," Fosse said. He raised up and took aim, and another French soldier fell.

"But they ain't shooting," Whitteney said. "They're just marching toward us as we blow their damned frog heads off."

Jennet paused in her loading and surveyed the scene. Whitteney was not completely correct, because as she watched, someone—no, it was Ensign Townsend—jerked back and fell off his horse as a ball took him in the forehead. But most of the soldiers with muskets were not firing them. They looked like toy soldiers at this distance, wreathed in smoke from musket and rifle fire.

Another figure joined them, falling heavily to his knees and cursing. It was Corporal Josephs. "It was an ambush," he said. "They should have signaled a retreat. We're outnumbered."

Jennet stared at him. Outnumbered?

She turned her attention on the French once more, and her stomach lurched. Another rank of Frenchmen had emerged from the tree line, following the first. Rifle fire all around her echoed in her ears, deafening her, and more French soldiers fell, but there were so many of them there was no way her company could survive this. The rain fell harder now, not enough to obscure her vision, but enough that shooting would soon become impossible. Which meant she needed to account for as many of the enemy as she could now.

She resumed loading and scanned the lines for a French officer. That was the strategy, kill their officers so no one remained to give orders. But she saw no one, no horses, no standard. Beside her, Whitteney let out a grunt of satisfaction as his next shot took down an enemy. But the French merely moved to close up that gap in their ranks. Jennet looked around for the captain, for Lieutenant Falconer, for any officer who could tell them what to do next.

She saw Adair finally. The captain sat his horse as placidly as if a battle were not raging around him. He appeared to be looking for something, or someone; he had his attention fixed on the distant tree line. Jennet brought her rifle to bear on him, but hesitated. His odd behavior aside, she had no proof he was a traitor. This might all have been a mistake. She could not shoot her commanding officer on a hunch.

She crouched with her rifle lowered and once more assessed Captain Lord Adair's emotions. He was not afraid; he was pleased. Pleased at how well the attack was going. Then Adair spurred his horse into a gallop, heading for the trees. Jennet incautiously raised her head, watching him go, and heard the whine of a musket ball pass far too close to her face. She let go of Adair's emotions. What he felt no longer mattered.

She raised her head again in time to see a long, long row of horses emerge from the tree line. Their riders' uniforms and insignia marked them as officers. She brought her rifle to bear on them, though they were definitely too far and it would take a miracle for her to hit anyone at that range. Instead, she watched, and waited for them to move forward. "Officers!" she shouted, though she did not know if any of her comrades understood her.

She wiped rain off her face and scanned the line, looking for a good target, and was stunned to see a figure dressed all in grey standing between two of the horses. Jennet blinked, rubbed her eyes, and peered again through the smoke and rain. Lady Ashford. What could *she* be doing with the French? She did not appear restrained in any way, but she also did not move. Jennet rose into a crouch, preparing to move forward again, but she stopped as another person caught her attention.

At the center of the line, a grey horse and its rider stood very still. Jennet had the strangest feeling the man was looking right at her, though she was sure that was impossible. And she was right; the man's head turned to right and to left, surveying the field. He wore the hat and coat of an officer, and medals glinted on his coat facings, though again Jennet was too far away to make out details.

A curious sensation swept over her. It felt like being gently prodded by invisible fingers, but inside her body rather than against her skin. Something nudged her, for all the world like an errant memory she wished to recall that was just out of reach. She steadied her rifle again, waiting for the man on the grey horse to walk forward.

Then the shooting stopped.

Confused, Jennet lowered her rifle and looked around. Fosse and Sadler had laid down their guns, and Whitteney and Corwin stopped midway through reloading. Josephs had dropped his weapon and ramrod. All five of them wore identical astonished expressions, as if someone had told them something startling they could not quite believe. Jennet caught up Whitteney's emotions, and then the other four, and found them all in the same state of astonishment.

"Corwin," she said, grabbing the nearest man's shoulder. "Corwin, what—"

A shudder passed through every man within Jennet's sight. Then, those who were on the ground rose to join the others until all were standing. Jennet felt those tangles of emotions shift from astonishment to joy to the same kind of love she had seen in Adair and finally to adoration. With another shudder, every man fell to his knees.

Horror and dread filled Jennet. She watched as the man on the grey horse walked his mount forward a few steps. He was definitely watching her now, the only one left standing in the field. Feeling numb, Jennet could not even pretend she had been affected, could not drop to her knees or do anything but stare.

That was Napoleon. And he had Coerced the entire company.

Jennet turned and fled.

CHAPTER 12

IN WHICH JENNET FLEES, AND A LONG JOURNEY BEGINS

F ear as she had never known pulsed through her. Napoleon. She tried, as she ran, to Coerce those she passed out of their adoration, but unsuccessfully. She had never been good at Coercing a mob when she did not have several moments of stillness to collect herself, and she did not dare stop. There was no way Napoleon did not know what she was, and no way he would let her escape if he could stop her.

She ran, heading for the trees the company had just marched past, her breathing loud in her ears, tripped on the wet ground, and rolled headlong with her pack pulling at her and her rifle still clutched in her nerveless hand. She could not help herself; she looked back, her heart pounding. The soldiers were rising to their feet, leaving their rifles on the ground, and the wagon drivers had climbed down and were walking like men in a dream toward the French line, and—

Jennet drew in a sharp breath. Five British soldiers ran toward her at top speed, rifles jerking back and forth in rhythm with their steps. Fear shot through her again before she remembered Napoleon was no Speaker, and he could not command them to chase her with the power of his mind simply because he had Coerced them to adore him. She rose and stood like a fool, completely uncomprehending why those five should have resisted Napoleon's Coercion.

Past the running men, she saw more horses, Captain Lord Adair's dull brown animal that had almost reached Napoleon's line—and beautiful black Suleiman, whose rider rode in the same direction with a deliberateness that broke Jennet's heart. She could not bear the thought of Falconer being Coerced, not after she had striven so powerfully to avoid Coercing him herself. Then she became angry. No. He would *not* be Napoleon's slave, not him of all people.

More musket fire rang out, and one of the running soldiers jerked and fell to his knees. His companion hauled him to his feet, and the two stumbled along behind the others. Shots whined past Jennet, and she ducked, but never took her eyes off Falconer. He was nearly fifty yards away, but her talent was limited only by line of sight.

She drew in a breath and gathered up her sense of Falconer's emotions. The ecstasy he felt at being so near Napoleon infuriated her. She did not take the time to coax his emotions safely through a natural range; that would take too long. Instead, she reached within for the terror she had felt and sent it surging through Falconer's innermost self.

The results were spectacular. Falconer's head jerked, and he wrenched on Suleiman's reins and turned the horse around so fast its hooves skidded on the wet, unplowed ground.

Then the first fleeing soldiers were on her, and hands grabbed Jennet around the arms and dragged her, making her lose sight of the lieutenant. Her shako fell off, but she had no time to retrieve it. She got her feet under her again and wrenched away from the grabbing hands, turning to run as fast as she could for the trees.

Two of the others outpaced her, not stopping to look back. Jennet ran as she had never run before. Her feet kicked up clods of wet earth, her heart pounded as if it wanted to escape her chest, but a surge of fear pulsed through her, giving her the strength to go on running even as the rest of her body demanded she stop.

She flung herself between the trees and grabbed hold of a rough bole to stop herself. Panting, she looked behind her. The entire company, even the women and the wagon drivers, walked at a measured pace toward Napoleon's troops, who had laid down their weapons and stood aside to let them pass. They did not even try to shelter from the increasingly heavy rain. Revulsion at the sight threatened to overwhelm her. She clung to the tree and closed her eyes, trying to calm her breathing.

"God's blood," someone said. "What in the *hell* was that?"

It was Sadler.

Jennet opened her eyes. Sadler and Fosse sat nearby, breathing as heavily as Jennet was. Farther on, Corwin leaned against a tree face-first with his head resting on his folded arms that were propped against the rough bark, and Whitteney knelt, leaning on his rifle as if he would fall without its support. All four of them had also lost their hats, and their faces were red with exertion. Behind them, Corporal Josephs squatted with his hands on his knees, sucking in air as roughly as if he had forgotten how to breathe.

Jennet immediately guessed what had happened. She had been in contact with each of the five when Napoleon Coerced them, and had not thought to release them when she fled in terror. She had communicated her fear to them, overriding Napoleon's Coercion with her own. For the first time in her life, she was grateful to her talent.

"I am shot," Whitteney gasped. He collapsed to the ground, put one hand to his thigh, and brought it away bloody.

Corwin pushed away from the tree and staggered to Whitteney's side. He prodded the injured leg. "The ball passed clean through," he said, "but the wound is deep." He slung his pack off his shoulders and dug through it, coming up with a shirt he slashed into wide strips for bandaging.

Whitteney was breathing heavily, and his eyes were dilated nearly to blackness. "What was that? That feeling? I wanted to throw myself at his feet."

"I felt—" Fosse drew in a deep breath. "I loved that man, and then I feared him as I have never feared anything else in my life. What *was* that?"

Jennet remained silent, but her heartbeat sped up again. They would realize any moment that Napoleon had Coerced them, and if they guessed their unnatural fear had been Coercion as well—

"That was Napoleon, damn me if I'm wrong," Sadler said. He looked close to vomiting. "Napoleon, here, attacking us."

"That can't be," Fosse said. "Why? The great Emperor, with his army in the middle of nowhere rather than at the gates of Paris?" He wiped sweat from his brow and drew in a deep breath.

"And yet we were Coerced," Sadler said. "It couldn't have been anything else."

"But we escaped," Corwin said. His deep, slow voice caught as he struggled to regain his breath. He tied off the bandage and helped Whitteney to rise. "And we must keep moving if we wish to stay free."

"No one escapes Coercion," Whitteney said. "No one." He looked back the way they had come. "Marie. I must—" He took a step, and his injured leg collapsed, pulling him away from Corwin.

Jennet grabbed his arm, supporting him. "You cannot help her now. You would only become a slave. Don't fear, Whitteney. No one will harm her." She was not entirely sure of this, but she also was not sure Marie would not go willingly to some French soldier. That was not anything she would tell Marie's husband.

"So, why us?" Josephs demanded. "Why should we—"

The pounding of horse's hooves interrupted him. Falconer burst through the trees and pulled Suleiman up sharply. His eyes were as wide as the horse's and his hair was disordered, giving him a manic, terrified look that said he was on the verge of fleeing again. He gasped, "Flee—do not stop, you fools, we must—" He wheeled Suleiman and sidestepped Corwin, who was in his path.

Jennet seized hold of his emotions. The fear she had induced in Falconer was too great. He might ride for hours in his terror, into who knew what danger. Feeling guilty both for having caused that fear and for interfering with his emotions further, Jennet Coerced him into a calmer state, slowly as she had not done when rescuing him from Napoleon. He would have no reason to believe his emotions had been altered. She told herself that made her sin less.

Falconer's body relaxed and he stilled Suleiman before he could ride on. He let out a deep breath. "That was Napoleon," he said. "It could be no one else. You all are free of Coercion?" He looked at Jennet as he spoke. She managed to hang onto a frightened, confused expression.

"We believe so, sir," Fosse said. "We don't know why." He had lost the ribbon tying his queue, and his hair straggled around his face.

"Nor do I," Falconer said, "though I have heard a different powerful emotion can rid someone of a Coerced one. I felt such fear..." He let his voice trail off. "Is that man wounded?" he said, his voice sharp and focused now.

"I can walk," Whitteney said. He pushed himself to one foot, but when he tried to rise fully, he let out a pained gasp and collapsed again. Corwin got a hand beneath his arm and helped him stand. Whitteney leaned heavily on him, his face ashen and pinched with pain.

Falconer looked behind them. He let out a deep breath. "Get him on the horse. We must go quickly. Napoleon will send men after us, either his own or his newly-Coerced troops. He cannot afford the chance that even one man might escape to warn Lord Wellington." He guided Suleiman around. "Hurry, now."

Jennet followed his gaze. In the distance, the men of the 3rd had reached Napoleon's soldiers. As she watched, a dozen of them turned and ran back the way they had come. Back in Jennet's direction.

Fear shot through her again, but this time, it was overcome by anger—anger that Napoleon had controlled her comrades and sent them in pursuit of their friends.

She glanced at the others, who were engaged in helping Whitteney onto Suleiman's back. Then she turned her attention on the pursuing soldiers and gathered up her sense of their emotions. Napoleon's Coerced feelings of adoration were obvious this time, and she set about undoing them. Immediately, she felt resistance to her Coercion. Napoleon had a tight hold on their obedience. She might unravel his grip, but it would not be in time to prevent the men reaching them.

So she ignored what Napoleon had done and set about evoking a new emotion. The men were weary already, in body and spirit; she took hold of that weariness of spirit and made it grow and spread into indifference, into a lack of desire to keep following. The soldiers' pace slowed until they were walking, then plodding. It would not last, but it might be enough to give her and her companions an edge.

"Graeme!" Falconer shouted. "Come now!"

She turned her back on the soldiers and followed Suleiman.

They ran after Falconer, who kept Suleiman's pace slow enough not to outrun them. Thunder rumbled, and the heavens opened up, drenching them. Jennet's curls were immediately soaked, and she reminded herself that it would be almost impossible for any pursuing soldiers to find them in this downpour. She ended up near the end of their little group, running more slowly because she could not stop herself looking in every direction for soldiers, either French or, more terrifyingly, their own, and then hurrying to catch up.

Despite her care, she was still startled when Corwin, right ahead of her, came to an abrupt halt. "Stop," he cried out. "There is a horse—I believe it is one of ours."

The others all came to a halt as Corwin approached the animal, slowly so as not to spook it. It was one of theirs, one of the pack horses, though it had lost most of whatever load it had been carrying and now wore only its saddle and a few bags. Corwin took hold of its bridle and led it back to their group.

Falconer dismounted and took the bridle from Corwin. "What a fortunate find," he murmured. He turned to the others and said, "Which of you is the best rider?"

They all exchanged glances. "Me, sir," Corporal Josephs said.

Falconer assessed Josephs' frame, his short and slender body, and nodded. "You will ride west for Paris," he said, handing the bridle over. "Make your way to General Harrison in that city and report Napoleon's presence here. He will have Speakers to convey the information to Wellington."

"Yes, sir," Josephs said. "But, sir, what of the rest of you?"

"We will continue north," Falconer said. "I will not lie to you, corporal. Even if Napoleon's main army is here and not advancing on Paris as we were told, there are still French forces between here and Paris. Getting through those troops may be far more dangerous than our journey north. But it is a risk we must take. Someone must reach Wellington, and our chances are better if we separate."

Josephs saluted and mounted the horse. "Very well, sir. Good fortune to you." He was gone before anyone else could return his good wishes.

Jennet watched Falconer, who stood still until Josephs was out of sight. "Sir," she ventured, "should we not continue?"

Falconer nodded, but with a distracted air. He looked at Whitteney, who clung white-knuckled to the saddle and looked close to passing out, then spoke quietly to Suleiman, tugging on his reins. The others followed, but Jennet cast one backwards glance and spared a thought for Josephs, riding into who knew what kind of danger. Dwelling on her own danger could not help their situation.

They hurried on through the storm. Jennet once more fell into her position at the rear, even more alert now that they had actually spotted something. For a while, she saw no movement, nothing but the incessant rain. Her eyes told her they had outpaced their pursuit for now; her heart told her that was foolishness. When she finally saw a pale shape dart behind a tree, it was with a sense of relief. She aimed her rifle at the spot and said, "Come out of there now!"

To her astonishment, someone did. Jennet lowered her rifle and exclaimed, "Veronique!"

Veronique came toward her, her whole body trembling and her hands supporting her heavy belly. She had been weeping, but now her eyes were dry, and despite her pale, frightened face and her soaked gown, she stood up tall. Jennet hurried toward her. "Veronique, what are you doing here?"

Veronique shook her head. "I felt the Coercion, and I ran. I did not know what they might do with me. I was so afraid."

The others had halted some distance away when they realized Jennet was no longer with them. Now Falconer dismounted and approached, his eyes on Veronique. "Mrs. Appleton," he said. "Graeme, how did she escape?"

Jennet, who had been about to take Veronique's hands to calm her, put her hands casually behind her back. "You are a Discerner," she said, ignoring Falconer for the moment. "Only a Discerner is immune to Coercion. Why did you not tell us?" Likely Veronique could not Discern Jennet's talent if Jennet was not actively using it, but Jennet had no desire to take that risk by touching her.

"It is no one's business but my own," Veronique said, a spark of defiance in her voice. "And it is not as if Discernment is useful, not like Bounding or Speaking. So I told Simon not to mention it."

"She says she is a Discerner, and thus immune to Coercion," Jennet told the others in English. "That is why she was able to flee."

Falconer closed his eyes and shook his head slowly in a gesture of frustrated resignation. "Would that I had known we had a Discerner already. This whole disaster might have been avoided."

"How is that, sir?" Sadler asked.

"There is no time for discussion," Falconer said. "Can she ride, Graeme?"

Veronique shook her head when Jennet relayed this question. Falconer's lips pressed tight together for a moment, but that was all the annoyance he betrayed. "Help her to mount—Suleiman can carry two for a time. We must outrun our pursuers."

It took three of them to help Veronique onto Suleiman's back. When they again set off, Falconer did not slow for Veronique's sake. They ran, rested briefly, and ran again. The rain let up only slightly, so it became merely a downpour and not a deluge. Jennet continued vigilant, but saw no other movement save their own.

After the first few terrifying minutes where they fled across open ground, they entered a forest of lindens, which grew far enough apart that even Suleiman could move with ease. It was no true shelter; sparse growth meant sparse cover, and without the storm's concealment, their path would be obvious. But it kept some of the rain off, and some shelter was better than none. Jennet had lost track of which way they ran, but she thought it was north and a little east.

At the next rest, she leaned against a tree to catch her breath. The sky was partly visible, and it looked lighter than it had. "The storm is passing," she said.

"Aye, moving on to drench someone else," Fosse said. "We cannot assume we have outrun them. Dear God, we are fleeing our own people."

"The storm protected us," Falconer said. "But you are correct, we cannot make assumptions. We will have to travel through the night, and let darkness protect us as well."

"We should eat something, sir," Jennet said.

"Have we any food?" Falconer said. "There are no farms nearby, and we dare not divert from our route to enter a town. And there is no time to hunt game. We cannot spare but five minutes." He helped Veronique down.

Sadler and Corwin got Whitteney off the horse; he was short, but solid, and they staggered under his weight before lowering him to the ground. The cloth wrapped around Whitteney's leg was scarlet with blood. Whitteney closed his eyes and bowed his head, but he remained seated upright.

Jennet unslung her pack and, setting aside the tent canvas strapped atop it, knelt on the ground to rummage through it. She had only the few possessions she always had: two spare shirts, two pairs stockings, a blanket, a comb and other toiletries, a useless shaving kit she kept for camouflage, and a little box of writing supplies. A sizable handful of coins, mostly shillings, but some guineas, was stitched into the pack beneath a false bottom. Powder and fifty-two rounds of shot, what remained after the battle that morning, finished out her load.

She was more concerned with her food supplies. Soldiers were supposed to carry three days' worth of bread and two days' worth of meat, plus a large water canteen. In the Peninsula, this was a custom more honored in the breach, as bread in particular was either worm-riddled, hard, or nonexistent, but in France they were usually well supplied. She had eaten some of her bread, but their evening's meat as they traveled had come from the quartermaster's wagons, and she still had all of the dried meat she had been given at the march's outset. She had also purchased a cheese before leaving Soissons, a largish wax-coated lump the size of her doubled fists, and half of that remained.

Beside her, the others also removed their food and silently put the bread and meat in the center of their loose circle. There were a few extra items, as Fosse also had a round of cheese, larger than Jennet's, and Whitteney contributed two potatoes and a handful of carrots and, to some exclamation, an orange. It glowed in the last light of the sun.

"It was a treat for Marie," Whitteney said, "Bounded here special from Spain." His voice was hoarse, and Jennet carefully did not look at his face so as to give him what little privacy she could for his grief.

"She will be well," Fosse said, clapping the man on the shoulder. "No one will harm her."

Whitteney nodded and swiped an arm across his eyes.

They put away the food that required cooking and handed around the bread, which they chewed in silence. Jennet watched Falconer covertly. His handsome profile looked no different than it usually did, but he had raked his fingers through his wet hair, making tufts stand on end. The sight made Jennet's heart beat faster, as if his careless grooming made him less of a beautiful statue and more of a man. She turned away, commanding herself to stop being foolish. They were all in mortal danger, and her ridiculous attraction was completely inappropriate.

"Sir, do you know where Wellington is?" she asked to distract herself.

Falconer looked grim. He pushed his hair back from his face with one hand again and stilled Suleiman with the other. "With the main body of the Army in Belgium. They were to rendezvous with the Prussians in preparation for an attack on Paris."

"Belgium," Sadler said. "That's hundreds of miles from here."

"It is." Falconer took a few steps away from his horse. "And we cannot be seen. Even were we to outrun our ground pursuit, Napoleon has

Coerced Lady Ashford, which means he has aerial surveillance in addition to however many Bounders he might have. The journey will be long and arduous."

Jennet glanced up through the branches. She had forgotten Lady Ashford in her haste to get away. Now the storm seemed even more like a friend than an inconvenience.

The lieutenant pinched the bridge of his nose as if his head pained him. "If only I had acted sooner. Had I challenged Captain Lord Adair immediately I became suspicious of him, we might not have walked into that ambush."

"You said you had no way of doing so, sir," Jennet said.

"What does it mean, you were suspicious of him, sir?" Sadler asked.

Falconer shook his head. "I suppose it no longer matters what anyone knows." He looked at each man in turn, though, as if impressing on each of them the seriousness of his words. "I now believe the captain was Coerced into betraying us. He must have encountered Napoleon at some point before joining the Army at Soissons. That Coercion led him to murder Ensign Mondy to prevent him reporting on Napoleon's troops in this vicinity, and to bringing our company where it could be ambushed by those troops. And I regret harboring ill thoughts of my commanding officer. I believed him to have thrown in his lot with the French willingly."

"But he spoke so freely of his hatred of Napoleon," Jennet dared say. "I have heard those who are Coerced do not realize it—should he not have openly declared his new allegiance?"

"The captain is extremely intelligent, and surely knew he could not succeed at his goal of aiding Napoleon if he revealed himself." Falconer looked as if he had swallowed something bitter. "I can even imagine his anger stemmed from being unable to act openly, which would have felt dishonorable. What I do not understand is how that Coercion lasted despite Captain Lord Adair's many rages, which to my understanding should have supplanted any other Coerced emotion."

Jennet knew the answer to this—that a new, strong emotion could supplant a Coerced one only if the victim experienced it shortly after being Coerced, within a few days at the most. But she could hardly tell the others that. Guilt filled her at not having recognized the captain's strange feelings of love, with no object Jennet could perceive, as Napoleon's Coercion. It was nothing she had ever seen before, did not look the way adoration did when she Coerced that emotion, and it made her fear Napoleon more for his obvious skill with his talent.

"At any rate, it no longer matters," Falconer continued. "We cannot help the rest of the company except by getting word to the Army so the allied forces can defeat the so-called Emperor." He mounted up. "Pray, assist Mrs. Appleton and Private Whitteney, and make haste."

"So Mondy was murdered so he could not scout ahead and discover the French army," Fosse said as he offered Veronique his hand. "But...no, I see. Word of Napoleon marching on Paris came from Captain Lord Adair, and his statements are all suspect."

"No doubt there are others spreading the same word," Whitteney said. He struggled to rise, and Jennet helped him to stand and lean on her. "Whatever forces attack Paris are a ruse. Which means our Army is looking in the wrong place."

"And may well start for Paris at any time," Falconer replied.

"Then we cannot afford to be slow, sir, isn't that true?" Sadler asked.

"We can barely afford this delay," Falconer said. "But if we exhaust ourselves, we will be useless to the Army."

"What of our uniforms?" Jennet asked. "If we remove them, we can travel unnoticed, but we would be considered spies if the French catch us." She did not add that they would be executed as such if they were caught.

"They leave us with a terrible predicament, Graeme," Falconer said. "We might well be executed if we are caught in uniform as well. If we are somehow immune to Coercion, Napoleon can have no use for us."

No one had a reply to that. Jennet could not reveal the truth about why they were no longer Coerced, but for them to go on believing they were immune could be dangerous if they met Napoleon again. They would simply have to keep moving and prevent that happening.

She took her now-customary place at the rear and tried to let the rhythm of her running feet quell her fears, but memories of that commanding figure on the grey horse would not subside. The idea of confronting Napoleon filled Jennet with dread. He was so powerful, so skilled, and he was capable of Coercing more individuals at a time than she had ever done. It was true, she had broken his domination over a few men, and she suspected that made her his equal in that small regard, but she lacked the control that would have freed the entire company. If she had years to learn, perhaps, but she did not have years. She suspected she might not have days.

She did not understand why Napoleon had not been at the head of his army. Surely he was too important to command a mere handful of soldiers? She did not realize she had said this out loud until Sadler, running to one side, said, "What was that, Ned?"

She startled. "Oh! It just seems odd that Napoleon should have been there at all, when he has so many generals who might lead his troops," she said, somewhat breathlessly from running.

"Almost could believe he intended to capture us," Corwin said.

Falconer turned briefly to look behind him. "Of course," he said. "The French only shot a few times, and I believed that to be because we were not yet in range. But suppose the purpose was not to kill, but to Coerce?"

"Which is what they did, sir," Fosse said. He exchanged glances with Sadler. Jennet guessed they both wondered at Falconer's slowness to grasp the obvious.

"I mean, Fosse, that capturing the company was the entire purpose of that encounter." Falconer sounded as if he had had a terrible epiphany. "The Rifles are the cream of the Light Division. The men are well trained and deadly at range, and are also among the most experienced regiments thanks to their many battles in Spain and Portugal. The French have nothing like them. I can well imagine Napoleon wishing to have them fight on his side. No wonder he needed the captain's cooperation."

Jennet's heart beat faster at the awful image. "Where is the rest of the 95th, sir?"

"Most of them traveled north to join the rest of the Army." Falconer shrugged. "Dividing the regiment was supposed to provide support for those battalions guarding the way for our allies to advance. I am certain this possibility never occurred to anyone. And now we will be fighting our own troops."

"Damn Napoleon," Sadler muttered under his breath. "Damn Extraordinary Coercer. Thank God there's only one of them."

Jennet kept her head lowered so he would not see her face.

CHAPTER 13

IN WHICH JENNET HAS AN UNCOMFORTABLE NIGHT'S SLEEP

They ran spread out between the trees—the narrow band of lindens could not be called a forest—for what felt to Jennet like forever. The linden trees grew low enough to the ground that she occasionally had to duck the branches with their rich green leaves. Suleiman and his passengers had it worse, though Falconer avoided most of the lowest branches, but Veronique did not complain. Whitteney rode in pinch-lipped silence.

Still, Jennet at the rear of their group could not help watching nervously in all directions, even above. The pattering of rain in the trees soon faded in her hearing, she was so accustomed to it, as did the sound of her footsteps over the rough, weedy ground. Very little grew beneath the trees, mostly tufts of wet, dead grass, last season's growth, surrounded by shoots of fresh green Jennet crushed beneath her boots. She gave the ground only as much attention as she needed not to trip over exposed roots; the rest of her was preoccupied with scanning the fields for blue French uniforms or the green of her own fellows.

They had gone a handful of miles when Jennet realized their path had curved northward, and the band of lindens had broadened enough to permit them to spread out further. Though the rain had mostly stopped, the sky was no more clear than before, and Jennet suspected the storm was not yet finished with them. Yet she still heard the rushing of water—

and just as she recognized the sound as the flowing of a stream, they came out on its banks. It was not broad and did not appear deep, and it ran very fast, throwing up little wavelets along its banks.

Falconer let out a relieved breath, as if the stream were an old friend he had thought never to see again. He guided Suleiman to drink deeply. "So long as it remains dark, we may follow the streambed to obscure our trail."

"We cannot walk along the bank without leaving a mort o' tracks," Fosse said. "Look at the mud. And hoofprints are even more distinct than boots."

"Then I suspect we are going to become quite wet," Falconer said.

They all knelt to refill their canteens. Jennet scooped water in her hands and drank as thirstily as Suleiman did. Shortly, Falconer said, "Quickly, now. It will give us a guide through the night."

Jennet walked into the rushing flow without hesitation. Her boots were not so waterproof as to keep out the water forever, but even through the leather, she felt how cold the water was, and it made no sense for her to wade barefoot until her feet froze.

She realized at least some of the dimness was the sun setting. They had been running longer than she had realized. Ahead of her, Fosse stumbled, caught himself before he could fall, and muttered, "This is going to be a long night."

"Indeed it will," Falconer said, startling Jennet again because she had thought him out of earshot. Though, now she came to consider the matter, she supposed a Shaper might Shape his senses to beyond normal human capacity, and Falconer's hearing might be acute. "We must take advantage of the hours of night, and hope to outpace our pursuit enough to snatch rest before we are exhausted."

"Do you know the countryside hereabouts, sir?" Fosse asked.

"I can get us as far as Rheims, I believe." Falconer still looked as composed as if he were in a fine drawing-room. "From there, we must proceed north to Belgium. North and perhaps west—it will depend on what news we have of the Army and its disposition as we go."

"It is at least a week's journey," Sadler said.

No one spoke in rejoinder to this. A week's journey.

They continued walking, stopping every so often to give Suleiman a rest and for all of them to drink. Jennet's feet grew gradually wetter and colder, but she pressed on, grateful for the stream despite her discomfort. At one point, they passed a small village the stream curved around as if avoiding contact with it. No one was about at that hour, but the fields were patches of rich, dark loam turned up in long furrows for a late planting.

Jennet imagined the smell of the earth and was transported to her childhood, to running past the fields belonging to Mr. Robertson and racing the plow horse, not an easy thing for her short five-year-old's legs. Plowing, and planting, and growing, and harvesting—every year, regular as her father's pocket watch. An unexpected ache filled her chest, not longing for her lost family, but a wish for life to be as simple as a plowed field. Impossible, because she would soon grow bored by farming if that were her livelihood, but after the events of the day the idea was for once appealing.

The rain had finally stopped, but the skies were still leaden with clouds, and beneath the branches, all was still and dark. The trees now grew thickly enough to be considered a forest, and the lindens mingled with other trees, mostly ones Jennet did not know the names of aside from the occasional beech. A wind had risen, rustling the leaves until they whispered in what sounded like unintelligible speech. Between the wind and the rushing stream and the splashing of their feet, the night was nothing like peacefully quiet, but it also did not resound with the sound of pursuit.

She knew she should not relax, that not hearing pursuers did not mean the soldiers of the 3rd were not still chasing them, but between fear and exertion, weariness began to catch up to her. It was full dark now, with the overcast blocking what moonlight there would normally be, and the stream was a rippling trail of shimmering blackness edged with slightly paler lines where the water cut through the soft soil. She watched her steps, aware that her tiredness might make her clumsy, and made sure she did not walk too close to Fosse for fear of tripping on his heels.

How long they walked, she had no idea. Occasionally Falconer called a halt, and at those times they stood like trees rooted to the streambed. At every rest, Jennet was convinced she could never walk again, and every time Falconer urged them onward, she discovered new reserves within her.

Finally, there came a time when Falconer not only said, "We will stop now," but led Suleiman away from the stream. He helped Veronique slide down and steadied her when she alit. Jennet splashed out of the stream and walked to their side. Veronique looked exhausted despite the relatively small exertion of perching in front of Suleiman's saddle. Whitteney slid down and landed in a heap. He looked like he might never move again.

"It will be dawn in a few hours," Falconer said, surprising Jennet; she had not realized she had lost track of the hour to that extent. "We will stop now, and sleep a few hours. It is safer to travel by cover of night."

"Do you believe we have lost our pursuers, sir?" Jennet asked.

"I believe we have stolen a march on them, but I am not so foolish as to assume that makes us safe." Falconer lifted the bags away from Suleiman's back, the ones they had taken from the pack horse, and rummaged through one of them. "Someone's spare clothing," he said, handing Jennet the other bag. "I believe it is Captain Lord Adair's. I hope he will not begrudge me its use."

Jennet expected Falconer to change his shirt, but to her surprise he removed Suleiman's saddle and proceeded to wipe the horse down with Adair's spare shirt. In her weariness, this struck her as the funniest thing she had ever seen, and she turned away so as not to burst out laughing. To distract herself, she opened the second bag, which was squishy yet firm and wet without being soaked through. A damp, faintly sweetish scent rose from the contents. "Oats," she said. "If we can ever make a fire, we will not starve."

"We can eat regardless," Sadler said. "There's still bread, and if we've stopped for a while, we can soak beef for later."

"And there's plenty of water," Fosse said. He removed a tin cookpot from his pack and brandished it like a sword. "We are practically civilized."

Corwin got Whitteney off the stream bank and onto a patch of soggy grass, and Jennet helped remove the bloody bandage and replace it. The blood had stopped flowing, though it started again in a sluggish trickle when they pulled the bandage free, and the new cloth did not redden immediately. "'Tis nothing," Corwin said in his gruff voice. "You will be walking again in no time."

Whitteney gave him a weak smile. "Ned, give me a hand," he said. "I never thought I would be hungry again, but I daresay I could eat a morsel."

They sat in a little circle as if there were a fire rather than bare ground and shared out bread and cheese and sections of golden, sweet orange. Jennet sat next to Veronique, who wrapped herself in her cloak and nibbled in silence. Jennet said, "You must eat. Think of the child."

"I think of nothing but," Veronique said bitterly. "That, and my fears for Simon, are all that preoccupy me. He must be dead."

"It is more likely he was Coerced when his scouting brought him in contact with Napoleon's troops. You should not despair." Jennet considered putting a comforting arm around Veronique's shoulders, but it was not something Ned Graeme would venture, and she still feared the Discerner learning her secret.

"He promised to protect me." Veronique took another bite of cheese and chewed and swallowed angrily. "Now I have no one, and this child will be born in sorrow."

"We will take care of you," Jennet said, feeling awkward about promising what she was not certain she could perform. And in truth, leaving Veronique behind was safer for Jennet, as she need no longer fear her secret being exposed. But the idea filled her with inexplicable guilt.

Across the circle, Fosse said in halting French, "You do not fear. It is well. We you do not... do not desert."

"I did not know you speak French," Jennet exclaimed in that language.

Fosse grimaced and made a little back-and-forth gesture with his hand. "I speak enough to make my meaning clear to the ladies," he said in English.

"I might have known," Sadler said with a grin. Fosse elbowed him in the side.

"What does she say?" Falconer asked.

Jennet repeated her short conversation with Veronique. Falconer shook his head. "We will find a safe place in one of these villages for her to stay. A nunnery, perhaps. This will be a terrible journey, and she will find it hard going even if she rides. And she will slow us, as well."

"She would be a stranger, with no one by her," Jennet protested, "and to deliver a child in such circumstances would be cruel."

"More cruel if we are overtaken. We cannot guarantee the men pursuing us will be gentle with a woman, even one with child." Falconer sighed and stretched out his legs, tilting his head back to look up at the black sky visible between the branches. "And we do not know how far ahead of our pursuit we are. Nor how large a force Napoleon has sent. Though it is unlikely to be his entire army."

"Where else might he go, sir?" Whitteney asked.

"I wish I knew." Falconer sounded tired. "If his decoy troops to the west have not done so, he might go west and take Paris, now that he has at least one British rifle company as a prize. He might move south to Troyes to attempt to Coerce the troops there. The Austrian army will approach from the east, and our battalions were intended to hold the line along which they should advance, preventing Napoleon's forces from overwhelming them. If Napoleon can control our Army at Troyes and farther east, he will overcome or Coerce the Austrians. Perhaps not easily, but with little opposition."

"But we must behave as if he intends on capturing us," Jennet said.

"Yes. We cannot be complacent. Even if Napoleon sends only a fraction of his forces after us, he, too, cannot be complacent about the possibility of our warning Wellington of his true intent." Falconer turned his gaze on Jennet, and it chilled her in its bleakness.

"Surely our Bounders will see where Napoleon's army actually is," Sadler said.

"If they know to look in this direction, yes," Falconer replied. "But I have no doubt the information that Napoleon marches on Paris has been widely spread, and our reconnaissance efforts will be turned on Paris and points south. And if the decoy army is large enough, it can conceal the fact that Napoleon is not with it."

Jennet felt as bleak as Falconer looked. "Aye, and Bounders, unless they are Extraordinaries, have limited skipping ranges," she said, "so they can only see so much."

"Which is why we will bring the news quickly," Falconer said. "Travel by night, hunt or forage as we go, enter towns only as a last resort."

"Paying for aught in towns might certainly be a last resort," Sadler said. "I have but sixpence, and no francs."

"That is a consideration," Falconer said. "I have some few francs, and not much more in shillings. I hope we will not need more than that."

Jennet held her tongue. She did not begrudge her companions the use of her money, but she had kept it hidden for so long, in her pack and in the lining of her jacket, she did not like to reveal how wealthy she was. Time enough for that when the need became urgent. She also did not remind anyone of her silver pocket watch. She did not know if their situation would ever be desperate enough for her to part with it.

The others revealed they had a little coin, though none of it was in francs or centimes. Jennet was the only one whose money—the pocket change she admitted to having—was mostly French. "Keep it for now," Falconer said. "If we must purchase food, we can divide the money then." His words ended on a wide yawn. "It is likely to rain again before dawn, so pitch tents, and Fosse, you will take the first watch."

Jennet unfolded her tent and then caught sight of Veronique, still huddled into herself, and realized their predicament. "We have only a few tents," she said to Sadler in a low voice, "and Veronique and the lieutenant will require shelter."

"I'll bunk with Fosse," Sadler said. "Veronique can have my tent. You give the lieutenant yours, and see if there's room in Corwin's tent for you."

Jennet nodded. She swiftly pitched her tent with Sadler's aid, then walked to where Falconer was tending to Suleiman. He brushed the beautiful animal's withers and flanks, murmuring softly as he worked. Jennet hesitated before approaching, it seemed so much like disrupting a divine rite. "Sir, will you take my tent tonight? As yours was left behind?"

Falconer turned his gaze on her. "And where will you sleep, Graeme?"

"Oh, I will share with one of the others. It's no trouble at all, sir." His regard made her even more uncomfortable, as if he could see through to her skin and know her secret.

Falconer glanced over the tents. "Which is yours?"

Jennet pointed.

"It's larger than the others," Falconer said.

"Is it?" Jennet had never noticed this, and now she realized it was slightly bigger, though not in any way that stood out. "Aye, I suppose. Not by much, sir." She couldn't imagine why Falconer would care about the size of the tiny tent.

"Enough that it makes more sense to sleep two people there than in the others." Falconer resumed grooming Suleiman.

"I suppose, sir." Jennet did not understand this any more than his first statement.

"Then I'll bunk with you, if you don't mind."

Jennet's heart lurched against her ribs painfully hard. "Oh, sir, but you shouldn't—"

"If you are concerned for my rank, you needn't worry. I am well accustomed to sharing quarters." Falconer did not look at her. "Unless you snore."

Jennet choked on an unexpected laugh. "Nay, sir, not I."

"Then it's settled. Get to your bedroll, Graeme. I will finish here."

Jennet hurried back to her tent and laid out her bedroll so it left plenty of room in the tent for a second person. Her heart still beat a crazed tattoo of nerves and excitement. She was being utterly foolish. It was not as if they were anything to one another but officer and rank-and-filer, or even officer and servant. Yet sharing that space was such an intimate thing Jennet could not calm her emotions. It was a pity she could not Coerce herself.

She removed her jacket and boots and huddled beneath her blanket with her face toward the tent canvas, closed her eyes, and waited. Shortly, the canvas shifted, and Falconer entered. Jennet heard the rustle of fabric as he removed his jacket, and then the quiet noises of someone settling in to sleep. Jennet remained motionless. Finally, Falconer was still, and all she heard were the noises of insects chirruping and whirring and whistling all around them. In the distance, a hunting owl cried, *tu-whoo, tu-whoo.*

Jennet breathed out slowly. She could not hear Falconer's breathing even though he was right next to her. He was so quiet she might have imagined herself alone had she not heard him enter. She had not shared sleeping quarters with anyone in years, not since that little Portuguese town whose name she had never learned where her company—her previous company—had been billeted, and she had slept in a loft with three other men, all of whom did snore. This was entirely different.

"Graeme," Falconer said.

Jennet's eyes flew open. The interior of the tent was nothing but grey shadows. "Sir?"

"These men. Fosse and Sadler, Corwin and Whitteney—they are your friends, are they not?"

The usual pang of guilt struck Jennet. "We have marched together for many months, and I trust them," she said. Calling them friends was too great a lie even for her.

"That is unusually fortunate, that the five of you and Corporal Josephs were the only ones unaffected by Coercion. A fortunate coincidence, in fact." Falconer sounded as if he were mulling over this statement. "I wonder why that is."

Jennet's heart beat fast for a completely different reason. "I did feel something, at first," she lied. "A compulsion, or even a kind of adoration, as if the object of it—Napoleon—were someone holy, someone deserving of worship. Then it was gone, and I felt nothing but fear." She did not like talking about Napoleon's Coercion at all, but that was what the others had experienced, and they would no doubt tell Falconer if he asked, so there was no point dissembling.

"That is what I experienced, as well." Falconer still sounded slightly distant in contemplation. "A terrible longing to be in that man's presence, to fall to my knees and worship him. And then, fear as I have never known. It makes no sense, unless—"

Jennet had a terrible feeling she knew what he would say next. "You did say some other emotion could take the place of a Coerced one," she said, hoping to distract him. "And it was frightening, facing all those French soldiers who kept advancing. There were so many of them."

"I did." Falconer shifted, sounding as if he had rolled over. "There was certainly enough to be frightened of. But I wonder about that."

Jennet could not believe he could not hear the sound of her pounding heart trying to escape her ribcage. She kept silent. Finally, Falconer said, "It is nothing. Pray, ignore my mutterings. We must rest, especially given the day we face tomorrow. It is a long, long march ahead."

"Good night, sir," Jennet said. She moistened her dry lips and added, "You did not say if *you* snore, sir."

Falconer chuckled. "If I do, I will have to Shape myself out of it. Good night, Graeme."

Jennet closed her eyes again, but it was no use—now she knew where Falconer was, and she imagined she could feel the heat of his body against her back. If she moved at all, she would brush up against him. The idea of touching him, even accidentally, made her heart race again. He had to hear the sound; it was impossible he was so ignorant of her presence as to be insensible of the pounding of her heart. She concentrated on breathing, in and out, slowly so she gave the impression she was falling asleep.

She berated herself silently. He was beautiful, but so was a statue, and statues did not disorder her senses the way he did. She was a fool to be so affected by his proximity. For ten years she had been indifferent to every man she encountered when she did not actively despise them, had sworn she would never look on a man with desire. And now a handsome face and a shapely body had turned all her oaths inside out in a way she had believed impossible.

None of that mattered. He knew her as Ned Graeme, no one he would ever find attractive, and likely that would remain true even if he knew her to be female. But these facts were not enough to stop her imagining what it would feel like if he touched her with desire. She wished she could take herself out and give herself a good drubbing, clear her imagination and restore her to where she had been before she ever saw Lieutenant Falconer. She did not need a man to care for her, she did not need romantic companionship, and she certainly did not need physical intimacy.

But it took her more than an hour to fall asleep.

CHAPTER 14

IN WHICH THEY FIND A POTENTIAL REFUGE, AND A DIFFERENT THREAT ARISES

When Corwin woke Jennet for her turn at watch, the rain had stopped and the sky had lightened, enough that she could see her surroundings clearly. Her boots, which she had set inside the tent against their being soaked again by the rain, had dried enough that with a new pair of socks, she was not very uncomfortable.

With her rifle in hand and her bayonet where she could reach it quickly, she circled the area where they had pitched their tents, listening to the birds twittering to one another. They fell silent whenever she neared, only to pick up their song again when she moved on. Their silence might warn her of the enemy's approach, but anyone who came that close would be visible, so the birds were not something to rely on.

She neared Suleiman and observed that someone had groomed him recently, as he was not wet at all except for his mane and tail, which were still damp. Suleiman regarded her placidly. The ground near him was bare of grass, and his jaw moved as he chewed. Jennet stroked his thick mane. "You are a nuisance," she murmured. "The French have taken all the horses, and they would certainly want a handsome fellow such as you."

Suleiman rubbed his nose against Jennet's shoulder, making her smile. "But I understand why the lieutenant would not abandon you," she said, patting the horse's cheek.

She continued her circuit, varying her path to avoid leaving an obvious track, though with seven of them and a horse, concealing their presence would be difficult no matter where she walked. Nothing moved aside from the trees, their leaves rustling in the morning breeze; she heard no sounds except the birds and the leaves and the rushing stream, louder than the leaves and burbling over its bed in an endless flow.

The sky's overcast was lighter than before, and Jennet watched the bright disk of the sun rise higher in the sky, obscured sometimes by the branches. When she judged a few hours had passed, she woke Falconer. "I have seen no sign of the enemy, sir."

Falconer nodded and ran his fingers through his hair, though this did little aside from disordering it further. "Rouse the others. We should move on soon."

Corwin and Sadler moved through their campsite as the others packed up tents and possessions. There was only so much they could do to conceal the presence of a group of travelers, but Jennet marveled at how they hid the signs of bodies sleeping and a horse grazing. Their work would not fool an experienced scout, but it would deceive the casual eye.

They ate as they walked, chewing beef softened by water and the hard, dry remains of the bread. Spread out as they were beneath the trees, they made less of a target to a Flying observer, but Jennet was still conscious of the trail they must be leaving. Her Coerced comrades from the 3rd, if they were the ones following, had extensive experience in tracking after years in the Peninsula. Dwelling on that possibility made her weary and dispirited, so she focused on watching in all directions, even upward.

Ahead and to the right and left, Sadler and Fosse were doing the same, though they rarely looked behind them as if they knew Jennet would alert them to a threat from that direction. It was good to have companions to rely on. She had never regretted so much Coercing them into friendliness. They were worthy of being actual friends.

Whitteney looked much better after some sleep and food. He sat upright in the saddle and was even able to give Veronique some support. But he spoke little, which was so out of character for him Jennet guessed he was still in pain. He did not even whistle a cheerful bird song to echo the ones they heard in the trees.

While staying alert to the possibility of danger, she watched for food sources as well. After six years in the Army, she knew well the need to take advantage of food wherever she found it: orchards, hedges rife with berries, even gardens. Jennet preferred finding abandoned gardens on properties whose owners had left in advance of the troops, or who had gone in search of more hospitable territory. She never liked raiding gardens when it meant others would go hungry, even though she understood the necessity.

A rabbit startled out of hiding by their approach dashed away, and she let it go with regret. Rabbits were good eating, but with no opportunity to light a fire, killing them was pointless. Jennet did not believe they were yet so desperate as to eat rabbit raw.

They ate at nightfall without stopping, hard bread from their supplies, making Jennet regret the loss of the rabbit even more sharply. Shortly after the ersatz meal, Falconer called a halt. "We will turn east again now that it is dark. There is a place nearby we may leave Mrs. Appleton."

Sadler shifted his rifle in a restless, uneasy gesture. A frown replaced his usual cheery smile. "What place is that, sir? Not a village, surely."

"It is a nunnery outside Sommesous, sufficiently far outside that we need not reveal ourselves to any but the nuns. I learned of it when I was with the 43rd and we passed through the village." Falconer eyed Sadler. "We cannot continue as we are. Mrs. Appleton will be safe there."

"Aye, sir," Sadler said, standing more erect. He did not meet Falconer's eyes.

Falconer took another step toward him. "You disagree, Mr. Sadler?"

"No, sir, just—" Sadler took a deep breath. "No, sir."

"This is our best choice," Falconer said. "Graeme, explain to Mrs. Appleton while we walk."

"Veronique," Jennet said, "the lieutenant knows a place where you will be safe. A place you can give birth. We will take you there."

Despite the dimness, Jennet clearly saw Veronique's expression change from curious to afraid. "But you will not leave me with strangers?"

"It is not safe for you to travel with us. And we must go swiftly in any case. It is not that we are leaving you—"

"But you are, and I shall be alone," Veronique exclaimed. "I have lost Simon, and you are all the friends I have in the world."

Jennet felt sick, and she wished Veronique had not said anything. But Falconer was correct; they could not continue as they were. "You will be safer," she persisted. "They will care for you, and someday you will return to your family. And all will be well."

Veronique looked at Jennet with such a bitter expression Jennet was taken aback. "I have no family who will accept me," she said, "so this place is as good as any." She turned away from Jennet, her chin lifted high.

Falconer glanced from Veronique to Jennet. "What did you say?"

"Nothing but what we intend," Jennet replied. "She would rather travel in danger and uncertainty than take shelter."

"Her desires are immaterial when it is a matter of safety, hers and ours." But Falconer did not sound as convinced as he had before. Then he shook his head and added, more firmly, "I regret causing her pain, but there truly is no other option."

"I know, sir," Jennet said, and retreated to her position at the rear so she would not have to look at Veronique any longer.

In another half an hour, the forest ended, and broad, grassy fields stretched out before them. The skies had finally cleared, and the moon had not yet risen, so the stars were undimmed and blazed brilliantly against the stark blackness of the sky. Far to the east, the low shapes of houses huddled on the horizon, darker than the fields and speckled with a handful of lights warmer than the stars.

Nearer to hand, perhaps a quarter mile away, lay another, smaller cluster of buildings, equally dark save for a single lamp illuminating the large wooden door and the stone wall into which it was set. What was visible of the building looked very old and very sturdy, its roof peaked sharply, the doorstep a lighter color than the wall.

"That is the place," Falconer said. He nudged Suleiman forward.

"Bide a moment, sir," Corwin said. His gruff voice startled Jennet. She had not heard him speak all day, not since waking her for her watch. "'Tis something not right about that stable."

Jennet looked where Corwin pointed. In the darkness, she could not clearly make out the different outbuildings, but the largest one lay outside the low stone wall fronting the nunnery, and as she peered into its black interior, she made out several shapes, barely moving, that might be mules.

"I see animals moving," Falconer said after a moment. "What do you consider amiss?"

"Animals, yes," Corwin said. "But two of them are horses. Think ye the French would leave good horses behind, even horses belonging to nuns? 'Tis reet peculiar."

Falconer took a few steps forward as if that would make a difference to what he saw. "We need more information. Corwin, scout ahead and bring us word."

Corwin saluted and ran toward the nunnery. Jennet watched him go, willing him to move silently—but he was one of the best scouts she knew, and would be cautious. Soon enough, he disappeared behind the stable.

She returned to Veronique's side and explained what Corwin had seen. Veronique nodded, but said nothing. Jennet rested her hand on Suleiman's withers and examined the dark stable. The movement was clearer than before, but it was only the usual restlessness of horse or mule drowsing in its stall, not the more agitated movement of animals reacting to a stranger's presence. Wherever Corwin had gone, he had not disturbed the stable's occupants.

Time passed. Jennet checked her pocket watch, but could not read it by the dim starlight. She put it away and watched Fosse pace, restless as always when he had nothing to do but wait. As he stood still as a post when he stood sentry, this tendency amused her. At the moment, she was too intent on Corwin's return to tease him. Whitteney watched, as still as Fosse was not, but his stillness was tense as if he were so intent on the nunnery he had forgotten his pain.

Falconer took a step forward. "He is returning."

Moments later, Corwin rejoined them, approaching from a different direction than the one he had originally taken. "It is our men," he said in a low voice, "men of the 3rd, I mean. They have placed pickets—there, one of them has come around to the front."

They all backed deeper into the shelter of the forest as a man, little more than a moving shadow, emerged from around the left side of the nunnery and walked past the front door, all the way to the corner where the stables were. He stopped briefly, looked inside the stable, and then walked back the way he had come. Jennet let out a long breath when he was once more gone.

"Took me some doing to avoid them," Corwin went on. "They're reet good at watching. And I recognized two of 'em, Ericks and Kersey."

"Excellent work," Falconer said. He did not look pleased. "They moved more quickly than I expected."

"But they couldn't have followed us, sir, or they'd have caught us," Fosse said.

"Like as not they guessed where we might go, and rode straight for

Sommesous rather than tracking us direct," Sadler said. He cracked the knuckles of his left hand, one at a time, with a series of noises like cracking walnuts. "'Tis both good and bad."

"Which means there are likely more searchers at the approaches to Sommesous, and had we been foolish enough to go there, we would have been apprehended," Falconer said. "We will need to press on. Graeme, will you explain to Mrs. Appleton the situation? I fear we cannot escort her to the door, but she will be safe on her own."

"Beg pardon, sir, but I don't know as you see the problem," Corwin said. "Ericks and Kersey, at least, they are not the kind of men to let a woman pass unmolested, no matter her condition. I heard Ericks talking to the other man, the one I don't know, about the nuns, and it weren't nice talk. Mayhap it were nothing but talk, and mayhap it weren't, but I don't know what's happened here. If we send Mrs. Appleton there, might could be we send her into danger." His gruff face looked even more villainous than usual.

Falconer looked past him at the nunnery, where another shadowy figure crossed from right to left and paused at the left-hand corner to talk to his companion. He said something Jennet thought was profanity under his breath. "We have no choice," he said, more loudly. "We cannot permit ourselves to be captured, regardless of what those men intend." He turned away, taking Suleiman's reins and leading him back into the forest. "But I will not abandon another woman to whatever fate they have in mind."

"Where are we going?" Veronique asked.

"You must remain with us for now," Jennet replied. "There are men at the nunnery who might do you harm. It is not safe."

"I see," Veronique said.

Jennet chose to ignore how satisfied the woman sounded.

They once more followed the stream northward, staying with it when it made a turn to the west and then straightened out northward once more. Jennet could not stop seeing those shadowy figures near the nunnery. Corwin's assessment of Ericks and Kersey, at least, was correct; they were casually cruel to anyone they considered weaker and loved to boast of their conquests, which were not limited to the camp followers.

She watched Falconer, who once more rode Suleiman, and wondered what he saw. She guessed it sat ill with him to leave the nunnery in the hands of those who would abuse the inhabitants—she did not believe any of them were happy about that. But he was correct; they had a mission more important than individual lives. And Jennet had not been in a position to use her talent to spare those women. She could have Coerced the soldiers free, or Coerced them to feel kindly toward the nuns, but not without revealing herself to her companions. That was unacceptable. Selfish, perhaps, but still unacceptable.

When the sky again paled with dawn's approach, Falconer led them away from the stream to a place where the trees grew close together and dismounted. "I fear we have seen the last of the storm," he said. "Now we must take added precautions against being seen from above."

As he spoke, he tilted his head back to survey what little was visible of the sky through the branches. Then he began walking, still looking at the sky, only glancing down now and then to avoid tripping or walking into trees. The others followed him to a place where the trees thinned out into a clearing like an upside-down horseshoe, hemmed in on three sides by the forest.

When Falconer did not immediately speak, Jennet said, "Is something wrong, sir?"

"I fear so, Graeme." He continued staring at something far to the west.

Jennet followed the line of his gaze, but saw only a flock of birds wheeling and diving in the western sky. "I don't understand."

"We have been very lucky so far, Graeme." Falconer pointed at the birds. "I believe we may have already had all the luck we are going to get."

Jennet could not at first see what troubled him. They were just birds, and not large ones at that. She watched them circle again and then fly northward, all but one. Jennet's heart thumped once as she realized that was no bird. "Lady Ashford," she breathed.

"Almost certainly." Falconer shot one last look at the distant Extraordinary Mover as she dove, circled low over the forest canopy, and shot away to the west. "She is only one person, and cannot be everywhere at once, but we have no guarantee she will not Fly this way. And we still cannot assume we have outrun our pursuers. We must stay beneath the trees, and continue to travel by night."

"Was that Lady Ashford? How close was she?" Whitteney asked. He leaned forward in the saddle and then winced in pain.

"Not close enough to see us, but close enough that we should not dawdle." Falconer tugged on Suleiman's reins. "Let us make haste. No tents today, and conceal our camp as best you may."

This time, Jennet took the first watch. Though her body ached with weariness, she felt alert enough to know she would only lie awake staring into the branches and letting the noise of the birds irritate her. Birdsong was pretty enough, but when one was attempting to sleep, it was as good as a signal whistle for disturbing one's rest. She circled the camp as the others built a rough shelter to conceal Suleiman, who even beneath the thickly-growing leaves stood out against the lighter ground. She took the opportunity to fill her canteen while they worked, then ranged farther away as they settled into their bedrolls.

She reflected on the many times she had manned the pickets, night and day, and how she remembered them by their smells: the dusty dryness of the wilderness of Spain, the sharp bite of the scrub growth covering the low hills of Portugal, the damp greenness of the French countryside. At the moment, standing watch smelled of cool water from the stream and the warm, leaf-scented humidity of air heated by the rising sun. It had not felt like summer for several days, but Jennet anticipated the day would prove hot and uncomfortable. Even had they not been running for their lives, sleeping through the daylight hours might be wise.

She heard someone approaching from behind and spun around, lowering her rifle when she saw Falconer. "All is quiet here, sir."

"Thank you, Graeme." Falconer stood beside her, scanning the trees as she did. "I wish I could guarantee it would stay that way."

"We can defend ourselves if someone comes upon us, sir."

Falconer smiled. "Let us hope that does not become the case." He sighed, and glanced upward at the sky, clear blue and cloudless. "It is breakfast time for civilized folk. What a pity we cannot have tea. I am very fond of tea in the morning, as I'm sure you know."

"Aye, sir. But you are right, we could not light a fire even if we had tea leaves. We do not even have cups."

"A real pity." Falconer shook his head, but he was still smiling ruefully. "My mother would be horrified to see me now, traveling rough across France with no tea in sight."

Jennet choked back a laugh. "Because no tea is a terrible deprivation?"

"Because she is under the impression soldiering is a genteel profession." Falconer chuckled. "So much of what is reported in England downplays the less savory aspects of our lives, Graeme. She hears of officers riding to the hunt, or playing cricket, or attending balls, and believes my life is little different from what it would be at home. Though of course I cannot be perfectly comfortable in foreign parts where garlic is a primary ingredient in every meal."

Now Jennet did laugh. "I am not civilized, then, because I have grown fond of garlic."

"So have I. I fear I will find English cuisine bland by comparison when I return."

Falconer was watching her now, his eyes alight with humor, and without considering the impropriety of the question, Jennet asked, "And where is your home, sir? Where do you return to?"

"My family is from Surrey. We have property south of Guildford, a house in London, another outside Oxford. We are not noble, but we are well enough off." Falconer dug a short furrow in the ground with his toe. "And you are from Scotland. Where did your people come from? Or—perhaps that is an insensitive question, as you said your family is dead."

For the first time in years, the memory of her family was not one of fire and screams. "We lived in a wee town you won't have heard of near Loch Lomond. My father was a minister in the Presbyterian faith, my mother kept house, and my brothers and I roamed free over the hills."

"That gives us something in common," Falconer said. "I ran wild as a boy until I was sent away to school." He hesitated, then said, "May I ask what happened?"

That, Jennet could never tell him, not even if he knew she was female. "House fire," she said. "I was...not there at the time. So it was only me that was spared." Spared because of those men who— She closed her eyes briefly, willing away memories that were surprisingly distant. Perhaps there would be a day when they did not hurt at all.

"I apologize if I gave you pain," Falconer said quietly. "You must have loved them dearly."

Her eyes ached with tears she refused to shed. "I did," she said, and hoped he would say no more.

To her relief, he merely nodded and said, "Wake Sadler in two hours," before walking away to his blanket. Jennet blinked rapidly until her eyes no longer felt swollen and paced her circuit of the camp, keeping watch over the others.

She took care not to walk too close to where they all slept, but she could not stop herself observing them, as if her notice gave them extra protection. When she came near where Falconer lay, she watched him sleep for a moment, feeling shy as she did so, as if she were intruding on his privacy. He looked less like a statue when he slept, his face relaxing, his mouth barely open. He had no bedroll, only a blanket, and it occurred to her that he might well have demanded one of them give up their bedding on the grounds that he was an officer. But he had not.

He was not at all what she had believed at first; he was not arrogant, he cared about justice and the fates of the men under his command, he respected her even though she was nothing but a common soldier, and he was compassionate in a way she had never expected from an officer.

It occurred to her that he could have deserted them. He had Suleiman; he could have ridden off and left the six of them to fend for themselves, or even left them to be captured so he might make his escape. But as far as she could tell, that possibility had never occurred to him. The knowledge made her heart swell. At least, if she were to develop an attraction to a man, it was to a man worthy of admiration.

She watched for her allotted time before shaking Sadler awake. He came awake as slowly as always, blinking and yawning and looking at her as if he had never seen another human being before. "Ned," he said with another yawn. "Is there meat?"

"I doubt it has soaked long enough, but you may have some if you wish," Jennet said. "Unfortunate that we cannot have a fire, as I saw rabbit spoor not far from here."

"A soldier's best friend, rabbits." Sadler sat up and popped his neck joints, twisting his head one way and then the other. He grinned at Jennet's grimace and scratched one armpit vigorously. "Ah, you don't know how good it feels to have a bit of a stretch in the morning."

"I do not sound like a sack full of unshelled walnuts in the morning," Jennet retorted.

"Nay, you do not." Sadler stood and stretched fully, letting off a string of pops and snaps that made Jennet laugh. Sadler clapped her on the shoulder and added, "Off to sleep now, Ned, and dream of returning to the Army as heroes. Or dream of hot, roasted beef. Both are as likely as each other, at least today!"

With a smile, Jennet found a spot to lay out her bedroll, not close to

Falconer—that felt like indulgence—but not far from any of her companions. Talking to Sadler had lightened her heart. She liked pretending to herself that it was true camaraderie, that she deserved their friendship. It was impossible, of course, but she liked the pretense.

Real friends. She had not had real friends in almost ten years, not since she discovered her talent. It was a compelling notion, one that cheered her until she remembered that she would never be able to learn if it were true. And she dared not act as if it were true; she was still guilty of having Coerced them, and she could not permit herself to forget that guilt. Not until she had atoned for her sins.

Despite her bleak imaginings, she fell asleep easily and woke refreshed a few hours before sunset. Fosse was on watch and nodded at her when she passed him in search of some privacy. Entirely relieved, she returned to camp to find everyone awake and engaged in packing away the supplies. They spoke rarely, but in cheerful, quiet tones, even Corwin, who usually did not speak at all. Jennet felt better rested than she had in days, even before Napoleon's attack. Even her fears of being overtaken by the enemy could not suppress her good mood.

They resumed their journey about an hour before sunset. It seemed all of them felt as hopeful as Jennet, even Veronique, whom Jennet caught in a smile once or twice. Jennet's position at the rear meant she saw almost nothing of her companions' expressions, but Whitteney whistled bird calls as he rode, and Fosse walked with a spring in his step she had not seen since Soissons, and even Falconer's occasional words sounded cheerful.

Just at sunset, they came to a road, its surface rutted and uneven from the last rain. Falconer called a halt at its edge. The trees grew right up to the road's edges, leaving no verge, and the canopy grew well over it, leaving only a narrow strip of sky where the branches of trees nearly met.

"It's still visible from above," Sadler said. He rotated his left shoulder, making the joint pop, but gave no other sign he was worried.

"That will not matter come full night, when Lady Ashford cannot search," Falconer said. "And we will travel more swiftly on a road, without leaving tracks—or at any rate, without leaving tracks that must belong solely to us. We will follow beside the road, well spread out, until full dark."

Fosse nodded. "Sadler and I will scout ahead, then."

"Unless we—" Sadler began.

Falconer raised a hand. "Quiet," he said.

Fosse and Sadler stilled. All the men brought their rifles to the ready. "Sir?" Whitteney asked in a low voice Jennet could barely hear.

Falconer shook his head. "Something moving nearby. Something, or someone. It may only be a traveler, but we should be wary."

He began walking again, but slowly. The others followed. Jennet did her best to make no noise, straining to hear what Falconer had. Even the birds had stopped singing, which worried her. Possibly it was simply that sunset had come, but if there were something, or someone, else—

Dark figures emerged from the trees on the other side of the road. Jennet saw pistols aimed their way. As the figures spread out to encircle them, one of the pistol wielders stepped forward and said in French, "Give us your money, and no one has to die."

CHAPTER 15

IN WHICH A FATAL ENCOUNTER LEADS TO ANOTHER, MORE SERIOUS PROBLEM

Falconer stopped, bringing the rest of them to a halt as well. "Graeme?" he said, his gaze never wavering from the speaker and his pistol.

"They demand our money," Jennet said.

Immediately three pistols were trained on her. She heard someone's breath hiss, but she could not look away from the enemy. Her hand closed tightly on the barrel of her rifle. She did not know if she could bring the rifle to the ready before the men fired, but that was irrelevant as it was not loaded. The bayonet at her hip, however, needed no ammunition.

"Put your weapons down," the first man said, still in French. "Then toss us whatever valuables you have. You see this is a civilized exchange."

"Robbery is not civilized," Jennet said in the same language.

The man smiled. He and his companions wore dirty white shirts and trousers stained with old food and, Jennet guessed, blood. Their hair was matted and greasy and none of the eight were shaven. In all, they did not look as if they intended anything but theft. "I can be much less civilized if you cross me," he said. "Weapons, and money. Now."

"They do not speak French." Jennet was unnaturally calm, even in the face of death. "Permit me to explain the matter to them. If you are interested in being civilized."

The man laughed. "Indeed," he said with a shrug. But the pistols did not waver.

Jennet's hand slid down the barrel toward the bayonet's hilt, a fraction of an inch at a time. "Bayonet" was the wrong word despite its intended use; the thing was a small sword, twenty-three inches of good steel. To keep the bandits' attention on her and not her hand, she turned her head away so she was looking at Falconer and not the bandits. Her heart screamed a warning at her, but she did not twitch. "Sir, they say we must put down our weapons, and they will let us go if we give them our money. I do not believe they are telling the truth."

"Neither do I," Falconer said. His voice sounded unusually strained, and he stood very still as if he were afraid even though most of the guns were not pointed at him. Jennet was embarrassed for him. So he was confident until actual danger struck. She could not believe he was so cowardly.

Falconer drew in a shaky breath. "Very well. All of you, prepare to draw swords when they are distracted." Before Jennet could ask what he meant by "distracted," he took a step forward with his hands held wide. Instantly every pistol shifted to point at him.

"Sir," Jennet said, "you cannot——"

"*Now!*" Falconer shouted, and lunged forward, faster than Jennet believed possible.

Several guns discharged, and Suleiman screamed and reared up, making Veronique scream as well. Jennet shouted a warning, but Falconer had impossibly dodged, ducking low, and not one of the shots struck him. Jennet's hands had already dropped the rifle to the ground and wrenched the bayonet free.

Shouting a challenge, she leaped at the nearest bandit, slashing broadly to force him back. He brought his pistol to bear on Jennet. She swung again, and as swiftly took hold of his emotions and sent fear surging through him. The man's face purpled, and he staggered backward, tripped, and fell. Jennet was on him like a hound on a hare, thrusting for the heart.

She rose, bringing her bloody blade to the ready, and snatched up the bandit's loaded pistol, which for a miracle had not gone off when he dropped it. All around her, her companions fought in the silent precision they had been taught, and bandits fell or ran away. Jennet brought her captured pistol to bear on one of the men threatening Fosse and shot him in the head, making him fall in a spray of blood and bone fragments.

And then it was over. The others stood or knelt over their victims, breathing heavily. Falconer wiped his sword on the shirt of the bandits' leader; the dead man lay on his back, his eyes staring sightlessly at the sky. Falconer's gaze fell on Jennet. "Very clever of you to keep him talking," he said. "It gave me time to Shape myself to a better form."

"You—" Jennet's assumptions embarrassed her. He had not been afraid; he had been concentrating on his talent. "Such rapid Shaping is painful, is it not?"

Falconer nodded. He rose, wincing slightly. "And it is painful as it wears off over the next few hours. But I hardly resent the discomfort." He looked around. "Is anyone injured?"

Fosse shook his head. Sadler collected his rifle and sheathed the bayonet. "I do not see Corwin or Whitteney," he said.

"We are here," Corwin said from beyond where Suleiman stood. "We have a problem."

Jennet at first believed he meant Suleiman had been injured. The horse stood as placidly as ever, after that one frightened movement. Then she realized Veronique no longer sat the horse's back. Dread sickened her, and she hurried with the others to where Corwin knelt.

Veronique sat, supported by Whitteney, whose face for once was not ashen with pain. She looked terrified, her eyes wide and her breathing loud and ragged, but she did not appear to be injured. She hugged her belly with both arms as if clutching it to her. "I fell on my stomach," she said, her eyes imploring Jennet for help. "The babe—it is not injured, surely? I could not stop myself falling, the horse—"

Jennet knelt beside Corwin and took one of Veronique's hands in hers, momentarily forgetting her reservations about touching a Discerner. "It will be well," she said without considering her words, then in English, to Corwin, she said, "Did she hurt herself? She must have landed hard."

Corwin's normally gruff face looked even more villainous than their attackers' had. "She is uninjured. But her waters flowed." He gestured at Veronique's gown. Now Jennet saw the large wet stain down Veronique's skirts. Dread spiked into fear.

"What does it mean?" she asked.

Corwin took Veronique's other hand. "The child must come now. That is what it means."

Reflexively, Jennet glanced around. The trees grew close to the road here, no doubt why the bandits had chosen it for their ambush, and there was no sign of civilization, not even the sounds of an unseen farmhouse. "But it cannot come now. There is nowhere for her to give birth."

Corwin shook his head. "It will yet be a few hours. A first birth takes longer. But when the waters flow, there is nowhere left to protect the child, and it must be born. We must needs find a place."

"What is he saying?" Veronique asked. Her voice trembled and was higher than usual.

"He says the child will be born in a few hours, and we have time to find a place for the birth," Jennet told her. "Can she ride?" she asked Corwin.

"Until the pains grow too strong, and she can no longer sit the horse." Corwin helped Veronique stand. "Sir, we must go quickly. If there is a settlement anywhere near—"

Veronique gasped in pain, silencing him. She put both hands on her belly. "You are certain the child does not come now?"

Jennet controlled the fear that surged through her. "Certain," she said. "Private Corwin knows of these things."

Veronique's body relaxed. "The pain passes," she said. She still looked frightened, but not as terrified as at first.

Falconer turned his attention from Veronique to the others. "We will make our best effort, but I cannot promise anything. I am not sure how far we are from Châlons-sur-Marne, which is the next large town on our route." He gazed northward as if he could see through the trees. "There is farmland outside that town, and we are likely to find help there, even at this hour."

"If we reach it in time," Fosse said. He and Sadler both shifted nervously, and neither would look at Veronique.

"Then we must go now," Falconer said. He looked Veronique up and down. Veronique's face was pale and her eyes were glassy with fear. "Whitteney, keep her from falling."

Jennet explained the situation to Veronique as Whitteney mounted with Sadler's assistance. It took three of them to get her safely atop Suleiman, in front of the saddle with Whitteney's arms securely around her. Veronique bit her lower lip nervously, but otherwise controlled her fear. Jennet was not sure she could have been as stoic in Veronique's place.

They walked on at a brisk pace, spread out around Suleiman like an honor guard. Jennet kept her bayonet close at hand, ready to fight if any other bandits attacked. But they saw no one as they traveled. Even the wind was silent, and the stillness of the air grew oppressive despite the continuing coolness of the weather.

The air smelled of new growth, a smell Jennet had as a child believed was the smell of the color green, just as the scent of water meant blue and the smell of wood burning meant gold like fire. But with the leaves unmoving and the birds no longer singing, with the darkness beneath the trees deepening, the smell of green was not as comforting as it normally was.

It was another mile before Veronique gasped again, bringing everyone to a halt. Veronique's face was puckered with pain, but as Jennet watched, the pained look subsided, and Veronique let out a deep breath. "I know the pains are to grow closer together, but I do not know how fast that happens. What am I to do?"

Jennet relayed this question to Corwin, who said, "It doesn't matter. They come when they come. When they are within seconds of each other, that is when the babe will be born. But it don't help her to know this."

Jennet had no idea how much of this to tell Veronique. She settled on, "It is still some time yet before the child is born. You should dwell on other things, like how happy Simon will be to see his child!"

That was a mistake. Veronique's face scrunched up again, this time with misery. "He will not see the child. He is lost."

"You shouldn't believe that. He is just Coerced, and someday we will rescue him." Jennet's tongue tangled on the words. Maybe it was wrong of her to encourage Veronique in false hopes, but there was no reason to believe Appleton dead rather than Coerced, not when Coercion gave Napoleon one more rifleman in his Grande Armée. "It is something to anticipate, presenting him with a son or daughter."

Veronique ducked her head, avoiding Jennet's eyes. "He will not care."

"Of course he will!" Jennet was not fond of Appleton, but she could not imagine him so lost to feeling as to be indifferent to such an event as childbirth.

"No," Veronique said. She bit her lip and hunched into herself. "It is not his child."

Jennet stopped, and Falconer nearly walked into her. "Not his child?" she exclaimed.

"What was that?" Falconer said.

Jennet realized she had in her surprise spoken in English. Her face reddening at her faux pas, she said to Falconer, "It is nothing—pray, let me speak to her more." To Veronique, she said, "Did you…I beg your pardon, it is none of my concern. Does he know?"

Veronique hunched further into herself as if feeling the weight of her humiliation, but she nodded. "It was another soldier. An English soldier. He was killed in battle. We were not married, but I, well." She ran a hand over her belly, then that hand stilled and her face creased with pain. When the pain passed, she continued. "Simon knew of my condition. He offered to marry me, for my protection and to give the child a father."

That did not sound at all like the Appleton Jennet knew, the man who was so rigid in his compliance with rules and regulations he might well have loved only them. "That was generous of him," she said.

"He is a good man." Veronique's eyes filled with tears. "He never touches me so I will not be overwhelmed by his emotions. I do not believe he loves me, but he is kind and honorable."

All kinds of observations Jennet had made without knowing slotted into place, like pieces of a fiendishly difficult puzzle. "But you love him," she said, not caring that this was not a thing Ned Graeme would say. "Veronique, I am certain—"

"Please, say nothing more," Veronique said. The tears spilled over her cheeks, and she wiped them away with the back of her hand. "It does not matter. Even if he is not dead, no one escapes the Emperor's Coercion. I should not grieve when so many have suffered more than I, but I am weak and foolish and I can see only the sorrow that lies ahead for me and the babe."

Jennet knew of nothing to say to that.

Then Veronique smiled, a lopsided expression equal parts amusement and sadness. "Private Whitteney is worried," she said. "He fears I have revealed something terrible."

"It is your own business and none of theirs," Jennet retorted. "I will tell them nothing is amiss."

"No, it matters nothing to me who knows now." Veronique glanced at the lieutenant. "He trusts you, I feel it. And I know you trust him, too."

Jennet remembered taking Veronique's hand and suppressed a flash of fear. Veronique was no Extraordinary Discerner, to feel others' emotions without the need for a touch, but Jennet knew even ordinary Discerners were good at ferreting out lies, and she had no desire for her lies to become known.

She said, in English, "Veronique's story is not what I believed," and told them everything she had learned about Appleton and Veronique. In the middle of her account, Veronique's body again stiffened as pain took her, her eyes squeezed shut, but she made no sound. Jennet fell silent until she recovered. She could not help wondering, despite what Corwin had said, how close the pains were and how much stronger they might grow. The forest showed no sign of ending, and she heard nothing that might indicate a town or even a farmhouse.

When she came to the end of the story, no one spoke for a few moments. Then Fosse said, "I wouldn't have guessed it. Never in a million years."

"He's still a bit of an ass," Sadler said. "Just not the way I imagined."

"I hope, for both their sakes, he is alive," Falconer said. "I'm afraid I don't know the man well, but he struck me as rather rigid. I suppose it's true that no one is ever only one thing."

"I feel bad about judging him so harshly," Whitteney said. "If we'd known, that would have changed things."

"Mrs. Appleton's privacy is her own," Falconer pointed out. "But I take your meaning. And I believe—" He jerked his chin in the direction they were going. "I believe we may find shelter soon."

Jennet looked that way. The trees were thinning out, drawing back from the road so their little group was not so hemmed in, and in the distance she saw open land. "Close, now," she said.

Veronique hunched in on herself, and a little cry of pain escaped her lips. The noise brought all of them to a stop. Jennet caught Corwin's eye. The gruff man was expressionless, but his stubbly jaw was rigid. He shook his head, the tiniest motion.

"We must hurry," Falconer said.

They emerged from the forest a few minutes later. Jennet had her pocket watch out and despite herself was timing the spaces between Veronique's pains. There was no point to it, but it gave her a distraction from her fears. Seven minutes. Then six.

Fosse, walking nearest Jennet, glanced at the watch. "Don't see how you can even read that," he said. "Not with how dark it is."

Jennet held the watch close to her eyes. "The light is enough. Though it hardly matters what time it is. It brings me comfort, that is all."

"You are lucky in your good memories. My father was a drunk who beat his children when he could catch them and his wife when he couldn't."

Jennet had never heard the cheerful Fosse sound so bitter, nor had he ever spoken of his life before the Army before. Speaking of her love for her own father suddenly felt wrong, as if it would be a taunt aimed at his private pain.

Fosse let out a breath with a slow hiss. "What's past is past, right? You hold onto that watch, Ned. Better to remember the good than cling to the bad."

"That's true," Jennet said. She searched for something she could say that would not sound fatuous or condescending, and came up with, "We neither of us have aught to go back to, have we?"

"Which makes the Army as much a home as anything." Fosse's wry comment made him sound more like himself. "And us brothers in arms. Life could be worse."

Jennet's face warmed at his off-handed words. For a moment, she forgot her concern for Veronique in contemplation of what he had said. Brothers in arms. It was not so terrible an idea, if only Jennet were not who she was.

The road unrolled before them like a spool of thread unwinding between the fallow fields. There was no sign of farmland, not even fields still stubbled with last year's harvest that had not yet been tilled. The forest stretched out to east and west, and on the west it curved around until the road disappeared into its northern expanse, far ahead. The stars blazed in a clear midnight sky, indifferent to human concerns. It was a beautiful night, and perfect for traveling, or would have been had Jennet not been so afraid for Veronique.

Six minutes. Then five.

They reached the place where the forest once again engulfed the road. Jennet's nerves urged her to give in to despair. They would find nothing, and Veronique would give birth in the open under a tree, with no swaddling blanket or cloths for cleaning. Of course, they would not have those things even if they found a farmhouse or a shed, but somehow the thought of delivering a child in a forest made the lack seem greater.

Veronique gave another gasp, and Jennet automatically checked her watch. Not quite five minutes. But Veronique said, in a normal voice, "Is it so bad? Whitteney's worry has grown more intense. And the lieutenant looks so concerned."

Jennet walked faster until she was even with Falconer. "Sir, Veronique asks if there is something wrong. She says she can feel Whitteney's concern. And I agree you look worried."

Whitteney grunted and tried to withdraw from Veronique, but they sat too closely together for him to avoid contact. "I beg pardon, Veronique, I forgot myself—Ned, tell her it is nothing."

Falconer let out a short bark of laughter. "There are no secrets where a Discerner is involved. I had hoped not to impose my worries on the rest of you. But I see no end to this forest."

Jennet decided to be open with Veronique, who after all could not be worse off for knowing the truth. But when she had translated Falconer's words, Veronique said, "I am no longer afraid. Things are what they are, and this child will be born regardless of anything we do." She winced, and let out a hiss of pain. "I wish it to happen soon, even if we are in the woods when it does," she added.

Fosse, leading the way, suddenly broke into a trot. "Look there!"

Jennet ran with the others to where the forest came to an end and the road emerged into the open again. They stood at the top of a short rise that made a gradual descent into the plain before them. In the darkness, all that was visible was the regular lines and edges of tilled fields lying like quilt squares across the plain—and, less than a mile away, the dark, squat shape of a farmhouse, sturdy and reassuring but unlit.

Falconer let out a breath of relief. "Make haste," he said.

Veronique's pains were coming a little more than three minutes apart when they made the turn onto the dirt path leading to the farmhouse. Though a thin stream of grey smoke spiraled from the chimney, the house was not very prepossessing, with its shutters hanging askew and holes in its roof where shingles were missing. Broken boxes and a wheelbarrow missing its wheel littered the front yard, and up close, it was obvious even in the dimness the windows had not been washed for some time.

Falconer brought Suleiman to a halt some twenty feet from the splintery, faded front door. "Graeme," he said, "I am not certain what to ask for. I would imagine this place abandoned if not for the plowed fields surrounding it."

"I will see what he has to offer," Jennet said. She put away her pocket watch and stepped up to the door. There was no knocker nor bell, so she rapped hard with her knuckles.

Immediately a ruckus of barking sounded from somewhere inside the house. Jennet guessed at least four dogs. Why they were all indoors, she did not know, but she was grateful she did not have to fend them off, or worse, flee from their attack. Coercion did not work on animals.

The barking continued. Jennet was about to knock again when light bloomed in the nearest window, and the top half of the door opened. An elderly man peered out at her. His thin white hair was mussed as if she had caught him sleeping, his shirt was not buttoned all the way to the top, and a dark brown stain like meat juice spread across the left side of his shirt. "What?" he demanded in a voice that creaked like a roof in a high wind.

"I beg your pardon, sir," Jennet said, "but we are in need of assistance. We are traveling with a woman whose time has come upon her, and she needs a place to give birth. Can you provide us perhaps a room, or a shed?"

"English soldiers with an expectant woman?" The man's voice rose higher in surprise. "Didn't think you all cared about the fates of the women you defile. Which of you is responsible?"

Jennet managed to control her impatience and her anger enough that her reply came out more politely than she felt. "She is French. Her husband is a...a captive, and he asked us to care for her."

"Only six of you," the man said, peering past Jennet. She hadn't expected his eyesight to be so good. "Where's the rest of your company? Tramping through other people's property, no doubt, stealing whatever honest folk have——"

"Sir." Jennet's grip on her patience was weakening. "How many we are is irrelevant. This woman is in need. Please, help us, or tell us you won't help a fellow countrywoman and we'll find someone who will."

"So testy. I could almost imagine *you* were the one dragged from his bed at near midnight." The man half-turned and shouted, "Shut up, the lot of you." Then he unfastened the bottom part of the door and slipped through the narrow crack, shoving unseen animals back with his foot. "Come this way. And don't get ideas about stealing. My dogs are champion hunters and they care not whether they hunt hares or men."

Despite a lurching limp, the man moved surprisingly fast. He led Jennet around the side of the house and beyond to a stone building something between a barn and a woodshed in size. It looked sturdier than the house, with an intact roof and no missing stones in its walls. A cow lowed, and the smell of fresh manure filled the air. Jennet relaxed. Any man who gave more care to his animals than himself could not be entirely selfish.

The old man wrenched the door open wide and stepped within. "You can use the barn," he said. "It's probably cleaner than the house, anyway. The well is beyond the barn, but if you are going to light a fire, do it in the yard and not inside, you understand?"

It was far, far more assistance than Jennet had expected. "Yes, sir. Thank you so much."

"Just don't come bothering me for anything else. And do not expect food. I've enough to sustain me and that's all." The old man nodded sharply and limped away, passing Falconer and Suleiman and the others who had followed in their wake.

Jennet hurried into the barn ahead of the others and found, as expected, a cow in a stall. There were actually two cows, which she had not expected given the apparent lack of prosperity the house evinced, and room for more, suggesting the property had not always been so impoverished. A small mountain of hay was piled against the back wall, permitting someone to climb to the roof, though as there was only the one room and no loft, that would be pointless. The barn was warm and smelled of cow and manure, and Jennet had never smelled anything so wonderful in her whole life.

Corwin was already busy dragging armfuls of hay into one of the empty stalls, the one farthest from the cows. "We need a bed," he said. "Fosse, bring that scrap of canvas, will you? Ned, find a place to start a fire and see if there's aught for carrying water. The rest of you, build up this hay pile."

Jennet hurried outside and scanned the yard. It was all packed earth, bare of plants, but there was a woodpile against the house. Jennet took the old man's words as tacit permission to help themselves to wood. Well, it wasn't as if they would not recompense him.

"What can I do, Graeme?" Falconer asked.

He stood next to Suleiman's head. Whitteney was still mounted, his arms supporting Veronique, who was breathing heavily. Jennet said, "They will make a bed for Veronique, sir, so if you help her down when that is ready, that is enough." She dragged wood to her chosen spot and reached for her belt knife to hack splinters from one of the short, split logs. Her hand found nothing. Cursing, she patted herself down anyway, but her knife was gone.

"Take mine," Falconer said, extending the beautiful Spanish blade.

Jennet hesitated. "It's far too fine."

"We are in no position to care about that." Falconer thrust the knife toward her. Jennet took it and, inwardly wincing at what she was doing to the edge, hacked at the logs until she had a small pile of splinters. She thrust the knife through her belt without thinking, but Falconer said nothing more.

Jennet busied herself with the wood until the fire caught and burned merrily into life. Then she rose just as the men emerged from the barn. Corwin strode to the horse and reached out for Veronique, who made an agonized sound just as Whitteney changed his grip on her to hand her down. Everyone froze, watching.

When Veronique had subsided into gasping breaths, Whitteney and Corwin carefully lowered her to where Corwin could help her walk into the shed. Jennet and the others stood watching, not meeting each other's eyes. Having started the fire, Jennet was uncertain of what to do next. Water. Yes. She didn't see the well, which meant it was behind the barn.

But before she could take more than two steps, Corwin's voice stopped her. "It don't take more than a few for this," he said. "I can make do with just me and Ned."

"Me?" Jennet hated it when her voice squeaked, though she knew it made her sound more like a young man. "I don't know anything about childbirth, Corwin."

"You've got good small hands, and that's what matters." Corwin's gruff face looked sinister, but his voice was confident. "The rest of you, find summat to boil water. We'll need hot food after to give her strength, and water to clean up after. And if any of you has a shirt you don't need, maybe a couple of shirts, could use that too." He marched over to Jennet and took her by the arm to draw her, unresisting, into the barn.

Veronique already sat at the edge of the hay pile, breathing heavily and not appearing to notice them. Jennet took a step toward her. But Corwin did not release her arm. Instead, he pulled her to the back of the barn, near the cows and the hay pile. "That's not all," he said in a low voice. "I don't think as it's proper for those fellows to be at the birth. Not proper for me, either, but I don't see as we have a choice."

"So it's all right for me?" Jennet said. "Why is that?"

Corwin hesitated. Then his jaw firmed up, and he nodded. "Because you're a woman," he said.

CHAPTER 16

IN WHICH THEIR LITTLE COMPANY INCREASES BY ONE

Jennet did not flinch. "I am not," she said. "Just because I needn't shave yet and my voice cracks sometimes—"

"I been watching you for months, ever since you come to the 3rd," Corwin said, his voice level and his eyes never leaving Jennet's face. "You make a good show of it, you don't walk like a woman and you don't have a woman's curves, not sure how you manage that. But I've seen you without your jacket, and you've almost no Adam's apple showing. You never take advantage of the light-skirts as follow the Army, and that's a thing every boy your age does because he likes to prove he's a man. And the longer your hair gets, the easier it is to see you as female."

Jennet cast desperately about for something to say that would refute Corwin's deadly accurate observations. "I don't," she said.

Behind them, Veronique let out a low moan that caused both of them to look at her. Her face was pale, and her entire body tensed with pain. When she relaxed, Corwin put a heavy hand on Jennet's shoulder and turned her to face him. "We've no time for games, Ned, or whatever your name is. I hope to spare Veronique from having a passel of men staring at her in her laboring time. Will you help?"

He did not look angry, or accusatory, or anything but determined. Jennet gave up. "I will," she said. "You won't tell?"

Corwin's gruff expression gave way to a smile. "You'll have your reasons, no doubt, and who am I to give away your game? Come. I'll show you what to do."

Jennet's fears of having to do something messy or unpleasant did not come true. Corwin instructed her to help Veronique remove her gown so she was only in her shift, then to kneel behind the woman and keep her sitting upright through the increasingly powerful pains. "Lying down makes 'em come slower, is what my mam always said," he told them—or, told Jennet, as Veronique had withdrawn into herself and seemed mostly unaware of her surroundings.

Just then, another spasm struck Veronique, and she cried out more loudly than before. When it passed, she wept, "God help me, I cannot bear this!"

"It will be well, I promise," Jennet said. This was something a young man would likely not say, but Veronique was too caught up in her pain to draw any conclusions about "Ned Graeme."

"Pity the lieutenant's not an Extraordinary, as I hear Extraordinary Shapers can ease the pains of childbirth," Corwin said. "Makes 'em unpopular with those as believe children must be brought forth in pain and sorrow. Here, hold her still and I'll give her a drink."

Veronique swallowed water gratefully and returned to her inward-focused breathing, rapid and heavy. Jennet shifted her weight to keep her knees from going numb. "What if something goes wrong?" she ventured.

Corwin's gaze drifted to the back wall and the pile of hay, much smaller now. "Naught we can do about that. Best to assume it will all be well." He lifted Veronique's shift and did something Jennet could not see. "A few more minutes, now."

The time passed as slowly as the last drop of molasses flowing from a jar. Veronique's pains came more quickly, soon so quickly she barely had time to recover from one before the next was upon her. Jennet's legs and arms ached from supporting Veronique, but she did not complain. Her little pains were as nothing beside what Veronique endured.

Corwin again did something beneath Veronique's shift. He wiped his hands on his trousers and said, "It's time. Get her squatting and I'll tie her shift out of the way."

Veronique moaned weakly as Jennet got her into position, crouched on her haunches over the canvas spread across the hay and the barn floor. "I am so tired," she whispered.

"Just a little longer, and it will be over," Jennet said. She gripped Veronique's shoulders and used her knees to support both of them.

"Ned, how do I say 'push' in French?" Corwin asked.

"It is 'poussez-vous,'" Jennet replied.

"You push down—poussez-vous—when I say," Corwin told Veronique. "Then rest. Only push when I tell you, even if you feel the urge. Do you understand? Ned, tell her."

When these instructions were relayed, Veronique nodded. Her face screwed up in agony, and she cried out, a terrible sound that cut Jennet to the heart.

"Push now!" Corwin commanded. "Poussez-vous!"

Veronique's whole body tensed, and her face reddened with effort. Jennet felt the strain through Veronique's shoulders where she held the woman. Corwin knelt in front of them, his face positively villainous with concentration.

"Fine, rest now, breathe," he said.

"Is it coming?" Jennet asked.

Corwin flicked a look at her that made Jennet grow cold. "It will take time," he said, almost certainly for Veronique's benefit because his glance had told Jennet what he would not tell the laboring woman—something was not right.

Veronique's belly tautened again, visibly so. Jennet held her as she pushed again. Then again. And again. Minutes passed, and they fell into a rhythm of pushing and pausing and pushing again. Veronique's cries weakened as time went on, and Corwin's face grew ever grimmer.

"Is there nothing we can do?" Jennet asked at the end of one of these periods. Her voice was breathy, and she felt as weary as if she and not Veronique were trying to give birth.

"She grows tired," Corwin said. He sounded exhausted as well. "But the child does not come." He sighed deeply. "She must push. If she were invigorated, well then, but I know naught that will do such."

Jennet held Veronique as she pushed again. This time, the woman made no cries of pain, just panted heavily. Invigorated. Corwin was right; there was nothing that could give an exhausted person more vigor. But if it were simply a matter of accessing hidden reserves...

Jennet gathered up her sense of Veronique's emotions. Veronique's exhaustion communicated itself throughout her body, making her emotions numb. There was no way Jennet could Coerce Veronique; a Discerner was always conscious of which emotions were not her own. But fear was different. It had a strong physical component the way lust did, and that physical component would affect Veronique's body even if the emotion did not. And with death staring them all in the face, Jennet did not care if Veronique discovered her secret.

Jennet waited. They had been doing this for so long she knew the rhythm as well as Corwin and Veronique, but she held back, waiting for Corwin's command.

At the next *"Push!"* Jennet sent terror flooding through Veronique. Veronique's whole body jerked. There was a sucking sound like water going down a clogged drain. "A head!" Corwin exclaimed. "Be calm, now, just a little longer—yes, push again! *Poussez-vous!*"

Veronique shuddered in Jennet's grasp. "Is it well? Not injured?"

Corwin carefully removed the babe the rest of the way and swiped at its nose. "A boy," he said, and as if answering Corwin, the child drew breath and let out a cry far fiercer than Jennet had imagined a newborn capable of. Veronique let out a sound halfway between a sob and a laugh.

"Oh, do let me hold him," she said.

"Corwin, can she hold him?" Jennet said.

"Here, but we should clean the lad." Corwin cradled the infant carefully in his hands, unable to move far thanks to the cord, and laid him gently in Veronique's arms. "Help her lie back, Ned, and fetch those shirts."

Jennet eased Veronique onto the canvas-covered hay pile and hurried for the door. She found the others gathered around the fire; they looked up like a pack of hunting dogs when the signal goes. "It is a wee lad," she said, "and I need those shirts now."

Jennet took several spare shirts along with her own blanket back into the barn. Corwin rubbed the crying child as gently as if he'd done it his whole life, then wrapped him in another shirt and gave him back to his mother. "'Tis no afterbirth yet, but it will come, and then we may cut the cord and bury the lot," he told Jennet.

Jennet helped him remove the bloodstained canvas once that happened, and then made a new bed with her blanket and assisted Veronique onto it. The infant suckled peacefully at his mother's breast and showed no discontent at being moved frequently. He had wisps of dark hair and a red, squashed face, and Jennet believed he was large for a newborn.

Veronique, her eyes closed, lay back in a boneless attitude of exhaustion. Sweat-dampened hair clung to her forehead and neck, but she smiled as peacefully as if the last few hours had been nothing but a dream. "He is beautiful," she murmured.

"What will you call him?" Jennet asked.

Veronique's eyes opened. "I had not considered," she said. "What is Private Corwin's given name?"

"Ah, it is William, I believe."

"That is a fine name. And worthy." Veronique caressed her son's head. "William Appleton. A good English name."

"What is she saying?" Corwin asked. He knelt nearby, washing his hands in pink water.

"That she wishes to name the child after you, in thanks." Jennet crossed the barn to kneel beside him. Next to them, one of the cows let out a low moo and continued chewing a wad of hay.

Corwin sat back. "She should not," he said. He sounded harsh, and more cruel than Jennet had ever heard him.

Taken aback, she said, "Why not? It is a good name, William."

"I am no one a child should take as a model in any way." Corwin stood abruptly, his fists clenched. "Tell her."

"I will not," Jennet retorted. "It is a generous gesture, and you would throw it back in her face?"

"It is ill-omened." Corwin turned and made for the door, but Jennet, not knowing why, put herself between him and the exit.

"I know you have not always been the best of men," she said. "What, you believe you are the only one who watches his comrades? Aye, not the best of men before, but surely you have not sinned so greatly as to deserve damnation?"

Corwin looked down on her. He was only a few inches taller, but the breadth of his shoulders and his powerful girth made him loom. "You know nothing of sin."

Jennet swallowed a laugh, fearing he would believe she laughed at him. "So, because I am...what I am...I cannot do evil? I have done awful things, things I am deeply ashamed of, and yet I have hope that I may be forgiven. Nay, do not tell me what you did, because that is between you and God. But do not deny the good you do simply because you once chose evil instead."

"Pretty words," Corwin said. But the murderous light was gone from his eyes. "You don't understand. I have done things—" He swallowed. "My own mother on her deathbed did not know me, so wicked had I become. Everything I touch eventually turns to lead."

"That is not true. Whatever you once were, you are no longer. You are good to your comrades, and you saved Veronique's life and that of her child, I know." Jennet hesitated. "And I know you are a good friend." *Not to me*, she silently amended. She hated herself in that moment for the fear that had led her to Coerce him. She would never know if he might truly have become a friend.

Corwin blinked, astonished. Then he laughed. Jennet had never heard him laugh before. "You are a rare one, Ned," he said. "Nay, do not tell me your true given name. Ned you are, and Ned you shall be." He clapped Jennet on the shoulder. "We must introduce the child to the rest of our merry band. Small William, eh? It is not such a bad name."

Jennet smiled and followed him out of the barn. She hung back when the others paid their respects to the infant and his mother. What had possessed her to make that speech? It was all true, yes, but she had no business telling anyone else how he should live or what he should do to face his sins. She was not even certain she deserved salvation, however bold her words. She had Coerced a laboring woman, and however well she might justify it as saving two lives, she did not trust herself to be honest when it came to the use of her talent.

The sky had lightened with dawn by the time the birth was over and everything cleaned up. Jennet spoke once more with the old man, asking his permission for them to remain that day and paying him something for the firewood and the hay. It was wonderful to have a hot meal again. Spirits were high, and laughter and merriment spilled out over the farmer's fields, with even Whitteney regaining some of his good humor, but Jennet did not feel much like conversation. Aside from the exhaustion of helping with the birth, there was the fact that Corwin had spotted her for what she was. She could not help wondering how many others had seen through her ruse. How many of her current companions had done so? And if they knew, why did they not speak?

She excused herself after their meal of roasted beef and cheese toasted over the fire until it was runny and claimed one of the empty stalls for her own. Across the way, Veronique and baby William slept, still with Jennet's blanket. It would be a warm day, though, and Jennet did not mind the lack. Much.

She lay on her back and stared at the ceiling, which was nearly invisible in the gloom. She should Coerce Corwin again, make him adore her so he would not give her away. The idea made her feel ill and even wearier than before. Surely there would be a day when she no longer lived in fear, and could stop turning to Coercion to protect herself. Until that day—no. No, she would risk exposure rather than Coerce someone she wished were her friend.

And then there was Veronique. It was possible the woman had been too far gone in exhaustion and pain to realize where the fear had come from and had not guessed Jennet's secret. But that was not something Jennet wished to rely on. She would have to watch Veronique carefully, and if Veronique looked likely to give her away, Jennet would have to run. The idea filled her with horror, followed closely by misery. She should not have become so close to these men. Life was easier when one was not attached to anyone else.

She flung one arm across her face and tried to ignore the sounds of laughter from outside. Once they were reunited with the Army, Jennet would arrange to be transferred somewhere far away from her companions. Somewhere far from Falconer. And her inappropriate attachments would fade and die.

She wished the idea did not hurt so much.

๛

JENNET WOKE TO FIND FALCONER ASLEEP A FOOT FROM HER FACE AND managed not to make any noise in her surprise. Granted, there were not enough stalls for each of them to sleep alone, but she had not guessed he would not have claimed a stall for himself.

He lay facing her, his jaw relaxed and his mouth barely open, breathing so lightly she almost could not hear it. His eyelids twitched occasionally, but aside from that, he was perfectly still. The urge to touch him seized her, a desire to feel the lines of his face and the smoothness of his skin, and she had actually raised her hand before she came to her senses. She squeezed her eyes tight shut and drew in a deep breath, then let it out in a long, warm stream, willing it to carry her inappropriate desires away.

She carefully stood and exited the barn, where she brushed off her uniform and stretched mightily. Her aches of the previous day had vanished, leaving her clear-headed and rested. Her melancholy, too, had faded somewhat. She had been foolish to worry that anyone but Corwin had seen through her disguise. The others all believed her to be male, and would go on believing it—had not Corwin said she did not look or walk like a woman? And she need not leave their band.

It was late afternoon, and Jennet did not at first see the sentry, but then Sadler came around the corner of the barn and nodded at her. Reassured, she collected firewood and set about reviving last night's fire. She might see about begging tea from the old man, and then Falconer could have his favorite beverage. Veronique could use something hot, too, to replenish lost blood.

With the fire burning merrily and the pot set to boil, Jennet determined to beard the old man in his den. Unfortunately, he did not appear at her knocking, though the dogs made an unholy racket. She gave up and returned to the fire. Whitteney sat beside it, poking it in a desultory manner. The bandage around his leg was only barely spotted with blood. Nearby, Fosse cut meat, soaked into near-tenderness, into smallish pieces that he tossed into the pot.

"The lieutenant's tending to his horse," Whitteney said. "And Corwin is seeing to Veronique. That child is the quietest I've ever heard. Ain't heard boo out of him since he was born. Quiet as a lamb, he is." His color was better, and his face no longer looked pinched with pain, though he did not shift his injured leg at all.

"That's good for us," Fosse said. He dumped the rest of the meat into the pot and stood to greet Corwin as the big man exited the barn. His cheery smile faded in the face of Corwin's grim demeanor. "Is aught amiss?"

Corwin shook his head. "I'm no doctor nor midwife, but the babe is well enough. Eating like a champion, even. But Veronique cannot ride, not for more than a few minutes. She's still weak and she lost a mort o' blood." He turned his bleak gaze on Jennet. "You'll have to tell the lieutenant."

Jennet blinked. "Why me?"

"I don't know but as he's got it in his head we need to press on. We can't do that. And he listens to you, God knows why. Maybe you remind him of a younger brother or summat." Corwin's eyelid flickered in the faintest wink imaginable.

Jennet scowled. "He isn't a monster. He won't eat you."

"Then you've naught to worry over," Corwin said, relentless.

Jennet looked to Fosse and Whitteney for help. Both pretended to be busy at their tasks. With a sigh, she trudged off to the barn. The memory of waking next to him had not faded as she had hoped, and now the thought of facing him embarrassed her even as it excited her.

Falconer was, in fact, in the stall he had appropriated for Suleiman, grooming him and murmuring under his breath. "Good morning, Graeme," he said, as cheerily as Fosse ever dreamed of being. "I smell food. Pity there's no chance of tea."

"Sir, I have bad news," Jennet said, choosing not to tell him she had tried to acquire tea. That might sound ingratiating. "Veronique cannot ride."

Falconer's hands stilled. "Of course. I should have realized." His eyes unfocused. "That is unfortunate."

"We cannot abandon Veronique," Jennet said.

"Of course not." Falconer sounded appalled. "But if she cannot ride..." His voice trailed off, and his eyes were still fixed on some unseen vista, his jaw tight in thought. Jennet fidgeted, not wishing to rudely walk away but not interested in being a captive audience for his cogitation. Finally, when she could bear it no longer, she said, "What do we do, then, sir?"

"There is a large church in Châlons-sur-Marne, attached to a foundlings' hospital," Falconer said, in a distant tone that suggested he was still working through possibilities. "Mrs. Appleton will be safe there, safer than if she remains with us. And the child will receive the best of care."

"But—"

Falconer's gaze came to rest on Jennet. "We cannot afford sentimentality, Graeme. This will free us to speed north with our message. Mrs. Appleton will have to understand."

Jennet hesitated for a moment, then nodded once. Something of her continued disquiet must have shown on her face, for Falconer put a hand on her shoulder and added, "Your loyalty to your friend's wife is commendable. Do not feel guilty at putting our mission over that loyalty. Mrs. Appleton's ultimate survival, and that of everyone in

France, is more important than one individual's comfort. Do you see that?"

"I do, sir," Jennet said.

Falconer clapped her once more on the shoulder. "All will be well," he said. He stowed the brush in a saddlebag hanging nearby and gestured to her to follow.

All the others except Veronique and her child were gathered around the fire, passing around the one shallow pot they had for a plate. "Stand at ease," Falconer said when they all drew themselves to attention. "I'm informed Mrs. Appleton cannot ride. Now that her babe is born, it is time to find her a safe place to stay while we proceed north. I will take a few of you into Châlons-sur-Marne to inquire at the church as to the possibility of their giving Mrs. Appleton shelter. The rest will remain here with Mrs. Appleton until our return."

The others exchanged glances. "Sir," Fosse said, "are you certain she will be safe?"

"Safer than on the road with us," Falconer said. "But we will make sure of that before bringing her into Châlons-sur-Marne. I will not casually abandon any of us. Sadler, Fosse, and Graeme will come with me. Eat up, and we'll leave immediately. I wish to be on the road north by evening."

Jennet gulped her food and collected her jacket from the barn. After a moment's reflection, she undid the seam of the false bottom of her pack and gathered a handful of coin. Surely a priest should be generous in providing shelter to one in need, but she had known too many venal priests to fail to be prepared with a bribe. She stuffed the money into a small purse she tucked inside her shirt and hurried to join the others, avoiding Veronique's eye. The woman was intent upon her child, but Jennet did not like to take the chance Veronique might perceive her intent and fall into a weeping fit at being left behind.

It was just after three in the afternoon when the four of them, Sadler and Fosse, Jennet and Falconer, set off across the fields eastward. They soon came upon a road aimed straight for the town like an arrow. Most of the fields on either side had already been tilled, and they saw no one who might make note of their presence and report it. Ahead, a glimmering line revealed the presence of a river. Jennet tried to remember where they were. It might be the Marne, given the town's name. Beyond the river, houses and shops crowded one another, and the golden stone of a cathedral rose to tower over them. It was a pity they were not in a position to visit it.

Falconer came to a halt. "We should not enter openly, and take the chance of being reported," he said. "Which of you is the best scout?"

They all exchanged glances. "That's me, sir," Sadler said.

"Can you enter that town without being seen?"

Sadler grinned. "My own mam wouldn't notice me if I wished to be invisible. I'll see what's afoot."

Falconer glanced toward Châlons-sur-Marne again. "Be quick as you can. We lose more time the longer we wait—but you know that."

Sadler nodded once, a brisk gesture. His usual happy-go-lucky demeanor had vanished, replaced with a calm competence that reminded Jennet of Falconer himself. "I suggest the rest of you wait somewhere concealed, sir. Somewhere I will know to return to."

It took some time to find a good spot by the river, one heavily wooded where none of them were visible. As they settled in to wait, Sadler stripped down to his shirt and raked his fingers through his hair. He stepped out of their hiding place and let his shoulders droop, then walked away at a slow pace, kicking the ground and raising little puffs of dirt that made his boots filthy. In minutes, he had disappeared.

"Remarkable," Falconer said. He paced the length of their shelter, no more than fifteen feet along the banks where the willows grew. Jennet walked to the river's edge and watched the water flow, brown and dark blue beneath the willows, lighter blue where the sun's rays struck its surface. The water was too murky to see if fish swam within, though as they had nothing with which to catch fish, and she and Fosse had no skill at catching fish with their hands, it did not matter. And Jennet was not fond of fish, anyway. It was merely something to keep her from fretting.

Fosse came to stand beside her. "Quite an adventure, eh?"

"Not an adventure I would have chosen," Jennet replied.

"'Tis better than being Coerced and made a slave." The smile fell away from his face. "Whitteney's pain made him talk in his sleep. He worries for Marie's safety, I daresay more than he worries about his own, injury or no."

"No one will hurt her." Jennet nudged a clod of earth with her toe and made it splash into the water.

"No." Fosse sighed. "He knows what we think, that he's blind not to heed her flirtations. But he claims that is just her way, and he is sure she has always been faithful to him."

Jennet shrugged. She knew of no one so blind as a man in love. "Naught we can do about it, save—"

Behind them, Falconer said, "Hush. Someone approaches."

Jennet and Fosse jerked to attention. Fosse put a hand on his sword's hilt. But then Sadler said, "Nay, it is I," and ducked beneath the concealing branches.

"That was too fast. Were you unable to enter the town?" Falconer said.

Sadler shook his head. "Not that," he said. "I simply didn't have to go far to learn what we need to know." He was breathing heavily, but not, Jennet judged, with exertion. "Châlons-sur-Marne is crawling with Napoleon's soldiers."

CHAPTER 17

IN WHICH JENNET MUST PLAY YET ANOTHER ROLE

"Impossible," Fosse said. "They could not have advanced before us. We'd have seen them."

"It's them, no question," Sadler insisted. "They don't hide themselves, and the uniforms are distinct."

Falconer's left hand closed into a fist. "What else did you see?"

"Just that they'd taken over a house, a big house, for their commander." Sadler's breathing was returning to normal. "Based on the regimentals I saw, it's General Grouchy's forces."

Falconer turned away to pace once more. "I believed him to be much farther south. He was not there at Napoleon's ambush, and his presence here might have nothing to do with us. But we cannot assume they do not have orders to look for us. Napoleon has as many Speakers as the Army does."

"I saw a couple of soldiers harassing someone on the street. Some man," Sadler said. "I think as how they're looking close at anyone looks like they don't belong."

"Then what do we do, sir? Go back?" Fosse looked over his shoulder at the river as if he could see French soldiers advancing on their position.

"And what of Veronique?" Jennet said.

"There's no way we can take Veronique to that church," Sadler said. His sharpness of language and demeanor frightened Jennet because it meant Sadler believed the situation very serious. "She's too weak to walk far, and we'd have to put her on Suleiman. And *he* stands out by a mile."

Falconer let out a long, slow breath. His eyes once more focused on something Jennet could not see.

"Sir," Fosse began. "Perhaps Veronique—the farmer might take pity on her."

Falconer gave Fosse a look that made him redden with embarrassment. "The farmer barely tolerates us, and Mrs. Appleton still needs care," he said. "And I will not divide our party and leave some behind. Not when there is still a chance of us being overtaken. But we cannot remain here for her to recover. As we do not know the fate of Corporal Josephs, we may be the only chance the Army has of learning Napoleon's true position."

"Then what is to be done?" Jennet asked.

Falconer grimaced. "What I have been reluctant to do ere now, Graeme. We will need a wagon, or a cart, and we will need civilian clothes."

"Civilian—" Jennet's voice squeaked in surprise. "But we are soldiers, sir."

"I know. But we will need a cart to convey Mrs. Appleton if we are to make any progress at all. We cannot travel openly as British riflemen, not with Lady Ashford still searching, and a cart cannot be concealed beneath the trees. It is not what I would normally choose, but we have already taken so many risks one more cannot make a difference."

"Suppose," Jennet offered, feeling awkward and uncomfortable, "suppose you leave us and ride north, sir?"

Falconer jerked in surprise. "Leave you?"

"Well, sir, you did say the message is important, and we cannot go quickly in any case."

The look Falconer turned on her made her want to cringe. "If I leave you here," he said, "you will certainly be overtaken by whomever follows us. Even were Whitteney fit to walk, it will be days before Mrs. Appleton is well enough to continue, and she will slow you even then. And we cannot assume the only fate you would face is Coercion—or am I wrong, and you five would accept that willingly?"

"Not a chance in hell, sir," Sadler said, still with that cool, competent air.

Falconer nodded. "Were you all able to travel freely and speedily, I would choose differently. But I will not abandon you to possible death. We stay together." He glanced past Sadler toward the river. "Someone must enter the town secretly."

"We can't go in uniform, sir," Fosse said. "And none of us speaks French but Ned."

"I'll go," Jennet said. "I just need other clothes, that's all. We could maybe steal from one of these farms—"

Sadler was shaking his head. "They might go after you even if you look and sound French. It ain't safe."

"They will be looking at the men," Falconer said. "Not the women."

It took Jennet a moment to understand what he meant. Then she blanched. "I'm not a woman," she said, pitching her voice as low as she could.

"Of course not," Falconer said. "But you are young enough that with the right clothing, you could pass for one."

"No. I can't." If she dressed in women's clothes, it would all be over. She had no illusions about how she looked; she might be thin and lack curves, but her main protection had always been that people saw what they expected to see, and when she was in uniform they expected to see a young man. In a gown and bonnet, nothing would protect her.

"Come, Ned, it's not as if any of us will mock you," Fosse said. "It won't be awful."

"Though eventually we'll tease you," Sadler said with his customary grin. He punched her lightly on the arm. "We're only human."

"This is important, Graeme," Falconer said. "And you won't be alone. I'm coming with you."

All three of them stared at him. "But—you'll draw attention," Jennet said, for the moment forgetting her own problem. "And I don't believe you can Shape yourself female."

"I cannot, no. But you have not considered the whole of the matter. While the French soldiers will not be looking at the women as potential spies or British troops, they are still men, and there are some men who see all women as prey." Falconer's jaw was tight, and his eyes narrowed. "A lone man, or group of men, is a potential threat. A lone woman is a potential victim. But a man and a woman together…they are invisible."

"Sir, you don't speak French," Jennet pointed out. "You will give yourself away just by that."

"Then I will have to be mute." Falconer smiled, a sideways quirk of his lips. "Mute, and possibly slow of wit. Sister and brother, come to town for the marketing. What could be more simple?"

"No one will believe it," Jennet said sharply. "Not with the way you look."

Falconer raised an eyebrow. "The way I look?"

"Yes, the..." Jennet felt awkward about saying *You are more handsome than any man I've ever seen.* "Your appearance," she tried again.

"He means because you look like God's gift to women, sir," Sadler said.

A low chuckle escaped Falconer's lips. "I can do something about that. Give me half an hour."

Jennet opened her mouth to object again and then closed it. If Ned Graeme protested too much, they would want to know why he refused to do this one simple thing, and then Falconer might make it an order, and she would be discovered, after all. "Very well," she said. "But I don't want to hear a word about this, d'ye ken?"

"Not a word," Sadler said, drawing his forefinger across his neck in a throat-slitting gesture. "I'll go see what I can scrounge, sir."

"Take a little money," Falconer said. "I dislike being a thief."

Jennet handed over a few francs and watched Sadler leave again. Fosse gave her a lopsided smile and said, "Never mind the joking, Ned. No one thinks less of you."

Jennet merely nodded. Her heart was beating rapidly, and sweat slicked her palms. She wiped her hands on her trouser legs. Oh. She would have to undress in front of them. Her heartbeat accelerated until it hurt. She needed to find a solution to that little problem, fast.

"What money do you have, Graeme?" Falconer asked. "Any more French coin?"

She removed her purse from within her clothes and shook out the coin into his palm. Fosse gasped, but said nothing more. Falconer simply sorted through the varied coins. "This is a good deal more than I believed we had," he said. "Does this represent your savings?"

"It is more important we get that cart," Jennet said.

Falconer shook his head. "I will see you are reimbursed, Graeme. You should not have to suffer to meet our needs." He returned the coin to the purse. "Handing over English coin might be difficult, but there is more French money here than I hoped. You hold the money. As your slow-witted brother, no one will expect me to make purchases."

Jennet nodded. She was still furiously contemplating her new problem. Ask them to look away, pretending modesty? That would be incredibly suspicious. Depending on what Sadler returned with, she might remove her trousers after the gown was on, but what to do about her upper body? The cloth she used to bind her breasts was not inconspicuous, though she was not well endowed in that respect and did not require much cloth. It was still obvious she was female.

Falconer reached inside his uniform jacket and removed something that gleamed metallic in the shadows beneath the trees. He sat cross-legged on the grass and held the metallic object in both hands, bowing his head to look at it. Jennet approached, curious, and discovered the object was Falconer's steel mirror.

"How is it done?" she asked, curiosity overriding her dread for the moment.

"Very slowly, and very painfully, I am told," Falconer said.

"You are told? But you have Shaped yourself before, sir, haven't you?"

Falconer raised his head. "I have Shaped my muscles and bones before, but this is the first time I have Shaped my appearance, Graeme."

"That's impossible," Jennet said without thinking. "Not with how beautiful you are."

Falconer's eyes widened. Then he roared with laughter, more unre-strained than Jennet had ever heard him. "Oh, Graeme," he said. "You will do wonders for my self-love. No, I have never Shaped my appearance. What you see is the way I have always looked."

Jennet felt her head might pop off, she blushed so hard. "I apologize, sir, I assumed—"

"What everyone assumes," Falconer said. "Shapers are all vain, are they not? And why not Shape oneself a face that the gods would envy? I consider myself blessed in that respect, Graeme, though at the moment I wish I had more experience. I like pain no better than anyone, and I admit to feeling some trepidation. Suppose I cannot restore myself when this is over?"

To her astonishment, Jennet realized the lieutenant was truly uncertain and, even more surprisingly, a little afraid. Without thinking, she laid her hand on his arm and squeezed gently. "You know yourself well, sir. And if you do not perhaps return exactly to this form, no one will think any less of you."

Falconer blew out a breath. "I am a fool to permit something so ridiculous as my appearance to stop me doing what is necessary. If you can endure women's clothing, I can endure some ugliness, yes?" He turned his attention back to the mirror. "Pray, excuse me, Graeme, I cannot do this and talk at the same time."

Jennet retreated several steps, far enough that she could not watch his Shaping. It had not occurred to her before that Shapers who changed their appearance might not have some base state, so to speak, to return to. She hoped Falconer would remember his original appearance well enough to return to it. It was not only that it was a handsome visage, it was the one she knew and liked so much because it was his.

You fool, she berated herself as she so often did, but it was becoming increasingly difficult for her to believe she admired Lieutenant Falconer solely for his beauty the way she would admire a statue. He was competent, and caring, and his smile cheered her the more for its rarity, and he treated her with respect. But no, she was not in love with him, could never be in love with him, and perhaps leaving was a better option than she had initially believed, if it meant removing herself from his disturbing presence.

Sadler returned in half an hour with a bundle of cloth in his arms he dumped on the bank before them. "Couldn't find shoes for a man," he said. "You'll have to hope no one looks at your feet, sir. Ned, see if these fit." He handed Jennet a pair of women's shoes made of soft fabric. They did not look as if they could protect against anything. Jennet reminded herself that was not the point.

She picked through the pile of fabric. Sadler had found a bright red skirt, a petticoat, a shapeless garment that might be a large apron, and a scarf. "There's no shirt," she said.

"The only ones I saw were too small. You'll have to make do with your own. The scarf will help, and—" Sadler handed her a couple of rolled stockings. "You can use these to, you know. To fill out your shirt."

Jennet wanted to laugh. "Good idea," she said.

Falconer removed his jacket and traded it for the threadbare coat

Sadler had found. "I can't wear these uniform breeches," he said, "they're far too fine."

"Try these, sir," Sadler said, handing him a pair of brown knee-length breeches. Jennet swiftly turned her back on the men as Falconer began unbuttoning his breeches. She pulled the skirt on over her trousers and then removed the trousers, dropping Falconer's knife at her feet, all so quickly no one saw anything they should not.

The apron covered the lot, full-skirted with a top that tied at the back. Jennet stuck the rolled-up stockings inside her shirt and tightened the apron to keep them in place. She wrapped the scarf fichu-style around her neck to conceal the decidedly non-feminine cut of her shirt and tucked the ends away beneath the apron's top.

The shoes fit a little too tightly, but they would do for the short time she was in the town. The skirt was shorter than fashion in England dictated, but not by much, and she was grateful she would not have to hold it out of the way to keep from treading on it. Finally, she tied the white cap over her curls. It was impossible. They would see immediately she was female. She let out a deep breath and turned to face the men.

They were still fussing over Falconer's clothing. Apparently the breeches were too large, and they needed to find a way to keep them from sliding off his hips. Jennet waited, not willing to draw attention to herself. Eventually, Falconer did something with his braces that solved the problem. "Graeme, are you ready?"

Jennet suppressed a blush. Blushing would only make her look more feminine. She came forward, exaggerating her man's walk and holding her arms stiffly away from her body. "I feel a fool," she said, still in her deepest voice.

Fosse cleared his throat. "It's a good illusion," he said. "I doubt anyone will know. That is, you don't exactly look like a woman, but you look *enough* like a woman—"

"Don't stand so stiff, lad, everyone will know you've never worn skirts before," Sadler said.

"You'll be fine." Falconer's voice was a little rougher than usual, and Jennet looked at him fully for the first time since he had begun his Shaping and had to control a gasp. She had expected him to alter his appearance in some small way, anything that would keep him from drawing attention. But Falconer had made himself look grotesque. His cheeks were prominent bulges just beneath his eyes, which were set more deeply than before. His eyebrow ridges were similarly prominent, and the combination gave him a sullen, stupid look. He had also grown out his beard in patches, as if he had a skin disease.

He looked at Jennet and smiled, and in that moment she knew him again, for his eyes were the same. "Oh, sir," she said, "I believed the point of Shaping was for you to draw less attention, not more."

Falconer chuckled and tugged his peasant's hat, wide-brimmed and drooping, farther over his eyes. "People dislike noticing anyone who is visibly disfigured, and I judged this to give us more security. Are you ready?"

"Yes, sir." She handed him the knife, which he tucked away inside his clothes. Jennet had to agree it did not look like a weapon a farmer would own.

Falconer turned his attention on Fosse and Sadler. "You're to go back to the others. Wait until an hour after dusk. If we have not returned by then, make your way north to Valenciennes. There, you may find the Army. Understood?"

"Yes, sir," both replied.

Falconer straightened his ill-fitting shirt and nodded his approval. "I am grateful now that we kept Suleiman. We will need him to pull the cart once we acquire it, but taking him into a town full of French soldiers is the same as handing him over to them outright. You and I will pull the cart for now, Graeme." He gestured to Jennet, and the two of them left the shelter of the trees and made their way to the bridge over the river.

There was enough traffic on the road into Châlons-sur-Marne Jennet feared someone noticing that they had emerged from beneath the trees. But everyone they passed in both directions was intent on their own business, watching the road ahead or chatting with their companions. Jennet avoided meeting the eyes of the wagoners headed away from town. They could likely do her no harm, but after so many years of passing for male, she felt exposed, vulnerable to whistles or coarse comments on her appearance.

She glanced at Falconer. He had adopted a somewhat lurching gait that raised his left shoulder higher than his right, and his mouth was slightly open, giving him a dull, slow-witted appearance. The sight amused her. He apparently had an unsuspected talent for theatricals. Acting was a popular entertainment among the men and even more so among the officers, but Jennet had never seen the lieutenant participate in such activities. She hoped he was good, for both their sakes.

The sound of Falconer's boots clopping over the stones of the bridge disappeared into the other noises of wagon wheels creaking and big, heavy wagoners calling out to their big, heavy animals and the twittering laughter of a group of young women all leaving the city together. They paid no attention to Jennet, but stared at Falconer before turning away in disgust, twittering more loudly. Jennet caught the gist of what they were saying and was relieved that Falconer had been right about the effect of his grotesque appearance.

"They find you repellent," she said in a low voice.

"Excellent," Falconer replied, barely moving his lips. "This may actually work."

"Were you not confident?" Jennet's heart sank.

"Confidence is nothing when it comes to confronting an enemy." Falconer hunched his shoulder higher. "The best plan is only as effective as the enemy's reaction. Most of this is guesswork. Are you afraid?"

"No, sir, not with you," Jennet said, and immediately felt stupid and sentimental.

But Falconer did not react to her moment of foolishness. "We will go first to where we might buy a cart. That, too, is a risk, as there may be no one interested in selling. But it is a risk we cannot avoid."

They left the bridge behind and were immediately surrounded by the houses of Châlons-sur-Marne, most of them two or even three stories half-timbered above and stone below. Ahead, the cathedral's spires rose above the nearest buildings, its stone glowing yellow in the summer sunlight. Many of the other buildings were of the same yellow stone, and the overall effect was of a summer day despite the coolness of the morning.

A village of this size in Scotland would have many thatched roofs, but these were all ruddy tile or grey slate, and they gave the houses a solid appearance, as if they had stood against invaders for hundreds of years and would continue to stand for centuries to come. It was an illusion; if Napoleon's forces chose to assault Châlons-sur-Marne, it would fall immediately. But it was an illusion Jennet cherished.

They made their way through increasing throngs, jostled by other passersby but not accosted or given suspicious looks. Jennet was just reflecting on how she had seen no French soldiers when a trio of men in blue and red came out of a tavern almost on top of her, laughing and clapping one another on the back. Fear thrilled through her at their proximity. But they ignored her and cast only the briefest horrified glance at Falconer. They walked as if they took up twice their actual space, forcing everyone around them to make way.

Jennet realized she had stopped and was staring after the soldiers. Falconer gripped her hand briefly, bringing her out of her stupor with a rush of fear—did her hand feel feminine? But he only muttered, "We should not stop. We have little time."

Jennet nodded. She let Falconer take the lead before stepping out behind him.

CHAPTER 18

IN WHICH JENNET'S
IDENTITY IS REVEALED IN A
MOST DRAMATIC FASHION

The streets of Châlons-sur-Marne curved confusingly, but Falconer guided her without touching her again, merely giving verbal instructions now and then. After a few minutes, they emerged from the street into a wagon-yard attached to a larger than usual building that might be an inn.

"Here is where you must be bold, Graeme," Falconer said quietly. "Some of these men will wish to cheat a young woman. I will back you up, but the talking must be yours. Understand?"

Jennet nodded. "Who do I speak to?"

Falconer cleared his throat and spat a gob that landed on the hard-packed earth some short distance away. Jennet choked back a laugh. "That direction," Falconer said. "He will not have anything for sale, but he will direct you to one who does."

Jennet looked in that direction. The wagoner nearest them did not look the sort who would be helpful. He looked, rather, as if he might tear Jennet to pieces and gnaw on her bones. Jennet swallowed. She reminded herself that she was a young woman, and had resources other than the ones Ned Graeme depended on. Before she could talk herself out of it, she walked across the wagon yard, reflecting gratefully that it was not muddy and full of puddles her silly women's shoes would not endure.

"Excuse me, sir," she said in French. "Can you spare a moment to help me?"

The man raised his head from where he had been contemplating his boots. Jennet lowered her eyes modestly, hating herself for trading on her femininity. She clasped her hands in front of her in a way she hoped made her look helpless and hoped he was the sort that liked being manly in front of a girl.

"What do you need, girlie?" he said. His voice was deep and rough and sounded as if he gargled with paving stones.

Jennet tilted her head slightly to one side. "My papa sent me and my brother to buy a new cart, ours having been taken by soldiers last week. You looked to be someone who knows where I might find one."

The man straightened, and Jennet had to control a flinch; he was well over six feet tall, and that combined with his burly shoulders and hands the size of small hams made her fear being accidentally crushed. "That your brother?" he said, pointing at Falconer.

"It is."

"Doesn't look like he's all there." The man peered at Falconer, and Jennet realized he was rather near-sighted.

"He's strong, but you're right, he's slow. He can do things if I explain very carefully what's to be done, and Papa says I'm to watch him closely and make sure he doesn't stray." Falconer was gently rocking back and forth in a slow, deliberate way that made the illusion stronger. A sense of longing struck her and vanished almost instantly.

"How big a cart?"

Jennet jerked herself back to the present. "Not too big. It's not a big farm."

The man nodded. "Eh, Matthieu!" he shouted. A man just leaving the inn changed his course and walked toward them. He had a large nose visible from across the yard, and a warty face, but his smile was pleasant. "Matthieu, this young lady is in the market for a cart. You still interested in selling yours?"

"I am, for the right price," Matthieu said. He indicated a cart standing near the stables along the yard's far wall. Its sides were glossy, not with varnish, but with much use, and the seat canted slightly to the left, but it looked sturdy enough. It was small enough that Suleiman could pull it alone with no effort, and large enough for two people to lie in the back and still leave room for a few supplies. "Found it abandoned by the *rosbifs*, with broken wheels, and I repaired it. But it's too small for my trade, and I could use a few extra francs. Surely *you're* not the one buying, not a pretty girl like you?"

Jennet's irritation rose. She ducked her head lower, pretending to shyness. "It's for my papa. He's busy with the planting. And I do all the buying for the farm, so it's not as if I don't know what I'm doing."

She regretted her bold words instantly. Matthieu's eyes lit up, and the curve of his lips took on a more sinister expression. "I'm sure you do," he said. "Then you won't object to paying four hundred francs. Since you'll know that's the going rate."

Jennet did not need to be a Discerner to know he was lying. Besides, she knew from talking to the wagon masters of the 3rd a cart of that size cost fifteen pounds to build, and she could guess at the rest from there. "That is nearly a hundred francs more than the going rate, as I'm sure *you* know. But that was a test, wasn't it? I'm glad I passed. Now. I have two hundred francs and five English pounds, is that acceptable?"

Matthieu didn't blink. "English coin? I don't think so. I'd have the devil of a time changing it. Three hundred seventy-five francs."

Jennet could feel Falconer's attention on her like a needle boring into her back. "Your cart is used, and we both know English coin is as solid as French. Two hundred francs, and seven English pounds." She was reaching the edge of what she had stowed in her purse. If she could not come to agreement with this man, the odds of her buying a different cart were not good.

Matthieu hesitated. Jennet pounced. "Just think how nice a cart you can buy with all this extra money," she said, hoping she did not sound too brash. She could not remember how girls behaved, even though she *was* a girl. So much easier to deal straightforwardly!

The man's enormous nose quivered like a fox on a scent. "Done," he said.

"Thank you so much," Jennet said, remembering to curtsey. She did it so awkwardly, surely someone would believe she was male; her hands felt overly large, and the skirt fell in a tangle over her legs.

She carefully counted the agreed-on amount into Matthieu's hand. Her heart cried out at seeing her hard-earned money vanish, and with it her chances at a life outside the Army. She knew Falconer meant well, but it was unlikely he could get the Army to restore her lost funds. But there was nothing for it unless she was willing to desert, strike out on her own, leave Ned behind and become Jennet once more—and be forced to depend on her talent for her protection even more than she did now.

"Um...Alain, come with me," she said, inventing a name for Falconer and gesturing to him. "Alain, this is our new cart. Pull the cart, Alain." She remembered in time that Falconer did not speak French and mimed pulling at the shafts.

Falconer grunted and took hold of one shaft. Jennet grabbed the other. They wheeled the cart around and away out of the wagon yard, down the street and out of sight.

When they were well away, Falconer murmured, "Excellent work, Graeme. This cart will do nicely."

"Thank you, sir," Jennet said, and fell silent. She had not Coerced those men. She had not even peeked at their emotions. And she had got what they needed without either of those things. Her heart ached, not with sorrow for once, but with happiness. She had not needed Coercion. If she could avoid it in this instance, perhaps she could do so again. And she might not be damned, after all.

Falconer hunched his back again. "Let us make haste. If they decide to report their new acquisition of English coin to the authorities, we should be gone before anyone can search for us. We need food for at least five days' travel, and more blankets. And a camp kettle. And *tea*."

Jennet suppressed a smile and hurried on.

It took longer than they had hoped to find what they needed. Most of the shopkeepers' supplies were low thanks to the demands of both armies, and what little there was cost dearly. Falconer's desire for tea had to go unsated, as there was none available. Jennet pointed out that they could hardly light a fire to boil water, not if they were still being pursued.

They had worked their way almost to the inn in their expedition and now turned back toward the bridge, their cart not laden as heavily as they wished. Jennet's purse was nearly flat by now, and she had grown numb to the prospect of spending her coin more than half an hour before.

She had also become accustomed to walking past French soldiers in the street without so much as a twitch. Aside from walking as though they were the lords of creation, with no need to give way to even the frailest grandmother tottering on sticks, they paid no attention to anyone not either a male citizen or another soldier. Jennet had dared glance at one or two of them, careful not to catch their eyes; she did not know if Falconer's presence would be enough to stop them accosting her.

"You! You there! The ugly one!"

Someone grabbed Falconer and spun him around, making him drop the shaft of the wagon. "Stop!" Jennet exclaimed. Then she froze. The hand on Falconer's shoulder belonged to a French soldier.

The soldier was staring, not at Falconer's face, but his boots. His British military-issue boots. All the blood drained from Jennet's face. Falconer wore his usual dim-witted, gape-mouthed expression and showed no sign he understood he was in trouble.

"Please, sir, is something wrong?" Jennet asked, pitching her voice high and nervous in a feminine way. "That's my brother, sir, he didn't mean harm whatever he's done. He's not quite right in the head, see. So if he gave offense, he didn't mean it."

"Where did you get those boots?" the soldier said, leaning right into Falconer's face.

"Please, sir, he doesn't speak none," Jennet hastily added. "He got those boots off a peddler, sir, about a year ago. He's got big feet and we were grateful they fit, him not having had much in the way of footwear before that. Is something wrong?"

"Those boots were made for a British Army officer." The soldier's anger worried Jennet. Despite her earlier resolve, she gathered up her sense of his emotions. His anger was tied up with regret and pain, and Jennet felt ill, because that combination generally meant someone was caught up in painful memories that fed his emotions. Such emotions were difficult to Coerce, as smoothing one left the others in a heightened state.

"Were they? We only knew they're in good shape," she said, improvising desperately. She could not untangle his emotions; she would have to impose a new emotion instead. She had wished so desperately not to use Coercion again, and yet here she was embracing it once more.

"You're coming with me," the soldier said, moving his hand from Falconer's shoulder to his wrist.

Jennet held her breath. Anger was difficult to displace with any other emotion, even fear, and normally she would run her victim through a range of emotions leading away from anger, but there was no *time*.

Falconer turned his head slowly to regard the soldier's grip. Then, faster than thought, he broke free with a twist of his arm. With his other hand, he punched the soldier in the face so hard Jennet heard cartilage crunch. "Run," he said, and took off without waiting for her.

Jennet immediately followed him. Behind her, the soldier shouted, "Spies! Get them!" in a nasal, clogged voice that would have amused her if she hadn't been terrified. Falconer sped up, outpacing her. She gasped out a plea he could not have heard—except he did, for he turned and grabbed her hand to pull her along after him.

Ahead, two soldiers emerged from a shop. They saw Jennet and Falconer and clearly drew conclusions about two running figures by stepping into their path. Jennet focused her fear and let them both feel it like a blow to the chest; they shrieked, staggered backward, and one fell and tried to scramble crab-like away.

Behind them, more shouts told Jennet soldiers were in pursuit. She and Falconer whipped around a corner and paused, Jennet gasping for breath. Falconer did not look the least bit weary. "We need a place to hide," he said.

"No one...the soldiers...all afraid," Jennet managed.

"True, no citizen will hide us for fear of the soldiers," Falconer replied. "If we can get ahead of them—"

The shouts were louder now. Falconer pulled on Jennet's arm. Groaning inwardly, Jennet ran.

They dodged through streets and around corners, but as if this were a nightmare, more soldiers appeared wherever they went. Gradually, street by street, they were forced away from the inn and the cart, though Jennet did not believe there was any more safety there than anywhere else. But the cart represented freedom, and as the minutes passed, Jennet despaired of ever finding that again.

The next time they had a moment's rest, Falconer said, "I have an idea. But it depends on us getting closer to that house."

Jennet looked where he pointed. "That house" was a broad stone edifice wider than any other in Châlons-sur-Marne, with a lattice of black beams crisscrossing the creamy plaster of its upper stories and three chimneys sending plumes of thin, pale-grey smoke into the blue sky. Her mouth fell open. "You are mad," she said, not remembering he was her superior officer. "That is the house the French have taken as their headquarters. We should be trying to get *away* from it."

"I know," Falconer said. "Do you trust me, Graeme?"

Jennet nodded. "You know I do, sir."

"Then—run!" Falconer set off once again.

Jennet was sure she would die of exhaustion. Her legs ached, her chest burned, and she could hear nothing over the wheeze of the air in and out of her lungs. But she trusted Falconer, and as his path brought them ever closer to the French headquarters, she reviewed in her head what she could do to Coerce them out of danger.

Shouts meant they had once more been spotted. Her feet in their stupid soft shoes ached from running. Falconer pulled her around yet another corner and into a narrow alley down the road from the headquarters building. It was piled with trash and smelled terrible. Falconer immediately wrestled off his coat and hat and tossed them deeper into the alley. He leaned against the stone wall to remove his boots and stockings, which he tossed beyond the coat, well out of sight.

"Sir, what—" Jennet paused. The shouting was drawing nearer.

Falconer looked her up and down. "Take off the apron." He snatched the cap off her head, disordering her curls. Jennet removed the apron, which made her makeshift bosom slide.

"Sir, I don't understand," she said. "They will be on us in moments. What are you doing?"

"Making us invisible," Falconer said. "Against the wall, Graeme, and—forgive me."

Jennet backed up, now thoroughly mystified. The shouting was closer than ever, and Jennet heard booted, running footsteps. She closed her eyes and tried to Coerce the approaching men, but she could not see them, and that made Coercion impossible.

She opened her eyes just as Falconer took her in his arms and kissed her.

It felt as if an explosion had gone off in her head and sent shockwaves through her body, so utterly unexpected was his embrace. She barely heard the soldiers nearing over the roaring in her ears, barely felt the roughness of his new-grown beard, was conscious only of his arms encircling her and his lips on hers.

Without another thought, she kissed him back, drawing him closer with her arms around his shoulders. His hand moved from her waist to her thigh, pushing her skirt up to expose her leg, and his lips on hers were fierce and passionate, kissing her again and again. A distant whispering voice told her something was wrong, but she ignored it, knowing only that she wished him to go on kissing her forever.

The shouting had stopped, and she heard someone laugh. Then a male voice said, "Take care she don't make you wither and rot, friend!" Footsteps retreated rapidly, and after a moment, all was silent.

Falconer withdrew from her, his breath for once ragged and shallow. Jennet closed her eyes and willed herself calm. That had been—

Her heart contracted as if she had been shot. No. She had kissed Lieutenant Falconer. Kissed him the way a woman kisses a man. She had given herself away in the worst possible manner.

She could save herself. She would tell him she had been putting on a show for the French soldiers. After all, he had done the same, kissing her as if—

Jennet felt sick now as well as sore at heart. He had kissed *Ned Graeme* as if he were attracted to him. He believed she was male, and he had kissed her. It had never occurred to her that perhaps he was attracted to men rather than women, but of course that was possible. It all made sense now, how he had arranged for her to remain close to him, how he had brought Ned into his confidence, even how he had insisted on sharing a tent. Jennet wanted to weep. It was Ned Graeme he cared about. And that would not have mattered had she not fallen hopelessly in love with him.

Falconer's breathing had calmed. "We will wait a few minutes, and then leave. I hope the cart has not been stolen."

Jennet nodded. She did not feel capable of speech.

"Ned," Falconer said, then fell silent.

The immensity of her tragedy struck her. Thanks to her kisses, he believed Ned returned his interest. She could not permit him to pursue her in that way. Which meant she would have to give away her secret, after all, to prevent a truly colossal and embarrassing misunderstanding.

"We had to be close to the French headquarters because they would not believe we would take such a chance." Falconer's voice sounded dull, as if he had used up the last of his stamina on running. "And no man ever looks too closely at a man and a woman embracing."

"It was a good ruse," Jennet said. "Very clever."

Falconer leaned against the wall again and closed his eyes. "Does it make things better, or worse," he said, "if I tell you I know you are a woman?"

Again, shock rooted her in place. Much more of this and she would run mad. "You know? How long have you known?"

"At the risk of sounding crass, I do know a woman's body when I feel it." Falconer sounded weary beyond belief. "I apologize most wholeheartedly, particularly for exposing your body to their view, but I believed that display would be convincing. I should not have taken advantage of you, but when you returned my kiss, I was overcome. It was wrong of me to reciprocate when you were in no position to resist."

She did not know why this failed to comfort her. At least she was not dealing with a lover of men who believed she was a man who returned his affections. But her heart still ached with a terrible longing. "I understand. It must have been a complete surprise."

"The greatest surprise of my life." Falconer shook his head ruefully. "What is your real name?"

"No. What you do not know, you cannot accidentally reveal." First Corwin, now Falconer, and Fosse and Sadler must suspect something. Perhaps it did not matter if she told them all, but she had lived with this secret so long it felt like stripping naked to give it up.

"That makes sense. Very well...Graeme. Let us make haste. We have already lost more time than I care to contemplate." Falconer did not put his boots back on, but he did cram the hat back on his head, pulling it down over his ears with some ferocity. Jennet, seeing the sense in not appearing as they had done while they were chased, left her apron and cap off.

They returned to where they had left the cart. Jennet expected it to be gone, snatched up by a soldier or an opportunistic citizen. But no one had touched it. Jennet chose not to dwell on how miraculous that was.

Falconer dropped his boots into the cart and picked up one shaft. "Do you," he began.

When he did not immediately continue that sentence, Jennet asked, "Do I, what?"

He shook his head. "We will take a route away from the main streets, to encounter as few soldiers as possible."

Jennet took up her own burden, and with a heave, the cart rolled into motion.

CHAPTER 19

IN WHICH TWO UNCOMFORTABLE CONVERSATIONS RESULT IN DIFFERING ACCORDS

The battered, makeshift cart wobbled on uneven wheels, forcing Jennet to push hard on the shaft to keep the cart rolling in the direction she and Falconer chose. It moved as ponderously as if it were twice its size and fully laden, and Jennet's arms and legs ached with the effort of keeping it on a straight path after only a few minutes of walking.

Sweat streaked her back and dampened the cloth binding her breasts, not just from the exertion but from the sun. Jennet had not realized how much protection the ridiculous cap had been from the sun's heat. Its rays beat down upon her with unexpected ferocity. This might well be the hottest day of summer so far.

Beside her, Falconer's breathing was for once as heavy as her own. She was grateful for the exertion that limited speaking. Her tumultuous thoughts spun round like leaves caught in a river's eddy, tumbling past one another in confusion.

Falconer drew in a deep breath. "Graeme."

That sounded like the prelude to an unpleasant conversation. "You needn't say anything, sir," she said, hoping to forestall him, knowing that was unlikely. "We've neither of us anything to reproach ourselves for. It was all the necessity of the moment."

"I know. I simply wondered how long you have pretended to be male," Falconer said.

Jennet tripped and caught herself, rocking the cart sharply. "Six years, nearly," she said. "Since I joined the Rifles."

"Six years," he repeated. "And no one knew."

Jennet shook her head. "Who would guess? It is not as if I look feminine. People see what they expect to see." She drew in a deep breath and wished Falconer had not decided to have this conversation when they were both exerting themselves.

They turned a corner into a narrow street not much wider than the wagon. Falconer glanced Jennet's way, eyeing her closely. "I can see it, now that I know the truth."

Fear stabbed Jennet's heart. "You will not tell," she said. Promise to herself or no, she would Coerce him rather than permit him to reveal her secret.

Falconer's brow furrowed. "Honor forbids it," he said. "I would not betray you so. But in truth, I do not believe any of our little company would think less of you for learning your secret."

"That is not your concern," Jennet said, forgetting he was her superior officer for the moment. "I choose to be male. I can barely remember how a woman behaves. You might have done better to dress Sadler in this garb; he can play the part better than I."

Falconer chuckled, a rather breathless sound. "When I consider how casually I suggested you dress as a woman, I am astounded that I did not realize sooner."

His humor calmed her anger somewhat. "Then you will not treat me like a woman?"

"I will—"

They came to another sharp turn in Châlons-sur-Marne's twisty streets, and for a moment, both of them needed all their breath to manage the cart. The turn put them on the road to the bridge, and relief at nearly reaching their goal suffused Jennet. They trudged in silence for a moment or two, and then Falconer said, "You are a soldier, and I will treat you as such. Never fear."

It was what she hoped for, and at the same time his words made her heart ache again. He had kissed her out of surprise, not desire—and why would he feel desire for someone whom seconds before he had believed to be a young man? In any case, he felt nothing more for her than whatever friendship could lie between a soldier and his superior officer. Friendship, loyalty, comradeship, but not love. And love was what she felt for him.

Falconer straightened briefly and took a better grip on the shaft. "Where will you go, when this is over?"

Jennet blinked. It was not the question she had expected from him. "I suppose I will return to Scotland, sir."

"I thought your family was gone."

"My own family, sir. I have an aunt and uncle in Edinburgh. They took me in, after my family was gone, but I did not like living with them. They have a large family and it only reminded me of what I'd lost." And her aunt had expected her to work more than her share of the labor, like a slavey rather than a niece, but saying that would be asking for pity, even though it was not uncommon.

"But you cannot continue this ruse forever."

"Do you have a point, sir?" The thought of the future sharpened Jennet's tongue.

Falconer shrugged. "I suppose not. I apologize for prying. I simply find what you have done remarkable, and I am curious about the life you lead." Then, to her surprise, he laughed breathlessly. "Captain Lord Adair would be aghast to learn his best sharpshooter is a woman. He is convinced a woman's place is in the home."

Jennet smiled. "And you know better, do you, sir?"

"I have been revisiting all our interactions," Falconer said, "and seeing them in light of what I know now. Even had I believed women to be the weaker sex before, I could not maintain that belief now."

His words left her achingly empty inside again. He had sounded admiring, as if they had recaptured the camaraderie they had shared, soldier and officer. Admiring, but not affectionate—though, why should he feel that way? Lightly, concealing her inner turmoil, she said, "I would not like to arm-wrestle you, though, sir. Not with you having such an unfair advantage, as a Shaper."

Falconer laughed again. "There are all sorts of strengths, Graeme."

The nearer they got to the bridge, the more soldiers filled the streets. At least ten of them stood on either side of the bridge, looking very closely at every man leaving Châlons-sur-Marne. Jennet glanced at

Falconer and her heart thumped painfully. He looked as distinctive as he had all day, with that hideous face that no soldier could fail to forget.

"Your face," she murmured.

Falconer's eyebrows lifted, and he stopped walking. His grotesque features quivered. Then they visibly shifted. The high, pronounced cheek-bones disappeared like sand smoothed out by an incoming wave. His brows receded, and his eyes grew more prominent. Falconer clenched his jaw tight as if he were in extreme pain. Then he let out a whoosh of breath and wiped tiny beads of sweat from his hairline. He still did not look like himself, but he also did not look as he had when they were chased. The whole transformation had taken less than a minute.

"It hurt you," Jennet said.

Falconer nodded. He resumed his grip on the cart's shafts. "Rapid Shaping is always painful. But the pain passes."

"Even so," Jennet said.

"Do not pity me, Graeme, for that small sacrifice. Not when you—" He closed his mouth, eyeing the soldiers they now approached.

Jennet made a lightning-fast decision. As they drew nearer to the soldiers, she gathered up her sense of each man's emotions. Most of them felt an eager desire to find the intruders and drag them in as captives, and worse, spies. Two of them were watching the women rather than the men and felt more lustful than alert. Lust, or eagerness—both were the sort of heightened emotion that lent themselves easily to being diminished as one might trim a lantern.

Jennet took hold of their heightened emotions and soothed them, encouraging each soldier to feel instead indifference to those walking past. She watched their faces as she did so and saw the minute shifting of feet and shoulders that said they grew bored with their task, bored and inat-tentive. By the time she and Falconer dragged their cart across the street and past the soldiers, none of them gave any heed to the passersby.

Once they were safely on the bridge, just one of many rickety wagons and poorly-mended carts, Falconer said, "That was fortunate. I was not certain our disguises would be sufficient."

Jennet nodded.

The road past the bridge was deeply rutted and dry, and their feet and the cart's wheels kicked up clouds of dust that made Jennet cough when she incautiously opened her mouth. Further conversation was impossible. Jennet was grateful for the excuse not to speak. They could never go back to what they had been, and she had no idea what they were to each other now. It was one thing for Corwin to know the truth of her sex, because he was taciturn and kept his own counsel and would never do anything accidentally to betray her. But Falconer was an officer, and a gentleman, and officers and gentlemen had strong opinions about the treatment due a woman, even one who was not a lady. No matter what he said, it was possible he might give her secret away simply by a change in his behavior.

All her secrets stifled her. Her stupid, traitorous body refused to let go of the memory of kissing Falconer and being kissed in return. That would never happen again, and she needed to forget about it as soon as possible.

When they pulled the cart into the yard behind the farmer's house, they found the men seated around the fire, which burned low. They had removed their uniform jackets and wore rough trousers and peasant hats and looked as unlike soldiers as possible. All four looked up when the cart drew near. Whitteney whistled, loud and long. "And aren't you the prettiest lass I've ever seen!"

Jennet scowled at him. Sadler thumped his arm. "Shut up. Ned didn't have to humiliate himself, and you'll be grateful for the food his ruse bought us."

Whitteney grinned and pursed his lips, but instead of a lascivious whistle, he came out with one of his many bird songs, the raucous cry of a jay. Jennet could not maintain a scowl in the face of his good humor.

Falconer set down his burden and stretched his arms. "I need my mirror," he said. "I prefer not to look like this one moment longer. And I now no longer have any idea of my appearance."

Jennet examined his face. "You look more like yourself than not, sir," she said. "Except for the beard."

"I'm afraid there's nothing Shaping can do about hair that has already grown. I will need to shave. I hope I remember how." He walked away, and Jennet heard him mutter something that sounded like "God's gift to women" as he shook his head. Despite herself, she smiled. He had not lost his sense of humor, and Jennet was impatient with herself that she had given in to melancholy.

She strode into the barn. Falconer was not the only one who wished to look like himself again. Sadler and Fosse had put her uniform and boots in the stall where she'd slept the previous night, and she swiftly removed skirt and petticoat and flung them away, pulling on her trousers with relief.

"Why were you dressed like a woman?" Veronique said.

Jennet squeaked in a very unmasculine way and spun around, clutching her uniform jacket to her chest. Veronique sat on her hay pile, cradling baby William, who blew milky bubbles in his sleep.

"There were French soldiers in the town. It was a disguise." She cursed her carelessness. Veronique had probably seen enough of her body to know she was female, and that meant one more person who knew the secret.

"Do not be embarrassed. You did it for our sakes." Veronique shifted the baby in her arms and sat up. "Did they see you?"

Again the memory of kissing Falconer threatened to overwhelm Jennet. "They chased us, but we eluded them."

"And spent all your own money on a cart to benefit me." Veronique was not smiling. "You should not have sacrificed so."

"We leave no one behind," Jennet said in her roughest, deepest voice. She wished she might still wear her jacket. It made her feel better, as if her soldier's uniform were armor against discovery and weapons alike.

"Even so." Veronique looked away. "Private Corwin will not say, but I might have died in childbirth, yes? And the babe?"

Jennet did not believe in lying simply for the sake of avoiding unpleasant topics. Lying to protect herself, on the other hand, she had never felt guilty about. "Yes. You were growing weary, and could no longer push the child out."

Veronique nodded. She still was not looking at Jennet. "It is strange," she said. "I was tired, and then I felt such fear—the kind of fear that lets one run very fast for a few moments. That fear caused me to make a final effort. And the babe was born." She touched William's downy head.

Jennet remained silent. Veronique knew. She had to know. No Discerner could fail to recognize Coercion.

"It was a miracle," Veronique said. She finally looked at Jennet, with no expression on her thin features. "And miracles come from God, not the Devil. Do you not agree?"

Jennet blinked. "I don't know. If evil is used for good—"

"I believe that is impossible. Evil begets evil, always." Veronique regarded her steadily. "And if something we believe to be evil produces a good thing, perhaps that means we do not understand the evil thing."

"Perhaps," Jennet said. She swallowed to moisten a suddenly dry throat. "If that emotion ultimately brought you joy—"

"I do not resent it, of course." Veronique looked down at her child. "And I am grateful to it, wherever it came from."

"That is..." Jennet could not decide what to say. She cleared her throat. "We will leave soon. The load must be arranged to give you a place to ride."

"Thank you." Veronique struggled to rise and failed. Jennet stepped to her side and held out her hand.

"Permit me to help you," she said.

To her astonishment, Veronique extended the babe to her. "Hold him, please. I will regain strength faster if I exert myself in small ways."

Jennet gingerly took the child and held him the way Veronique had, supporting his head, which wobbled somewhat. William did not stir from his sleep. Sadler was right; he was the quietest infant Jennet had ever seen. Unpleasant memories of holding her aunt's youngest child surfaced. She remembered that babe as being loud and demanding and permanently red in the face from screaming.

Veronique got to her feet and gathered up Jennet's blanket. "He is beautiful," she whispered. "So perfect. I hope he does not grow up to be someone terrible."

"That is unlikely. Besides, how can you imagine such a thing while looking at him?" Jennet touched his small hand in wonder.

"I imagine no one expected a certain infant would grow up to be Napoleon," Veronique said, an uncharacteristic bitterness in her voice. Jennet handed William back and wiped her hands on her trousers for no reason she could explain.

The barn door eased open, and Fosse said, "We're ready to leave, Ned. And—you know we mean nothing by our teasing, right? It's all in fun."

Jennet rolled her eyes and threw the balled-up socks she had worn inside her shirt at him, making him duck and laugh. She would not have minded at all if the risk of exposure did not hang over her all the time. "Let us go, Veronique," she said.

She left the others to make space for Veronique and the supplies, and hurried to the farmhouse's front door. Once again, her knocking did not produce the old man, though the hounds reached new heights of howling protest. Wincing at the leanness of her purse, she left a few francs on the doorstep. He had not been friendly nor sociable, but he had provided such welcome shelter Jennet could not begrudge him a little extra coin.

By the time Veronique was settled, and they had hoisted Whitteney up, it was almost night. "We will not reach another town tonight," Falconer said, "at least, I don't believe we will, but we cannot afford not to make progress." He sat the cart seat as if it were a throne, his restored profile more noble than anything impressed upon a coin.

"Why were those frogs in Châlons-sur-Marne, sir?" Whitteney asked. "If they weren't the ones that took our company."

Falconer snapped the reins, and Suleiman stepped out. He did not look at all as if pulling a cart was beneath his dignity. "Châlons-sur-Marne lies on a line from the great cities of Prussia," Falconer said, "and based on the uniforms we saw, those are the forces of General Grouchy, whom I had believed to be much farther south. I assume Grouchy is there to prevent the Prussians from advancing west to join Wellington's Army."

"Does that mean Wellington don't know about them, sir?" Whitteney sounded appalled.

"Likely not, which means our mission just became a hundred times more important." Falconer flicked the reins again until Suleiman was almost trotting. "We will go until Suleiman tires and make camp then. I hope to reach Rheims by tomorrow, at which point my knowledge of the area ends. We will have to stay with the roads, and hope we look like ordinary travelers from above."

Jennet reflexively checked the skies, which were blue and cloudless and free from birds or Extraordinary Movers. It was hard not to hunch in on herself, nonetheless. Sadler had provided her with a wide-brimmed hat, which she pulled down over her ears.

They were able to travel another five or six miles before darkness fell and Falconer called a halt. Suleiman was visibly trembling when Jennet unhitched him, and she took a moment to stroke his neck, wishing Coercion worked on animals so she might ease his fears if not his exhaustion.

Hands took the reins and bridle away from her. "I will care for him, Graeme," Falconer said. "He needs water. Pray, prepare something to eat."

Jennet nodded. She began to walk away, but Falconer called her back. "Yes, sir?"

In a low voice, Falconer said, "I should not share a tent with you, now that I know the truth." He paused, and added, "I cannot devise a way to avoid it that does not look odd, and I have no way of providing you with your own tent as is proper."

"I would rather you not go to the trouble, sir," Jennet said stiffly. "It is not as if I have a reputation to protect. And I prefer not to rouse suspicions by you changing your habits for no apparent reason."

Falconer sighed. "Very well, Graeme." He led Suleiman through the trees in the direction of the stream that paralleled the road. Jennet watched him go before coming to herself. And so it began. She could admit his desire to protect her warmed her heart even as it also annoyed her. Had she not made her way in the Army for six years without a man's protection? Was she not a crack shot with the rifle and skilled at surviving off the land? Falconer's need to treat her like a woman might endanger her secret. And yet she found herself wishing she could openly be the woman he wished to protect. She cursed herself inwardly and dug through the supplies for something they could eat without cooking it.

The pace Falconer had set and the emotional distress of the past two days left them all tired and disinclined to chat. Jennet had bought bread in Châlons-sur-Marne, and by the time she had finished her portion she did not care who she shared a tent with so long as she was permitted to sleep. She crawled into her tent, wrapped her new blanket around herself, and did not even notice when Falconer joined her.

When she woke in the pre-dawn hours, she lay on her back for a few minutes listening to Falconer breathe. It was such a peaceful sound that for a moment, she imagined them sharing a bed somewhere far from this small tent. Then the moment passed, and she quietly left the tent, rubbing her eyes to stop the tears. When had she become so ridiculously feminine? She was a soldier, not a sniveling woman, and she refused to become maudlin over any man, not even Falconer.

She built a small fire, conscious of how it would draw the eye of an observer—but dressed as they were, how much stranger would it look for their little group not to light a fire? Then she fetched water from the nearby stream for a pot of porridge. The memory of preparing porridge for Captain Lord Adair made her smile as she recalled how little inclined she had been to eat it. But oats were cheaper and took up less space than meat, and they needed both money and space.

Falconer joined her as the water began to boil. "How I regret not finding tea in that town, Graeme," he said. "It is a bracing way to start the day."

"I am not so fond of it as you, sir, but I appreciate the smell," Jennet replied. She added oats in her usual slow fashion and stirred.

Falconer settled himself cross-legged on the ground next to Jennet. She braced herself for more questions, some comment on her true identity, out where anyone might hear. But Falconer said nothing, merely rested his hands on his knees and stared into the fire. It was such a comfortable feeling Jennet wished they were alone for her to confide in him.

More canvas rustled, and Sadler said, "Oh, *porridge*. Must we, Ned?"

"It is good for you, and you should not whinge," Fosse retorted from behind him. He had somewhere acquired a new ribbon—new to him; it was actually quite elderly and frayed—and was engaged in binding up his hair in a queue.

Jennet stirred the porridge, releasing a gust of hot, sweetish steam. "It's this or the last of the stale bread. It needs eating up."

"You sound like my mother, Ned," Sadler said. "'Tis as if you did not leave the skirts far behind."

He was joking, but his words made Jennet briefly numb. If anyone were to guess, it would be Sadler, with his quick wit and ready observation. Maybe they all needed to know. Keeping the secret was suddenly exhausting. But—no. She could not bear revealing herself intentionally. If they discovered it, she would endure, but she would not give away her secret herself.

CHAPTER 20

IN WHICH JENNET'S TALENT
SAVES AN EQUINE FRIEND

T hey ate, and packed up, and were on the road by half an hour
after dawn. William cried for a bit at the start until he was
offered food, and then he settled down. Truly the most agreeable child Jennet had ever known.

She marched behind the cart, feeling more naked without her rifle
than from the absence of her jacket. She had removed it and stowed it in
her pack when the others did and put her rifle and bayonet in the cart
behind the supplies, under a blanket. It would do her no good if they were
ambushed, but she had placed her sword where it could be easily reached,
and that would be better in a close fight than the rifle.

She hoped Lady Ashford was far from them, or failing that, hoped she
Flew so high they were even less noticeable. Removing her uniform felt
wrong, as if Jennet were denying her identity, and yet they had no choice if
they wanted to reach the Army undetected. It still felt wrong.

They spread out away from the cart, with Falconer driving and Jennet
marching alongside. The others stayed in the trees, barely within sight of
the cart. Even without their uniforms, they all agreed so many able-bodied
men in a group, particularly ones who spoke no French, would draw too
much attention. But the travelers they passed walked with heads bowed
and glanced fearfully at them when they did not ignore them, not even
glancing at Suleiman, whom they had smeared with mud in an attempt to

disguise his striking appearance. Some of them stepped aside for the cart to pass well before it was necessary, as if they hoped Falconer and Jennet would ignore them as well.

Almost everyone was headed north as they were. All of them bore heavy burdens, and the few who walked beside mules had loaded the animals to the limit of what they could bear. Refugees. Jennet had seen men and women like them in Spain and Portugal, and she recognized the dull hopelessness on their faces. She wondered where they were going, and what they had experienced of Napoleon's advance that had set them on this road.

All day they walked, with occasional rests for Suleiman. They ate on the march, apples and fresh bread and hunks of cheese, and kept an eye on the skies. Lady Ashford did not appear. No bandits ran screaming out of the trees intent on their destruction. They heard no sounds of French soldiers in a terrible marching line behind them. The day was warm and clear, and had they not been in enemy territory Jennet would have found the march invigorating. As it was, the constant strain of watching in all directions at once wore on her, making her long for a real bed. She had not slept in a real bed since last winter.

The sound of pounding hoofbeats turned Jennet's alertness southward, to their rear. She fell behind until the cart passed her, turning to listen to the rider's approach. That was no mule; the gait was too fast.

"Keep moving," Falconer said. "We are nothing more than travelers."

"Whoever it is, they are almost certainly French," Jennet said. She glanced behind her and discovered Falconer had resumed his ugly disguise, if not quite so extreme. He nodded and flicked the reins once, making Suleiman step out faster.

In another minute, the rider overtook them and turned his horse, coming to a stop in a little cloud of dust. He wore a road-grimed French uniform and rode a brown mare that reminded Jennet uncomfortably of Captain Lord Adair's mount.

He glanced into the cart, observed Veronique and the babe, frowned at Whitteney, and then turned his attention on Falconer. "You there," he said in French. "Where did you get that horse?"

"Beg pardon, sir, my brother can't speak," Jennet said.

The soldier's gaze settled on Jennet. "Is that so," he said. "Well? Explain yourself."

Jennet eyed Suleiman, who stood patiently and without twitching. The mud might work to conceal him from Lady Ashford's distant observation, but up close, he still looked far healthier than the few other horses they had seen in their travels. "He's been ours for years," she said. "Wish we'd known he has a weak heart before we paid good money for him. He's good for naught but pulling this cart."

The soldier examined Jennet closely, then turned his attention on Falconer, who stared vacantly into space as if unaware of their presence. "That's the sort of thing someone would say if they didn't want a prime animal to go to serve the Emperor's cause," he said, smiling nastily.

Jennet gathered up his emotions. "We can trade if you like," she said. "Our Pa would be grateful to have a healthy horse such as yours." The man was greedy—she did not need to be a Coercer to recognize that—but greed was close to desire, and desire was only a short step from revulsion. As she spoke, she nudged his emotions into a feeling of disgust at her offer.

The nasty smile vanished. The soldier said, "Try to fool me, will you? I wouldn't take your nag if you paid me."

"If you wish," Jennet said. She eased him away from disgust, though not so much that he would change his mind, and added, "You've come a long way, it seems." Carefully, she turned his disgust into contentment, the kind of satisfaction one feels after a long day of work and a good meal by the fire.

As she had hoped, the soldier said, "I have ridden since last night from Auve. Anyone but I would have taken much longer."

Pride. An excellent emotion to manipulate. "I am sure that is true," Jennet said. "Did you not stop in Châlons-sur-Marne? Or does your mission lie elsewhere?" She nudged his pride higher.

Now the man's smile was sly. "I am off for Rheims," he said. "In pursuit of English soldiers who may be headed north. Have you seen any such?"

Jennet widened her eyes. "The British Army, on this road? That cannot be so!"

"No, a handful of men, intent on carrying word of the Emperor's movements." The soldier's horse moved restively, and he quelled it with a tug on the reins. "They will not be traveling openly."

Jennet saw Sadler's sallow face peering out at her from behind a tree, past the soldier. She nodded, as much to her comrade as to the French soldier. "I have seen no British soldiers on the road, but there was a group of men whose paths my brother and I crossed early this morning." Jennet leaned on the soldier's emotions, making him want to believe her. "Many of them, all very hale, and they did not respond to my greeting, as if they did not understand. They went west, not north."

The soldier muttered something under his breath. "My thanks," he said. "It seems they are off to Paris, after all. You have saved me a journey in the wrong direction. Good fortune to you and your brother!" With that, he wheeled his horse and galloped off the way he had come.

Now Jennet saw Fosse as well as Sadler. She gestured a signal that meant "all is well" and said to Falconer, "He was looking for us, on orders that came from east of Châlons-sur-Marne. I told him his quarry was going to Paris."

Falconer's eyebrows flew nearly to his hairline. "You said that? And he believed you?"

Jennet shrugged, but her heart was pounding. "He was not very bright, and I told him what he wished to hear. This ruse will not convince his superiors, but I believe we have gained time on any pursuit."

"Well done, Graeme." Falconer snapped the reins, and Suleiman stepped out. "I heard him say 'cheval.' Horse. Did he try to take Suleiman?"

"He did. I offered to trade."

"*What?*" Falconer pulled up on the reins, making Suleiman protest.

Jennet grinned. "You must admit Suleiman is a beautiful animal any French soldier would be proud to own. I convinced him it would be a mistake."

Falconer shook his head. "You are more eloquent than I guessed. Thank you for saving my magnificent inconvenience of a horse." He closed his eyes, and his features settled back into their usual arrangement.

"Are we to proceed, then?" Fosse called out. He stood at the edge of the trees, casting his gaze up and down the road rather nervously.

Falconer blinked and worked his jaw as if it had stiffened. He turned when small William let out a fretful cry. "Let us continue. Graeme may have bought us a reprieve, but we must assume that messenger is not the only one."

The forest came to an end about two hours before dusk, and once more they were surrounded by farmland. This time, it was vineyards, rows and rows of greening vines as far as Jennet could see. Farmhouses, mostly of stone, dotted the landscape like dogs watching their property, and sometimes people moved along the rows, their actions imperceptible at that distance. They were dressed much as Jennet and her companions were, in white shirts and brown or black breeches, which relieved Jennet's mind slightly. Lady Ashford was unlikely to distinguish between them and the peasants working the fields.

They began to see more ordinary traffic on the road, mostly farm wagons pulled by enormous horses with feet the size of platters. The farmers paid them little attention, though their party must look strange, five men walking wide around a cart carrying a woman and infant. Without the shelter of the trees, they were more obvious regardless of their formation.

Soon, they came within sight of a broad river and a city sprawled around it. "Rheims," Falconer said. "I see no sign of the French army presence, so we will stay the night."

"In town, sir?" Fosse asked. "Is that wise?"

"Rheims is free from Napoleon's control as yet, and large enough that we can disappear into it," Falconer said. "We will scout out the town, though, and avoid any places where royalist sentiment is not clearly displayed. Anywhere we see Bourbon flags should afford us security. Since the French are unlikely to canvass Rheims, asking after us at every door, I do not believe it a risk—and were they to do so, it would mean the French army is here, and our cause lost. And we can use a rest."

Jennet stayed silent. That dream of a real bed seemed finally within her grasp.

Rheims was the oldest city Jennet had ever seen, its heavy stone buildings weighing down the landscape as if, having lasted this long, they would not be destroyed by any act of Man. The narrow streets were mostly paved with irregular cobblestones whose smoothly rounded tops felt slippery underfoot. Suleiman showed no sign that the slipperiness affected him.

Jennet closely examined those who walked nearby, watching for signs that one of them was suspicious of this group of men walking together. Her companions did well, but except for Sadler, none of them, to Jennet's eye, looked like anything but a soldier.

She saw no tricolor flags or bunting anywhere, which relieved her mind. But she also did not see any white flags, the color of the royalists.

She had hoped to see Rheims filled with obvious Bourbon loyalty, which would make the town, not safe, precisely, but safer than Châlons-sur-Marne. Even better would be the sight of English soldiers, or even their German allies. But the streets were thronged with ordinary citizens, none of whom acted suspicious in any way. That made her nervous. Surely their appearance must mean something to someone!

Jennet walked closer to Sadler to avoid pedestrians coming the other way, and occasionally put a hand on the rear of the cart to steady herself against someone who shoved past. "I have never felt so confined," she murmured, though no one nearby could hear her and likely none of those who could spoke English. "Living here would be like being entombed."

"Nay, lad, to me it feels cozy," Sadler replied. He smiled and nodded to a passing woman, who ignored him. "Have you never been to London? Its streets are as narrow."

"I spent half a day in London once. I prefer open country. There is so much life there."

Sadler drew in a deep breath with satisfaction. "Cities have a different kind of life to them. 'Tis almost like being part of history. I heard as Rheims has seen dozens of kings crowned here, and then there was that Joan of Arc."

Jennet frowned. "I didn't know you knew aught of history, Sadler."

Sadler shrugged. "Not much. Kings and queens, they mostly do as they please with no care for such as us. But here on the continent, it comes easy to pick up a snatch of history here and there."

Jennet gaped. "I like cathedrals," she confessed. "I'm not much for religion, but cathedrals are interesting."

"Ah, then you see it, too." Sadler jogged her with his elbow. "Makes me wonder what's at home I never noticed, eh? Certainly a mort o' cathedrals there, too."

Jennet nodded. A man holding a shielded taper came out of a door just ahead and lit the lantern outside the door, sending a glow across the grey stone. Up and down the street, more lanterns were being lit. Jennet had not realized how dark it had got until the lamps illuminated her surroundings.

"Aye, cathedrals, and castles, and manors," Sadler continued. "Something to show one's children, mayhap. Or to share with a loved one."

Jennet cast a skeptical glance at Sadler. "I suppose. I hadn't seen it that way."

"Yes, a young woman. Or a young man, mayhap." Sadler's gaze was suddenly very acute. Jennet's heart thumped once like he'd struck her in the chest with a mallet.

"A young woman," she managed.

"Or a young man," Sadler said. "That is, a young woman would want a young man to court her." He wouldn't stop staring. Jennet did not know what to say. He knew her secret, obviously, but why would he not come right out and say it?

"That's true," she said, frantically searching for something else to say that might put him off the scent.

Sadler shrugged and looked away. "I've always thought a soldier's past was his own business and none of anyone else's. I don't care who you were before you joined up, Ned. You've risked your life for me, and I'd do the same for you. *Whoever* you are." He was back to sounding as if this were a normal conversation. "Ah, looks like the lieutenant's found us an inn."

Jennet wished she could scream. First Veronique, now Sadler. Could no one simply say what they meant? Aside from Falconer and Corwin, who had been all too direct. It sounded as if Sadler wished her to know he knew the truth of her identity and did not intend to tell anyone else. Jennet was torn between gratitude that he would keep her secret and anger that she had given herself away even to someone inclined to support her.

She breathed out in relief at the sight of the inn, where finally a white flag flew. It hung crookedly, and it was not as clean as it should be, but it reassured her. Nothing else about the inn did. It looked small from the front, tucked away as it was off the street in a little courtyard barely big enough to hold all of them plus the cart. But Falconer did not stay to knock on the door; he continued around the corner, through an arched passage whose sides the cart scraped that was low enough to force Suleiman to duck, and into open air that smelled of manure and warm equine bodies. Lamps glowed above a row of stalls, some of them occupied. The lanterns' amber glass made the light feel like honey, warmer even than the last golden light of the sun that peeped beneath heavy clouds. Rain was coming, and Jennet was relieved at knowing they would not camp out in it that night.

Falconer guided Suleiman across the wide courtyard to one of the empty stalls, and Jennet helped Veronique out of the wagon as the lieutenant removed the horse's harness. Then Sadler and Corwin hauled the wagon into a corner and handed out each man's pack. Jennet worried about leaving the rifles buried beneath the sacks of supplies, but thus far they did not appear to be anything but ordinary Englishmen, and hauling rifles through the inn would dispel that illusion. Whether their packs, which to Jennet were clearly Army-issue, would give them away, she did not know.

"We should stand guard, sir," Sadler said. "The rifles might be too much temptation for whoever watches the yard all night."

"I agree," Falconer said. He looked at the men gathered around, and at Veronique, who had wrapped William up tightly and held him close to her chest. "Corwin, you'll take first watch. One of us will bring you something to eat. The rest of us—" Falconer lowered his voice. "This place is the safest I know of in Rheims. The innkeeper is French, but he is loyal to the Bourbons and was even when that was dangerous. He also owes me his life. But we must all stay alert."

Fosse twiddled the ribbon tying his queue. "We will keep to ourselves, sir."

Falconer nodded. "The innkeeper speaks some English, Graeme, but I would prefer you stand by, in case of miscommunications."

Jennet reflected that he had not touched her, even casually, since that disastrous kiss. "Understood, sir."

"And don't call me 'sir,'" Falconer added, including all of them in his command. "This inn caters to many nationalities, and some here will speak English, so we must be circumspect."

The idea of treating the lieutenant with the kind of informality that would not suggest he was her commanding officer made Jennet's head whirl. She resolved not to speak to him if she could help it. The fact that this decision filled her heart with a terrible pain told her it was the right one.

CHAPTER 21

IN WHICH TALKING TO STRANGERS DOES NOT END WELL

The side of the inn abutted the stables, a tall, windowless cliff with only one small door. Falconer led the way, followed by Veronique, and Jennet ended up near the rear, just behind Whitteney. He limped along, supporting himself on a long, wrist-thick branch Corwin had found, and refused Jennet's help even though he still moved more slowly than the rest of them. Jennet did not mind the delay. She had never regretted hanging back to assess her surroundings, though at the moment her view of her surroundings was blocked by Whitteney. It was still sensible behavior.

The door opened on a narrow, dark hall lit indirectly by the glow of lamps or candles coming from somewhere ahead. Jennet became aware of stairs leading down half a breath before tripping and descending them more precipitously than the builders intended. She followed the others into a cavernous room with stone walls and brick arches, lit by dozens of candles that made the room orange. She saw no windows, so the room would look this way day or night. The dimness, and the rough-hewn stone, gave her the impression of a room that had not changed for centuries.

A log as long as Jennet was tall burned in the long fireplace, warming the room to just more than was comfortable. Two trestle tables lined with wooden chairs paralleled the fireplace, and a handful of old men sat in small groups at both of them. They had the intent look of serious drinkers and did not look up as Jennet and her companions entered. Three steps at the far end of the room rose to a door barred with iron, one sturdier than the one they had entered by; Jennet recognized it as the inn's front door from seeing it briefly outside. Another set of stairs, much longer, rose into darkness beside it. Someone had set a delicate iron railing into the wall following the staircase. It looked so out of place in this medieval bastion Jennet felt absurdly sorry for it.

Falconer walked directly to the curve of pitted, polished oak beside the fireplace. "Remy," he said with a smile. "I see you have not changed."

The man behind the bar paused in his wiping of the oak slab. His left arm ended below the elbow, and a long scar creased his left cheek and dragged down the corner of his mouth. He smiled, recognition lighting his rough features. "Ah, Thomas!" he exclaimed. "You see I remember you. As beautiful as the day is long."

Falconer chuckled. "You will make me blush."

"No, no, it is not for a Shaper to make ashamed of his looks." Remy turned his attention on the others. "I see you have friends."

"Yes, and we need rooms for the night."

Remy's gaze halted on Veronique and the bundle in her arms. "*Mon Dieu*, Thomas, you bring a woman here?" He sounded more appalled than angry. "This is no place for a lady."

Falconer gestured to Remy to come closer. He said something in too low a voice for Jennet to hear all the words, but she made out "protection" and "husband" and "watch" and could guess the story Falconer was spinning, that they were escorting Veronique somewhere to be reunited with her husband. She wondered if Remy knew Falconer was a soldier, and if so, whether he guessed the rest of them were soldiers, also. Falconer must trust him, if he did not take precautions with their identities.

Then Falconer and Remy shook hands, and a coin passed between them. Falconer saluted Remy in a casual, non-military way and indicated the companions should follow him up the stairs. This time, Jennet was directly behind the lieutenant. The stairwell was as dark as the hall had been, and Jennet had to watch her step carefully until they emerged into a short passage lined with doors, lit by a single lantern whose glass was none too clean.

"There are four rooms free," Falconer said when they had all reached the top safely. "One is for Mrs. Appleton, naturally. Graeme, you'll bunk with me, and the rest of you will take the rooms at the end of the hall. I apologize for the close quarters—"

"It's all right, s—that is, a bed is a bed even if Fosse does snore," Whitteney said with a grin. Fosse elbowed him, making him wobble and clutch his stick more firmly.

"Ned's small, sir, wouldn't it make more sense for him to doss with one of us?" Sadler said.

Jennet held her breath. Sadler was looking at her in a peculiar way, and fear shot through her, fear that because he knew her secret he was interested in molesting her. Then his gaze turned on Falconer, and Jennet realized he was actually concerned about her proximity to the lieutenant, who as far as he knew did not realize she was female. She wanted to laugh, then weep, then laugh again.

"I may need to call on Graeme to run errands," Falconer said, as casually as if this were any other conversation. "As he speaks French, he will serve as a message runner. But the beds are quite large, and free from vermin—at least, they were when I was here last." He opened the nearest door. "Graeme, explain the situation to Mrs. Appleton, and if you'll give me your pack I'll stow your things."

Jennet handed over her pack and said, "Veronique, you and William will sleep here."

Veronique followed her into the room, which had a low ceiling and stone walls and a tiny window that at the moment was a square of black. Jennet lit the lantern on the small table just inside the door, revealing a bed with a straw-tick mattress and, surprisingly, a soft blanket spread over it.

"This is comfortable," Veronique said, sounding pleased. She sat on the bed and opened her gown to feed William. "I should not go downstairs again. Those men did not seem friendly, or open to the notion of a woman eating with them."

"Someone will bring you food," Jennet said.

She was at the door when Veronique said, "I suppose you cannot share this room with me, though likely you should. Not if they do not all know you are a woman."

This time, Jennet was prepared for the revelation. She shut the door and said, "You saw me undress."

"I did. You should be more careful." Veronique did not sound appalled, or surprised, or accusatory. She might as well have been conversing on tomorrow's weather.

Jennet sighed. "I take it you do not intend to tell anyone, or you would have done so already."

Veronique adjusted William's grip on her breast. Without looking at Jennet, she said, "You have many secrets, and I would be cruel and ungrateful to spread their knowledge abroad. Not after you have done so much for me."

"Thank you." Jennet breathed out slowly. "Thank you, Veronique."

She had her hand on the latch when Veronique said, "What is it like?"

Jennet blinked, and said, "Oh—they treat me differently, without the carefulness men use around women—"

"Not that," Veronique said. "The...other thing."

She was watching Jennet closely, and Jennet's heart constricted. Well, it was not as if her life was not already in Veronique's hands. "I see their emotions," she said. "Not as you do, not as if they are my own, but like tangles I can understand, and touch. And then a tug here, a tug there, and the emotions are in a different shape."

"So simple," Veronique said. "But you made me feel fear. I believed that impossible."

"Fear is tied to the body as most emotions are not," Jennet said. She could not believe she was having this conversation with anyone, let alone someone who could not be Coerced into keeping the secret. "Fear, and lust. The heart and nerves are caught up in those emotions, and I can make even you have that physical reaction."

"I am grateful, since it saved my life. It is simply peculiar." Veronique's eyes narrowed. "You have never shared that with anyone, have you?"

"I have not. It is surprisingly freeing." It was true. Jennet's heart was lighter than it had in years. Was it that confession truly was good for the soul, or was it that telling the truth was less of a burden than lying?

Veronique nodded. "And Coercion does not last forever?"

"I don't know. They say the Emperor's Coerced feelings of adoration do not fade, but...I don't know. Fear does not last long, and neither does lust, because the body cannot sustain such peaks of emotion without becoming exhausted. I believe anger is the same, though I rarely Coerce anger. It is too unpredictable."

"But you are not an Extraordinary, yes? So your talent might be different from Napoleon's." Veronique sounded distant, as if she were contemplating something else.

Jennet considered lying for the briefest moment. "No. I am an Extraordinary. I can Coerce anyone without touching them. It is coincidence I was in contact with you when I Coerced you."

Veronique's eyes widened. "Then it is no wonder Napoleon could not Coerce you. You may..." She bit her lip and fell silent.

"If you are about to say I may face him with impunity, that is not true. He did not bring his full talent to bear on me, so it may be that a Coercer truly can be Coerced with enough determination. But even if Napoleon cannot Coerce me, he still has much greater experience with his talent, much greater control, and his troops would overwhelm me before I reached him." Saying it made Jennet feel better, as if she had laid out all the reasons why she should not face Napoleon again and they made sense enough to give her permission not to.

"I see," Veronique said, and she sounded so disappointed Jennet's justifications shriveled.

"I cannot face him," she repeated. "And we must reach the Army in any case."

"I understand. It is just that I hoped—but you could not find Simon before you were discovered, in any case."

Jennet realized Veronique's disappointment was not disappointment in her. That did not ease her heart at all. "I wish for your sake I could. But I truly believe Simon is well. Napoleon will not wish to waste any riflemen. And someday..." She could not bring herself to promise Veronique she would eventually be reunited with her husband.

Veronique smiled, a weak, false expression. "Someday," she agreed.

"Someone will bring food," Jennet repeated, and fled.

The others were gone when she emerged from Veronique's room. She made her careful way down the stairs and found Sadler seated at the end of one rough table, carving into a roast fowl of some kind. It was more blackened than Jennet found appetizing, but it was food, and better yet, it was not boiled beef.

"We should take food up to Veronique. Where is the—Thomas?" Jennet asked. Saying his name felt odd and too-familiar, as if she had kissed him again.

"He left to care for Suleiman," Sadler said. "Whitteney retired upstairs to rest—I wager he is more exhausted than he lets on. And Fosse has made a friend." He jerked his chin in the direction of the bar, where Fosse stood chatting with an older man in between swallows of a very dark ale. Wrinkles swamped the man's eyes, but he did not look aged, just hard-lived. He laughed and clapped Fosse on the shoulder a couple of times.

Jennet eyed them both. "Is it not odd that he should have happened on a drinking partner who speaks English?"

"The lieu—that is, *Thomas* said people from all over Europe come here," Sadler said with a hearty belch. He wiped his lips with his sleeve and added, "Not so strange if one of 'em is from the old sod."

"But—" Jennet regarded Sadler in confusion. Had not Falconer said they were to be careful? Even if this was an Englishman, and no French sympathizer, they ought not be so casual in their associations. And yet Sadler and Fosse both were cynical and suspicious, and she had never known them to be careless when it came to security.

She turned her attention to Fosse and his companion. There was a light in the stranger's eye Jennet recognized. She had not had it turned on her in years, but any woman learned quickly to recognize when a man had a sexual interest in her. But surely the stranger did not intend to seduce *Fosse?* Fosse was definitely not interested in men, she was sure of that.

She swiftly examined the stranger's tangle of emotions. Oh, yes. Sexual desire was one of the stronger and more obvious emotions, and this man definitely had designs on Fosse. But he should be aware, should he not, that Fosse would not respond?

On a whim, she took a peek at Fosse's emotions, telling herself it was all right because she would not Coerce him. She saw nothing but friendly contentment, no disgust or anger. None of this made sense.

She was about to withdraw when the stranger again clapped a hand on Fosse's shoulder in a friendly way. Instantly, Fosse's emotions changed—not dramatically, but in a gradual way that left him feeling more cordial toward the stranger. Another touch, and that cordiality became warmer, more intimate.

Stunned, Jennet stared at the stranger, who still looked as normal as a person could. Of course talent did not show on the skin, but she needed no more hints—the man was a Coercer. One who intended to make Fosse love him.

CHAPTER 22

IN WHICH A BATTLE BETWEEN COERCERS HAS AN UNEXPECTED ENDING

J ennet scanned the room, hoping for inspiration. "Should I get Fosse? There'll be no food left if you go on pigging it up," she said, hoping she sounded casual, though to her ears her voice sounded shrill and tense.

"He's eaten already," Sadler said, chin deep in a drumstick. "Worry about yourself, Ned."

"But I don't think, um, Thomas wanted us to get drunk, and you know how Fosse is when he's had a few." Jennet felt that was inspired.

Sadler shrugged. "We'll keep an eye on him. There's no harm in tipping back a pint or two."

That was suspicious. Jennet assessed Sadler's emotions swiftly. She had never seen them so placid. "Did that man lay a hand on you?" she demanded.

Sadler glanced up from his meal. "What man?"

Jennet, despairing, looked back at Fosse. He was gone. So was the stranger.

She whipped around. "Where is he?"

"Who, Fosse? He just went out, probably for a piss." Sadler tore into another drumstick.

Jennet turned in time to see the front door close. "I...that's a good idea, I need a piss myself," she said, and ran for the door.

The one lantern over the door did not illuminate more than a tiny circle of cobblestones. Jennet cast about in both directions and saw nothing. Frightened, she closed her eyes and listened. To the left, away from the stables, she heard murmured conversation, and then nothing. Jennet walked slowly in that direction. She had no idea what she might stumble upon, and she recalled how large and well-muscled the stranger was despite his age. She kept walking. He might be big, and capable of beating her senseless, but she could not abandon Fosse.

The wall made a sharp turn after a few paces, into a sheltered nook. Jennet came around the corner and nearly tripped over the two of them. The stranger had Fosse in his arms and was kissing him, and Fosse was responding as passionately as if the stranger were female. It took no effort to discover Fosse was in the grip of sexual excitement, and Jennet wanted to be sick at how the stranger had manipulated him.

The two were so engrossed in what they were doing they did not notice Jennet. She drew in a deep breath, took two steps forward, and exclaimed in a loud voice, "Oh! Beg pardon, fellows, I did not see you there." As she spoke, she sent Fosse's emotions in a grand sweep from desire to pleasure to contentment, and from contentment to discomfort to frustration into, with a final tug, anger.

Fosse jerked away from the stranger's embrace, shoving the man back. He swiped an arm across his mouth. "What in *hell's* name," he breathed. "What did I—you *dared!*" He swung a fist at the stranger's face.

Far too swiftly for someone his age, the stranger dodged. "Now, this is all a misunderstanding," he said, grabbing Fosse's wrist and beginning to Coerce him again.

Jennet was ready for this. She was sure the anger she had Coerced in Fosse would protect him against most other Coercion for now. Instead, she turned her talent on the Coercer. She had been immune to Napoleon's Coercion, and this man might be immune to hers, but possibly a direct attack would work.

She threaded her Coercion around the stranger's emotions. He was angry but not furious, baffled and uncertain, and she built on those latter feelings slowly, encouraging them like teasing a fire into life. For a moment, the Coercer's uncertainty showed on his face. Then his eyes widened as if he had unraveled a terrible secret. "No," he said. "No! It's impossible!"

Fosse punched him again, this time hitting him in the stomach. The Coercer bent double, but when Fosse pressed the attack, the stranger's right hook came out of nowhere and laid Fosse out cold. Jennet gasped. The Coercer straightened, glaring at her.

"Another one," he said. "Damme, man, what the hell are we doing fighting one another? You care what happens to this long streak of piss?"

"He is my friend," Jennet responded, not caring that it was not strictly true. "And you have no right to use your talent for such vile purposes."

"As if you've never Coerced a girl to your bed," the Coercer sneered. He looked Jennet up and down, and the sneer broadened. "Maybe you haven't. Well, it's a matter of time, isn't it? We're neither of us like them. Kings of creation, we are!"

Fury filled Jennet. "I will never Coerce someone to love me," she said. "Never. And if that's what you believe you're entitled to do, I will stop you."

The man's eyes widened again. "Stop me?" he said, and burst out laughing. "What's a scrawny runt like you going to do to stop me?"

Jennet assessed him. He had probably Coerced hundreds, maybe thousands of people since his talent developed, years before. He was big and mean and accustomed to getting his way. But he was not an Extraordinary, and he was going to lose. Even if Jennet did not know how to make that happen. Yet.

She tested herself against his emotions, tugging at his pride. Altering it was more difficult than she was used to, mainly because he had a firm grip on his emotions. But it was not impossible. Pride becomes jealousy. Jealousy weakened becomes frustration. Frustration deepens into dejection.

The man's shoulders sagged. Then his jaw firmed, and his brows knitted together in fury, natural and not Coerced. "Don't you turn your talent on me," he said. In three swift steps he was on her, grabbing her arm. "I don't care if you are an Extraordinary, I'll see you dead first."

Jennet glared at him. All her fear had vanished as if she had Coerced it out of herself. She braced herself for a blow. Instead, she felt that same prodding, nudging feeling she had felt outside Troyes, when Napoleon had Coerced the 3rd. Fear tickled her spine. It was so obviously not natural she almost laughed, but she had no attention to spare for mirth. Whether an ordinary Coercer simply was no match for an Extraordinary, she did not know, but she brushed aside the stranger's Coercion and pressed on.

Dejection. Dejection becomes sadness.

The man's grip on her arm slackened. He blinked at her uncomprehendingly, as if she had struck him. "Why are you so cruel?" he demanded, his voice breaking.

Jennet did not release him. She drove his sadness deeper, into the bone-aching misery that drove men into madness or suicide. "You do not deserve my pity," she whispered, "and I will do the world a favor in stopping you."

The Coercer gasped. The sound snapped Jennet out of her concentration. A sick feeling washed over her. She had never killed anyone with her talent, and here she was on the brink of driving a man to take his own life. "No," she said. "I cannot."

The Coercer's head jerked up. Fear filled Jennet, terror like she had only experienced once in her life, and her grip on the man's emotions slackened. Almost immediately, she recognized the terror as false, but it was too late; the Coercer bore down on her as relentlessly as she had him.

For a moment, neither moved. Jennet cast about for an emotion that would stop him even as she deflected his jabs at her, his attempts to overwhelm her with fear. She needed something different, something he would not expect.

An idea came to mind, and immediately she set about implementing it. Gathering up strand after strand of pain or fury or sorrow, she soothed them all, stilling them past indifference into nothing. She had never tried eliminating emotion rather than stimulating it, and she had no idea what the result would be, but even if it simply stopped the Coercer from wanting her dead, even if all it did was give her a moment to break away, it would be worth it.

The Coercer's eyes dulled, and then he released his hold on her. "I don't," he said, and sagged. Jennet quickly stepped out of his reach, breathing heavily. The Coercer did not follow. Keeping an eye on him, she sidled around and crouched next to Fosse, who was stirring.

"Ned," he murmured. "Ned, get away from him...we need...oh, Lord, my head..."

"Everything is fine," Jennet said. She got a hand under his shoulder and helped him sit, then stand. Fosse staggered and could not keep a straight line, but he was mobile. "Let us go back inside."

"No. That man—Ned, he's a Coercer." Fosse's face was paler than usual even in the dim light, and he looked sick. "What he did to me, I can't believe—oh, *no*..." He jerked away from Jennet and fell to his knees, vomiting.

A heavy hand landed on Jennet's shoulder. "You whelp," the Coercer said. "I'll make you wish you'd never tangled with me."

Jennet tried to wrench away, but he held her fast. She braced herself for a blow that never came. Instead, the Coercer took hold of her other shoulder. His face was taut with concentration. "Fear me," he said. "Fear me, damn it!"

Jennet felt nothing, no prodding or nudging as of invisible fingers. She took hold of his emotions and saw anger being supplanted by fear. "You can't, can you," she breathed. "Your talent is gone." She had done nothing to the Coercer but Coerce his emotions, and yet—

The Coercer snarled again, "Fear me!"

Someone appeared at Jennet's right hand. "No, you bastard, fear *me*," Fosse growled, and slammed his fist into the Coercer's face, knocking the man's head back so sharply Jennet heard his neck bones pop. The Coercer released Jennet and dropped.

Fosse stood over the man, breathing heavily. "I should kill him," he said.

"Leave him," Jennet said. "He won't trouble us again."

"He's a damned Coercer, Ned. God knows how many men he's—" Fosse shuddered and wiped his mouth again.

Jennet could not explain to Fosse how this particular Coercer would never work his talent on anyone again. "We'll tell Remy, and he'll know who can take him into custody. We can't get involved or they'll pay too close attention to us, right?"

Fosse nodded. "Right. Right." He grabbed Jennet's elbow and dragged her away until she fought free and walked beside him. "You saved me," he said, stopping abruptly. "How did you know?"

"Needed a piss," Jennet replied. "It was just good luck."

"I'll take it. Thank you, Ned." Fosse gripped her wrist. "Thank you."

"It's what we do for each other, right?" Jennet said with a grin.

Fosse grinned back. "It is indeed."

When they returned, Whitteney had joined Sadler. She told the two her own version of what had happened—found Fosse with the Coercer, fought the Coercer, Fosse knocked him out—while Fosse had a conversation with Remy. That conversation ended with Remy and a couple of men who looked like sides of beef heading out the door armed with cudgels. Jennet worried that they might not bother calling for the guards, not with swift justice so readily available. Then she decided it was not her problem.

Falconer came in halfway through her story, requiring her to start over. He looked so grim Jennet was grateful he had not been present for the confrontation. She did not know what she would have done if Fosse had been conscious for that last battle of talent, or of what steps she might have taken to prevent Falconer from knowing her secret.

The others burst into rapid conversation when she finished, leaving her able to sit quietly and go over events in the privacy of her head. She had done something to that Coercer that either suppressed or destroyed his talent. Possibly only suppressed, as she could not imagine anything capable of removing talent from an individual, but even suppressing Coercion was supposed to be impossible. Yet she had done it.

It had to be her Coercion of apathy. She had removed all his emotions, and immediately he was incapable of Coercing her. She had never Coerced an absence of emotion before, because what would be the point? So much easier to guide someone's emotions into a useful state. She wondered what the effect would be on a non-Coercer and immediately banished the idea. Such a person would not have a Coercer's talent to lose, but nothing good could come of removing all emotion from a person.

"Graeme, are you well?"

Jennet blinked. "Yes, s—yes, I am well, but that Coercer laid a good blow on me before I dodged him," she told Falconer, whose lips tightened.

"You should have said something," he said. "We cannot have you injured."

"I am not at all bad off, and there is no reason it is worse for me to be injured than anyone else," Jennet said, glaring at the lieutenant. If he intended to treat her like a fragile flower, the two of them would have to have words.

Remy and his two friends came marching back in at that moment, talking loudly in French and laughing great booming laughs. "They are saying they beat the Coercer before handing him over to the guards," Jennet translated. "I am so glad they did not kill him."

"Why not?" Fosse demanded. "He's a Coercer. He has probably stolen and killed and...other things a million times. I say he's better dead."

"I do not like to encourage vigilante justice," Falconer said. "The city will take care of him. In any case, he will be unable to Coerce freely again."

"Why is that?" Jennet asked. He could not know what she had done to the man.

"France is direct and efficient in dealing with Coercers," Falconer said. "Once the guards have proved he is a Coercer, they will brand his face so no one will permit him to touch them and be Coerced. It is perhaps a brutal solution, but effective."

Jennet managed not to shudder. "I am glad. He should not be able to Coerce anyone, not if that is what he does with his talent."

"And what else should he do?" Sadler asked. "Don't say you are going soft, Ned."

Jennet realized that was not something a normal person would say and forced a yawn. "I mean Coercing others is evil. And I am ready to sleep."

The others all agreed, and they trooped up the stairs. Sadler took Jennet by the arm and drew her aside before she could enter the room she would share with Falconer. "I can make a stink if you don't want this," he said in a low voice. "You've chosen your path, and I won't treat you different, but you shouldn't..." His voice trailed off as he searched for words, likely ones that would express his concern about her sleeping in a bed with a man without stating outright that he knew she was a woman.

Jennet shook her head. "He won't lay a hand on me. But thank you."

Sadler nodded and released her. He gave Falconer a long, hard look the lieutenant returned with some perplexity, but neither said anything.

In the room, with the door closed, Falconer said, "You swear you are not injured?"

"Shall I strip naked and prove it?" Jennet said, weariness and exasperation loosening her tongue.

To her surprise, Falconer laughed rather than becoming angry. "I deserve that," he said. "You truly do not wish to be treated like a woman, yes?"

"I am a soldier, sir. I've proved my mettle on the battlefield. I deserve what I've earned." Jennet sat on the bed and removed her boots. The mattress sagged beneath her, but not as much as she had expected.

"You do indeed. Forgive my misplaced chivalry, Graeme." Falconer doused the light, and a moment later she heard the blankets rustle. The mattress sagged again with a heavier weight than her own. Then all was still in the dark room.

Jennet drew in a deep breath and released it quietly. She slid beneath the blankets, compressing the mattress further, and lay with her back to Falconer. His weight was greater than hers, creating a slope in the mattress she had to work at not sliding down to end up pressed against his back. Her heart pounded against her ribs hard enough to hurt. She had shared a bed with her cousins years ago, had slept next to her comrades all through the long Peninsular campaign, but she had never before shared a bed with a man whose body she was so exquisitely aware of.

She pulled her blanket up to her chin and tried to relax. Surprisingly, despite having walked all day and been in a fistfight, she was tired but not sleepy. The heat of Falconer's body scorched her with his nearness. Desperately, she cast about for something else to dwell on.

She remembered the fear, the natural fear, on the face of the Coercer when his talent did not affect her. The despair she had inflicted on him would have put him in the way of taking his own life, which to Jennet was even more despicable than if it had killed him outright. She could not believe she had been willing to do such a thing, even to avenge Fosse's violation. And it had been so easy.

"Sir?" she said before she could stop herself.

"Yes, Graeme?" Falconer did not sound sleepy.

"When you do something that makes you despise yourself, what do you do?" Again the words emerged without any consideration of how they would make her sound. She felt so foolish. "That is—perhaps you never do any such thing."

"I have done many things I regret," Falconer said. "And some of them have been despicable. I do not know that there is anyone who is completely free from regret over his actions."

"Then, what do you do? How do you live with yourself afterward?"

There was a pause. "I cannot speak for everyone," Falconer finally said, "but for myself, I do my best to make things right. And I try to act in a way I can be proud of, going forward."

"But that does not change the past," Jennet said.

"No. However, I see no benefit to dwelling on things you have tried to correct, even if they still fill you with regret. If you despise yourself, you can never truly repent, for you will always have one foot in the past."

Jennet had never looked at the matter in that light. "You are talking about forgiving oneself," she said.

"I suppose I am. At the very least, ceasing to berate oneself for mistakes. My mother says criticism should breed change, not contempt." Falconer chuckled. "I never realized how alliterative that was. Perhaps she has the soul of a poet."

Jennet pondered that for a while. She had grown so accustomed to berating herself for her sins she had never considered what the point of doing that was. Did she chastise herself so she would improve, or was it merely self-flagellation?

"But you—" Falconer began.

When he did not immediately go on, Jennet said, "I what?"

"I stopped myself before I could rather patronizingly say you cannot possibly have sinned in any great respect," Falconer said.

Jennet laughed. "Oh, sir, would that that were true."

"In seriousness," Falconer said, "I believe that there are few sins that cannot be expiated. I realize that is not Scripture, but it is my experience that much of the evils we commit are done without malice, and I cannot help feeling that God is more generous with our faults than we are. So— whatever you have done, Graeme, let it change you for the better."

Jennet had to remind herself to breathe. "I will, sir. Thank you."

"I'm not sure how deserving of thanks I am, given that I have trouble living that advice. Now, get some sleep. I want us out of here at first light."

"Yes, sir."

But sleep was even farther from her than before. Talking to him in the quiet darkness, sharing such intimate thoughts, reminded her why she loved him. Her whole body ached with the knowledge that he was right beside her, and this was a very private room, and they were sharing a bed. She clutched the blanket to her face. All she need do was roll to her other side and reach for him.

Likely he would respond with enthusiasm, the way any man would. They would share passion, and intimacy, and it would be wonderful. And then it would be over. After six years in the Army, Jennet knew well how men felt about the women they bedded: a soldier took comfort where he could find it, but no soldier respected the woman who warmed his bed. One glorious night was not worth seeing the man she loved look at her with disdain or, worse, indifference.

Falconer began to snore. It was a light, regular sound, not a snore she had ever expected to hear from a man. It was as beautiful as he was, and she muffled a laugh at her fancy. A beautiful snore—how absurd. Snoring annoyed her, as she was a light sleeper and easily wakened, but for once she did not mind. She loved the sound because it was his, and that made her a fool, but she did not care. Smiling, she let the sound carry her off into sleep.

CHAPTER 23

IN WHICH THEIR JOURNEY IS INTERRUPTED BY THE RETURN OF SOMEONE NO LONGER A FRIEND

A light rain fell the following morning, dampening their bodies as well as their spirits. The wind scattered the rain so it blew into their faces on occasion and chilled them further. Muttering curses at the weather under her breath, Jennet helped Whitteney rig a canopy from one of the tents to help cover the cart's passengers. The sky, ponderous with grey clouds blown by the wind, did not look as if the bad weather would let up any time soon.

They left Rheims behind and followed the road north and west, treading through the growing mud and murky puddles made by the ruts other carts and wagons had left. Soon Jennet's shirt was soaked at the shoulders, and she hoped the whole shirt would not become so wet that the cloth binding her breasts would be visible. But even that fear was distant. Most of her companions knew the truth; what did it matter if all of them did?

She fell back on running through a list of things that were not awful: the rifles were protected within the baggage, her boots proved as water-proof as she could have hoped, her stomach was full, she was not dead or Coerced by Napoleon. It was not a long list, but it cheered her.

The rain let up an hour after noon, and shortly the clouds dissipated, leaving the sky clear blue as if it had never heard of storms or clouds or chill rain. Jennet shook the rain out of her curls. Changing her shirt would be welcome, but they were in the middle of nothing, just fields as far as one could see, and she could go nowhere for privacy.

After the rain stopped, they paused for food and, at Fosse's suggestion, to change into drier clothes. Jennet had a moment's panic that subsided when Falconer, in a loud voice, said, "Gentlemen! We should discuss what lies ahead," and drew everyone's attention long enough for her to make the change unobserved. When it came time for him to put on a dry shirt, she looked away, feeling that restored the balance between them. She did not need to see his body to know she would love him no matter what he looked like.

They reached Laon after dark, and Falconer did not enter the city. "I am unfamiliar with it," he said, "and would rather not risk exposing ourselves to anyone who might report our presence. We will sleep out of doors and resume our journey in the morning."

Jennet reminded herself that she was a soldier, and living rough was what soldiers did, but it was hard not to remember the bed she had slept in the previous night and compare her bed on the still-damp ground unfavorably to it. She even envied Veronique her nest in the wagon, though not her bedmate. That was something else to be grateful for, that she had no child to care for.

They camped on the north side of the city, but did not pitch tents so as to save time and make themselves less conspicuous, though Suleiman's presence made that unlikely despite their efforts at disguising him. Jennet laid her bedroll near the wagon, tense with hope and dread that Falconer would sleep next to her. But he slept near Suleiman, on the wagon's other side, far enough that she could not even hear his snoring. She berated herself silently for being so smitten as to love his snore, and drew her blanket over her ears hoping sleep came quickly.

The lowering clouds threatened rain again the following morning. As they gathered up their bedrolls and possessions, Falconer said, "We will have a long, hard march today to reach Saint-Quentin by nightfall. I do not intend us to stay there, either, but it is as good a mark as any."

"We will need food," Sadler said. "Our supplies are running low, and if we ain't to stop in a city, we must needs forage."

Falconer nodded. "We should be out of this forest soon enough, and there will be farms and houses. But do not permit foraging to slow you down. We are already behind what I had hoped, and if we are still pursued, we cannot afford any more delays."

Rather than waste time with a fire, they ate on the march. As before, they spread out to either side of the road. Jennet pulled her floppy peasant's hat over her ears when drizzling rain began to fall. It was not much more than a mist, and she was not as soaked as before, but she envied her comrades marching beneath the sheltering trees.

After a few miles, they left the forest behind for more vineyards, stretching out over the gentle rises of the landscape. They passed two groups of refugees and one man on a mule, all of them heading south, then overtook a small family, husband and wife and three children. The youngest, no more than two years old, rode on her father's shoulders and laughed merrily at the birds that swooped overhead. She tugged on her father's hair as Suleiman and the cart drove past, and waved at Jennet, who walked wide around their little group. Jennet did not wave back. She had seen the look the man directed at them, that sullen glare that hides fear.

The sun dropped lower in the sky, lower and lower with no sign of a city. There were villages, here and there, and stone farmhouses squatting in the middle of lushly green fields, and the stream that paralleled the road grew gradually wider, but there was nothing that could be Saint-Quentin. Jennet recalled that Falconer had not said how far a journey it was, just that it would require hard marching, which in the Army meant a long road ahead.

At the next rest stop, Falconer said, "I want you all to spread out to forage. There are plenty of farms, and I have seen an orchard or two, so finding food should not be difficult. Follow the stream if you lose sight of us, and it will lead you to Saint-Quentin. Graeme, you'll stay with me in case we are accosted."

The men nodded.

Whitteney sat up and slid toward the end of the cart, dragging his stick with him. "I will go, too," he said. "You know I am the best at foraging."

"You will slow us," Sadler said. He flicked the stick with a fingernail. "That is not enough to make up the difference."

"Then you will stay with me, if you're afeared I will show you up," Whitteney retorted. He did seem to be moving more easily.

"Very well," Falconer said. "Watch yourselves."

Whitteney saluted him, then gave Jennet a lazier, mocking salute. "Take care you do not forget how to be a soldier, Ned," he said with a smile that said he was teasing.

"Hardly," Jennet said. "Do not enjoy yourselves too much without me."

Whitteney grinned and put his free arm around her shoulders in a brief, comradely fashion. His expression changed briefly, his eyes narrowing and his lips pursing in confusion, and he looked Jennet directly in the eyes as if he wished to question her. Jennet, her heart pounding, kept a friendly smile on her face. So, that was one more who knew, or at any rate guessed, the secret of her sex. Perhaps she should simply make an announcement, if they were all to discover it separately!

She and Falconer continued on with the cart as the others disappeared across the fields. After a time, Jennet became aware of louder water flowing some distance ahead, and soon they came within sight of a river. She did not know which one it was, but the road crossed it by an ancient stone bridge whose piled supports were green with muck as if the river was normally much higher.

"It is the Somme," Veronique said, startling Jennet, who had believed the woman asleep. "My home is near here—well, not near, it is at least twenty miles west. But it lies along the Somme."

"Your home? I did not realize." A brief, ignoble image of diverting to take Veronique to her home crossed Jennet's mind. It would not take very long, and then they would be freer to travel—but no, they could not afford any delay, and twenty miles was most of a day's travel.

"I say, my home, but it is not that, not any longer." Veronique's bitterness filled the air. "I left to follow my—the father of my child because my mother's husband would not endure a slut under his roof."

Jennet's brief resentment faded. "I see. Well, you need not return. We will care for you."

"I thank you, but—do not take this amiss, but I find myself wishing to care for myself. I simply do not know how." Now Veronique's voice was dull, as if she were once more contemplating a terrible future.

"What is it you do?" Jennet asked. "For a trade, or a craft. Or—perhaps you have no skills."

"No, I am an accomplished weaver." William made a fussy little cry, and Veronique soothed him. "But I know of no place to ply my trade."

"It is something, anyway," Jennet said. "Weavers are needed everywhere. Once we are with the Army, and Napoleon has been defeated, we will inquire."

"Do you believe that is possible? Napoleon's defeat?"

Jennet shrugged. "I must have hope, for despair does no one any good." But as she spoke, she had a momentary glimpse of a future in which Europe lay Coerced before its Emperor, with her the lone free person— only if that were true, she would not be free, she would be dead. She shook the image away and added, "Wellington is the most skilled military leader of his generation. If anyone can defeat Napoleon, it is he."

"I hope you are right," Veronique said.

They fell back into silence as the road stretched out, still with no sign of Saint-Quentin. On their left, the Somme flowed unceasingly toward a distant sea. Its rippling waters made a constant rushing sound that made Jennet thirsty, and she took a long drink from her canteen.

"What did you speak of?" Falconer asked.

"Veronique's home, and what she will do when this war is over," Jennet replied.

"I see. And what *will* she do? It is unlikely Private Appleton will return."

Jennet glanced at Veronique to see if she understood this statement, but she and William had fallen asleep. "She is in the same position many women are, their husbands lost to them, children to care for. But she will survive."

"I believe it." Falconer transferred both reins to his left hand and drank from his canteen with his right. "In truth, I believe she will make more of herself than I will."

"But you are an officer, sir. You have higher rank you will achieve— surely that is an accomplishment to be proud of."

Falconer chuckled. "Becoming a captain, or even a major, would indeed be a worthy achievement. But I am my father's second son, with a fortune settled on me, and have no need of the financial advantages to higher rank. And as I have no intention of remaining in the Army longer than they have need of me, my future is simultaneously set out for me as well as being unknown."

"Do you not like the Army, then?" Jennet asked, and then felt stupid. As if the Army were a favorite dish, or a pet, that one might prefer over other callings.

"It is more that I do not know whether I am truly serving my country well," Falconer said. "I have fought in many battles, been wounded and returned to the fight, and I believe the men respect my leadership. But when I remember Captain Lord Adair's erratic behavior, I cannot help but believe I should have acted differently."

"You could not have guessed he was Coerced," Jennet said. "No one could have." The lie curdled in her mouth.

"No, but I knew something was wrong, and I should have forced the issue and to the devil with the consequences." Falconer's jaw was tight, and he looked past Suleiman's ears at some vision Jennet could not see. "When I remember all those men who once looked to me for direction Coerced to love that foul Napoleon, all my reasons for not confronting the captain sound hollow. And then there are the many disasters surrounding our flight."

Jennet frowned. "What disasters? We are all well and unwounded, we have not been captured—"

"I should have sent Corporal Josephs west on Suleiman the instant we fled," Falconer said, his voice low and grim. "Or sent one of you north after Josephs headed west on the pack horse. We should have left Mrs. Appleton behind outside Troyes—she would likely only have been Coerced, and been safe with the company. We could have found her and the babe a place in Châlons-sur-Marne—"

"Stop," Jennet said. "I refuse to hear any more of this. Sir, you yourself told me we all have made decisions we regret, foolish or awful decisions, even decisions that are counter to what we know is best, and that we must live with them as best we can. I cannot believe you are the only officer in the entire British Army who has ever failed to act in perfect accord with military procedure."

Falconer looked down at her. "An officer's mistakes affect more than himself, Graeme. I cannot excuse my choices."

"To my knowledge, the only truly foolish thing you have done is hold onto your absurdly beautiful horse," Jennet snapped. "Suppose you had chosen differently in all those instances. You cannot know that events would have worked out for the better. Someone might have stolen Suleiman from whatever messenger you sent. Corporal Josephs might well be dead now. Veronique could have been killed by the soldiers or died alone in childbirth. Might-have-been is a fool's game, sir."

"And I suppose you have no regrets," Falconer said sharply. "No choices you would prefer to have back. You speak so easily of might-have-beens—"

Jennet realized how freely and foolishly she had spoken. She could not hold back her bitter laughter. "You are correct. So much of my past, I have wished undone. Forgive me, sir. I should not have spoken to you so familiarly."

Falconer pulled on the reins, bringing Suleiman to a halt. "Do you really believe that?" he asked, again speaking quietly. "That my choices do not condemn me?"

He sounded so in need of reassurance Jennet's heart turned over in her chest. "You have nothing to reproach yourself for, sir," she said, wishing she dared take his hand, or climb onto the cart and put her arms around him. "We are all alive and well, and you should rejoice in that. And if you have made mistakes, they are all the sort one can learn from."

"Mistakes one can learn from," Falconer said. "And what will you learn from *your* mistakes, Graeme?"

She could not bear to look at him. "I don't know, sir. I haven't finished making them."

His laugh startled her into facing him. He was smiling and shaking his head. "I still find it impossible to believe you have sinned greatly," he said, "but I am grateful for your insights." He snapped the reins, and Suleiman stepped out smartly. "Let us see if we can beat the others to Saint-Quentin."

In the end, they did not reach Saint-Quentin before the other four returned with their bounty. Loaves of bread, a few rounds of cheese, and a half-full sack of oats, as well as Sadler's hat full of apricots, cheered Jennet. It was not much, but they would not starve. Whitteney looked as if his wound pained him less, and stumped along as readily as ever, but when Jennet offered him a seat in the cart, he made no complaint.

The fields and vineyards offered no protection the way the forest had, and Falconer ordered them all to draw in closer, though he still set Corwin and Fosse to scout ahead and behind. In their travel-grimed clothing and wide-brimmed peasant hats, they did not look like soldiers, but none of them were wounded or missing limbs, and that made them stand out as much as uniforms would have. Jennet watched Falconer, who sat on the cart's seat as confidently as if their conversation had never happened. If he had reservations about their progress, they did not show.

The sun had nearly set when they came around a curve in the road that brought them close beside the river, which flowed darkly in the low light. And there, perched on the slopes of a low hill beside the river, lay the hunched buildings of a city that sparkled here and there with yellow lamp lights.

"We'll pass the city and make camp on the far side," Falconer said. "I see no obvious tricolors, but Saint-Quentin is no safe place for us regardless."

He sounded as confident as he looked, and Jennet's heart once more ached with longing. She watched Saint-Quentin as they passed it, wishing once more for a quiet room and a shared bed.

◎፠◎

THE FOLLOWING DAY WAS CLEAR AND HOT, AND JENNET ACTUALLY broke a sweat marching behind the cart. This time, they ranged wide of one another, but they still had no cover, and short of spreading out far enough that they had no contact with one another, there was no way to conceal they were a group. Falconer looked grim, but he said, "There is nothing for it but to press on. Corwin, continue to scout ahead. Graeme, stay back unless we are accosted. And you might all pray that God is on our side."

They encountered many more travelers going north, and only a handful going south. Once, a French soldier riding a lathered horse south-bound passed them without stopping, and Jennet held her breath until he was out of sight. They saw no one else in French colors.

Whitteney looked at her strangely whenever they stopped for a rest, but he said nothing. Jennet decided not to make an issue of it unless he decided to confront her. That made almost all of them who knew she was a woman. She realized, to her amusement, that none of them knew anyone else knew the secret, which meant four men and one woman were staying silent on her behalf. The knowledge warmed her heart.

Suddenly Veronique, lying back in the cart, gasped. "She is back," she exclaimed. "That Extraordinary Mover."

Jennet automatically looked up. The soaring, tiny figure of Lady Ashford swooped above them. Cursing herself, she immediately looked

234

down so Lady Ashford would not know she had been spotted. "Sir, don't look up," she called out, "but Lady Ashford is above us."

To their credit, none of the soldiers looked up at this news, though Sadler, walking ahead and to Jennet's left, hunched his shoulders as if in preparation for taking a blow. Falconer, driving the cart, did not so much as flinch. "Where above?" he asked.

"Slightly to our rear, sir. Maybe five hundred feet up."

"Watch for my signal. On my mark, make a show of noticing her. We are simple peasants, and an Extraordinary Mover is a rare sight, remember?"

Falconer continued to drive. Jennet refrained from tugging her hat lower in what Lady Ashford might see as a guilty gesture. She felt as if an enemy rifleman had targeted her, set his sights on the back of her neck. Sweat dripped down her back and prickled beneath her arms. Then Falconer said, "Look, up there!" and brought the wagon to a stop, pointing.

Jennet looked. The others were all crying out and pointing, so she did the same. Lady Ashford made a sweeping curve above them, not slowing. Jennet was sure Falconer's plan was madness. Lady Ashford would know they were not what they appeared to be, would swoop down and work her Moving on them to hold them in place while the French army approached to capture them. Jennet had heard it was difficult for a Mover to hold someone who resisted, but she also knew some Movers were extremely powerful, and if Lady Ashford was even only one of the five most powerful Extraordinary Movers in the War Office, that still made her a formidable foe.

Lady Ashford made another circle around them. Then, to Jennet's amazement, she waved and darted away southward.

Jennet let out a deep breath and scratched under her arms, not a very refined gesture, but the itching was becoming unbearable. The others burst out talking over one another until Falconer said, "Enough. We have fooled her for now, but we cannot slow down. Graeme, does Mrs. Appleton know what cities lie along this route?"

Jennet relayed the message to Veronique, and then said, "She says not. She has heard of a city called Cambray in this area, but she does not know if the road goes there."

"We will have to take our chances, then." Falconer snapped the reins, and Suleiman stepped out.

They walked more quickly now, all of them surreptitiously scanning the skies. Jennet wished more than ever for her rifle. It was near to hand, already loaded and stowed beneath a blanket beside Veronique, but that was not the same as having it slung over her shoulder. Carrying it would make her extremely conspicuous even from as high above as Lady Ashford Flew.

Of course, having her rifle meant turning it on the enemy, and it was difficult to remember Lady Ashford was that. She had been so friendly, so agreeable, and she had kept Jennet's secret. Jennet could not believe she had gone for six years in the Army with no one realizing she was female, and within the span of two weeks had given her secret away to five—no, six people. She was slipping.

A gasp from Fosse brought her back to herself. "She's back," he said.

"Keep moving. She will pass on," Falconer said.

Jennet stretched to give herself an excuse to look up. Lady Ashford Flew toward them, more slowly than before. She was clearly following the road, which filled Jennet with dread. She recalled the course of recent events and what Napoleon's men must have done: "spies" discovered in Châlons-sur-Marne, that news communicated to Napoleon's Speakers, the word going out to watch the road northward. Jennet had misdirected the messenger on that route back toward Paris, but that ruse could not have lasted. Which meant what they had always feared: that Napoleon's troops were again moving northward as well as west. But Napoleon was not stupid, and he would take precautions against the possibility that their little group had made it farther north than anticipated. Which accounted for Lady Ashford's presence.

Jennet trudged on, trying to make herself look like a peasant. She let her shoulders droop and kept her eyes fixed on the back wheel of the cart. So she had some warning when the cart came to a halt, and she did not walk into it.

She looked up. The others had all stopped, as well, and were standing in the tense poses of soldiers preparing to make an attack. Falconer sat straight on the seat, the reins gathered loosely in one hand.

Beyond him, standing squarely in the middle of the road, was Lady Ashford.

CHAPTER 24

IN WHICH JENNET PROVES HER SKILL AS A SHARPSHOOTER, WITH DRAMATIC RESULTS

"You nearly fooled me," Lady Ashford said. "How daring, to wave and draw my attention when you surely must have wished me not to notice." She sounded just as Jennet remembered, carefree and cheerful, and her smile was pleasant. Jennet could hardly see her past Falconer and Suleiman, but the sound of her voice was unmistakable.

"What gave us away?" Falconer asked. He, too, sounded as if they were two friends having an ordinary conversation.

Lady Ashford's mischievous smile deepened. She removed her goggles and slapped them against her open palm, a casual but somehow also sinister gesture. "Oh, you were very careful, lieutenant, but from above, the movement of so many able-bodied men draws the eye. And once I had noticed that, I could not help but notice your horse, who is striking despite your efforts to conceal him. What is in that cart, that you all protect it so assiduously?"

Jennet's morning meal turned to stone in her stomach. All their care, and it meant nothing.

"The cart is unimportant. We were simply careless." Falconer shifted his weight to rest one hand on the seat and lean on it. Hidden from Lady Ashford's view, his fingers flicked rapidly, but Jennet already knew what he meant. She looked at Sadler, who had his gaze fixed on the blanket covering the rifles.

"I'm not sure I believe that, but very well." Lady Ashford put her hands behind her back and took up a parade rest stance. On her, it looked strange, given that she wore no uniform but her odd grey coat and billowing trousers, but Jennet could not help seeing it as sinister as well. It was a reminder Lady Ashford did not need hands to stop them.

Jennet and Sadler exchanged glances. Sadler took a step toward the wagon and rested his arm along its side, further blocking Lady Ashford's view of Jennet.

"You've come a long way," Lady Ashford was saying. "It's really remarkable. But don't you see how mistaken you are? The Emperor will win. It's just a matter of time." She sounded as if Falconer were an errant child she was gently chastising.

"Forgive me if we do not share your Coerced opinions," Falconer said.

Jennet carefully slid one of the rifles toward herself, using the noise of the conversation as cover. Veronique, her eyes enormous, watched her with baby William clutched close to her breast.

"Coerced?" Lady Ashford sounded surprised. "I have not been Coerced. The Emperor's position is right and logical. You say I am Coerced simply because you and I are in disagreement. I assure you, my decisions are my own."

"This is not an argument I wish to have," Falconer replied. "Pray, move aside and permit us to pass."

"You realize I cannot do that," Lady Ashford said. "I have no desire to see you reach your destination, and take word of the Emperor's troop disposition to Lord Wellington. I hoped to make you see reason. I like you, Lieutenant Falconer. You are intelligent as well as extremely handsome. Please, do not force my hand. Turn around, and join the winning side."

Jennet shifted the rifle into a vertical position against her body, one hand on the barrel, the other on the stock. She had seen the speed of Lady Ashford's Flight. She would get only one shot.

"We will not return," Falconer said. He still sounded casual, but there was a firmness to his words that declared clearly he would not back down. "Feel free to return with more news of our location. By the time Napoleon's soldiers arrive, we will have reached our destination and it will be too late."

"Is that so?" Lady Ashford now sounded disappointed. "Very well. I suppose I shall simply have to take you with me. We will see how far they get without your leadership."

Falconer jerked. His hands closed on the cart seat. Fosse and Corwin, near the front, both shouted and dove for him. Jennet had time to observe that Falconer's posterior actually hovered two inches above the seat, and that his knuckles were white with strain, before she ran the few paces that would put her clear of the cart and give her an unobstructed view of Lady Ashford.

She brought the rifle to the ready and shouted, "Release him!"

Lady Ashford's attention focused on Jennet. Her mouth opened in astonishment. Then she darted into the sky. Jennet fired.

Lady Ashford jerked. Her body relaxed all at once, and then she fell, landing without trying to catch herself. Jennet flung down the rifle and raced to her side, gently turning her on her back. The rifle ball had torn a gash in her heavy coat, and blood soaked the Extraordinary Mover's side. She had also struck her head hard upon landing, and there was a contusion on her forehead with a long cut down its middle. But she was breathing, and it relieved Jennet that she had not killed her.

She gathered up her sense of Lady Ashford's emotions as the others crowded around her. Even in her semi-conscious state, Lady Ashford's devotion to Napoleon was a complex tangle threaded through every other feeling she had. It appeared natural, as every Coerced emotion did, but the strength of the devotion absent any object for it to focus on made it clear to Jennet that it had been Coerced. Devotion, and love, and a subtle adoration that made Jennet feel ill. She needed a solution fast, before Lady Ashford awoke fully.

She had never undone another's Coercion before, only supplanted it with some other emotion. It was too late for that; Lady Ashford had been under Napoleon's spell for far too long. But the false, Coerced emotion was still an emotion, and might still be altered.

Jennet tugged at the tangle of feeling. She had Coerced adoration before, to her shame, and she knew what led to it. Now she swiftly reversed that path: adoration to passion to love to admiration, making the intensity of the emotions diminish with every step. Then, sideways from admiration to pleasure, that warm feeling one has in the presence of the person cared for, and on from pleasure to contentment, from contentment to peace.

Somewhere in that path, she divorced Lady Ashford's unnatural attachment from its object and focused it inward. Finally, wishing it were not necessary, she took peace away and gave Lady Ashford a sense of loss. She did not wish for the woman to feel any pleasure associated with her captivity.

She became aware of the others around her, speaking loudly. "—did not kill her," Whitteney was saying. "She fell far enough, might have cracked her head open."

"You should have shot to kill, Ned," Sadler said, no trace of his usual humor in his voice. "She's dangerous."

"We ought bind her..." Fosse's suggestion died, likely as he realized binding a Mover was pointless.

"Move back, and give her room to breathe," Falconer commanded. Jennet drew back with the others. Falconer thumbed up her eyelids, one at a time. "She is coming to. All of you, back away out of her sight."

"Sir, you should not stay close," Jennet said. She was certain Lady Ashford was no longer under Napoleon's thrall, but she did not know how the woman would react when she discovered this. The memory of being Coerced to do evil could be powerful and sickening.

"Back away, Graeme," Falconer replied. Jennet could do nothing else.

Her foot kicked something as she stepped back. The rifle. She gathered it up, considered loading it, and decided there was no point. But better she hold onto it than one of the others, who might decide to shoot Lady Ashford out of hand.

Lady Ashford let out a groan. "You shot me," she said, her voice weak. "And my head aches. I cannot see clearly."

"Lie still," Falconer said. "You took a blow to the head when you fell."

Lady Ashford said nothing. She slowly raised one hand to touch the wound on her forehead and then winced. "You shot me," she repeated. "Shot an Extraordinary in service to—" Her hand fell. "I remember. I loved Napoleon. I adored him. Dear God in Heaven. I was Coerced." Her voice was still weak, but she sounded astonished. Jennet took hold of her emotions, just to be sure, and saw pain and confusion as well as a terrible aching sorrow and, unexpectedly, deep-rooted shame.

"Do not think to dissemble. We will not be fooled." Falconer's voice was flat and hard. "You are Coerced, and you wish us to believe otherwise so you may again betray us."

"No." Lady Ashford tried to sit up, but her body only quivered with effort. "No, I swear it. I don't know how it happened, but I no longer feel anything for Napoleon." She shuddered. "He made me adore him. I—" She shuddered again, and then she was weeping, sobs that wracked her body with their intensity.

Jennet, feeling uncomfortable, watched her companions. Fosse and Whitteney would not meet anyone's eyes, and Sadler was for once impassive. Corwin wore the ferocious expression that Jennet now knew concealed his discomfort. Veronique seemed confused the way anyone who had not understood that conversation might. She caught Jennet's eye and said, "What has happened?"

"She hit her head, and—" Belatedly, Jennet remembered Veronique knew the truth. "I removed Napoleon's Coercion," she said in a low voice, conscious that Fosse, who stood nearby, spoke a little French and might understand her words. "She says she is no longer Coerced, and they naturally do not believe her."

"Oh." Veronique again looked at the sobbing Lady Ashford. "Tell them I can know if she is yet Coerced."

"You should not lie for me," Jennet protested.

"It is no lie. If she still feels love for Napoleon, my Discernment will know." Veronique knelt beside Lady Ashford and put a hand on her shaking shoulder.

"Stay back, Mrs. Appleton, she is dangerous," Falconer said. "Tell her, Graeme."

"She says she can Discern if Lady Ashford is telling the truth." Jennet took a step closer. "It is worth the risk, sir."

Falconer hesitated. Then he stood and took a step back. "We should interrogate the countess, at any rate. Can Mrs. Appleton tell if someone is lying even if she does not speak their language?"

Jennet relayed this. Veronique nodded. "The lie is in the emotions, not the speech," she said.

"She says you may ask," Jennet said. "But, sir, I do not know if Lady Ashford can hear you. Her weeping seems real."

"Then let us discover if she is still Coerced." Falconer nodded at Veronique.

Veronique's hand closed more tightly on Lady Ashford's shoulder. "She feels profound sorrow and guilt," she told Jennet, "and a deep shame I do not understand. But there is nothing that suggests love for Napoleon." Veronique gasped then, and jerked her hand away for a moment. "I beg your pardon, it is just that when I said his name, I felt her revulsion. She is definitely no longer Coerced."

Jennet repeated this in English, making the others burst out in exclamations of surprise and disbelief. "Her head injury must have done something to break her free," Falconer said, shutting the rest of them up. "Still, I have no wish to be fooled." He knelt beside Lady Ashford and put his hand on her other shoulder. "Lady Ashford, collect yourself, please. I have questions."

Lady Ashford's sobs diminished. Soon, she wiped tears from her eyes and again made the attempt to sit up. Falconer did not act dismayed when she failed. "Did you communicate our position to Napoleon's troops?" he asked.

Lady Ashford began to nod, winced in pain, and said, "I did. I identified you when I flew past earlier, and I immediately returned to the battalion south of here to warn them to stop searching south of Saint-Quentin and proceed north." Tears filled her eyes again. "I believed it was the right thing to do."

Falconer looked at Veronique. Veronique nodded. "How far is the battalion?" Falconer asked.

"A day's march, perhaps a little more. But if they pursue a forced march, they will be upon you in much less time. Please, help me sit."

At Falconer's glance, Veronique nodded a second time. Falconer put an arm beneath Lady Ashford's shoulders and lifted. Lady Ashford let out a cry of pain and shut her eyes, but she managed to remain upright.

"Lady Ashford, how far are we from the British Army?" Falconer said. He wore again the haughty expression Jennet had not seen in weeks, the one she now suspected concealed feelings of dismay he did not want revealed.

"I am not certain. I did not Fly that far north, for fear of being captured." Her final words were choked as she clapped a hand over her mouth and convulsed. She rolled onto hands and knees and vomited. Jennet let out a hiss of dismay. Vomiting was a not uncommon reaction to realizing one had been Coerced, but she did not believe that was the case here.

"Sir," she said in a low voice, "she hit her head very hard, and I wonder if she has not cracked her skull."

"I suspect as much, Graeme," Falconer replied in the same low tones. "Whitteney, are you capable of walking? The cart cannot hold three."

"I can walk all day if need be," Whitteney said. His grip on his walking stick tightened.

"Bind her wound, and then help her into the cart," Falconer said loudly. "We must travel as fast as possible. If we can outpace our pursuit by one more day, they will be unable to follow farther without giving away the very information Napoleon wishes to prevent us bringing."

"I cannot Fly," Lady Ashford panted. Her head hung low, and her arms shook with the effort of supporting her body. "I do not believe I can even Move anything."

"That seems obvious. You will ride, but stay sitting up. Falling asleep could prove fatal to one in your condition." Falconer stood and stared back down the road south as if he could see the approaching soldiers.

Whitteney gestured to Corwin. "Help me get this coat off her," he said. Jennet hovered nearby as they bundled Lady Ashford out of the heavy coat, feeling inappropriately guilty at having caused the wound in the woman's side.

"How can I help?" she asked.

Whitteney glanced up at her. "Bring one of the blankets, and then help Sadler and Fosse rearrange the cart to lighten the load. And do not look so stricken. You saved her from Coercion."

A jolt of fear shot through Jennet before she realized he meant by indirectly causing the blow to Lady Ashford's head. She hurried away to find a blanket.

While Whitteney cut the blanket into strips, Jennet worked feverishly fast to make space in the tiny cart. She and Fosse and Sadler dumped the contents of boxes into the cart and then discarded the boxes, used the sacks of grain to make a support to keep Lady Ashford upright, and shoved the rifles even farther to one side. Jennet deposited the rifle she held atop the stack without concealing it. There was no point. She wondered if they ought to resume their uniforms, now that Lady Ashford was no longer an aerial threat, but that would be yet another delay, and they already had many of those.

Eventually, though, Fosse and Corwin carried Lady Ashford to the cart, and Veronique got in beside her and settled William on her lap. Falconer snapped the reins, and Suleiman stepped out.

They walked in silence, the creaking of the wheels the only sound. Jennet kept an eye on Whitteney, who limped along in front of her but did not appear in danger of falling or collapse. From her position at the rear she had a clear sight of Lady Ashford, who seemed to be remaining upright solely thanks to the bags they had packed around her. Her face was pale and yet damp from beads of sweat clinging to her hairline, she kept her eyes closed, and her chest moved perceptibly with her breathing.

She looked so unwell it worried Jennet. The wound from the rifle ball had been bloody but not deep, and Jennet did not believe it could affect her so profoundly. The head wound, on the other hand, was a problem; head wounds could kill even if they did not appear severe, and though Whitteney had washed and bandaged the cut, the swelling had not gone down.

The longer they walked, the worse Jennet felt. She repeated to herself what she had rehearsed silently after Lady Ashford's fall: they had not known the countess had already reported their location to the enemy, stopping her had been essential, and Jennet had been the only one in a position to do so. But she could have shot Lady Ashford before she took to the air, had she not been worried about Falconer, and had she not foolishly demanded Lady Ashford release him. Even her knowledge that it was a fool's errand to play the might-have-been game did not stop her telling herself that this was her fault.

When they stopped to rest and water Suleiman and eat something, Falconer leaned over the wagon's side to examine Lady Ashford. "Look at me," he demanded. Lady Ashford turned her exhausted gaze on him. "Is my image doubled?" he asked.

"Yes, doubled and tripled at times," Lady Ashford said. "And my head hurts, and I do not believe I should eat, for I would only expel the food, I am so nauseated."

Falconer's lips thinned into a taut, white line, but he said nothing. He pulled one of the water canteens out of the tightly-packed mess and held it to her lips. "You must try to drink, at least."

Lady Ashford swallowed twice and then pushed the canteen away. "That helps," she said. "I would like to lie down."

"That is not safe," Falconer said, but more gently than he had yet

BEGUILING BIRTHRIGHT

addressed her. "Rest as you may, and when we reach a city, we will see about finding you a doctor."

He turned and walked past Jennet, back down the road. Impulsively, Jennet followed him. "She is bad off, isn't she, sir?"

"She is, but I will not have you take the blame for that," Falconer said grimly. "You stopped her aiding the enemy further, and you saved her from her Coercion. You made the best decision you could."

That did not make Jennet feel much better, though his reassurance was welcome. "But she might die."

Falconer nodded. "She might."

"Why do you not like her?" Jennet asked, wishing to change the subject.

She had not realized how impertinent that was until Falconer gave her a very wry look. "And what makes you believe I dislike Lady Ashford?"

Jennet swallowed and decided to forge ahead. "You are curt with her, and have been in the past, before all this happened. She seems a kind woman, and to my knowledge has never done anything to you. But you seem impatient when you must deal with her."

Falconer shook his head. "You're impertinent, Graeme. And far too observant." He let out a sigh. "Lady Ashford may well have an estimable character, but she also believes because I am attractive, I am available for her flirtation. I dislike being viewed as a thing."

"Oh." Jennet was ashamed of how she had so often watched the lieutenant and admired his beauty. "But you—I apologize, but might you not Shape yourself to be less beautiful? Or is that wrong, that you should be expected to do so simply to avoid that sort of attention?"

"It *is* wrong." Falconer spoke with such vehemence Jennet was taken aback. "I do not see why I should disfigure myself to avoid unwanted attention. And it is a foolish quibble, to dislike an aspect of myself that benefits me so greatly. As if I am saying 'pity me, I am too handsome for words!'"

Jennet laughed, partly in amusement and partly because he had sounded more like himself then. "I did not believe men ever needed to deflect unwanted attention."

"Possibly it is my own quirk. After all, I did not choose this Shape, and I imagine those who do Shape themselves beautiful know what attention

245

they will receive." Falconer sighed. "Go and eat, Graeme, and you might pray that we reach a city soon."

Jennet nodded and returned to the cart.

She finished eating as they walked, tossing apricot pits into the grassy verge. Lady Ashford's appearance had not changed. Tentatively, for she had never prayed while walking, Jennet composed herself and bowed her head. *Papa, she is dying, and it may be my fault. I do not know how much guilt is mine, and it seems indulgent to pray for forgiveness when her life is at risk and she needs the prayers more than I. Please, let us find one who can help her, and find that person before it is too late. Bring us to a city and not a village. Let us outrun our pursuit. Thank you.*

The prayer did not ease her heart, but it changed her perspective. They were exerting themselves to their utmost, and had done everything they could to care for Lady Ashford, and now they traveled as fast as possible toward, she hoped, a city. The rest was in God's hands, and she should not try to change the Omnipotent mind.

CHAPTER 25

IN WHICH AN EXTRAORDINARY SHAPER MAKES AN EXTRAORDINARY DEMAND

They rested again in the late afternoon. Suleiman looked weary despite how much of the unnecessary load they had shed, and Jennet added his welfare to the silent prayers she said now and then. She glanced at her companions, not wishing them to know of her regard; they all looked tired, especially Whitteney, who snapped at anyone who inquired after his health. Despite this, Jennet suspected, if they felt as she did, that it was emotional weariness rather than physical.

But the weariness was short-lived. Only minutes after their last rest, Corwin called out, "There's a city ahead!"

Everyone shifted, shielding their eyes to see ahead. Jennet saw nothing from her position, but knowing the city was there cheered her tremendously.

They hurried faster now, even Suleiman, and the city grew gradually larger in their sights. Soon enough, there were farmhouses at long intervals, and then cottages closer together, and then the cottages became narrow buildings built close together, and with that, they were within the city. It was nearly evening, and the streets were not as thronged with traffic as they would have been earlier; most of the wagons and carts were headed back the way Jennet and her companions had come.

Jennet stared at the buildings that were three and even four stories tall, which shared common walls but whose differing construction and paint showed clearly where one left off and another began. Their windows were as tall and narrow as the buildings themselves, but they were paned with glass, giving the city a very prosperous look even in the dimness. The occasional sign advertised shops, though since the signs bore only surnames, Jennet had no idea what was on offer within.

Falconer steered the cart to one side, out of the flow of traffic, and said, "Graeme, to me."

Jennet hurried forward, dodging a couple of men who were not inclined to get out of her way. Suppressing her annoyance at their arrogance, she said, "Sir?"

"We need an inn, and we need a doctor," Falconer said. "I need you to ask around for those things. Sadler, go with him. I do not like the look of some of these men."

Jennet's annoyance surged. He had promised he would not treat her like a fainting maiden. Then she surveyed the crowd, and saw how many of its members were large, rough-looking men who also did not make way for anyone, and decided he might have a point. "We'll hurry, sir," she said. Then, after a moment's hesitation, added, "Will a doctor be enough, sir?"

"It will have to be." Falconer looked grim again. "I imagine there is little chance of finding an Extraordinary Shaper here, whatever the size of the city. Hurry, Ned."

Jennet plunged into the crowd, Sadler at her heels.

She soon discovered there was no shortage of individuals willing to point her in the direction of an inn. But no one seemed to know the direction of a doctor, and more frighteningly, a few people did not understand what she was asking for. There had to be a doctor somewhere in this town!

Finally, she and Sadler returned to the cart. "We should find lodging, and perhaps the innkeeper will know the information we need," she said.

Falconer nodded. "Lead the way, then."

The inn Jennet chose was on a side street, narrow and with stone arches twined with ivy rearing above the street every ten yards. It was narrower a street than in Rheims, and it worried her that there was no room for the cart to turn around should that become necessary.

To Sadler, who still walked beside her, she said, "I cannot believe I ever considered Rheims' streets narrow. If we are attacked, we will be like rats in a trap."

"Aye, as will our attackers," Sadler said with a grin. "No room for proper sword work at all. We may be reduced to battering at them with tooth and nail."

Jennet glared at him. "I do not see how you can feel such levity when we are still in danger. We know nothing of this town, and I see far fewer banners hailing France's king than I would like."

"My alertness is not lessened by my cheery face, Ned." Sadler nodded in the direction of an elderly man who approached them and then passed by without meeting their eyes. "I have been watching every man who passes us, making note of what they looked at. Almost every one of them watched the lieutenant and the horse, but none of them counted the rest of us or examined the cart for its load the way someone might who intended to report the presence of enemy soldiers. We should not be complacent, but I believe we're in no immediate danger."

Jennet watched the next man who approached and saw Sadler was correct. "You are not as frivolous as you would have us think," she said with a smile.

"Aye, and that's a secret you ought keep to yourself," Sadler retorted, jabbing Jennet in the ribs with his elbow.

When they reached the inn, Jennet regretted choosing it; it looked very small, possibly too small to admit all of them. But it was quiet, and the cobbles in front of it were clean of waste and dirt, and Falconer did not exhibit any dissatisfaction with her choice. He drove the cart into the small stable yard, and Jennet negotiated with the stable hand for the use of a stall for Suleiman and a place to stow the cart.

When she finished convincing the man not to charge them an exorbitant rate—and did so without resorting to Coercion, which elated her—she was alone in the yard. There was no door into the inn on this side, so she returned to the front door, blackened oak that looked blacker against the white stone wall of the inn, and hurried in search of her companions.

The tap room resembled so many French houses she had seen in the early days in France, before the General Order had forbidden billeting soldiers in civilian houses, for a moment she was transported back to the previous winter. Black beams the color of the front door crisscrossed the ceiling, which was a grimy white from years, possibly centuries, of smoke from the fireplace along one wall. Whatever had caused the fire to smoke had apparently been repaired, for it drew perfectly now, and Jennet smelled the crisp hot odor of flames and rich, garlicky soup.

Three trestle tables crowded the floor, surely too many for this tiny inn. None of them were occupied despite the hour. Jennet's worries about having led the others astray resurfaced. She crossed the room to where a man stood behind a much-worn slab of polished oak and said in French, "Sir, my friends, the English—where are they?"

The man jerked his head in the direction of the stairs, which were of heavy stone and rose up only five steps before sharply turning and ascending into darkness. Jennet nodded. "Thank you, sir, and did they ask you for the direction of a doctor?"

The man shrugged. "There was one spoke a little French, but he said only that they needed room. Someone ill?"

"A head injury. Please, sir, we are very concerned for her. Do you know of anyone at all? A doctor, or a surgeon, or...but there must not be an Extraordinary Shaper."

"An Extraordinary Shaper?" The man snorted derisively. "Of course there is. Do you imagine us so provincial? There is Madame Durand, who lives on Tournay Street. But she does not like foreigners."

Jennet could not imagine an Extraordinary Shaper who would let a dislike of foreigners interfere with Healing someone. "Oh, sir, that is good news! Can you direct me to her?"

"It will do you no good, but you may try." The man rattled off a series of directions Jennet made him repeat more slowly. When she was sure she had them memorized, she darted for the door.

"Please, if you would be so kind, tell them where I have gone, and that I will return soon," she said. The man just grunted. Jennet chose to take it as a "yes."

She hurried off in the growing darkness, counting turns and looking for landmarks. At the sign of the black boar's head, she turned right and hurried on, third left, second right, fourth right.

She had expected something to indicate an Extraordinary Shaper's home and was surprised to find only a discreet brass plaque with the name DURAND etched on it. She knocked on the door, as politely as she could manage given how tumultuous her feelings were. She would find someone to save Lady Ashford, and that would not be a death on her conscience.

The door opened. A man in evening wear just like an English butler or steward filled the doorway, staring down at her. "Yes?"

"Ah, sir, I seek Madame Durand, is she in?"

"Madame Durand is not at home to urchins," the man said, and began to shut the door.

Jennet grabbed hold of his emotions and wrenched him abruptly from supercilious pride to curiosity without touching the intervening steps. She did not believe she could get away with making him fond of her. "I have an intriguing proposition for her, and a chance to perform a Healing."

The door swung open again. "Truly?" The man's curiosity echoed in his voice. "What proposition?"

"It is for Madame Durand's ears alone," Jennet said. "*You* understand." She nudged him back in the direction of pride, this time pride that he had a position of responsibility in an Extraordinary Shaper's household.

"Pray, enter, and I will bring your request to Madame." The man bowed slightly. Jennet walked past him into the house.

The house was one of the narrow ones Jennet had first observed, but its entry was brightly lit by several shielded candles and a chandelier perfectly sized to fit the room. The light, and the brightness of the white walls, made the room seem less narrow. Stairs stained a warm chestnut filled most of the space, with the hall extending farther into the house and out of sight. Had Jennet not been anxious, she would have liked the house very much. It was the sort of place that made one feel instantly at home despite its emptiness.

The butler, or steward, said, "Wait here, sir," and ascended the stairs. Jennet waited. She smelled nothing but the faint hint of furniture polish, no smells of cooking supper, which was as well because she was hungry and the smell of food would have agitated her empty stomach.

Finally, the man returned. "If sir will follow me," he said, and Jennet followed him up the stairs and around a corner into a drawing room that was as unwelcoming as the foyer had been friendly. It was stuffed with étagères and cabinets groaning under the weight of more knick-knacks than Jennet had believed existed in the world. Her aunt was fond of china figurines, and her drawing room in Edinburgh overflowed with them, but this collection put her aunt's to shame. Everywhere Jennet turned, she stood in danger of knocking something over.

"Interesting," a woman said. "Gervais, you may leave us."

The man bowed and let himself out, shutting the door behind him.

Jennet regarded the speaker. She was slim and beautiful, though far from young; Jennet put her age at nearer sixty than fifty. She wore a rose satin gown with a deep neckline, and her white hair was piled high atop her head. Around her neck she wore a string of diamonds from which fat pearls depended at intervals, and a diamond pin gathered up the folds of her gown at her breast. She sat, or rather perched, on a chair that looked too small for a person, leaning forward to examine Jennet.

"I don't like lies," the woman, Madame Durand, said. "Why did you tell Gervais you were a boy?"

Jennet chose not to react with surprise. "I didn't, madame. He drew that conclusion himself."

"But you dress in a masculine manner, which implies you wish for people to make that assumption." Madame Durand's eyes narrowed. "I ask again, why is that? Are you not proud of how God made you?"

Her heart sinking, Jennet said, "I wished to be a soldier, and women cannot do that. So I pass as male." She was starting to understand what the innkeeper had meant about her not having a chance with Madame Durand. The woman was clearly sure of herself and of how the world ought to run, and had no interest in kindness or charity.

"I see. And when you told Gervais you had an 'intriguing proposition' for me, that, too, was a lie?"

"No, madame. That is, I believe it to be a challenge, but perhaps you will not feel the same. I apologize for wasting your time." Jennet turned to go. If she were fast, she might yet locate a doctor who would be willing to treat an Englishwoman.

Madame Durand ran a thin finger over the diamonds of her brooch. It had a strange shape, curved at the top and with a small gold cross at the bottom. "I decide what is a waste of my time," she said. "What is this challenge?"

It was not as if Jennet had not already lost time. "I have a companion, an Extraordinary Mover, who fell from a great height and hit her head. She complains of doubled vision and nausea and cannot use her talent. I believe her skull is cracked and her brain is swelling. That is not a thing anyone but an Extraordinary Shaper can treat. I hoped you would be willing."

"And what will I get out of this in return?" Madame Durand smiled, not widely, but Jennet had no trouble seeing it as the smile of a predator.

"I had not considered that far. She is English, and perhaps you choose not to treat foreigners," Jennet said.

"I will treat anyone so long as they have the right amount of money." Madame Durand gestured with a pale hand. "It is how I live as I do. Have you money?"

Jennet mentally assessed her remaining coin. "I have some. I do not know what you would consider enough."

Madame Durand said, "I will accept five hundred francs."

Jennet blanched. She did not have that much, unless she took extraordinary action. "I have it," she declared. "You save my friend's life, and I will pay what you require." She carefully did not use the word *demand*, in case Madame Durand was insulted and refused to help, after all.

Madame Durand rose. "Tell me where this Extraordinary Mover is."

Jennet's mind briefly blanked as she could not recall the inn's name, only the many turns that had brought her from it. "It is the Moon and Stars Inn," she finally said.

Madame Durand's expression did not change. "I have never heard of it, but my driver will know. I pay him to know every address in Cambray. Go, and I will follow shortly. And do not think to cheat me. I will not be mocked."

Jennet gabbled thanks and hurried away, down the stairs and outside. She stood for a moment, breathing as heavily as if she had run much farther than the stairs. Five hundred francs. She had almost two-thirds that sum.

Slowly, she reached inside her shirt and removed her father's silver pocket watch. It was worth at least two hundred francs, possibly more. And it was all she had left of her father. Her hand closed over it more tightly. Her father's memory, set against a woman's life. It should not be a difficult decision, but it was all she had.

Angrily, she thrust it back within her shirt and took off running. Perhaps Lady Ashford was already dead, and Jennet would not need to make the decision. She hated herself for even considering the possibility.

Back at the inn, she burst through the age-blackened door to find Fosse and Whitteney at one of the trestle tables. "Where have you been?" Fosse demanded. "Lieutenant was fair ready to scour the town for you, he was that upset."

"I found an Extraordinary Shaper," Jennet gasped. "Please, tell me it is not too late."

"Lady Ashford lives still," Whitteney said. He shifted his stick to make room on the bench. "Sit, Ned. You look done in."

Jennet shook her head. "I must tell the others to expect her—excuse me—they are upstairs?"

With the assurance that they were, Jennet bounded up the stone steps into a short hallway whose floorboards creaked loudly enough to wake anyone sleeping beyond its six doors. One of the doors stood open, and light and voices came from within. Jennet pushed the door open all the way.

The room was not large, and it was the smaller for the bed within. Lady Ashford sat with her back against the headboard. In the candlelight, her color was better, but her eyes remained closed and her head lolled as if she could barely support it. Veronique sat on the edge of the bed, nursing William. Her attention, however, was not on the babe but on Lady Ashford.

Corwin and Sadler stood just inside the door, talking in low voices. "Ned," Sadler said, serious for once. "You should not disappear like that. Go tell the lieutenant you're here before he sets us to searching this city for you."

"It is only that I found an Extraordinary Shaper that I left. She will be here soon. I hope it is not too late." Jennet glanced at Lady Ashford again.

"For an Extraordinary Shaper, it's not too late unless it's death," Corwin said. His frown made him look murderous, but his voice was compassionate. "We will watch her. Go, Ned."

Jennet returned to the hall and surveyed the closed doors. Only one of them had light coming from beneath it. She rapped lightly on the door. "Sir, it's Ned Graeme."

The door sprang open instantly. "Thank God," Falconer said. "Never do that again."

"I was perfectly safe," Jennet said, annoyed.

"You disappeared into a strange city we know almost nothing of." Falconer drew Jennet into the room and shut the door. "This is not about your sex, Graeme. I would say the same to any man under my command. Having come so far, I am disinclined to lose any of you on the doorstep of victory, so to speak."

Jennet's annoyance disappeared. "My apologies, sir. My wish to find a doctor made me reckless. But I found an Extraordinary Shaper, sir and she will be here soon. And now I must leave again."

"Leave? Why?"

Jennet drew in a breath to calm herself, though she felt anything but. "The lady's price is five hundred francs. I must arrange for her payment."

Falconer grabbed Jennet's arm. "What do you mean? I am sure we don't have that much remaining."

Jennet found she could not meet his eyes. "There is something I can sell to make up the difference. But I must hurry before everything is closed."

"Something you can sell?" Falconer looked puzzled for a moment. Then his eyes narrowed, and he swore, a blistering word that made even Jennet the hardened soldier blush. "I won't have you sacrificing anything of yours, not while I am still in command," he said. "You have already given up most of your savings, and you are not to give more. Don't imagine I don't know what you have in mind."

"It's mine, sir, and Lady Ashford's life is more important." Jennet's hand closed on the watch again and drew it out. "It is worth quite a lot, I imagine."

Falconer took it from her hand and opened it, making her protest. "'J.G.,'" he read off the inside of the case. "Who is J.G.?"

Jennet swallowed. "My father, sir. John Graeme."

"You are not to sell this," Falconer said. "Not for any reason. I will find the money, not you. It is my responsibility."

"You cannot make me do anything," Jennet retorted, forgetting for the moment he was her superior officer, "and it is my fault she is injured."

"I am an officer, and that makes this my responsibility, regardless of the proximate cause." Falconer pressed the watch into her hand and closed her fingers over it. "Graeme, you will regret losing this for the rest of your life. I am certain of it. Now, what coin have we left?"

After collecting what remained in the bottom of her pack, and slitting the seams of her jacket to retrieve the rest of her savings, Jennet was surprised to find she had the equivalent of more than four hundred francs. It was not enough, but it was closer than she had hoped. She gathered it into a purse and handed it to Falconer. "But how——" she began.

Someone rapped on the door, and Sadler poked his head in. "Sir, the Extraordinary Shaper is here."

Jennet trailed behind Falconer as he hurried down the stairs to greet Madame Durand. The Extraordinary Shaper was enveloped in a fur-trimmed pelisse of emerald wool over the silk gown and had added diamond ear-drops to her ensemble. She examined the tap room with curiosity; it was likely, Jennet guessed, that she had never seen one before. "Show me the patient," she said.

Jennet hung back, feeling superstitiously that Madame Durand could read their insufficient funds on her skin and would refuse even to look at Lady Ashford. She waited in the doorway as Madame Durand removed her pelisse and took Lady Ashford's wrist between her thumb and forefinger. The silence stretched out so long Jennet wanted to scream. Finally, Madame Durand said, in English, "I will take payment now. Five hundred francs."

"We have four hundred and seventeen francs," Falconer said. He was back to looking haughty. "That will have to be sufficient."

Madame Durand dropped Lady Ashford's hand. "I told your...young man...my fee. He assured me you could pay. I dislike being lied to."

"He believed we had the money. It was no lie," Falconer said. "Four hundred and seventeen francs is a princely sum."

"It is. It is also eighty-three francs short of what I require." Madame Durand smiled, an expression even more arrogant than Falconer's, and stood. Her diamond brooch winked in the low light. "Excuse me, gentlemen. And thank God you have enough there for a funeral."

"You won't save a life because we can't pay?" Sadler burst out. "Of all the—"

"Enough, Mr. Sadler," Falconer said. "Madame, I see I cannot convince you. Pray, permit me to escort you out. The rest of you, remain here."

Jennet stepped hastily aside as Madame Durand and Falconer exited. Neither of them paid her any attention. When they were gone, she shut the door and leaned against it with her eyes closed. *Myfaultmyfaultmyfault* ran a mocking chorus through her head. And to think she had the means to save Lady Ashford, if only Falconer had not convinced her to keep the watch!

Corwin touched Lady Ashford's forehead. "She's burning up," he said. "Like as not it won't be long now."

Jennet heard the floorboards creak and moved in time not to be shoved by the door opening. "Sir, it's—"

Madame Durand sailed across the room and sank gracefully onto Lady Ashford's bed. "Out. All of you. I do not need an audience for this Healing," she commanded.

Jennet found herself in the hallway with the others without quite knowing how she had got there. She and Sadler stared at one another. "What in the hell was that?" he said.

"Madame Durand changed her mind," Falconer said.

Now all of them except Veronique stared at him; Veronique was still looking at the closed door and likely had not understood his words in English. "She changed her mind, sir?" Jennet said. "Just like that?"

"I convinced her of the benefits of generosity," Falconer said.

"With all due respect, sir, I say you are lying," Jennet said. "What did you do to convince her?"

Falconer turned his haughty look upon her. "Never accuse your commanding officer of lying, Graeme. And I said nothing out of the ordinary. Perhaps she has untapped reserves of the milk of human kindness."

"You know that's not true, sir, that woman has the heart of a snake," Sadler said.

"Very well, I suppose you are correct. Shall we have something to eat? And I daresay I could use a glass of wine, it has been a very long day. Private Sadler, take a turn at watch in the yard. I would hate to be the victim of theft." Falconer turned and descended the stairs without another word.

"What is wrong? Will that woman not treat Lady Ashford?" Veronique asked.

Jennet relayed what had happened, leaving out only that she was certain Falconer was lying. He had done something to change Madame Durand's mind, something he refused to admit to. Something they would all object to if they knew the truth.

"It is a relief," Veronique said. "For her to die would be an ill omen for the rest of our journey."

Jennet nodded. She cast one backward glance at Lady Ashford's door before descending the stairs. Perhaps Falconer had a valuable possession Madame Durand had been willing to accept, or he had made her a promise drawn on his family's wealth. But neither of those things was embarrassing or worth lying about. No, he had sacrificed something, and Jennet intended to ferret out what that was. However he tried to conceal it.

CHAPTER 26

IN WHICH A JOURNEY ENDS IN AN UNEXPECTED CHALLENGE

Thshey ate together in silence, roast chicken and boiled root vegetables and crusty bread too fine for the establishment. Jennet, seated next to Falconer, shot him covert glances from time to time, but he ate completely unselfconsciously, not even displaying the discomfort he might feel at eating with the men. If she could get him alone, she might winkle the truth out of him, though she no longer felt as confident as she had in the hall upstairs. Falconer was good at keeping secrets, as she well knew; he had never so much as hinted to the others that she was female. But she could not be comfortable until she knew what he had sacrificed.

Madame Durand had not come downstairs by the time even Fosse, who despite his lanky figure ate enough for two men, had finished his meal. Jennet watched Falconer again, this time openly. He held a glass of wine casually between finger and thumb and sipped occasionally, his attention fixed on the fire.

Jennet shifted uncomfortably. "Sir, should we do something? Is it a bad sign, that Madame Durand is still upstairs?"

Falconer glanced her way, then returned his attention to the fire. "Shaping someone whole, particularly someone with a head injury, takes time, Graeme. We will not rush Madame Durand."

"Particularly since she did not wish to help us," Jennet persisted. "Sir, what did you—"

"Another glass of wine, I believe," Falconer said. He rose from his seat and picked up the bottle, filled his glass, and walked away. Jennet's annoyance grew. He had to know his behavior only made them all more curious. On a whim, she assessed his emotions; he felt the satisfaction of having eaten a good meal, as well as the deeper satisfaction of having accomplished something difficult. Neither of which told her anything.

Soft footsteps sounded on the stairs, and Madame Durand appeared. She was fastening her pelisse around her shoulders so it obscured all her glittering jewelry and much of her silk gown. "She will live," she said. "But with an injury such as that, there is a chance of inflaming the brain a second time. She should rest, and make limited use of her talent, to be safe. I make no guarantees if she chooses to ignore these instructions."

Falconer set down bottle and glass. "You have our gratitude," he said, bowing.

Madame Durand did not extend her hand to him. She twitched the pelisse to cover her bosom more fully. "Safe travels to you, if only because I hope never to see you again."

Falconer bowed again, smiling pleasantly. Madame Durand gazed at each of them in turn. When her eyes lit on Jennet, they narrowed, but she said nothing. Then she swept out of the tap room, letting the door close loudly behind her.

"Sir, what did you do to her?" Sadler asked, rather plaintively.

"I did nothing," Falconer said. "What do you imagine—that I threatened her with violence? I would never behave in such a dishonorable manner toward anyone, not even a despicable woman such as she is. And now I will finish my wine, and speak with Lady Ashford if she is awake, and then take to my bed."

Jennet decided not to hover. He might suspect she had not given up on interrogating him, and leaving now might diminish those suspicions. So she climbed the stairs to Lady Ashford's room.

Lady Ashford was lying down, but not sleeping; her eyes were clear and alert and turned on Jennet when she entered. "Ah, it's you," she said with a smile. "I ought to hate you for doing this to me, but this is how war goes. And—" Her smile fell away. "I thank you for indirectly saving me from Coercion. I cannot believe I did not realize I was enthralled."

"No one ever does—that is, so I have heard." Jennet sat where Veronique had sat earlier. "I am glad to see you restored."

Lady Ashford touched her head where the wound had been, then looked at her fingers as if expecting to see blood. "The Extraordinary Shaper Healed my side as well. I am grateful you are not a better shot, or we might not now be having this conversation."

"Oh, I am an excellent shot," Jennet retorted, "unless you believe it pure luck I wounded you in a non-lethal way that nevertheless brought you out of the sky."

Lady Ashford's eyes widened. Then she laughed. "I had not considered that. You are correct, that was first-class shooting." She sat up so she was propped on her elbow. "For that, and for...the other thing...I am in your debt. Call on me at any time, for anything, and I will do everything in my power to assist you."

Jennet felt uncomfortable. "Lady Ashford—"

"My name is Clemency," Lady Ashford said. "I will not ask your true name, for I am sure you prefer your privacy. But when we are alone, I would prefer you use my given name."

That made Jennet even more uncomfortable. "Clemency, you need not feel yourself indebted to me, truly you need not. It is only what I would have done for anyone."

"I was Coerced to a man's bed," Clemency said. "One of Napoleon's generals."

Jennet gaped. "I—you do not need to tell me anything, that is—"

"Napoleon made me adore him, and he made me love the man he chose," Clemency continued. "I was that man's reward. Napoleon filled me with desire for him, and I—I have never lain with a man, not before now, and Napoleon made me believe it was right and natural. And even as I remember that now with revulsion, there is a part of me that remembers what it was like to love that stranger. You saved me from that nightmare. Do you imagine there is *anything* I would not do for you?" Tears rolled down her cheeks she made no move to brush away.

Jennet remembered Coercing Clemency out of Napoleon's unnatural affection, how there had been love as well as adoration in the Extraordinary Mover's heart. She had removed both without considering why Napoleon would have Coerced both emotions when only one was necessary to keep Clemency in thrall. Jennet's discomfort faded, replaced by an aching sympathy and, more distantly, fury that anyone might believe himself entitled to treat a woman so. "I did not realize. I assure you no one will think the worse of you, but do not—it is private, yes?"

"I intend to tell no one, but I believed you deserved to know the extent to which you have saved me." Clemency lay back and wiped her eyes. "I should sleep, but in the morning, I will Fly to find the Army. They must know of Napoleon's advance."

"The Extraordinary Shaper said you were not to Fly, not if you wish to remain well."

Clemency grinned, a roguish expression that made her seem once more the woman Jennet remembered making a wagon soar through the air. "I have not reached the rank I have by caring for my own well-being. And I do not believe your small company has scouted out how far Napoleon's forces have come. I am more than willing to risk myself for the sake of defeating him."

Jennet nodded. "Is there anything you need?"

"Just sleep. But thank you."

Jennet rose and let herself out, nearly running into Falconer as she did. "I told her of Madame Durand's instructions, and she wishes to sleep," Jennet said in a low voice.

"Then I shall not disturb her," Falconer said. He stepped back to let Jennet exit fully and close the door behind her. "I thought to provide you with a room of your own," he said, "but I fear Madame Durand's fee has put us in straitened circumstances. We can barely afford the four rooms we require."

"I don't mind, sir."

They entered the room Jennet had found him in earlier, where Jennet discovered her pack had already been stowed. She removed her boots, then took her uniform jacket from her pack and spread it out over the end of the bed. It was terribly wrinkled and smelled musty even from only three days in the same space as her dirty socks, but perhaps a night's airing would help.

On the other side of the bed, Falconer had set his own boots aside and was stretching. "I hope tomorrow our journey will be over," he said with a yawn.

"Lady Ashford said she would Fly ahead of us and take word." Jennet yawned in tandem with him.

"Did you not tell her Madame Durand said that was dangerous?"

"Lady Ashford is not the sort of woman who cares about not endangering herself in a noble cause." Jennet nudged one boot with her toe, aligning it more perfectly with the other.

"I suppose that's true." Falconer lay back under the blanket and closed his eyes. "Douse the light, would you, Graeme?"

Jennet walked around to his side of the bed and stood there with her arms crossed over her chest. "How did you convince Madame Durand to Heal Lady Ashford?"

Falconer raised an eyebrow, but his eyes did not open. "I did nothing to her, Graeme. Go to sleep."

"You said something," Jennet persisted, "and whatever it was, you wish us not to know. Was it something despicable?"

"It was not. Graeme—"

"Then it was embarrassing. Or—but I do not believe it was dishonorable. Not from you, sir."

One eye opened. "I do not intend to share the details with you, Graeme. Now, sleep."

"Did you give her something valuable? Or was it a promise of aid, or money?"

The other eye opened. Falconer glared at her. "Go to bed, and that is an order, Graeme."

"Sir, I can keep this up all night."

Falconer sat up. "Do I have to—oh, hell, I cannot have you flogged, can I?"

"No, sir." Jennet leaned forward. "Please, sir. Whatever you did, it spared me giving up all I have left of my family. I cannot bear not knowing."

With a sigh, Falconer swung his legs around to sit facing Jennet. "What I say now, you can never reveal, or I will be forsworn. Understood?"

Jennet nodded.

His eyes narrowed. "Did you notice Madame Durand's jewelry?"

"Aye, sir. I could hardly help noticing, sir, there was a mort of it. That gaudy necklace, and her diamond ear-drops, and the pin."

"Yes. The pin. What did you make of it?"

Jennet frowned. "It had an odd shape, sir. I recall wondering if it was upside down, as it's my understanding a cross should be above and not below."

Falconer smiled. "Very observant. It was, in fact, upside down. Though with how encrusted it was with diamonds, I am not certain you realized its correct shape. It was an Imperial crown."

"But Napoleon was the Emperor. Why would she wear his symbol?" Jennet asked.

"Napoleon's rule never extended this far north and east, and these cities were not Coerced," Falconer said. "However, he had supporters throughout this area, and those supporters did not disappear when Napoleon did last year. I was with the 43rd until early this year, stationed in Marne, and the officers of the 43rd were taught to look for signs of secret supporters of the erstwhile Emperor. And one of them—" He tapped the center of his chest— "is the Imperial crown. Worn as jewelry, usually a small pin, but kept concealed until needed."

Jennet gaped. "She wore that thing openly. And it is nothing like a small, inconspicuous pin."

"My assessment of Madame Durand's character is that she is extremely confident in her social standing and her wealth, and she enjoys thumbing her nose at those around her." Falconer's smile was wicked. "But she is not so confident that she did not listen when I threatened to expose her to those in authority."

"Then, you blackmailed her." Jennet could not believe the words coming out of her mouth.

"As I said, Graeme, I did nothing." Falconer's smile deepened. "I could have gone to the mayor of Cambray and revealed the presence of a Napoleonic sympathizer. These northeastern towns take such things *very* seriously, as they are conscious of how close they came to Coercion. They are not fond of traitors, not even wealthy and talented ones. But I did not do that. And Madame Durand exercised her talent on our behalf, and I will leave in the morning, taking my dangerous knowledge with me."

"It's still blackmail, sir." Jennet immediately regretted her words, they sounded so judgmental and priggish.

Falconer's smile disappeared. "I know," he said. "You recall what I said about doing things that make you despise yourself? I have never resorted to anything so dishonorable before, but the truth is, Graeme, I do not regret it. I did what had to be done, and I will atone for it however I may."

"You should have permitted me to sell the watch," Jennet said.

The smile returned. "Now *that* would have been truly dishonorable. I can live with a little tarnish on my soul to know that your father's memento is safe." Falconer lay back and rolled on his side to face away from her. "If you have any more impertinences for me, I refuse to hear them. Lights out, Graeme, and no more snoring."

"*I* do not snore, sir," Jennet protested. "You, however, are a champion."

"How unfortunate that I do not know the Shaping that would stop it," Falconer said. "You had better fall asleep fast, then."

Jennet snuffed the candle and settled in to sleep beside him, unable to stop smiling.

CLEMENCY LEFT EARLY THE NEXT MORNING, STOPPING ONLY TO RAP ON Jennet's door to say goodbye. "I will likely not return," she told Falconer, "but I will warn them you are coming. I am glad you are soldiers and not Extraordinary Movers, or we might compete over who arrives faster."

"It matters more that the Army knows the danger," Falconer replied. "Safe journeys to you, my lady."

"I hope to see you again eventually," Clemency said, but the smile she gave him lacked the warmth Jennet remembered from her previous flirtations. Falconer bowed politely and said nothing.

Then Clemency turned to Jennet. "Remember what I said. You may call on me at any time, for anything within my power."

"Thank you," Jennet said. Her earlier annoyance with the woman over her treatment of Falconer vanished in her memory of what Clemency had confided in her.

When Clemency had gone, Jennet said, "I believe she is a nice person, sir."

Falconer shrugged. "She means no harm, and I admit she refrained from paying me those attentions I find offensive, so perhaps you are correct." He returned to the room and donned his uniform jacket. "We no longer need hide, Graeme, so get dressed, and let us make a good start."

Wearing her uniform again comforted her, like coming home after a long absence. Its weight was like armor, protecting her against all comers, and she tucked her watch safely inside, rejoicing that it was still there.

With Falconer gone, she re-wrapped the cloth binding her breasts, put on a fresh shirt, and felt altogether new and clean.

As they left Cambray, she looked at each of her companions in turn. They had all been comrades for months—well, not Veronique or Falconer, but the others—and yet this journey had brought them together in ways she could not have expected. And when it was over, that closeness would disappear. She remembered contemplating Coercing someone into reassigning her elsewhere. The idea struck her with an almost physical pain. Maybe her companions did not feel a natural friendship for her, but she cared about them in a way that had not been Coerced, and it would break her heart to leave.

Their road wound northeast, through farmland and the occasional copse of trees. The others seemed not to suffer Jennet's melancholy. Whitteney amused them by whistling bird calls so realistic they would have fooled a bird's own mother, and Fosse and Sadler traded ribald jokes Falconer laughed at and responded to with a few of his own. Even Corwin, who normally marched in silence, let out a deep chuckle now and then. It felt more like a pleasure stroll than a march, though they strode as rapidly as always. Falconer had assured them that if they did not dawdle, there was now no chance of their pursuers overtaking them. It was now only a matter of finding the Army, which should be in the vicinity of Valenciennes.

"Unless they have already moved out, of course, but we will be able to follow their path easily," Falconer had said over breakfast. The knowledge did not comfort Jennet. Regardless of whether they found the Army today or next week, the end of their comradeship was near.

It was an hour and a half after noon, by Jennet's watch, that Falconer brought Suleiman to a halt and said, "We have found them."

Jennet shielded her eyes and squinted into the distance, but saw nothing. Falconer's Shaped vision was much more acute than hers.

"They do not appear to be moving out," Falconer added. He did not sound happy.

"Is that bad, sir?" Fosse asked.

"It could mean Lady Ashford did not reach them, or that they did not take her report seriously. I would have imagined they would marshal their forces to meet Napoleon's army. But they remain in position." Falconer flicked the reins. "There is no point waiting here and wondering. We must join them if we wish to know what is afoot."

In another hour's march, Jennet could see the Army's forces, as well as the picket lines. She did not understand much of what the military did on a grand scale, but even she could see this was a typical encampment, not alive with movement the way they were when a regiment or even a company marched out. Her nerves, already on edge, tightened further. But Falconer did not seem unduly upset, so she calmed herself, wishing once more she could Coerce her own emotions.

The Army was situated at the base of a low rise, spread out like so many marching ants with tents of all sizes lined up in rows throughout. Falconer drove the cart to where the first picket line hailed him. "Lieutenant Thomas Falconer of the 3rd of the 95th," he told the corporal, "and I have urgent news for the commander. Will you direct me to him?"

"That's Major General Waldroup, sir," the corporal said, and indicated where Falconer should go. Falconer saluted him and drove on.

They were not stopped again, and it even seemed to Jennet that no one noticed them at all, not even to stare at the lieutenant's beauty. This made her even more nervous. Surely someone ought to realize they were well away from their company, if not that they had crossed half of France to bring this message to the general. Now that they were here, her earlier desires were reversed; she longed to deliver the message and be set free, so she and her friends could disappear back into a company. Even one not their own.

Finally, Falconer stopped the cart in front the spacious command tents and climbed down. To the sentry standing outside, he said, "I am Lieutenant Thomas Falconer, and I have a message for Major General Waldroup, if you would be so good as to inform him?"

The sentry nodded to his companion and ducked inside the tent. The second sentry gave no indication he noticed Falconer or any of them or even Suleiman and the cart. Jennet's nervousness grew, though Falconer looked haughty again and as calm as ever.

Presently, the tent flap moved, and a soldier emerged, saying, "You will join the general now."

To Jennet's strained nerves, the command sounded sinister, though it was nothing out of the ordinary. Falconer strode into the tent with his head held high, looking as princely as ever despite the road grime and missing shako. Jennet let the others precede her, giving Veronique a final, hopefully reassuring look.

Within the tent, three officers gathered around a map, with two soldiers standing near the door flap. The officers' attention was on Falconer, who faced a thin, white-haired man wearing both a major-general's insignia and a Speaker's knot. Major General Waldroup's skin was darkened from years of exposure to a much hotter sun than shone over France, and he looked as tough as seasoned wood. Despite being shorter than Falconer, he held himself as if he towered over the lieutenant. "Lieutenant Falconer," he said, his voice perfectly polite and more aristocratic than Jennet had expected given his appearance. "Lady Ashford told us of your approach."

"Then our message was delivered, sir," Falconer said.

"Indeed." The general sounded as if he did not actually care about the message. Jennet's nervousness turned into apprehension, though she could not imagine what danger they might be in. "Lady Ashford reported here this morning, and I sent her west, to the 33rd."

"I observed many details of the forces at Napoleon's command," Falconer continued, "and I can show you where they are positioned, if you will permit me access to your map, sir."

"That won't be necessary." The general gestured to the soldiers. "Lieutenant Falconer, I am placing you under arrest."

CHAPTER 27

IN WHICH JENNET ONCE MORE RESORTS TO SUBTERFUGE

F alconer's mouth fell open in the least controlled response Jennet
had ever seen in him. "Arrest, sir?" he said.

"For desertion," Waldroup said, as calmly as if this were a normal
conversation. "You and these men were reported missing nine days ago,
presumed deserted. You will turn your sword over to me, lieutenant, and give
me your parole that you will remain confined pending your court-martial. You
five—" He waved in their direction— "will also submit to confinement."

"Sir," Falconer said, visibly regaining control, "this is a mistake. The 3rd
was Coerced by Napoleon nine days ago, and we are the only ones who
escaped. We have come to warn—"

"Lord Adair has been in regular communication with me, personally,
ever since the 3rd left Soissons." Waldroup looked Falconer up and down
with continued polite indifference. "He has reported no enemy
encounters."

"Captain Lord Adair was Coerced before his return to Soissons."
Falconer's tone matched the major general politeness for politeness. "He
led the 3rd to where it could be taken. He lied to all of us from the moment
he left Paris, and he lied to you, sir."

"That is a serious allegation, and one for which you have no proof. I
have known Lord Adair for years, and I would know if he were Coerced."

268

Waldroup signaled one of the soldiers standing nearby. "Fetch the provost marshal." The soldier nodded and left the tent.

Indignant protests choked Jennet. She did not dare speak out of turn, even in the face of such gross unfairness. She examined the major general's emotions, searching for evidence that he, too, had been Coerced—it was the only explanation for why he would ignore their sworn words. But she saw no tangle of unfocused adoration as she had in Lady Ashford. Waldroup did not even feel smug satisfaction at having bested Falconer. His emotions were calm and indifferent and showed none of the fear someone might have in the knowledge Napoleon's army was advancing on his poorly-defended position.

She started to Coerce Waldroup into an emotional state that would incline him to listen, but his calmness gave her nothing to work with. Frustrated, she set about making him fond of all of them, which was a difficult balance to strike between mere interest and outright love, but not impossible. Surely if he felt affection toward them, he would not be so resistant to their message.

As she Coerced Waldroup, she was distantly aware of Falconer speaking. "I assure you we are telling the truth. Why would we walk deliberately into an Army camp and present ourselves to its commander if we were deserters?" he was saying.

Waldroup's feelings for Falconer were now those of a fond parent. He seemed intent on Falconer's words, which were so logical Jennet was relieved. Waldroup could not maintain his opposition now.

"Yours is an interesting story," Waldroup said. "And Lady Ashford was equally insistent. But I repeat, the 3rd has not been Coerced. They are moving west to join the regiments attacking Paris in an attempt to regain it from Napoleon. I regret more than I can say having to confine you, lieutenant, because I am fond of you, but we cannot permit desertion to go unpunished." He turned his gaze on Sadler, then examined each of them in turn. "The rest of you will begin your punishment in the morning. I am reluctant to resort to flogging when it is clear you were suborned by your superior."

"But we—" Whitteney began, sounding outraged. Jennet stepped hard on his foot, and he subsided.

Waldroup turned on him the sad, regretful look of a disapproving parent. "I truly do regret this," he said. A soldier wearing the armband of the provost entered, and the major general said, "Take them away."

"Sir, you must listen," Falconer said. "Napoleon's army was no more than two days behind us. If you do not take steps, he will come upon you unawares and cut you off from the allied support. *Please*."

Waldroup shook his head. "I must say, this is the most dramatic defense anyone has ever mounted against desertion. Never fear, lieutenant, you will have the opportunity to speak for yourself at your trial." He extended his hand.

Jennet, bewildered, watched Falconer detach his sword belt and wrap it around his sword before giving it to the major general. He was fond of Falconer, saw them all as his sons—he should give Falconer's words credence, not turn them over to the provost for detention. Her Coercion had never failed her before.

There were other soldiers wearing the armbands of the provost's office standing nearby. Jennet did not even consider running. Where would she go? She watched her friends for signs that they might do something foolish. Corwin looked stolid and villainous as always. Fosse and Sadler seemed ready to burst into violence. Whitteney had his attention on—

—no, they had left Veronique behind! She sat in the cart, tending a crying William and trying to attract someone's attention. Veronique would be an impeccable witness to the Coercion of the company, as a Discerner was aware of Coercion, but she did not speak English well and was a woman, and if Waldroup had disregarded the report of a female Extraordinary Mover who was English, he was unlikely to care what a Frenchwoman had to say.

The provost marshal's men marched them to a tent that looked more solid than the one Jennet slept in, as large as the major general's. Jennet felt a moment's relief that they would at least be confined together, though how that might work to their advantage, she did not know.

The provost's men stopped at the tent door and gestured them all inside. Jennet hung back. "Please, sir," she said, "please, that woman we traveled with, she has recently given birth and her husband is lost—will you see that she is given somewhere to sleep? She is on the strength, sir." Feeling desperate, she roused his emotions to encourage him to feel affection for her. It was the same ploy she had tried on Waldroup, and if this time, it failed, she did not know what she would do.

The young soldier's face softened. "We'll see to it," he said.

Jennet, relieved, backed into the tent, where a quiet argument was going on. "We must break free," Fosse was saying, low enough to be barely audible. "If this general won't see reason, we must find someone as will."

"Break free when we're being held in the middle of the camp?" Whitteney said. He looked white around the lips, as if he were nearing the end of his resources. "You're mad. We can only try to reason—"

"He's not reasonable," Sadler said. "He's full of himself and not going to listen to the likes of us."

"Even if all we do is get him to send scouts south," Whitteney said. "That would do it."

"That's enough," Falconer said. The others fell silent. "General Waldroup is a fair man, but he believes himself too canny to be deceived, certainly not by someone he knows and respects like Captain Lord Adair. I am not sure why he would be fond of me, as we have never met before today and I know of him only by reputation, but that peculiarity aside, he will see we are treated fairly. Which is the only good thing I see about our situation."

"It won't matter in a few days," Jennet said. "Because Napoleon will overrun us, and there will be no need for a court-martial."

"Don't be so optimistic, Ned," Sadler said with a lopsided smile.

"No, Graeme is correct," Falconer said. "We are in the terrible position of having a duty to perform and being unable to perform it. We can hope Lady Ashford, having been disregarded here, made her way to the 33rd as General Waldroup said and delivered her message there. But we should not give up simply because it is impossible."

"Pity we can't send Ned out dressed as a woman," Fosse joked. "He could seduce the guards, and we might all run free."

A horrible awkward silence descended. Jennet could not think where to look. Certainly not at any of the men who knew her secret. Definitely not at Falconer. Fosse glanced around. "What's wrong with you fellows?" he demanded in a whisper. "Ned, 'twas a joke, you know that."

Jennet sighed. It was entirely possible her secret would come out at court-martial, and if they were convicted—if there were time before Napoleon's advance, that is—she realized she did not want to take her punishment under a false identity. "Fosse, I am a woman," she said.

Fosse laughed. "Sure you are, Ned."

Jennet glared silently at him. Fosse's laughter died away. "Ned, you... but you can't be. I've seen you take a piss standing up."

Jennet refused to blush. "That just takes practice. I'm sorry, Fosse."

Fosse looked at the others. "Did all you lot know?"

Sadler nodded. Corwin shrugged. Whitteney said, "I wasn't sure."

"But, isn't it illegal?" Fosse said.

"The legality is not the issue," Falconer said. "I have heard of it happening before, not just in the British Army but in our allied forces. Most women are found out immediately. Some go for years undetected. Graeme is the best shot in the 3rd—would you care to lose that by telling her secret to the world?"

"*You* knew, sir?" Fosse said. "And didn't say?"

"I judged Graeme's fervent desire to pass as male worthy of keeping that secret." Falconer was not looking at her, Jennet noticed. She was not sure how she felt about that.

"Then..." Fosse's voice drifted to silence.

"It changes nothing, Frank," Sadler said. "Ned's a fine companion and a good friend. I don't much care whether he sits or stands to piss, though to hear him tell it he's good either way."

Everyone chuckled, and the mood lightened somewhat. Jennet ignored the miserable knot Sadler's declaration of friendship had tied in her stomach and said, "Thanks, fellows. I don't know as it matters much now, but I'd rather that general not know the truth. I don't believe he respects the word of a woman much."

"I wouldn't tell, Ned," Fosse assured her. "O' course, now it seems obvious, looking back, but you make a fine lad." He clapped her on the back in a comradely way.

"And now that we have that secret aired, we still need a solution," Falconer said. "Let us get to work contriving one."

THEY HAD COME NO NEARER A SOLUTION BY THE TIME A SOLDIER CAME bringing supper. The meal consisted of a hearty soup, fresh bread Jennet guessed came from a nearby town, boiled beef, and chopped, boiled turnips. The turnips tasted sour, as if they were last year's harvest, but the rest of the food was surprisingly good. They were even given ale to wash it down with. Jennet tried not to dwell on the tradition of a hearty last meal before execution.

While Fosse sat near the tent flap and sang loudly and tunefully, the others continued their whispered conversation. Jennet had remained quiet throughout the discussion and, to her relief, none of them seemed to notice. She had come up with three different ways to free them and two to convince Waldroup to listen. All of them required Coercion; none of them permitted her to act unnoticed. Giving away the secret of her sex was one thing, but she could not reveal she was an Extraordinary Coercer. That was not a thing any of her friends would understand or forgive.

"I believe we are in agreement that escaping is impossible," Falconer whispered. "I did not actually give my parole, but that is sophistry, and I would consider myself forsworn were I to break that tacit oath."

"*We* swore no oath, lieutenant," Sadler said. "We might try it."

"That is true, Sadler. But even setting the question of oaths aside, escape would mean making our way through the entire camp, and as our riflemen's uniforms are different, we would almost certainly be spotted." Falconer paced in a tight circle, his hands loosely clasped behind his back.

"We only need to find a Bounder, and he can take us wherever we need to go." Whitteney gestured in a way Jennet believed was meant to indicate a Bounder disappearing. "You said there are other officers in nearby divisions who will listen. Maybe even Wellington himself."

"And *I* said, how are we supposed to get a Bounder to listen? They all are keen on duty and regulations," Sadler said. "He'd just turn us in again, and then we'd be guilty of desertion twice."

"So we don't escape," Whitteney said. "We stay and plead our case. But that means getting the general to hear us out."

"He is not stupid, and he is not punitive," Falconer said. "I feel certain we will win the day at court-martial. But we do not have time to wait on the general's schedule."

"Which leaves us back where we started, begging your pardon, sir," Fosse said.

"Not quite," Falconer said. "I will request speech with the general, and I will convince him to believe me."

"How are you going to do that, sir?" Corwin's voice startled them all. He had spoken little more often than Jennet. "He's got no reason to listen."

"I don't know, Corwin, but we have no chance if we don't speak to him at all." Falconer did not look haughty, and Jennet's heart sank. She did not need to Coerce him to know when he felt unsure.

At that moment, the tent flap opened. Fosse stopped singing mid-word. Jennet instinctively backed away. Despite their precautions, the provost guards might have overheard, and Waldroup's Coerced feelings might not be enough for him to overlook them planning an escape.

But the person who entered was Veronique.

Everyone made exclamations of surprise and worry. Jennet took Veronique by the hand and led her further in. "Where have you been? Are you well? What of William?"

Veronique shifted the sling to reveal William sleeping soundly. "I have tried to learn what has happened. You are to be tried at court-martial, is that it? Why did they not hear your warning?"

"The general in charge is a Speaker, and Captain Lord Adair lied to him repeatedly. He believes those lies over our report." Jennet crossed the tent to peek outside. The provost's sentries ignored her, though the one she had asked to see to Veronique still felt fondness toward her. "How did you convince them to let you in?"

"I told them Private Sadler was the father of my child and that they were cruel to keep us apart." Veronique smiled impishly. "They seemed very uncomfortable at the idea."

"Why did she say my name, Ned?" Sadler asked.

Jennet ignored him. An idea grew in her mind. "Then they did not look too closely at you?"

Veronique shook her head. "Why does it matter?"

"Wait one moment." Jennet turned to Falconer. "Sir, I can see a way to get one of us free and to a Bounder."

Falconer's eyes narrowed. "Even were you to pass as female—and yes, Graeme, I see the irony—you would still have to convince the Bounder to convey you. And even if all of that were successful, you would also need to convince whatever officer you spoke to of the truth of your words. It is far too risky."

"At worst, they catch me and return me here, and we are put under heavier guard, sir." Jennet hoped she looked sufficiently resolute. Aside from that one moment facing Napoleon, she had never Coerced Falconer, and she could not bear the idea of doing so now.

Falconer's jaw tightened for a moment, and he turned away. "You know this is our one chance," Jennet persisted.

Falconer nodded. "That does not mean I have to like it," he said. "Very well. Everyone, turn your backs and give Graeme and Mrs. Appleton some privacy."

"Ned, you can't possibly," Whitteney began.

"He did it in Châlons-sur-Marne," Sadler said. "He'll be fine."

To Veronique, Jennet said, "We need to switch clothes. Do you mind waiting here for a while? They will discover the ruse eventually, probably when William cries, but for now—"

"You are far braver than I," Veronique said. She removed William from his sling and handed him to Falconer, who took the child with a look of bewildered nervousness that made Jennet's heart ache with love for him.

In silence, she and Veronique undressed down to the skin. Jennet unwound the cloth binding her breasts and rubbed to rid herself of phantom pressure. Then she dressed in Veronique's shift and gown and pinned up her hair with the few pins Veronique had left after their journey. She and Veronique were of a size, though Veronique was shorter, and their hair was nearly the same color.

Veronique looked very odd in Jennet's uniform, with the sleeves draggling over her hands and the trousers baggy at the knees and ankles. Jennet put on Veronique's shoes, which were surprisingly large, and walked a few paces to become accustomed to them. Her boots were too small to fit Veronique, to everyone's surprise, so she stashed them under one of the benches next to the canvas wall and said, "I'm ready, sir."

The men turned around. Sadler whistled. "That's a change and no mistake," he said. "No one will take you for male, I warrant."

Jennet nodded. She was too nervous to feel embarrassed at their scrutiny. She adjusted the sling around her body so it was not obvious it was empty. "This will work," she said, mostly for her own sake.

Veronique retrieved her child from the lieutenant, who looked relieved. "You will have to go straight to Wellington," he told Jennet. "There is no time for anything else. He will know what to do."

Jennet nodded. Falconer gripped her shoulder briefly and released her. "Good fortune, Graeme," he said in a low voice, and held the tent flap for her. Jennet hurried outside, cradling the sling and ducking her head as if weeping. She let out a sob as she passed the sentries, giving each a little nudge of Coercion to boost their embarrassment so they would not look closely, and was soon out of their reach.

It was about an hour before sunset. Jennet had lost track of time in the windowless tent, and she had believed it to be much later. The sight of the sun heartened her. She walked through the camp, staying well away from anyone who might be inclined to question her. There were plenty of women, for which she was grateful, and even some children running about. Thus far, her ruse had worked.

She did not know where the Bounders might be. In a battalion or regiment, there would be several, and they would have a section of camp to themselves where their portable Bounding chambers were set up. But although all military camps were organized along the same lines, the Bounding chambers were always placed away from the main body of the camp to increase their efficiency, and this was a large camp, so they might be anywhere. She would have to take a risk.

She kept walking, knowing that a woman walking somewhere was believed to have business there, and would not be questioned. After a few minutes, she saw what she needed: a gathering of women engaged in cooking supper and gossiping around the campfire. She veered over to speak to them.

"Excuse me," she said, pitching her voice high just in case, "my husband, Major Kelson, and I are new to this regiment, and I would like to speak with the Bounders to establish their ability to Bound me to London as needed. Would you tell me where they are?" As she spoke, she altered the feelings of one of the women to a greater friendliness toward this stranger. There was a very real chance these women of the rank and file might feel antipathy toward an officer's wife, but she had no time for a different ploy.

"They're on the north and west, about a hundred yards from the horse pickets," the woman said. "Major Kelson? I've never heard of him."

"We're new," Jennet repeated, and hurried away.

It took her a moment to orient herself. Ultimately, she followed the sound and smell of horses to their corral. Suleiman was among them, relieving Jennet's mind that he had been cared for. She turned her back on the horse lines and walked casually toward the cluster of tents nearby. Some of them were full-sized; a handful were narrow and tall and completely closed off to the outdoors. Those were the Bounding chambers, made for the use of Bounders who were not Extraordinaries. Jennet had seen inside only one in her time with the Army, but she knew each had a unique, complex symbol painted on one wall that served as a signature, or focus, for a Bounder to Bound to. Surely one of these Bounders knew a signature that would lead to Wellington.

There were no people visible when she arrived at the Bounders' quarters. She shut away her fear that they had all Bounded elsewhere and said, "Excuse me, sirs? I have need of a Bounder."

Something rustled behind one of the tent flaps, and a moment later, a tall, powerfully built man emerged, ducking to avoid hitting his head on the tent roof. He was in his shirtsleeves and held a grey and blue jacket in one hand. "Oh," he said, pausing halfway through putting the jacket on. "I believed this to be official business."

"It is, sir," Jennet said. "I need to be Bounded to speak to Lord Wellington."

"You do?" The Bounder finished donning his jacket and tugged it to lie straight across his broad shoulders. "You're not even a soldier. What kind of business could you have with my lord?"

Gently, Jennet tugged on his emotions. He was curious, that was good, and he was bored, which was even better. "It's a private message I've been entrusted with," she said, rousing his curiosity. "Something I can't share, even with you—and you have the major general's highest confidence, of course, so you can see how very private that must make it."

"General Waldroup would never give a woman that kind of responsibility." The Bounder had come closer, though, and Jennet felt his boredom ebbing of its own accord. She diverted some of his curiosity about her mission into curiosity about her, and then turned it into attraction.

"He didn't wish to," she improvised, "but I'm sure you know how Lord Wellington finds women intriguing. The general believed Lord Wellington would give the message greater consideration if I delivered it."

The Bounder was right next to her now, peering at her face. "You're not Lord Wellington's type," he said, then seemed to realize his gaucherie and quickly added, "that is, not that I should comment on my lord's personal life, but you are rather young."

Jennet ducked her head further and lowered her lashes, tilting her head slightly in a demure way. "Oh, but surely you don't believe anything untoward might occur between myself and Lord Wellington? I am meant only to charm him, not to force him into a certain course of action. You don't take me for a *Coercer*, do you?"

She laughed, and the Bounder joined in after a moment, only a little uncertainly. "Of course not," the Bounder said. "No one would believe such a thing of a pretty young lady like yourself."

"How sweet of you." Jennet fluttered her lashes again. The Bounder's attraction to her was perfect—not too intense, not too weak. "Then will you convey me? I really shouldn't take up more of your time."

The Bounder nodded. He moved to take her in his arms, then hesitated. "I really shouldn't—that is, it's improper for me to touch a lady in such an intimate way."

Frustrated, Jennet ground her teeth and shifted his attraction to her into something more physical. The Bounder's eyes brightened. "On the other hand," he said, "this *is* an important message, you say?"

"I am assured, lieutenant, that you hold me in the highest respect," Jennet said, and extended her arms to him. The Bounder swept her up, lifted her—

—*light, floating though there is no air*—

and they were elsewhere.

CHAPTER 28

IN WHICH JENNET TELLS THE DUKE OF WELLINGTON A LIE TO CONVINCE HIM OF THE TRUTH

The Bounding chamber was very dim, lit only by a single lamp with very thick, translucent glass behind which the flame seemed hardly to move. A black and grey symbol that looked like a pyramid crossed with a leafless tree was painted on the canvas immediately opposite Jennet. From outside came the noise of people walking past, their feet loud on wood or stone, she could not tell.

The Bounder had not released her when they arrived. "There, I believe that's deserving of something," he said, and before she could pull away, he drew her close and kissed her.

His mouth was unpleasantly wet and tasted of boiled beef and red wine gone acidic. Jennet endured his embrace for the length of time it took to change his attraction to her into mere fondness. Then she stepped away, smiled, and said, "Thank you so much for your cooperation, lieutenant." With that, she backed away, feeling for the tent flap with her left hand, and escaped.

Despite the warning the sound of feet on a hard surface had given her, she was surprised to discover the Bounding chamber had been set up inside a house—a very large house, given the size of the room she was in. She guessed it had once been a ballroom, what with the beautiful parquet floor and the hooks in the ceiling that might once have held chandeliers. Floor to ceiling windows illuminated the room perfectly with warm, late-afternoon light. Like Madame Durand's house, this room was so welcoming Jennet regretted having to leave.

There were five Bounding chambers in the ballroom, none of them apparently in use. She did not check to see if her Bounder assistant had gone back to the Army; she headed for the door.

Despite the hour—it was now nearly sunset—Wellington's headquarters bustled with movement. Jennet stood in the ballroom doorway and watched people hurry past in twos or threes, conversing in low voices. They filled the entry hall and walked or ran up the stairs, which matched the ballroom and the foyer in scale. Jennet contemplated having to interrogate man after man, searching for Wellington, and in the end decided not to bother. She ran up the stairs, dodging officers, and hurried in search of the great man herself.

She did not have to Coerce indifference to avoid being accosted, which relieved her mind. Indifference was perilously close to apathy, and she was still a little afraid of what might happen to someone whose emotions she Coerced away. But these men were all preoccupied with their own business, and if some of them might ordinarily have stopped her on the grounds that no woman dressed as she was belonged here, she encountered none such.

On the second floor, she noticed the flow of traffic was all heading one way, and she took a chance that it was the direction she wanted. She followed the officers to an open door, beyond which was a drawing room. Most of the furniture had been removed, and a couple of desks had been added; they were so heavy and ornate it was impossible they had been original to the rather delicate décor of the drawing room. Jennet wondered briefly whose house this was, and what city it was in. Then she pushed past an officer leaving the room and stepped to one side, waiting to be noticed.

In addition to the men thronging the drawing room, delivering messages or carrying them away, three officers, two of them major generals, sat at the desks, going over paperwork. The larger of the desks bore an enormous map, the details of which Jennet could not see aside from that it was a map of Belgium and France. The third officer leaned over the map with a pen in hand. He appeared to be in his mid-forties and had a lean, handsome face and dark hair that was slightly disordered, as if he were in the habit of running a hand through it.

Jennet had expected to wait a while to be observed, but this man, glancing up as someone addressed him, noticed her immediately. "Who are you?" he demanded. "What are you doing in this room?"

"Sir, I have a message for Lord Wellington," Jennet said.

One of the major generals chuckled. "I wonder what kind of message," he muttered.

"I beg your pardon, Honeycutt?" The handsome officer turned a keen glance on Honeycutt, who blanched.

"My lord, I beg your pardon," he said. "It was ill-considered."

"Well, let's see that you consider your words more carefully in future." The officer straightened. "I am Lord Wellington, young lady. And I must request that you bring personal messages to my quarters. This is a place of official military business."

Jennet swallowed to moisten a suddenly dry mouth. For an instant, she forgot she was a Coercer, and then she remembered and felt even worse. She intended to Coerce this man? At least with Napoleon, she knew what danger she faced. Wellington had power the likes of which she could not comprehend.

"My lord, my message *is* military business," she said, for the moment falling back on fact and reason. "I bring word, my lord, of Napoleon's troop disposition. He is not in Paris. His army is advancing north through the Aisne department and he intends to come upon the British Army from the east."

She had to speak louder and louder until she was nearly shouting because every officer in the room save Wellington himself had started talking over her. Wellington stared her down as if he were an Extraordinary Discerner to ferret out her lies. When she finished, he made a gesture that silenced the others. Then he said, "Young lady—"

"I beg your pardon for the interruption, my lord, but despite appearances, I am male," Jennet said, pitching her voice as deep as she could. "My name is Ned Graeme, and I am a rifleman of the 95th regiment. I dressed this way so I could reach you, as I had no other way of escaping confinement."

Wellington looked at her even more intently. Jennet swallowed. If he saw through this lie, it was all over, but she could not convince him of the truth unless he believed she was a soldier. Finally, he said, "Confinement?"

"It is a rather long story, and we have no time," Jennet said. She assessed Wellington's emotions and found curiosity, and the beginnings of worry, and amusement, which worried *Jennet*. She did not Coerce him, judging his emotional state to be just what she wanted for the moment. "It's up to you, my lord, but I suggest you clear the room so there are no more interruptions, and then I will gladly tell you everything."

Wellington stood. "Honeycutt, Bertelmy, and Daubney, if you please, I will have you remain. The rest of you, carry on."

The room cleared rapidly, though there was a great deal of muttering and sidelong looks at Jennet. She remained still and tried to capture Falconer's calm demeanor, though not his haughty look, which might be disastrous. When only three men plus Wellington remained, Wellington resumed his seat and said, "Pray, continue, ah, Private Graeme?"

"Yes, sir." Jennet drew in a breath. "About two weeks ago…"

She told him almost everything—not the personal details, not the events that had drawn her and her friends closer, but everything about Captain Lord Adair's Coercion and betrayal and their flight northward, all the way to Major General Waldroup's refusal to believe and their confinement pending court-martial. "According to Lady Ashford's reconnaissance, Napoleon's army was no more than two days from Major General Waldroup's position," she concluded.

"Lady Ashford," Wellington said. "And why did she not report directly to me?"

"I don't know, my lord." Jennet had wondered this herself. "Major General Waldroup said he had sent her to report to the 33rd, and that is all I know of the matter."

Wellington said nothing. One of the other generals, a portly man with a red face and Speaker's insignia on his left breast, said, "You confess to breaking out of confinement, to a second count of desertion, and you expect us not to simply court-martial you out of hand?"

"Sir, had Major General Waldroup listened to our story, we would not have been confined," Jennet replied. "I know this looks bad, sirs, me putting on women's clothes and sneaking away. It's not the kind of behavior expected of a British soldier. But we were desperate, and—sirs, I risked my life bringing this news because I don't want Napoleon Coercing the whole Army. Please forgive my subterfuge."

"You're quite right it's not honorable behavior! I say—"

"Enough, General Bertelmy," Wellington said. "Private Graeme, Major

General Waldroup is a soldier of long standing and excellent repute. If he says he has not been fooled, why should I disbelieve him on the word of a soldier I do not know?"

"Sir, I have seen Coercion. I do not believe General Waldroup has. He does not understand what happens to those who are Coerced. I know General Waldroup believes he has not been fooled, because he is Captain Lord Adair's friend and the captain himself does not believe he has been Coerced. Have someone send a message to Lady Ashford—she will explain better than I can." Jennet drew in a breath and let it out slowly. "My lord, what is more reasonable—that I am a deserter who deliberately walked into your headquarters and spun you an unbelievable yarn to prevent being punished, or that I am a loyal soldier who escaped Coercion and walked hundreds of miles to warn you of Napoleon's imminent attack?"

Wellington's eyes narrowed again. "And that, to me, is the unbelievable part of your story. How did you escape Coercion if no one else of your company did?"

"Sir, Lieutenant Falconer—he who led us north—he believed a different strong emotion can overcome Coercion. I know I felt tremendous fear, facing Napoleon's forces and knowing he must have more in reserve." Jennet did not look away, though she disliked how those eyes bored into her. "I know it's not done to confess to fear on the battlefield, but since it seems to have saved me and my companions, I'll own to it gladly."

"My lord," one of the other men said, "this young man speaks sense."

"I agree, Major Daubney," Wellington said. He beckoned to Jennet. Jennet approached cautiously, still not certain what to expect. Wellington pushed the map so it was nearer Jennet's side of the desk. "Where was Napoleon's army?"

The map was upside down from Jennet's perspective, but it was large enough she could read it with some effort. She made note of the marks that indicated the British troops and the advance of the Prussians on the east, as well as the incorrect position of the Grande Armée surrounding Paris. Then she traced the line of their journey—how strange that it had taken more than a week to travel what she could mark with her finger in a few seconds! "I am not certain whether this is General Waldroup's regiment," she said, tapping one of the larger marks, "but this is Valenciennes, and we met them before we found that city."

She drew a circle with her fingertip around Châlons-sur-Marne, and then a line north from that. "Here is where we encountered a French battalion, here in this city. We recognized their regimentals as belonging to General Grouchy. Lady Ashford said they moved north in pursuit of us, so Napoleon's forces—I mean, the ones with him at their head—must have been joined by General Grouchy's men."

"Marshal Grouchy," Wellington said absently. "We had word Napoleon made him a Marshal of France." He tapped a long finger against the map. "Daubney, what is the latest news from our Prussian allies?"

"They were still moving west this morning," Daubney said. "You don't imagine—"

"I try not to borrow trouble, Daubney." Wellington once more turned his gaze on Jennet. "You have my thanks," he said, "for having endured much, and dared greatly, to bring me word. Now I intend to see what I may salvage from this colossal failure of intelligence. You will wait while I dispatch Bounders to verify your story."

Jennet held her tongue. It was what Waldroup should have done, standard procedure, and she reminded herself it did not mean Wellington disbelieved her.

General Bertelmy tipped his head back in the attitude of a Speaker for a few moments. When he lowered his head and opened his eyes, he said, "I have instructed them to send the Bounder directly to headquarters upon his reconnaissance."

Wellington nodded. He stood and, with lowered head, examined the map in silence. Jennet watched him, nerves making her feet twitch. She could not permit impatience to get the better of her, but she felt horribly conspicuous in Veronique's gown. Her imagination supplied her with scenarios in which the Bounder did not observe Napoleon's army where she had said it was, followed by her own arrest and court-martial—

A light rap on the door prompted Major Daubney to rise and open it. A tall, well-built Bounder in grey and blue stood at attention there. Wellington turned to face him. "Well?"

"My lord, the French army is massed south of Valenciennes," the Bounder said. "I did not dare surveil fully, as I was immediately attacked by French Movers who attempted to detain me. I apologize for not being able to provide better intelligence. I can confirm the forces are where I was told to look." His ashen face suggested just how unnerving his experience had been.

Wellington closed his eyes and let out a deep breath. "Send word to our forces in the 33rd and the 51st, General Bertelmy, to ready themselves to move out at first light. Major Daubney, organize our Bounders for transportation. And someone find me a new map."

"What should I do, sir?" Jennet dared ask.

"Get out of that dress, for one," Wellington said. "I will admit it is a convincing illusion, but I warrant you would prefer a uniform."

Jennet gradually realized she had succeeded. Awareness that she had not Coerced Wellington at all followed quickly. She assessed his emotions once more and did not understand why his amusement had deepened.

Then she caught his eye once more. He looked her over from head to toe. And he winked.

Relief warred with confusion, and relief won. "Yes, sir, I certainly would," she said with a nervous laugh that barely escaped being a giggle. She made herself shut up, saluted, and backed away while Wellington barked out a rapid-fire series of orders and General Bertelmy tipped his head back in a Speaker's attitude. Her relief manifested in an unexpected weariness, and when it became clear that she had been forgotten, she leaned against the wall and let her eyelids droop.

"You there. Gramm?"

"Graeme," Jennet replied automatically, opening her eyes. A sergeant stood before her, a bundle of dark green cloth in his arms.

"I've a change of clothes for you, and then you're to report back to the 51st. Major General Waldroup's forces," the sergeant explained when Jennet looked mystified. "Come with me, and I'll show you where you can get out of that gown." He smirked. "Though you're pretty enough to be a girl, in that garb."

Jennet scowled at him, making his smile broaden. "'Tis a joke," the sergeant said. "I heard tell as how you crossed half of France just a step ahead of Napoleon. I say, a man does that, he can dress as he likes."

Jennet followed the sergeant down the stairs and into the servants' quarters, where he showed her a room that smelled of water and soap, though it showed no sign of either. "Used to be the laundry," the sergeant said, "before his lordship took over the house. Go to the Bounders' room when you're done, and tell them your name."

To Jennet's relief, the sergeant did not stay to talk. She quickly shed Veronique's gown and shift and donned the uniform, which was only a little too big. It was also, to her surprise, a rifleman's uniform rather than ordinary regimentals. The sergeant had not provided boots, and Jennet was forced to retain Veronique's too-large shoes, but she did not care about looking ridiculous.

Then, in rapid succession, she waited in the ballroom for a Bounder, who was not the man who had Bounded her there; was caught up in the Bounder's grip and whisked away to another Bounding chamber; and emerged to find herself once more in Waldroup's camp. It was, to her surprise, as quiet and peaceful as when she had left it.

Fear that Waldroup had refused to obey Wellington's orders, whatever they had been, surged over her. She made herself consider the situation logically. Even though Waldroup was a Speaker and could receive orders directly, the regiment could hardly march in the dark, and breaking camp tonight made no sense.

She made her way across the camp in the growing darkness, though she had no idea where she should go. In the end, she sought out the women who had given her directions. Their numbers had swelled with the return of their husbands and lovers, and Jennet's heart almost failed her before she remembered she was a soldier and the equal of any five of them. "A young woman came to this camp today," she said. "A woman with a newborn child. Did any of you see her?"

One of the soldiers, a burly man sporting sergeant's stripes on his sleeve, let out a deep chortle. "Where have you been that you don't know?"

"Know what, sir?" Jennet did not like the way the others glanced at each other with secretive, amused looks. It was the kind of amusement she was sure was at her expense. After the day she had had, she had no desire to be the butt of some unknown joke.

"That woman helped one of the prisoners escape," the sergeant said. "Walked right in to the provost marshal's tent and gave her clothes to a young soldier who walked right out again, under the sentries' noses."

Jennet felt ill. "What did they do to her?"

"Naught, as far as I know. She has a newborn babe, so what could they do?" The sergeant laughed again. "Took the others to General Waldroup, though, on account of that lieutenant put her up to it."

Jennet did not like the sound of that. "When was this?" They would not execute the others out of hand, surely, but Jennet had a very bad feeling something was wrong.

The sergeant shrugged. "Mayhap an hour gone. Why do you care?"

"Thank you," Jennet said, and darted away.

CHAPTER 29

IN WHICH JENNET BETRAYS
HERSELF

Despite the short grass trampled to mud that covered much of the ground, her feet in their inappropriate footwear seemed to land painfully on every stone and twig possible. She ignored the pain and ran on, passing the empty, unguarded tent where they had been confined and hurrying on to Waldroup's headquarters. Again, sentries stood at attention outside; again, they ignored her even when she ran up to them, breathing heavily.

"I have a message for General Waldroup," she panted. "He is within, yes? Pray, permit me to pass." She heard several voices, none of them speaking loudly enough to be intelligible.

The sentries stared ahead at nothing. Neither spoke or acknowledged Jennet in any way.

Annoyed, Jennet shouted, "Sir? General Waldroup?"

One of the sentries shifted his weight, drawing attention to the sword he wore. It was big and heavy and notched along one edge of the blade. It was also silver-bright even in the lantern light and looked capable of taking Jennet's head off. The other glared at Jennet, clearly warning her away.

Frustration filled her heart. All of this could have been avoided had Major General Waldroup been a reasonable man, but he was not. Jennet was filled with the sudden unshakable certainty that his unreasonableness was going to get someone killed, very likely someone she cared about.

As if someone had Coerced her, that frustration abruptly turned to anger. She did not have to put up with this kind of treatment.

She took hold of both sentries' emotions, observed that one felt curious and the other felt the self-satisfaction that marks a true bully, and sent fear shooting through both of them—not dramatic fear, but a creeping uncertainty about the rightness of their cause. At the same moment, she said, "You will both be in a great deal of trouble for not passing me through."

Both jerked, and took a step sideways away from one another. Jennet took that as permission, and shoved through the flap into the tent.

The conversation came to a halt when she entered. Seven people turned to stare at her. Jennet knew six of the seven: they were Falconer, Fosse, Sadler, Whitteney, and Corwin, as well as Waldroup. The stranger wore captain's insignia. He looked perplexed at her interruption. Her friends all gazed her in varying degrees of astonishment. Falconer looked so haughty she knew he was concealing some stronger emotion.

Major General Waldroup, on the other hand, did not seem to recognize her at first. "What is this—" he began, peered more closely at her, and said, "Ah. Our deserter. I'm surprised you returned."

"Sir," Jennet gasped, "did you receive word about Napoleon's advance?"

The general stared her down in silence. Jennet began running over terrible possibilities in her mind: he had not been informed, he had been informed and chose to disbelieve, he believed but was angry with them anyway—

"General Bertelmy Spoke with me half an hour ago," Waldroup said. "It seems you took your information to Lord Wellington directly. Unnecessarily, as I intended to investigate your story." He did not sound angry, was as outwardly calm as before despite his glare, but Jennet's awareness of his emotions showed her his chagrin at having foolishly passed up the opportunity to prove his military merit to Wellington.

"General, as I said," Falconer began.

"Silence, lieutenant." Waldroup continued to glare at Jennet. "Young man, you abandoned your uniform, you escaped confinement, and you went above my head to gain your point. Tell me why I should not dispense with the formality of a court-martial and simply have you shot."

"General—"

"Lieutenant Falconer, be silent or I will have you removed." The major general's words were as calm and polite as everything else he had said. Jennet felt oddly separate from what was going on a foot in front of her. She had expected the major general to become angry, or shout, or make loud threats the way Captain Lord Adair had. But he was the very image of a gentleman officer. It left her not knowing what to do, save brazen it out.

"Sir," she said, "I apologize for my ruse. And I apologize for—I don't know what it's called when one goes behind an officer's back to petition a higher authority. But, sir, you are an excellent officer. Lord Wellington said it himself. It's not your fault a friend lied to you. You did what you had to, sir."

Waldroup raised an eyebrow. "And now you think to patronize me, soldier?"

Jennet's heart sank. "No, sir. Speaking my mind, sir."

She examined his emotions again, feeling at a loss. She had never found anyone immune to Coercion, or, more accurately, anyone whose emotions could be manipulated but who did not react instinctively to the manipulation. She saw anger, thankfully held in check, and pride, and a knot of feeling she did not immediately recognize, it was so complex.

"I'll thank you to keep your mind to yourself, soldier." Waldroup turned to the unknown captain. "Summon the provost marshal to take them all into custody. This time, the sentries are to let no one through." Without waiting for the captain's assent, he tilted his head back as he Spoke to someone.

The captain left the tent. Jennet turned to Falconer. "Sir—"

Falconer shook his head, the smallest gesture, but one that clearly conveyed the need for silence. Jennet desperately wished she had heard the earlier conversation to know whether Waldroup intended to follow orders. Wellington *had* said he was a respected officer; surely that meant he was obedient, too?

"What is your name, soldier?" Waldroup said, causing Jennet to turn back around.

"It's Graeme, sir. Ned Graeme," she said.

"Ned Graeme." Waldroup shook his head. "It is a shame one so young should be so corrupted. Lieutenant Falconer, that is another charge I will lay at your door."

"No!" Jennet shouted.

"Graeme, let it go," Falconer warned her.

"My orders are to move east," Waldroup said as if neither of them had spoken. "It is too dark now to send Bounders to investigate, but they will leave at first light, and we will wait on their report. In the morning, I will hold a court-martial—"

"No!" Jennet shouted. "You damned fool, how can you prate about courts-martial when Napoleon is on your flank and like to take a bite out of your regiment? Is that how you obey orders?"

"I beg your pardon?" Waldroup said, for the first time sounding angry.

"I take responsibility for Graeme's outburst," Falconer said at the same time. "He is weary from our travels and does not know what he is saying."

"I should imagine you do," Waldroup said. "I make allowances for his youth. Now, in the morning, while we await the Bounders' report—"

But Jennet had stopped listening. This fool was going to ruin all Wellington's plans. His refusal to move—Jennet was no strategist, but even she could understand the careful marks on Wellington's now outdated map. Napoleon's army would drive a wedge between the British Army and the Prussians, cutting off Wellington's support and circling the Army. From there, Napoleon had only to press westward, bring his other army east from Paris, and squeeze.

She wrapped her Coercion around Waldroup's emotions and took a closer look at the unfamiliar knot. Her sick feeling grew as she prodded it. Embarrassment and pride tangled with a deep desire to save face—it was a type of arrogance she had only rarely seen before, and one she did not know how to alter. More specifically, she did not know what new form the emotion could smoothly be guided to take.

She realized the general had addressed her, and said, "I beg your pardon, sir, did you say something?"

"If you can be bothered to listen to your superiors, Graeme, I asked you what, exactly, you told Lord Wellington," Waldroup said.

Jennet took a deep breath. She could see only one path forward. "I told him what we told you, sir," she said, and with a single fluid movement Coerced the arrogance into apathy.

Waldroup stiffened. His eyes, which Jennet now saw were a very pale blue, blinked at her. "What would be the point of that?" he said.

"Exactly, sir, since you already believed us," Jennet said. All Waldroup's emotions had vanished, leaving her free to Coerce a new emotion. They needed him to take them seriously, they needed him to obey Wellington's orders, and they needed him to let go his mania for courts-martial. Jennet teased his apathy into a willingness to believe—a dangerous move, as it left the Coerced person open to believing everything, but it only had to last a minute or two.

"I believed you?"

"Yes, sir, that Napoleon is mere days from this position," Jennet said.

"Of course he is," Waldroup said. "I believe you."

Behind her, Falconer twitched. Jennet had no attention to spare for him. She coaxed a new emotion to twine with Waldroup's gullibility, a desire to act on his beliefs. "And you believe Lord Wellington's communication that supports what we told you. His Bounders have scouted the area, and there is no need to wait on further reconnaissance in the morning," she added, and brought a third emotion into play: pride, but not an arrogant pride, rather the pride that is akin to patriotism. She needed Waldroup to link the need to follow orders with a sense that doing so would save his country.

Waldroup straightened. "Lord Wellington knows what is best for this Army," he said. "I would never second-guess his orders."

"Neither would we," Jennet said, "us being loyal to the Army and all that. Which is why we walked hundreds of miles to tell you, so you could lead this regiment to victory over Napoleon." With the gullibility having done its work, she made it fade until it was the merest shadow over Waldroup's new pride in his position.

"Of course," Waldroup said, "of course. Very good work, men."

Jennet considered bringing up the court-martial and decided not to push her luck. "Thank you, sir," she said. "May we be excused?"

"Speak to the quartermaster about shelter tonight," Waldroup said. "In the morning, you will join us as we move out. It is a shame about the 3rd, good men all, but with luck we will free them from Coercion, yes?"

Waldroup smiled and clapped Falconer on the shoulder. Jennet did not dare look at the lieutenant. Now that she had won, the sick feeling had returned. Surely that had not been as obvious a Coercion as it felt? True, the general's behavior had been odd for a minute or two, but no one would draw the conclusion from it that he had been Coerced. Not that it mattered. She had done the only thing that would bring the general around to following Wellington's orders.

She followed the others out of Waldroup's tent. Falconer did not pause or acknowledge the sentries; he continued walking, to Jennet's eye at random, through the camp. She gingerly avoided the worst stones and wished desperately for her boots. "Sir," she said, then subsided, fearing his response.

Falconer ignored her. He kept walking until they were almost at the horse pickets. The scent of horseflesh wafted to Jennet's nose, and for once the smell did not reassure her. Falconer stopped abruptly and drew in a deep breath. Jennet watched him hold it for a moment and then breathe out in a long, slow stream.

"That was odd," Fosse said. "Don't you all call it odd?"

"And he didn't say naught about a court-martial, not the second time," Sadler said.

Jennet remained silent. She was watching Falconer, who had not turned around. His shoulders were tense and his head bowed, and one hand was closed into a fist.

"He changed his mind, and I say that's all we ought care about," Whitteney said. "Come, lads, let's away to a tent. I declare I could sleep for a year."

"Something wrong, lieutenant?" Corwin said in his deep, slow voice.

Falconer turned around. His eyes met Jennet's. For the space of half a breath, she believed she had got away with it. Then she registered how still his expression was, how devoid of emotion. It was not even the haughty look he wore when he was hiding how he felt. It terrified her.

"Sir," she said, grasping for something, anything that would break through his reserve. She could come up with nothing to excuse herself, no plea for forgiveness, no reminder that she had done it all for their sakes. For his sake.

Falconer let out another deep breath. "It was you, wasn't it," he said, still deadly calm. "You are responsible."

"What are you saying, sir?" Whitteney asked.

Jennet pleaded with him silently. She could barely endure him knowing what she was; if they all knew, her life truly was over. With wide eyes, she silently begged him not to tell.

Falconer's eyes never left hers. "You did it," he repeated. "You Coerced the general."

The other four immediately took a step back, leaving Jennet standing alone. "I don't understand," Sadler said, glancing from Jennet to Falconer and back again. "Ned's not a Coercer."

"Were you that arrogant, that you believed you could get away with Coercing him where all of us could see? That we wouldn't notice?" Falconer's voice cracked. "How many times have you Coerced *us*?" *Coerced me*, his eyes said.

Jennet's mouth was so dry she could barely speak. "I," she began, and fell silent again. She could not say she had never Coerced them. That would be a lie.

One by one, horror dawned in the others' faces. "You made us like you," Whitteney said. "Made us care so we'd protect your secret. Both your secrets."

"Did you even really rescue me from that other Coercer," Fosse demanded, "or were you working together?"

Jennet's heart felt ready to crack in two. She could not even ask their forgiveness. Fleeing was all that was left to her. She turned and tried to run, but Corwin was there, blocking her path, grabbing her shoulders. "Tell us the truth," he said, his voice rough.

In desperation, Jennet wrenched free of his hands and sent terror shooting through all five men. As they gasped and cried out, Jennet ran. She did not look back, not even when Falconer shouted her name.

CHAPTER 30

IN WHICH JENNET CALLS ON AN ALLY TO MAKE HER ESCAPE

Fear and despair made Jennet fleet-footed. If Falconer recovered from her Coerced fear soon enough, he would catch her, for no one could outrun someone whose legs and lungs were Shaped to perfection. And she could not face him again. She cared nothing for punishment; she simply could not bear to see the horror and betrayal in his expression. That would be more than she could endure.

She ran the first dozen strides at random before realizing she had to find real footwear if she intended to make good her escape. She changed direction and ran for the provost marshal's tent.

The quiet peace of the camp after dark set her nerves on edge rather than soothing them. At any moment, someone might lunge out of the darkness to apprehend her. She might not have time to Coerce an assailant she did not see coming.

Movement nearby made her jump and swerve, ready to defend herself. Her heart beat painfully hard, as if she and not Falconer were the one Coerced into fear. She realized it was a tent flap moving, lighter against the dark background, and ran on before whoever had opened it tried to stop her.

The provost marshal's tent was still empty. Jennet breathed out in relief that one thing had gone her way and ducked inside. The windowless space was close and humid compared to the cool evening outdoors, and it was so dark Jennet had to stop where she was and wait for her eyes to adjust. Then she threw herself to the ground and felt around at the side of the tent, beneath the bench.

Her grasping hands fell on the rough leather, caked with dried mud from walking from Troyes to Valenciennes, and she snatched up the boots and hugged them to herself in relief. She kicked off Veronique's shoes and crammed her feet into the boots, which felt odd since she wore no stockings, then stood still and considered. She needed to get out of the camp, get far from the Army, but how? She dared not walk south or east, where she would run into Napoleon's Grande Armée; if she walked west, she would only find more of the British Army; and she did not know what lay immediately north. She was afraid to try Coercing another Bounder, since that delay would offer Falconer another chance to apprehend her, not to mention she was heartsick and weary and did not wish to Coerce anyone ever again.

An idea came to her. Briefly, she was aware that this action would make her truly a deserter, but the awareness had no force behind it. She was a woman, and not a true soldier, so the question of whether or not she was actually capable of deserting seemed irrelevant.

She hurried toward Waldroup's tent. He was himself a Speaker, so she might be wrong about the location of the Speakers' communication tents, but in all the other regimental camps she had seen, the Speakers had their post near the commanding officer. She could not recall whether she had seen them before, as she had been preoccupied all the times she had gone in to speak to Waldroup, but it was worth taking the chance. She reflected that she had already taken so many chances that night God might believe she was due no more good luck, but she refused to give up. Not when the alternative was seeing that horrible, betrayed look on Falconer's face.

Jennet's relief at seeing the broad, high-roofed tent near Waldroup's, a tent with a Speaker's standard in front, eased some of her pain. The flap was open, and lantern light spilled out in a wedge in front. The Speaker's standard, a bronze owl with its wings half-open and its mouth wide in a silent cry, had been driven into the ground at an angle that made the owl seem ready to drop off its perch.

She stopped and peeked inside. If Waldroup were there, she should not risk him noticing her and ordering her elsewhere, perhaps with a guard. But there were only three people present, all of them seated on camp stools with writing desks on their laps. Two of them wore the pale blue of the Speaker corps. The third, a woman with thick chestnut hair pinned in a braid around her head, wore the black-on-black of the War Office. An Extraordinary Speaker. Jennet did not know what to make of her presence there.

"Excuse me," she said in her deepest voice.

One of the Speakers did not respond. His head was tilted back in silent Speech. But the other two looked up from their desks. "Yes?" the other Speaker said. He did not sound impatient, or irritated, or even suspicious. Jennet did not permit herself to believe that made him inclined to be helpful.

"I have a message to relay to the Extraordinary Mover Lady Ashford," she said. "I am not certain where she is, except that I am told she was sent to the 33rd this morning."

"That's not enough information for me to help you," the Speaker said. "I can relay the message to one of the 33rd's Speakers, but it may take some time to locate Lady Ashford."

The Extraordinary Speaker set her desk aside and rose. She was tall, taller even than Falconer, and whip-thin, with bright green eyes and a scar down the left side of her face that dragged the corner of her mouth down. "That won't be necessary, Lieutenant Jersey," she said. "I know Clemency and I can Speak to her directly. What's the message, private?"

Jennet had not seriously considered the possibility that she would succeed right away, and had not given much thought to the wording of her message. "Ah, tell her—ask her to meet Ned Graeme south of this camp for new orders," she said. Immediately she regretted it. New orders? South of camp? If Clemency did not arrive promptly, it might be too late for Jennet. But the Extraordinary Speaker nodded as if the message were not at all bizarre. She tilted her head back and stilled. Jennet waited, impatience and worry making it difficult not to jig in place.

After about a minute, the Extraordinary Speaker looked down at Jennet. "I have no way of knowing her response, unfortunately, but I did ask her to find someone to relay—oh, excuse me." Once more she tilted her head back. Jennet wanted to scream. "I beg your pardon, that was a much quicker response than I expected," the woman said when she was finished Speaking. "Clem—that is, Lady Ashford says she will meet you at the designated place, and 'anything for Ned Graeme,' my contact says."

The Extraordinary Speaker raised a puzzled eyebrow. "Are you Ned Graeme? What are these new orders?"

"I apologize, but I am not free to divulge them," Jennet said, trying to sound sad at having to disappoint an Extraordinary rather than arrogant.

"But you're not an aide-de-camp," the Speaker said. Jennet had forgotten he was there. "You, relaying orders?"

The conversation was slipping out of her control. Hating herself, she Coerced lack of interest in both of them and said, "I was the one available, and you know how General Waldroup is about making good use of resources." She did not know whether that made any sense, but either it was logical or her Coercion made it so, because neither Speaker nor Extraordinary Speaker did anything but nod knowingly. Jennet took the opportunity to flee.

She hurried through the camp, along the route her friends—no, not friends, they would never be friends again—her traveling companions had taken that afternoon, following Falconer and the cart. There were fewer campfires on this side, as most of it was taken up by the quartermaster's wagons and the oxen waiting patiently for the slaughter. Jennet slipped past the few tents and the men talking and laughing loudly near them. In the darkness, in her dark green uniform, sneaking past them was not difficult.

The pickets were more alert than the quartermaster's men, but she moved with assurance instead of walking furtively, and Coerced them into a lack of interest just to be safe. Despite these precautions, she still walked as quickly as possible, soon putting herself beyond their reach. She had learned over the past six years that inattention and complacency could get a soldier killed faster than charging an emplacement over bare ground.

Soon enough, she had left the camp behind for the road south. There was no moon to guide her path, but Jennet preferred the cover of darkness and gratefully stayed beneath the sheltering trees rather than walking the verge. She walked until she could no longer hear the sounds of the camp or see its fires, and waited. The sound of millions of insects singing under the night sky blended together in a single high-pitched whine that drilled into Jennet's skull until she learned to ignore it. She looked up at the stars and then away again when the vast crystal-studded blackness made her feel dizzy.

She wished she had asked the Extraordinary Speaker when Clemency would arrive, how many minutes. Restless, she paced beneath the trees. Falconer and the others would have overcome their Coerced fear by now. The memory of how terrified they had looked stabbed her heart, bringing her to a stop. If only she could have explained—but what was there to say? Everyone knew Coercers were evil, and she could not defend herself against their accusations. Likely now they were all revisiting every interaction they had ever had with her, finding more proof that she was a monster.

She reached for her watch. She could not read the face with so little light, but it would be a distraction from her horrible thoughts. And its smooth surface always comforted her.

Her fingers brushed the lining of her green rifleman's jacket and found no pocket. She groped further, believing she had made a mistake, and touched nothing but fabric. Her watch was gone.

Frightened, Jennet tore off the jacket and prodded it all over. She found nothing—no watch, no specially sewn pockets, no fraying where the lining had been slit. Breathing heavily, she clutched the jacket to her chest. This was not her jacket; it was the one provided by Wellington's people. *Her* jacket was with Veronique. And Jennet had left her watch inside that one.

Jennet slowly donned the jacket. She had not been so close to weeping in the ten years since her family's death. Weeping over a watch, how pointless and self-indulgent. It was just a thing...the one thing she had left of her father. He had taught her to tell time by it. She had stolen it from her uncle when he had claimed it for himself. She had carried it through six years of war, six years of privation. Falconer had sacrificed his honor so she need not sell it. Her throat ached with unshed tears.

She rubbed her fists against her eyes. She had not cried in ten years, and she would not cry now nor ever again. She could mourn the loss of her watch without tears. Perhaps Veronique could sell it to support herself and William. That would be a worthy cause, and one that ought not make her heart ache as much as it did.

Jennet paced along the verge again. More memories emerged, bitter and painful. Corwin arguing with her over Veronique giving her son his name. Sadler teasing her about how she looked in skirts. The look Whitteney had given her when he first realized she might be female, and Fosse's astonishment when he learned the same.

She did not want to remember Falconer at all, but as if her weariness had lowered her resolve, she found she could remember nothing else. She should have contented herself with admiring him from afar, like the statue he resembled, but instead she had been drawn to his confidence and competent power, to his compassion and his well-concealed sense of humor. And he had kissed her. Even if he had not meant it, his kiss had been the most extraordinary experience of her life. It had made her realize her infatuation had turned to something more profound. She hated herself for so many things, but most of all she hated herself for falling in love with someone she could not help but betray.

With no moon in the sky, she did not know how much time had passed before a large shape swept over her and alit some dozen feet away. "Is something amiss?" Clemency said. "I was never so surprised as when I received Miranda's communication."

She sounded so sincerely concerned tears welled up again in Jennet's eyes. She blinked them ferociously away and said, "I need a favor, Clemency, and you cannot ask me for an explanation."

"That is a favor indeed, as I am of a most inquisitive nature," Clemency said with some amusement. "But—" She stepped closer, removing her goggles, and looked at Jennet's face. "I perceive this is not a time for levity. Very well. I will not ask, but I assure you, if you choose to confide in me, I will not abuse your trust."

Jennet nodded. "It is not entirely my secret to tell," she said. "And you may not choose to help me if you know the truth." She listened to her own words and realized she could not make another person an unwitting party to her desertion. "What I can tell you is that I must leave the Army. It is not strictly desertion, but I must leave, and I need you to convey me somewhere they cannot reach me. I understand if you feel you cannot abet my actions."

"It is true, I should not." Clemency still had the inquiring, puzzled expression, as if Jennet were a difficult text she needed to translate. "But I am with the War Office, not the Army, and my obedience is to a different master. And you—forgive me, but I can see you are in great distress. I cannot help but feel compassion for you, whatever predicament brought you here."

"Thank you." Jennet released a deep breath of relief. "I wish I could explain. Will you take me to...to Brussels, I suppose?" It was the nearest large city she could think of that was not Paris. "And I hate to ask more of you, but I have no more money."

"You spent your money to save my life—ah, you did not realize I knew that, did you?" Clemency's smile was visible even in the darkness. "I told you, anything you need that is within my power to grant, I will give you. And do not imagine I consider us even, not when this request is so very small. Brussels, eh? And you do not wish to wait until morning, no doubt. A night flight can be dangerous, but I have never been afraid of a little danger."

"Danger does not matter to me," Jennet said. In truth, she could not bring herself to care about the possibility of dying, even of falling from a great height, and she further did not care that she did not care. Once she was in Brussels, perhaps, she might exert herself to live again. "I am ready to go whenever you are."

"Then relax, and permit me to Move you." Clemency settled her goggles over her eyes and rose a few feet into the air. An invisible hand wrapped itself around Jennet's legs and waist, gripping her firmly but not painfully, and in the next moment she, too, had left the ground. She tensed, and Clemency said, "Do not fight it, as that makes Moving more difficult."

"Not impossible?" Jennet asked. Her voice came out as a squeak, and she swallowed and added, "You tried to Move the lieutenant."

"Yes, and Moving a Shaper who is in a position to cling to something is one of the more difficult things a Mover can attempt." They rose higher now, and the ground beneath was a dark-colored expanse with the darker blotch of the Army camp to the north, speckled with lights. "A Shaper can become extremely strong, and that combined with his will makes him almost impossible to shift," Clemency continued. "I do hope you are not afraid of heights."

"I don't believe I am. Besides, it is too dark to see how high we are." Jennet craned her neck, not wishing to overbalance herself, if that were possible. It was true, she could not tell how far up they had risen. Wind battered her body and tried to steal the breath from her lungs.

"I will go faster, if you are comfortable," Clemency shouted over the wind. "I will not Fly so high you will freeze, so there are no worries on that hand. And do not fear, I won't drop you. I am rated at just over nine thousand pounds lifting capacity, and your weight is nothing, because I do not tire the way someone carrying you bodily would."

"Faster, yes," Jennet said. The wind swept her words away, but Clemency nodded as if she had heard Jennet. The wind picked up, and Jennet screamed with excitement, for she was suddenly moving faster than she ever had before, soaring through the air with Clemency above and behind her.

Now she regretted not being able to see the ground, as she was certain that would make their speed even more noticeable. She spread her arms wide and let the wind buoy her up, laughing. Clemency said something that was lost in the wind, and their speed increased again until Jennet had to close her eyes to keep the wind from tearing her eyeballs from their sockets.

Flying blind, she had no idea where they were or how much time had passed, but eventually their speed decreased, and Jennet was able to open her eyes again. In the distance, a city loomed, its few lights marking its contours. Jennet's temporary elation fled. She knew nothing of Brussels except that many of its citizens spoke French. On the other hand, it was well away from the Army, and perhaps that was all she needed.

Clemency set them down at a crossroads outside the city. "Do you have a place to stay?" she asked. "I feel great uncertainty at abandoning you to a strange city."

"I will make my way as best I can," Jennet said. "Thank you."

"It really is the least I can do." Clemency reached inside her heavy grey coat—it was new, Jennet noticed, not the one Jennet had destroyed with her shot—and removed a large purse. She dug out a handful of coins and extended them to Jennet, who hesitated, then took half of what was offered.

"Please, take it all," Clemency protested. "You will find it much easier to make your way if you are not impoverished."

"This will be enough," Jennet said, and pocketed the money.

Clemency put her purse away, then, hesitating, said, "Are you certain you can tell me nothing? You have the look of someone bearing a great burden. I would help if I could."

Jennet felt awkward at having judged Clemency poorly just because of her interest in Falconer, an interest Jennet herself shared. "I—thank you. That means so much to me, I cannot express. But this is not a secret it will do me any good to spread knowledge of. I wish you luck in the coming fight."

"Napoleon is still moving, isn't he?" Clemency sounded more curious than afraid.

"If the 51st cannot hold him, he will cut the Army in half," Jennet said.

"That is my understanding, as well," Clemency said. "But you did not leave the Army because you are afraid of Napoleon, did you?"

Jennet shook her head. "Nor did I leave because I did not wish to be on the losing side. Lord Wellington is a great commander. This war has not yet been lost."

"I see." Clemency nodded. "Good fortune to you, Ned Graeme." With a rush of air, she leaped into the sky and was gone.

Jennet did not watch her go. After a moment's consideration, she removed her rifleman's jacket and threw it into a bush. Turning it inside out would conceal her identity, but the idea of keeping it, whatever its condition, sickened her. She would rather look strange in shirtsleeves than wear a uniform she no longer deserved.

She turned on her heel and wearily walked toward Brussels. With luck, she would find an inn still open, and a bed, and then...she could not bear to think past the next few minutes. Things would look better in the morning.

CHAPTER 31

IN WHICH A CONVERSATION CHANGES JENNET'S PERSPECTIVE ON MANY THINGS

Jennet woke late the following day, confused by the unfamiliar slant of the light and the musty smell of her bedchamber, so different from the mildewy dampness of her tent. For a few moments, she lay on her back, staring up at the underside of the roof. It was dingy, swirled with dirty marks that her idle mind turned into pictures: a dog, half a table, a man's profile stretched out like warm wax. Then she remembered where she was. Brussels. She had found the inn late last night and spent a few centimes for a bed to herself in a dormitory at the top of the house.

She sat up. She was alone in the hot, sun-drenched room. Her hand reached for her watch to discover the time, and her heart contracted when her fingers found only cloth. Quickly she slapped her trouser pockets and breathed out when she discovered Clemency's money was still all there.

Memories returned. She had dreamed they were all back on the road to Valenciennes, walking endlessly through the forest, and it took a little while for the dream to fade. She would not go down to breakfast with the others, would not greet Falconer or joke about his snoring keeping her awake. Jennet closed her eyes and made herself breathe slowly until the pain in her heart subsided.

The inn was a hostel, and did not offer meals, so she walked in search of food, though she was not hungry. She found a street vendor selling hand-sized meat pies and bought one. It was not very good, but it suited what remained of her appetite. By the position of the sun, it was just after noon. She had not slept so late in years.

She licked meat juice off her fingers and wiped her hands on her trousers. They did not have an obviously military appearance, and her somewhat grimy white shirt looked like ones worn by every other person she passed. True, most men wore coats, but even in shirtsleeves, she did not draw too much attention. She had made a clean escape.

Her feet carried her onward, through the quiet but poor neighborhood she had ended up in late last night and past shops and houses to an enormous open plaza surrounded on all sides by tall, elegant buildings of creamy stone. Jennet had never seen so many windows in her entire life. She stopped in front of a stone edifice whose towers rose at all four corners and from its center. The central tower sprouted smaller towers and spires so Jennet had the impression of a spiky flower unfolding before her. She did not believe it was a church or cathedral, based on how many people were going in and out of it, but it shared some of those holy places' beauty.

She wandered around the plaza, drinking in the sights. The vast space was crowded with people, many of them talking loudly in French or Flemish or even German. All of them sounded agitated, some angry, most afraid. As she walked, she heard the same things repeated over and over again: Napoleon's army on the move, the Allied forces powerless to stop him, soldiers might overrun Brussels at any moment. Jennet was sure the last was not true, but the words filled her with guilt nonetheless.

She left the plaza and headed west until the road she was on crossed a canal. She walked to the center of the bridge and stopped to look over the side at the water rushing past. It never stopped moving, and Jennet considered how that would feel, to drop into the water and be carried downstream, all the way to the sea. Unless this canal did not go to the sea. Jennet found it did not matter to her where it went.

Her hands curled over the railing. It would be so simple to climb over and jump in. The drop likely would not kill her outright, and she could follow the water until she sank beneath it. So simple.

She closed her eyes and sighed. It would not be simple, because well-meaning people would wish to rescue her, pull her from the water's embrace and warn her of the dangers of jumping off bridges. And she was not completely certain she was ready to die, despite everything that had happened in the last twenty-four hours. She might be fully damned now, but she did not relish the idea of meeting her eternal fate just yet.

She crossed the bridge and kept walking, following the twisting streets of Brussels until they led her back to the canal. By that time, the sun was setting, and her body suggested food was a good idea. She had no appetite still, but she bought a wedge of cheese off the last vendor in an open-air market and ate it as she walked back to the plaza. Perhaps the crowds would be gone, and she could see if they lit those marvelous windows at all after dark.

Ahead, men crowded the steps of one of the elaborate mansions, a house easily fifty feet long and, like the other buildings, covered in windows. Jennet slowed her steps to watch, idly curious for the first time all day.

A carriage drew up to the steps, and a footman hopped down from the rear to open the door. A man stepped out and was instantly mobbed by the crowd. Jennet's first impression was that it was a very genteel mob, as none of them attacked the new arrival or tore at his clothes. Her second realization was that the man was Wellington.

She froze, certain he would see her and remember her and know exactly what she had done. There was nowhere to hide on the street, nowhere to run that would not draw attention. But Wellington did not look her way. He gestured, and the crowd, while remaining loud and outspoken, parted like the Red Sea to permit him entrance.

Jennet did not move until the door shut behind Wellington, and the crowd dispersed and the carriage drove away. She reminded herself that the great man was unlikely to remember all the faces he met once and never saw again. She had not known his headquarters was in Brussels, though it was a location that made sense, central to the Army and well out of where Napoleon might immediately strike. Wellington Coerced by Napoleon...it did not bear dwelling on.

The draw of the great plaza had diminished. Jennet avoided it and retraced her steps to the hostel. She paid for her bed and lay sleepless on it as men entered and left the room. Some of them occupied the other beds, ignoring Jennet, who was relieved that she did not have to Coerce anyone into not molesting her. To her surprise, none of them snored. She ruthlessly refused to dwell on Falconer sharing a bed with her and tried her best to sleep.

This time, her early night meant an early morning, and she woke to the sound of church bells just as dawn pinked the sky. A sudden impatience gripped her, impatience with her melancholy and despair. If she did not intend to take her own life, she needed to return to living it. But she had no idea what that meant. She had no skills anyone would pay her to use on their behalf, she had no family she was willing to own, and worst, she had no desire, nothing she wished to achieve. She could not simply remain in Brussels, wandering the streets endlessly until the war came this way.

In the back of her mind, a tiny voice whispered *You abandoned your goal* and would not be dispelled no matter what else Jennet made herself dwell on. She had been a soldier, with a duty to stop Napoleon, and she had left that life behind. "I had to go," she said aloud in English, and ignored the passersby who overheard her and gave her quizzical looks. She could not have stayed. Falconer would have believed it his duty to reveal her talent to Waldroup, at least, and likely to the other officers of the high command, and they would have...she did not know what they would do with her, but it could not be anything good. She could not have stayed.

Her walk this day took her down narrow streets thronged with people as the plaza had been. A closer look revealed how heavily-laden many of them were, how they moved slowly as if wearier even than those loads would suggest. Most of them traveled in groups, with dirty-faced children in tow. More refugees. Their haunted expressions, the cries of their children, unsettled Jennet, and she walked faster, eager to leave them behind.

Emerging from the warren, she passed an urchin on a street corner, selling broadsheets. She considered buying one, but it was in Flemish, so she continued on, telling herself it was destiny that she not know the news. But the next news seller had broadsheets in French. She paid for one and found a quiet corner to read it.

She had not seen a newspaper since the Peninsula, when the company Bounders brought them weekly from England; that practice had not died out when the Army entered France, but Jennet had lost interest once she could not laugh at the differences between what the English newspapers believed and what was actually happening in the field. These French broadsheets were not much different from English ones, she noticed, in their desire for sensationalism. This particular one reported that Napoleon continued to advance northward and that the Prussians had been cut off from their British allies. That could not be true. Jennet still did not understand how newspapers were permitted to reveal military secrets like troop movements, but in this case, they were reporting lies.

Unless they weren't.

Jennet folded the broadsheet small and tucked it under one arm. Surely Waldroup's change of emotion had come soon enough that he could bring his regiment against Napoleon's in time to halt the Grande Armée's advance? Sick worry built in her stomach. If it had not been in time, Jennet had revealed her secret and lost everything she cared about for nothing.

She continued walking, not seeing her surroundings. It did not matter. She was just one person, not even a soldier anymore, and she had done what she could to prevent Napoleon's advance. She had nothing left to give. *You abandoned them* rang silently in her ears, and she shook her head to dislodge the horrible words. She had had no choice.

A carriage rushing past brought her back to herself, startling her into taking a step back from danger. The driver did not even shout at her. Jennet tried to summon up outrage, but felt nothing, as if she had success-fully Coerced apathy in herself.

She looked around and discovered her path had brought her to a church, not large enough to be a cathedral, but obviously a place of worship. Its dark grey stone walls rose high and forbidding to spires on every corner, and above its massive iron-banded front doors, a bell tower extended, higher than the spires and more solid. Jennet walked its length, examining the stained glass windows, which depicted elongated figures kneeling or praying or raising their arms in praise to God. She wished she knew more about the Catholic faith to interpret the stories the windows told.

On a whim, she trotted up the shallow steps to the door and pushed it open. It gave easily, and Jennet slipped inside, pausing to permit her eyes to adjust to the dimness. Then she walked forward into the nave.

The chapel appeared unoccupied. Rows of pews gave the space an angular, forbidding appearance at odds with how Jennet believed a church ought to be. She walked down the center aisle, stopping well away from the altar and the carved screen behind it. Paintings of cherubs welcoming the Christ child decorated the screens to either side. Jennet did not like cherubs. They always seemed to be plotting something.

"Are you in need?" someone said in French.

Jennet turned to see a priest garbed in black standing a few feet behind her. "I am a visitor to Brussels and I was curious," she said. "I am not of your faith. I apologize if I should not be here."

"A house of God welcomes all who seek, not only those who follow a particular creed." The priest approached her, both his hands tucked together in his sleeves. "We have a beautiful church. Would you like to see it?"

"Oh, but surely you must have more important things to do," Jennet said.

"I confess I was drawn to this chapel today," the priest said, "and I choose to interpret that as a sign that this is the most important thing the Lord has in mind for me this day. Please. Permit me to show you the chapel I love."

Jennet hesitated a moment longer, and the priest extended a hand to her, gesturing her to follow him. "Here is something you may not have seen before," he said, leading her through the pews to the wall. Beneath the stained glass windows, friezes had been carved, great marble panels that looked satiny smooth in their curves and angles. The light coming through the colored glass was not bright enough for Jennet to immediately make out the carvings' subjects.

She stepped closer and peered at the first. "They are stoning that man," she said.

"This relief is dedicated to St. Stephen, first of the Christian martyrs," the priest said. "Do you know the story?"

"He preached of Christ to the Jews, and they accused him of blasphemy," Jennet said, "and stoned him when he would not recant." The words came so effortlessly they surprised her. She had not remembered the story until that moment.

"Ah, so you are no Catholic, but also no heathen," the priest said with a smile.

Jennet examined the contorted figure of Stephen, its exaggerated torment. "This is very old, is it not?"

"It is. Come, allow me to show you the others."

Jennet followed him around the chapel walls, marveling. Aside from that initial discovery, she was unfamiliar with most of the saints depicted. Some of them were also martyrs: St. Sebastian, pierced with arrows, and St. Peter, crucified upside down. Others were less dramatic: St. Christopher, wading neck-deep in a flood with the Christ child on his shoulders, or St. Anthony, depicted with his hand raised in exhortation, surrounded by cringing figures overwhelmed by the power of his preaching. "They called him the Hammer of Heretics," the priest said, running a finger along the line of St. Anthony's shoulder. "A powerful way of saying he brought many back to the true faith."

Jennet was uncomfortably aware that from the priest's perspective, she had strayed from the true faith. "So, what is the purpose of a saint?" she asked. "Do you worship them?"

"Say, rather, we revere them as holy figures," the priest said. "They intercede on our behalf, and they set an example we lesser beings may follow."

"Set an example." Jennet glanced back at St. Anthony. "But surely no one can be as holy as a saint."

"Setting aside the fact that every saint was once an ordinary person like you and me, who is to say what calling God has for each of us?" The priest smiled, a surprisingly impish expression. "And I do not believe we need to be holy to be God's hands on earth."

His words struck Jennet to the heart, and she did not know why. "How are we to know?" she asked, her words sounding like a plea in her ears. "If we have a purpose, how shall we know what it is?"

"That sounds as if you fear receiving an answer, child." The priest's smile fell away, but he sounded compassionate rather than critical.

"I fear more coming to my purpose too late." The words burst out of Jennet, and again she did not know where they came from. But she felt in her bones they were the truest thing she had ever said.

"Sometimes prayer is the answer." The priest laid a hand on Jennet's shoulder. "Sometimes we study the words of God to discover what He wishes for us. And sometimes the answer comes from another person. But I believe seeking, however we do it, holds within it the promise of an answer."

"Then tell me," Jennet demanded, forgetting she spoke to a man of God. "For those of us with talent, what is our duty?"

"Do you believe your talent comes from God?" The priest looked mildly interested, and not at all as if he already knew the answer.

Jennet let out a deep breath. "I don't know. My talent is more curse than blessing, and yet I cannot bear the idea that it comes of the Devil, for would that not make me damned for something not of my choosing?"

"A curse." The priest's grip on Jennet's shoulder tightened. "You are not the first to come to me with that question. And yet." He was no taller than she, and their eyes were on a level. "Have you considered that no one who is truly damned would care about that question?"

Jennet gaped. "I—"

"If your talent is what I imagine, you have my sympathy. I have, as I said, encountered many with your talent. Most of them are hollow inside, seeing other people as things. A few of you seek a different path." The priest smiled, and Jennet shivered at the depth of compassion in his expression. "Do not despair. I find it difficult to believe God would entrust anyone with a talent save He also provided him a way to use it in His service."

Jennet's throat ached. "I have done so many things I should not," she said, her voice rough. "I have hurt those I loved. I cannot forgive myself, so why should God forgive me?"

"Oh, my child." The priest moved his hand to rest on her head. "'For all have sinned and do need the glory of God.' Do you know that one?"

"The Epistle to the Romans, chapter three, verse twenty-three," Jennet replied automatically.

"Very good. What comes next?"

Jennet strained to remember. "It is 'being justified freely through his grace,' but I cannot recall the rest."

"That is enough. St. Paul understood that truth better than anyone—have you never considered how much he had to repent of? We are all sinners, and we are all qualified for redemption. The scripture does not say 'except for Coercers.' All of us, young man. You and I and the King of France and even Napoleon Bonaparte. You have sinned, and were you a Catholic, I would offer you the confessional. As it is, all I can offer you is the promise that in choosing to do good with your talent, insofar as that is possible, you choose a path away from damnation." He smiled again. "And a promise that if you continue to seek absolution, you will almost certainly find it."

Jennet rubbed a sleeve across her eyes. "How can you promise that?"

"Because you were drawn here as surely as I was. Because you asked the right questions. I see great strength of purpose within you, my child. You will not be satisfied until you have made right the wrongs you have done."

Jennet shook her head. "It is what I wish most," she said, "but I do not know how it is to be done."

"That, I cannot tell you. But it would not hurt for you to examine your talent and identify how it might be used for good."

The low tolling of the bell silenced them both. "Excuse me," the priest said. "I should have prepared for Mass several minutes ago."

"I beg your pardon, I have kept you too long," Jennet said.

The priest smiled again. "Mass happens every day. It is only rarely I have the opportunity to speak with such a young man as you are."

Impulsively, Jennet said, "Sir, I am a woman—I know how I appear, and there are reasons—but I do not wish to lie to you, even by omission."

The priest's smile widened. "Truly extraordinary," he said. He made the sign of the cross over her. "Go with God, child, and remember—the Devil does not give gifts, only God."

Jennet nodded. She hurried through the nave, where men and women were seated on the pews. She had not even noticed their entrance. A few of them looked at her as she ran past, but idly, and she made it outside the church without being stopped.

There, she stood on the steps as more people passed her to enter the church. Her heart lightened in a way it had not in years. It had never occurred to her that she might be carrying burdens she did not deserve, but if the priest was right—and she felt in her bones that he was—she was not damned simply for being a Coercer. And everything she had done that hurt people—well, if that were to her damnation, should not the ways in which she helped people be to her credit, if not her salvation?

She drew in a deep breath. Then she set off running for Wellington's headquarters.

She arrived on his step breathless and sweating. The sun burned hot in the summer sky, and that plus her exertion made her long for a swim in the canal. Instead, she banged on the door. She did not like to enter unannounced, as if this were any public place, and perhaps Wellington lived here as well as working here and would not like strangers barging in.

The door opened. A man in a Speaker's uniform gazed down at Jennet; he was the tallest man she had ever seen, taller than Falconer, taller than the Extraordinary Speaker who had summoned Clemency. His brow furrowed. "Yes?"

"I would like to speak with Lord Wellington," Jennet said.

The Speaker's brow furrowed even deeper with perplexity. "You believe the Duke is available to every urchin who walks in off the street? Begone, now, and trouble this house no more."

That, to Jennet, sounded hopelessly pompous. She belatedly wished she had only turned her rifleman's jacket inside out and not got rid of it. That dramatic gesture had robbed her of some measure of respectability. Determining not to resort to Coercion unless it became essential, she said, "I am no urchin, I am a soldier of the 95th. I know what my appearance is, but I have come a long way to deliver my message. Please, sir, will you permit me entrance? I swear I will not take too much of Lord Wellington's time."

"A rifleman?" The Speaker sounded astonished. "You are out of uniform, soldier."

"I know, and I can explain, but I would prefer to explain to Lord Wellington." Jennet looked up with what she hoped was an appealing expression. Her dependence on Coercion meant she rarely had to concern herself with appearances.

The Speaker's brow furrowed. "I have no evidence you are what you claim. Move along."

"But—" Jennet bit back a lengthier retort. It was time for drastic measures. For a moment, she felt her usual guilt over using Coercion to get her way. Then she remembered the priest's words. Coercing this man would save lives, possibly hundreds of thousands of lives.

She gathered up her sense of his emotions. Despite his demeanor, he was afraid—more afraid than Jennet could see a reason for. She soothed his fears, and immediately the worry lines disappeared from his forehead. Then she twisted his fear into a state where speaking his fears would ease his mind. "Surely it would not hurt for me to speak to Lord Wellington for five minutes?" she said in a low, confiding voice.

The Speaker's brow relaxed further, and he bit his lip nervously. "That would be difficult," he said, "as my lord Duke has already left Brussels."

As he spoke, his fear spiked, and Jennet quickly soothed it. If he was so worried about something that his natural emotions could overcome Jennet's Coerced ones, he was far more afraid than he ought to be if Wellington had simply left Brussels for the battlefield. "Sir, is this the last big push?" she asked, and Coerced his fear to a different pitch, back into the state where speaking his fears would relieve them.

"Napoleon's troops moved faster than we expected," the Speaker said in a low, confiding voice. "He has driven a wedge between the Army and our Prussian allies. Both allied forces are moving to circle around and come at the Grande Armée from the north. But it might not be enough."

"Where did Lord Wellington go?" Jennet pressed.

The Speaker hesitated. Jennet leaned on his fears just a little more. "Somewhere north of Nivelles," the Speaker said. "The armies will meet in that area. Nobody knows more than that."

"Thank you, sir," Jennet said. She ran down the steps and sped away.

She had no idea where Nivelles was, and the first two people she stopped were newcomers to the city and did not know either. But the third man said, "Twenty miles south along the main road. But the French army advances from that direction—have you not seen the refugees filling this city? You will be walking into a nightmare."

"I know," Jennet said, and ran south.

CHAPTER 32

IN WHICH JENNET HAS A DILEMMA NOT RESOLVED BY A GOOD MEAL

She kept a steady, rapid pace all the way through the city until her chest and legs ached and she had to slow to a walk, and never mind her sense of urgency. The road heading south and east ran through tilled land laid out in neat if irregularly oriented squares. The day was as sunny as before, but the air was hot and heavy and damp. Clouds massed on the horizon, big, heavy, pendulous grey clouds that promised rain before nightfall. Jennet eyed the clouds and guessed at how soon they would arrive. She would need shelter before that.

The road was as crowded as Brussels' great plaza had been, both with travelers on foot and heavy farm wagons. All were headed toward the city, making a great current of people against which Jennet swam. She stopped a pedestrian, a man bearing an enormous sack over his shoulder, and said, "What news have you of the army?"

The man shook his head. "I've no time to chat. The army advances without mercy. Leave me be, and look to your own concerns." He brushed past her and hurried on.

Jennet tried again, several times, to speak with the refugees. The ones who did not simply ignore her spoke as curtly as the first man. Frustrated, she trotted alongside one of the wagons and shouted, "Sir, please tell me, how close is the fighting?"

The wagon driver, a heavyset man with a thick blond beard and shaggy eyebrows, let out a short, mirthless bark of a laugh. "Close enough," he said. "You are not going south, are you?"

"I must," Jennet replied.

"The more fool you," the wagon driver said. "You ought turn round and see what shelter you can find in Brussels, little fellow like you. Hop up, and I will give you a ride."

"Thank you, but I cannot stay. Have you seen any fighting? Where have all these people come from?" She took a few running steps to keep up with the still-moving wagon.

The wagon driver shrugged. "I left my village when men fled Nivelles. I chose not to wait to be overrun by the army. So I was well ahead of the fighting. But those as came from the south said the British were barely holding back Napoleon's advance. I heard the former Emperor had Coerced everyone in his path. That was enough for me."

"But if he had Coerced the British Army, surely they would have stopped fighting?"

"I don't know anything about that." The man slapped the seat beside him. "Last chance. You won't make it ten miles before you run into the battle."

Jennet shook her head. "It is kind of you, but I must move on. Good luck to you."

She pushed past more wagons, more families laden down with sacks and children, and spoke to a few other people. All of them repeated what the first wagon driver had said, though they gave different opinions as to how close Napoleon was and did not agree on the fate of the British Army.

After these encounters, Jennet's initial optimism fled. She intended to find Wellington and do what, exactly? She could not imagine herself coming into his presence and declaring she was an Extraordinary Coercer who wished to defeat Napoleon. Wellington was not likely to believe her unless she Coerced someone as proof, and then he would fear her, and that had its own problems. It was foolishness, but she had no other plan.

She contemplated her other options. She might, instead, seek out Napoleon directly. The idea made her shiver with dread. He was more skilled and more experienced than she at Coercion, and he would be surrounded by his most loyal men, none of whom she was likely to be able to Coerce to her side before the others killed her. And she also did not believe stopping Napoleon from Coercing anyone else would bring the war immediately to an end, not when there were so many other generals and Marshals commanding so many men.

She came to a stop, breathing heavily from exertion. Perhaps this was a fool's errand. She was only one person; why did she believe she was anything special? She should return to Brussels, and...

...and sit doing nothing, reading the reports of Napoleon's advance and the allied forces' attempts to stop him? No, even if all she managed was to be given a jacket and a rifle and sent to the front, she had to do something.

After a few miles, the stream of refugees dwindled, though she remained the only one heading south on the road. She walked on, more slowly, keeping an eye on the clouds. They drew nearer, turning the light odd shades of brass and blue, until she imagined she could see the rain pouring down in the distance. Then she ran again, looking for a house with a barn she might shelter in.

Most of the farms along the road looked more like English keeps than mere houses. High stone walls shut out the world, and peaked red roofs were all that was visible of the buildings within. Jennet's hope of sneaking quietly into a barn and waiting out the storm faded.

The storm was near enough now that Jennet could definitely hear the sound of hard rain striking the parched ground. She sprinted the last several yards to the next farmhouse-keep and pounded on the gate, which was a heavy iron-banded thing that made the house's resemblance to a fortress even greater.

There were two windows no bigger than Jennet's doubled fists in the gate, both of them barred, both of them shuttered so she could not see into the keep. She jigged with impatience. If the farmer would not give her shelter, she would simply have to get drenched, but she wished to know which of those lay in her future sooner rather than later.

A shrill wooden creak drew Jennet's attention to the right-hand window opening. Most of a face became visible behind the bars. "Yes? What is it?" he said in oddly-accented French. His voice was high for a man, but his heavy brows and thick mustache gave away his sex.

"I am a traveler, and I seek shelter from the storm. Please, may I—" The first hard, warm drops struck Jennet's head. "I'll take anything, sir, but it will be very wet out here soon!"

The face disappeared, and the window clapped shut. Jennet took a step back, annoyed at the man's abrupt dismissal. Then she heard the latch draw back, and half the door swung inward. "Inside," the man said. Jennet did not need to be asked twice.

She ran with the man across a courtyard of packed earth as the rain poured down, slapping the ground with hard little *tocks* as if the rain were gravel and not water. It felt almost as hard striking Jennet's head and shoulders, and she suppressed an unmanly squeal. Chickens squawked and flapped to shelter in a neat hut where the ground, looser and stirred up in swirls, showed signs of poultry habitation. A couple of dogs, long-limbed with big floppy brown ears, scrambled after Jennet and her savior, and they all tumbled in through the door of an ancient stone farmhouse together.

Jennet took two steps and immediately tripped over a dog. She caught herself on a stone slab of a counter just inside the door and, breathing heavily, got her feet beneath her. The tall, dark room smelled of onion and garlic, and it was comfortably warm, not hot as it was outside—or as the weather had been before the storm descended. The dogs bumped around her legs, whining for attention. She scratched the head of the nearest one. "Thank you," she said.

The man shook his head. His longish dark hair and beard were as thick as his mustache, his eyebrows looked like a couple of black caterpillars, and black hair covered his forearms. "Could not leave you out to drown," he said. "Mother, can we have a sop and a brew?"

The woman he addressed as Mother looked far too young to have a son his age. Jennet guessed he meant she was his wife, the mother of his children, though there were no signs of children present. Mother nodded silently and turned to the soup kettle over the fire. She was slender and fair-haired, but her sleeves pushed back over her elbows revealed strong arms. She stirred the pot, then put a couple of slices of thick bread on a toasting fork and settled it into a clever contraption that held it in place, freeing her hands to slice cheese.

In no time, Jennet had a dish of toasted bread with cheese melted over it, drenched in beef broth and curls of onion, and a large mug of dark ale. Her appetite, which had been gone since leaving the Army camp, returned full force, and she dug in happily. The man and his wife ate heartily as well; Jennet was surprised at the woman joining them, as she knew in many French households the men and the women ate separately. But Mother did not behave as if this were anything out of the ordinary.

The rain had not stopped by the time their plates were empty. Mother rose and silently put the dishes in the large ceramic sink, then pumped water and began washing. The man stared at Jennet. "Where are you headed, traveler with very poor luck?"

"To Nivelles," Jennet said, "and you were so generous, I'm not sure I should call it bad luck."

The man smiled. His teeth were unexpectedly white in his dark-bearded face. "It's bad luck if you hoped to reach Nivelles tonight. This storm is like to last until dawn."

"Oh." Jennet's heart sank. She reminded herself that the armies were still chasing each other, and it was unlikely they would clash before another two days, at least from what she remembered of Wellington's map. "I should not impose on your hospitality more, but if you don't mind, I can sleep in the barn."

"We have room. It's a big house." The man rose. "I am Gerard, and this is Amélie."

"Ned," Jennet said, deciding at the last minute not to reveal her true sex. "Thank you." It occurred to her for the first time to wonder where everyone else was. Surely a farm this size required more workers?

She followed Gerard down a dark hall to a staircase, past doorways looking into somber, empty rooms, or rather, rooms that felt empty even though they were all furnished. At the top of the stairs, Gerard pushed open a door, revealing a small bedroom with an iron-frame bed topped by a white counterpane. A wash stand beneath the window held a china pitcher and basin. "This is very generous, sir," Jennet said.

"As I said, it's a big house."

Gerard turned to leave. Impulsively, Jennet said, "Sir, where is everyone? It cannot be only you and Amélie."

Gerard fixed his dark gaze on her. "War is coming," he said. "Most of our workers left for the city, out of fear or out of hope they'd make a better life there, who knows? But my family has owned this place for a century, and I'll not be driven away out of fear."

"Do you know if Napoleon is near? Where he might be?"

Gerard looked at her as if she were demented. "'Tis not Napoleon we fear, 'tis the English," he said. "I can see how you'd see it different, you being English. But I don't hold that against you. In truth, we'll suffer no matter which side attacks first." He nodded politely and shut the door.

Jennet thought about sitting on the bed, contemplated the condition of her trousers after her long walk, and instead sat on the chair behind the door that had been revealed when the door was shut. She had not considered how the folk of Belgium might feel about the various armies approaching, British and Prussian and French. To her, Napoleon was such an obvious threat her sympathies were all with the British and their allies, but as Gerard said, it did not matter who struck first if either side's attack meant overwhelming this little farm.

The grey light entering the room grew ever dimmer as the invisible sun sank in the western sky. Jennet removed her boots and, after some consideration, her trousers. Gerard and Amélie were unlikely to enter her room at night, and if they did, she would feel terrible about Coercing them, but she would do it to defend herself.

She lay awake listening to the sound of the rain rattling the shingles and considered her situation. She still had no idea what she should do. Approach Wellington, and hope for the best? Or try to reach Napoleon, and pray she was not Coerced? She fell asleep feeling dissatisfied with all her options.

CHAPTER 33

IN WHICH JENNET SEARCHES FOR ALLIES, AND IN THE END CREATES HER OWN

The morning dawned wet, but clear. Jennet ate eggs and bacon with her hosts and bade them farewell by the time the sun cleared the horizon. Gerard had assured her the road she was on would lead straight to Nivelles. "It's another fifteen miles," he had said, "an easy stroll for a strong young lad," and Jennet had smiled with him.

The rain had churned the road into muck, so Jennet kept to the verge, walking at a faster than leisurely pace. Fifteen miles meant she would reach Nivelles after noon, and by then, she hoped to have a plan.

But it was difficult to plan effectively when the day was so beautiful. The air was muggy, true, and clung to Jennet's skin like a caul, and there was no breeze, and the pace she set raised a light sweat, but the sky was a brilliant blue, and the air was filled with the scent of wildflowers, and Jennet had trouble remembering that war was on the horizon.

An hour later, the road entered a forest, and Jennet slowed, feeling uncertain at not having good visibility. She had met no one coming or going, but that did not mean there might not be bandits or even soldiers, though she doubted enemy soldiers could have made it this far north without her noticing.

Then she heard the boom and crack of artillery fire, southwest of where she was. Another thunderous clap, nearer than the first, resounded through the forest. But the armies could not possibly be so close? Jennet broke into a run she maintained for half a dozen yards before coming to a halt. Running toward the cannons was stupid, particularly since she did not know whose cannons they were. And yet staying here was just as stupid.

So she walked, keeping a steady pace, as the thunder of cannon fire grew louder. The cannons were a good deal closer than the ten more miles it was to Nivelles; they were perhaps five miles away. She wished she knew what had happened, whether Napoleon had pushed forward or the British and Prussians had successfully cut off his advance. In either case, it meant battle had been joined, and there was no more time for Jennet to dither.

She came out of the forest to see a little village ahead, teeming with furious movement. Her pace slowed to a halt as she watched men and women hurrying toward her. Some of them drove carts harnessed to mules, while others chivvied animals ahead of them, dogs and goats and even a pig or two. Jennet saw the now-ubiquitous loads borne on backs, great burlap sacks knobby with their possessions. The sounds of frightened animals and crying children drifted toward her.

Jennet came to herself and ran to meet the fleeing villagers. "Have you seen the army?" she demanded. "How far?"

No one stopped to speak to her. One old woman perched atop a load in a rickety cart shook her fist in the direction of the village and screamed, "We'll all die! British or French, it's all the same to them—we are nothing in their path!"

The closer Jennet drew to the village, the more crowded the road became, until the traffic forced her to abandon it and run wide of the narrow, muddy streets. She tried again to speak to the fleeing villagers, but the only response she got was from a gangly youth who merely turned and pointed with a shaking hand southward. Jennet looked in that direction, past the houses, and saw more refugees headed north.

The pounding of artillery was very close now, only a few miles away. Jennet pushed past a family driving two goats ahead of their wagon and ran, her boots clumping through the churned-up ground, until she neared the next village. Rather than fight her way through the crowds of refugees, she veered east and ran through the fields, trampling the new crops.

She crossed more planted fields, occasionally glancing toward the road and its steady stream of travelers. Their stolid, constant movement unnerved her, that slow but inexorable plodding north. For some of them, their flight was already too late.

She returned to the road when she was past most of the fleeing crowds and hurried along, cursing last night's rain and the morass it had made of the road. She passed another village, and another, tiny little collections of houses that would not show on even the most detailed map. And, finally, she came to what she had been looking for: the churned-up ground that indicated a large body of men had marched through here, tearing up the earth on both sides of the road.

She ran faster, following the Army's path up and down the low rises of the countryside. At the top of every rise, she strained to see the kind of movement she remembered from battles in Spain and Portugal, the regular formations and bright colors of soldiers. Rise after rise passed, and Jennet's pace had slowed with tiredness, before she came over a final rise and saw the movement she had walked so far to see: lines of infantrymen, behind which were mounted soldiers. Almost certainly reserve forces.

Relief surged through Jennet, and she ran, stumbling over rough ground until she could see the uniforms clearly. They were nothing she recognized, solid black broadcloth, though not the black-on-black of the War Office, with bright silver badges in their caps, but what mattered was that they were not French.

Two of the riders saw her running toward them and turned away from their unit to stop her approach. "*Halt! Komm doch zurück!*" the first said.

Jennet did not understand the words beyond recognizing that they were German. "I am an English soldier, and I have a message for Lord Wellington," she said, slowly and clearly. She was aware that speaking slowly and clearly would not magically cause these men to understand her language, but perhaps if they spoke a little English, it would help.

The soldiers, one a captain, the other a major, glanced at each other. The major said, in heavily accented English, "You are not a soldier. Leave now. This is a battlefield."

"I am a soldier. Pray, direct me to the duke." Jennet planted her feet and threw her narrow shoulders back, defying him. Part of her quivered at addressing a superior officer so bluntly, even if he was not, strictly speaking, her superior, but to her surprise, she felt no fear now that she had achieved her first objective.

The two men conferred quietly in German. Jennet waited patiently.

Now that she had a moment's peace, she saw neither was completely unscathed; while they did not appear wounded, their uniforms were torn and bloody, the sign of men who had been injured and then been under the care of an Extraordinary Shaper. However quiet things might be here and now, these soldiers had seen battle recently.

She wished she understood what they were saying, to know whether Coercion would be needed. Then, to her surprise, the captain dismounted and put a hand on her shoulder. "You are a messenger?" he said.

Jennet nodded.

The captain's hand fell more heavily upon her. "Speak your answer," he said.

Only a Discerner would behave so. Before she could control herself, fear surged through her, and the captain gasped and snatched his hand away. "A spy," he said, drawing his sword.

Jennet flung herself backwards, away from his attack. Then she ran.

She heard nothing to indicate they were following her, no hooves pounding the squelching, muddy ground, but she did not stop to look behind her until she had disappeared over the nearest rise. The major had ridden a short distance toward the rise, following her, but as she watched, he wheeled his horse and returned to where the captain had mounted up again. Clearly he did not wish to be drawn into an ambush.

Breathing heavily, Jennet bent over with her hands on her knees and considered her options. She could not return to the soldiers, even if that was the most direct path to Wellington. It occurred to her that perhaps finding Wellington was not the best choice. After all, what would he direct her to do? Either he would not believe she was an Extraordinary Coercer and would put her to use as a mere messenger, or he would tell her to approach Napoleon directly and attempt to stop him. And that was something she could do without being instructed.

It was madness. Incapacitating or even killing Napoleon would not break his Coercion, and he had dozens of generals who all were committed to fighting this war regardless of his involvement. But it was the only thing she could do. The only thing that would prevent him Coercing all of Europe and forcing people to do his will. Jennet remembered Clemency's stricken face as she spoke of what she had endured, and her resolve hardened. She would make her best effort, and whatever it meant for the outcome of the war, she would have done the one thing no one else had the ability and the inclination to do.

She left the rise behind and ran west, circling well behind the German soldiers, who might see her and believe her to be an enemy spy. If any of them were Shapers, they would be capable of outrunning her. But she left the soldiers behind without drawing attention to herself. Then she kept running, watching the southern horizon. Tiny figures hovered high in the air, Skipping here and there or Flying in smooth paths. She wished she had an Extraordinary Mover's view of the battlefield, which should surely tell her something that a ground-level vista could not. She had a sense of the battle's edges from the smoke, but that did not tell her where Napoleon was.

After she had run for ten minutes or more, and her lungs ached with exertion, she began to wonder if she had passed everyone and was merely running on a line that would eventually take her to the sea. She decided to head south, which might be dangerous but would at least put her within sight of *something*.

She had stopped hearing the artillery fire some minutes before, not because it had ceased, but because like any other repetitive sound, it had eventually lost all meaning. Now she realized she no longer heard it because it had, in fact, stopped. At that moment, more cannon fire exploded nearby, and Jennet heard screams like she had only ever heard on the battlefield. She was far closer than she had believed.

She dragged herself up a low rise and, heedless of the danger of silhouetting herself against the horizon, stopped to catch her breath. From this vantage, she could see more clearly the squares and lines of the various regiments, even with the smoke drifting across the battlefield. She noticed two French eagle standards, one at the limit of her vision and nearly obscured by smoke, the other bright gold in the sunlight, taunting its enemies. She did not see Napoleon's standard anywhere. But someone carrying an eagle would know where his Emperor was.

The crack of musket fire brought her back to herself, and she flattened herself on the hill. She could not cross that killing ground to Coerce someone into giving away Napoleon's location. She needed help.

She surveyed the field, a more difficult proposition now that she did not have the advantage of height. Below her, crossing the tilled fields with no care for the crops they trampled, was a company of British soldiers.

Their uniforms looked strange, and it took Jennet a moment to recognize that this was because they were a darker red than usual and they lacked the white facings kept brilliantly bright with white pipe-clay. Their hats, too, were not typical shakos, but flat with a short brim and a golden badge Jennet could not make out. Then she recognized them. It was a company of Scorchers.

Jennet hurtled down the hill toward them. They were marching perpendicular to her path, and at first she had visions of herself screaming and waving her arms to attract their attention. Then the major at the head of the company commanded the others to halt, and he strode toward her. In halting French, he said, "It is to be danger. You go back now. Is very much danger."

"I am English, major," Jennet said.

The major looked relieved for only a moment. Then, in tones of great concern, he said, "Miss, what has happened to you, that you are garbed so irregularly?"

Jennet did not permit his accurate identification of her sex to discomfit her. He was Scottish, but she did not believe their common heritage would make a difference. "It does not matter, major. I need to go south."

"Miss, you should not be here. Pray, return northward." The major's red mustache quivered as he spoke. Jennet looked him over, looked all of them over, and made a decision.

"You do not understand, major," she said. "I wish all of you to go south with me. Now."

The major's eyebrows furrowed in confusion. "That's quite impossible, miss. I will send two of my men to escort you to safety."

He was a good man. And what she was about to do might well ruin him and every man in this company. For a moment, Jennet hesitated. She was not at all certain that what she intended would succeed, and if it did not, these men might face court-martial for dereliction of duty. But she had to try.

She gathered up their emotions, all ninety-four men, and smoothly swept them through a range of feeling that ended in adoration of her. For a moment, she was conscious of what she had done and how much power that gave her. Then the moment was gone.

The major blinked. "Miss," he said. In the next moment, he and every man in the company dropped to their knees before her.

Jennet ignored the sick feeling in her stomach. "I must reach Napoleon," she said. "You will get me to him."

"We will succeed or die trying, miss," the major said.

The sick feeling grew, and once again Jennet pretended it was not there. She could not tell herself this was not to her damnation. All she could hope was that the good she achieved outweighed the evil.

"Then let us go now," she said, and as the Scorchers rose to their feet, their faces shining in worshipful adoration, she led the way down the hill and south.

The major, whose name was Plaskett, marched beside Jennet and described to her the Scorchers' role in the battle. "We are to break the fighting at a farm called Hougoumont, which has been hot all morning," Plaskett explained.

"Then the French are occupied there," Jennet said.

Plaskett nodded. "The intent is to drive them back—"

"We will go around the fighting," Jennet said. "We have no time to fight through. Our goal is that French eagle, just there." She pointed at the glint of gold that was all that was visible of her target.

"I have my orders, though," Plaskett said.

"I know. But you will do as I say, won't you?" Jennet watched his emotions carefully. She had never known Coercion to break, even under the duress of conflicting orders, but that did not mean it was impossible.

Plaskett's indecision showed in the tremble of his lips and the creases in his forehead. "Of course I will. You are beloved to me above all others," he said.

Jennet leaned on his adoration a little more, and his face smoothed out. "Most beloved," he added with a dreamy smile. Jennet had to look away.

"But we cannot hope to avoid the fighting entirely," Plaskett said. "The French line extends too far."

"Then you will fight to defend me," Jennet said.

"To the death, miss." Plaskett's smile continued so beatifically happy Jennet wished she could kick herself for betraying a good man.

They came within earshot of Hougoumont before they saw it, as another rise prevented a clear line of sight. Jennet did not pause at the top of the hill. She had seen much battle in the last six years and did not need to see more to know it was brutal. But she could not help hearing the sounds of shouts, and screams, and rifle fire—no. Please, not rifles.

Despite herself, she scanned the walls and houses of the farm, which was as large as the one in which she had spent the night and filled with outbuildings. The commotion was too great for her to make out details, not even to see green jackets in contrast to red or blue ones. She ran on.

Then there were blue coats ahead, and men bringing muskets to bear on her and her Scorchers, and Major Plaskett shouted, *"Burn!"*

Fire bloomed mere yards away, and the screams of dying men were suddenly much louder. The scent of burned flesh filled the air, choking Jennet, who ran on without stopping, because stopping meant death. Muskets exploded practically in her face, the smoke of gunpowder made it impossible to see more than a foot in front of her, but Major Plaskett was still by her side, and fire consumed the French troops, and after what felt like an eternity and like two seconds at the same time, they were through.

"Move, move!" Major Plaskett shouted. Jennet shot a look behind her, but could not tell if they had lost any men, not with how fast she was running.

When Plaskett called a halt, she outran the Scorchers for a few paces because she had forgotten there was anything in life but running from the French. She walked back and caught her breath. It did not seem the Scorcher company was any smaller than it had been, but that might mean only a few had been lost. "Is everything well?" she asked Plaskett.

"Yes, miss. We are the best Scorcher company in the Army, and my men know their business." Plasket was breathing as heavily as she was, and there was char on his uniform and cap. Jennet finally saw the badge clearly; it was of a bird spiraling upward from a base of flames. A phoenix. Given that Scorchers, unless they were Extraordinaries, were not immune to fire, the badge seemed inappropriate.

"Where are we now, major?" she asked.

"We have passed the first line of the French. But the reserves are yet between us and our goal. And I fear I do not know Napoleon's exact location." Plaskett sounded almost distraught.

"Never mind, major, if you get me close enough to that eagle, I will find him." Jennet almost patted his shoulder in reassurance, he sounded so forlorn.

"Of course, miss. May I ask your name, miss?"

Jennet shook her head. "You don't need to know."

"Very well, miss." He did not sound disappointed even by such a blunt refusal. Jennet did not understand how anyone could believe Coercing adoration was anything but evil. She made herself stop dwelling on the many, many sins she would commit this day and instead reminded herself that she would stop a true monster or die trying.

CHAPTER 34

IN WHICH EVERY ROAD LEADS TO A SINGLE POINT IN TIME

They rested only a minute or two before continuing eastward through what felt like a strip of unearthly calm. Though the artillery now pounded ceaselessly away, they saw the enemy at a great distance, too great for the French to see them as a threat. Jennet no longer knew where she was. She had, aside from the German troops and her Scorcher allies, seen nothing of the Allied forces. But they had to be somewhere. And among them, somewhere, were those she had once hoped to call friends.

They must have been sent to another rifle company. Waldroup, now that he was in his right mind—she cringed inwardly to put her Coercion of him in those terms—would not wish to waste good soldiers, especially not a good officer like Falconer. Which meant they were out there, being shot at and in danger of cannon fire, and she should have been with them, but that was impossible. She deliberately refused to remember them again.

Major Plaskett suddenly ran faster, forcing Jennet to race to keep up. "'Ware Scorchers!" he shouted. "Be ready, men—*burn!*"

Once more, fire erupted in front of them, but this time it was joined by fire in their ranks. Jennet dodged a soldier who had become a greasy screaming pillar of fire, choked back nausea at the smell, and kept running. She wished more than ever to have some view of the battlefield that would tell her what was going on or if she were even running in the right direction. There was nothing but smoke and noise and tumult, and she was terrifyingly aware she had no weapon with which to defend herself. She had never longed so much for her rifle with its reassuring sword-bayonet.

Then they were again, miraculously, in a pocket of clear ground, with dying men in both French and British uniforms lying sprawled in every direction. Nearby, the charred standard and glowing golden eagle lay in the mud, still clutched by a French officer who lay on his back, his eyes staring. Jennet gasped to clear her lungs and choked and coughed on a stray wisp of smoke. To her astonishment, Major Plaskett remained at her side. He had lost his cap entirely, revealing a prematurely balding head. "Napoleon is not here," he shouted. Jennet could not tell if he had shouted because it was still noisy or because they were both deafened by artillery and musket fire.

"Then I will ask," Jennet said. She took three paces and fell to one knee beside the wounded French officer clinging to the eagle. His face was blackened, and blood covered his chest, but he still breathed. Jennet leaned over him. "Where is Napoleon?"

The French officer stared at her uncomprehendingly. Jennet realized she had spoken in English and repeated herself in French. The officer's face screwed up in pain. "I will not...tell an English...you may choke..."

Jennet braced herself for contact with his emotions. She felt them ebbing toward nothingness, a dwindling that always meant death was near. Without any subtlety, she made him love her, and repeated her question.

The soldier smiled. "Oh, my dear one. The Emperor is on the road south of here some two miles. But you will not abandon me, surely?"

Remorse struck Jennet's heart as it had not in all her other Coercions. "I will not leave you," she said. She held his hand and sat with him as the musket fire grew louder, listening to air bubble out of his damaged lungs until finally he drew no more breath.

"Miss, we must go, they are making another attack!" Major Plaskett said, in the tone of one who has spoken at least twice before already.

Jennet laid the dead man's hand across his shattered chest and rose. "South," she said, and surrounded by what was left of her escort, she ran once more.

It soon became clear that they had left the fighting behind, and Jennet slowed to a walk. "You should leave me," she told Plaskett. "What I do next, you cannot help me with."

"We could not abandon you miss, not if staying meant our death," Plaskett said in an injured tone. "And there will yet be others to fight."

Jennet hated the idea of more of these brave men dying for her sake. But she dared not release the Scorchers, who would likely be infuriated when they were free of Coercion. She could not fight them and Napoleon and whichever of Napoleon's officers remained. "Very well," she said.

They marched up a hill, from which, if Jennet looked back, she could see the fighting. From this distance, it did not look like much of anything, certainly not the kind of battle that ended with men's gory deaths. She turned back around as they came to the top of the hill, and froze.

Ahead, hundreds of French soldiers gathered in ranks, blocking the road. Where they had come from and why they were there, Jennet did not know, but she could not help imagining them drawn up in position, waiting for her. She was indescribably grateful that Plaskett had not left her. Then she felt sick again. There was no way even Plaskett and his loyal Scorchers could defeat this many enemy soldiers.

"That is the Emperor's standard," Plaskett said.

Jennet jerked into alertness. Just beyond the soldiers, a small white inn surrounded by trees stood next to the road, looking so peaceful, so normal, Jennet could not believe it was real. A few French officers waited in the yard. They had not as yet noticed the Scorchers. And planted next to the door of the inn was a battle standard. Jennet had seen many French eagles in her time in the Peninsula, but this would never be mistaken for a typical French standard.

She let out a breath. For a moment, she considered Coercing those French troops to her side. It would spare Plaskett and his men's lives, and it would spare many French lives as well. But Napoleon was there some-where, and Jennet could not count on him being unable to wrest those soldiers away from her. And whatever she did next, she would need all her resources to do it.

"I need to get past those soldiers, major," she said. "Can you do that?"

"We will do anything you ask," Plaskett said. "Ready, men? Then—have at them, lads, and make them *burn!*"

This time, Jennet held back so she was near the middle of the remaining Scorchers. She knew they were truly in danger when one, then another of her soldiers were flung into the sky by a French Mover, screaming as they hit the apex of their arc and then falling to strike the ground with a sickening thud. Plaskett had drawn his sword and was laying about him, snarling like a demon and setting little fires here and there. They were tiring, Jennet realized, and that meant she needed to move faster.

She shoved her way through the battle, inciting fear when she could not pass any other way, and to her surprise made it into the clear without injury. Panting, she kept running until she neared the inn. The officers she had seen had only just drawn swords and looked ready to enter the fight themselves. Jennet had not realized how fast that encounter had gone, even though she had fought in many battles and knew well that time meant nothing when you were facing down a foe.

The officers turned puzzled gazes on Jennet. One of them brought up his sword for a killing blow. Jennet grabbed hold of his emotions and prepared to terrify him. And a voice from behind the men said, "No, let her pass."

The officer lowered his sword immediately and stepped aside. Jennet watched the speaker's approach. It was the man she had seen outside Troyes, the one with the grey horse. He was shorter than she had realized, though not truly short; when he drew near, Jennet realized they were of a height. He had his hat tucked under his arm, and his dark hair, the same color as Jennet's, was slightly tousled. The mad notion that they might be mistaken for father and daughter crossed Jennet's mind, but she found it impossible to laugh.

"I remember you," Napoleon said. "Near Troyes."

"Yes," Jennet said, and could not imagine what else to say.

"You surprised me," Napoleon continued. "I have never encountered another like me. An Extraordinary, you understand—small Coercers are like millet seed in France. But you fled rather than approach me. Why was that?"

"I was afraid," Jennet said. Lying seemed pointless, and she did not believe he could hurt her with the truth. "I had never met another Coercer of any kind, and I did not know what you would do with me."

"I suppose that depends on what *you* intended for *me*." Napoleon cocked his head back and squinted at the sky. "I can only imagine you have some ridiculous notion of stopping my reign of terror, given your rather dramatic approach. I take it you Coerced those men into following you?"

Jennet did not respond. Behind her, the noise of fighting had diminished, but she was afraid to take her eyes off Napoleon to see whether her Scorchers had survived.

"We won't go into our respective moralities, or whether it is acceptable for you to do in the name of Good what I have done to supposedly enslave a nation." Napoleon returned his gaze to her. "It matters little to me what you choose to do, as I accord you the respect I would myself. We are the pinnacle of talent, do you not see? Ours is a talent that can build countries —well, obviously it has."

"Or destroy them," Jennet said.

Napoleon's eyes widened. "The economy of France is booming, its laws are gradually liberalizing, and we have driven the rot of Bourbonism from the country's heart. What in all of that suggests destruction?" He shook his head. "I realize we have different perspectives. Let us set all that aside. I would like you to join me."

Jennet jerked in surprise. "*Join* you?"

"Of course! Your talent is yet young and undeveloped. I offer you an opportunity to exercise it to its fullest, openly and to the praise of men. You have kept it secret until now, have you not? That is abhorrent to me." Napoleon made a face of disgust. Then he smiled, and said, "Join me. Be my heir. I would have you rule the Empire when I am gone."

Jennet felt as if he had punched her in the chest. When she regained control of herself, she said, "You cannot be serious."

"I am always serious on matters of statecraft. This war will be over soon, the back of the British resistance broken. I will teach you the subtleties of Coercion so you may maintain what I have won."

There was a ringing in Jennet's ears as if she still was not breathing properly. He could not be offering her—*her*—control of a nation! It was a trick.

"Imagine it," Napoleon was saying. "You will have your pick of advisors, your pick of lovers—the wealthy and powerful of Europe will bow before you—no more slaving in obscurity or bowing before your inferiors. I will take great joy in having you by my side."

Jennet's mind caught on part of his speech. "Lovers?"

Napoleon's smile became warmer and more amused. "You need not even Coerce them to your bed. Men, or women, as you choose. Great talent is a powerful aphrodisiac."

In that moment, she remembered kissing Falconer, how it had felt to believe even for a few seconds that he loved her and desired her. She still did not see Napoleon's trick, or why it benefited him to lie to her, but it no longer mattered.

"Do you remember Lady Ashford?" she asked.

Napoleon looked puzzled. "Who?"

Jennet let out a deep breath. "I had a feeling you would say that," she said, and wrapped her Coercion around his.

He had not been as unprepared as he seemed, for his Coercion was half a breath behind hers. In that first moment, they faced each other unmoving, like two wrestlers who enter the ring uncertain that a bout will actually take place. Then they collided, and Jennet felt dizzy, because as skilled as she was at manipulating emotion, Napoleon was a master. In quick succession, she felt anger and fear and love, each time breaking Napoleon's grip on her emotions before he could control her. And each time, it took longer to break his hold.

Breathless, she tried Coercing him, tried fear and then anger, but he slipped away so easily it seemed like he was mocking her. She was barely aware of his physical form, so she did not know if mockery showed on his face and she did not care. She tried adoration, knowing it would fail, then blocked his second attempt to make her love him.

Once more, she made herself breathe; her concentration was such that she had lost contact with her body and remained upright solely out of habit. He was too powerful for ordinary Coercion, and soon, if she did not find a solution, she would be his adoring slave.

There *was* only one other solution, one she had not attempted because it was difficult enough when one was not batting away someone else's powerful Coercion. But if she were doomed anyway, she might as well try. She fell more deeply into her sense of Napoleon's emotions, embracing them without trying to alter them, and set to work soothing each one.

She knew her efforts to stop him Coercing her were fading, for the new emotion of triumph emerged from the tangle of feeling at Napoleon's heart. She left it alone for the moment—if she removed his feeling of triumph, he might figure out her ploy—and pursued his anger, mild enough, and his pride, towering over the rest, and his pleasure at trapping her and his powerful sense of entitlement. As she worked, she could feel herself weakening, was tugged between fear and love so she wanted to weep, but if she did, she truly would lose.

She also could sense Napoleon was so intent on Coercing her he did not realize what she was doing to his emotions, for he put up no defense at first. Emotion after emotion fell to Jennet's attack, until finally that sense of triumph was all that remained. Then Napoleon's attack paused. Distantly, as if he were speaking through water, he said, "What are you doing?"

Jennet ignored him. She had no breath for speaking, and what little she could see was ringed in a red haze. Then Napoleon came after her in earnest. She felt his Coercion pressing down on her, twining around her emotions, but she already felt nothing he could manipulate, no anger, no fear, not even determination to succeed.

She wrapped her Coercion around his sense of triumph. Once more, she swung between the Coerced emotions he tried to impose on her, but now she knew they were false. Dizzy, she clung to what she knew was real: herself, tearing apart the most powerful man in the world's last vestiges of triumph and hope until, with a final cry she was not sure was audible, she wiped him clean of all emotion.

Napoleon sagged. Instinctively, Jennet put out a hand to keep him from falling. The erstwhile Emperor gazed at her dully, his mouth slack. Jennet withdrew from her sense of his emotions and sucked in a huge breath. The red haze cleared from her vision, and she blinked dry eyes and swallowed.

The nearest officers had not moved. Jennet was sure neither of them had realized the battle going on under their noses. Carefully, she gathered up her sense of their emotions and disentangled their feelings of adoration for their Emperor, replacing them with emptiness and confusion.

Both men jerked as if they had been suddenly poked with a stick. "What in—" said the officer who had tried to attack Jennet. "I don't understand. Why did I imagine this was the right course of action?"

The second officer looked at Jennet, then at Napoleon, and drew his sword. "I should rid the world of you," he growled.

Jennet stepped between him and Napoleon. "He is harmless now," she said, "and your efforts would be better spent stopping this battle. If that is possible."

Both officers stared at Jennet open-mouthed. "You cannot know that," the first officer said, and he, too, drew his sword.

"I can," Jennet said, "and I apologize."

She hated Coercing them a second time, after Coercing Napoleon's control from them, but not enough not to send them fleeing down the road in terror.

She eased Napoleon to the ground and took a step back—and into the point of someone's sword. "You foul doxy," Major Plaskett said. "You Coerced me and my men—you made us fight and die believing we loved you—woman or no, I swear I will kill you."

Jennet carefully turned around. A few French soldiers remained, backing away from the Scorchers with their empty hands held high in surrender. She had forgotten about both troops, and blessed her good fortune that Major Plaskett's men were as competent as he claimed. Some of the Scorchers looked confused, the rest angry. She guessed they had been freed from her Coercion either by Napoleon's manipulation or by her own inability to hold them as she fought that silent battle. "I believe that means Napoleon's Coercion will fade now that he is unable to maintain it," she mused.

The sword point wavered slightly. "Do you have any defense for yourself?" Plaskett snarled.

Jennet looked back at him. How strange, that an hour ago he had been nothing to her, and now she felt a tremendous affection for him and for his Scorchers. "None," she said. "None at all. I wish I could make amends, but you made all this possible, and I hope someday that will matter to you." With a tremendous effort, she gathered up every man's emotions, trying not to dwell on how much fewer there were of the Scorchers than when she had Coerced their adoration, and sent fear surging through them.

Major Plaskett's face reddened, his eyes bulged, and he cringed from her. Then he dropped his sword and ran, chasing after his remaining men and the fleeing French.

Jennet watched them go. Then she picked up Plaskett's sword and checked to see that it had not been damaged. She did not know what else to do with it, so she carefully stood it point-down next to the inn's door. Someone would find it and return it to him eventually.

Napoleon continued to stare dully at the ground. Jennet crouched in front of him. "Can you understand me?" she asked.

"I can," Napoleon said. "Not that it matters."

Jennet considered things she might say to him. Dramatic, eloquent things that might be quoted years or even centuries in the future. But she felt numb herself, not precisely apathetic, but as if she had accomplished something so tremendous nothing else could outdo it. "You're right," she finally said. "It doesn't matter."

Then she stared into the distance, imagining she could see past the hill to the distant battle. In a sense, she had not accomplished anything. France's generals and Marshals still fought for Napoleon's cause, and since she could hardly walk the length of the battlefield, removing their Coercion—she had no strength for such a thing even had it been practical—the loss of their leader would change nothing. She simply had to pray that Wellington was the general everyone claimed he was, that the Prussians had not been cut off from the allies' support, and that God was on their side, after all.

She dusted her hands off on her trousers. She had done what she had come for, and it felt strangely hollow. Likely no one would ever realize what had happened to Napoleon, and if they did, they would not attribute it to a simple soldier called Ned Graeme. She laughed softly to herself. Ned Graeme was dead, left behind in the fields of whatever this battlefield would come to be called. She wished with all her heart she had been able to say goodbye to the men she still considered friends. That would have been a true victory.

Without looking back, she set off south, away from the battle and toward she knew not what.

CHAPTER 35

IN WHICH THAT WHICH WAS LOST IS RESTORED

September brought cool weather to London, breaking the terrible heat. Jennet supposed it was not actually as hot as, for example, Spain in mid-July, but the many stone buildings of the great city trapped heat at the bottom of the manmade canyons and kept it clutched there throughout the interminable nights. But by September, the air remembered it was supposed to move, and the breezes off the Thames, as noisome as they were, also stirred the blood and made one imagine the scents of wood smoke and falling leaves in Hyde Park.

On this day, the weather was actually chilly, enough to warrant Jennet wearing her cape over her muslin gown. A few more weeks, and she would need a wool gown instead. She pinned her curls neatly back, tied her bonnet over the arrangement, and gathered up her key and pocketbook, both of which she kept inside the cape.

Her room was small and dingy, with the whitewashing having faded in places, and it would likely become very cold in full winter, but it was hers, rented at a good rate from a respectable yet impoverished gentlewoman named Mrs. Frobisher. "I don't take renters, dear, I host guests," Mrs. Frobisher had told her. "That makes it essential my guests be perfectly respectable, and you certainly meet that description."

Jennet had refrained from laughing. She had also refrained from

Coercing her landlady into a better rate, or a free one. She had not Coerced anyone in three months.

She walked the short distance from Mrs. Frobisher's establishment to the tea shop where she worked. It, too, was respectable and slightly shabby, catering to those who were not precisely well-off but maintained a certain standard of living. Jennet had stumbled on it early upon her arrival in London, just as the owner, Miss Geary, was in need of a hard worker, young, female, must be attractive, experience with serving a plus. She had not Coerced Miss Geary either.

Initially, she had kept track of all the times she had had opportunity or need for Coercion and did not use her talent. After a week, she had stopped. It surprised her how easy it was to interact with people without making them bend to her will, far easier than remembering how to live as a woman. She did not lie to herself that this meant she was forgiven, or that she was free to relax her vigilance; it simply reassured her that forgiveness was not impossible.

Inside the tea shop, she hung up her bonnet and cape behind the counter and straightened her hair. It had grown out more quickly than she had expected, but was still not quite shoulder length. That was still more than enough to require pinning. She had gained weight, too, and no longer looked starved in the face. Her lack of obvious curves, she could do nothing about, but the male customers of the tea shop seemed to find her attractive regardless. She smiled at the ones who flirted and learned how to dissuade the overly-attentive ones without resorting to her talent. She felt an odd sense of pride whenever she did this.

Miss Geary was just bringing out the first rack of cakes to the display. "Oh, Jennet, isn't it a lovely day," she said. Her voice always sounded musical, as did her accent, which Jennet had never been able to place. "Lovely, lovely, lovely."

"Yes, Miss Geary." Jennet stepped into the back to start the fire and boil water for tea.

"I never will fathom how you make that fire start, first time, every time," Miss Geary trilled. "You're not secretly a Scorcher, are you?"

Jennet laughed along with her. "It's a knack."

"Well, it's a knack worth having, so far as I'm concerned." Miss Geary swept past again with another tray. She would have been in hours before, making the little confections that made her shop so well-liked, though not quite a la mode. Jennet had been to Gunter's once, the most famous tea shop in London, and been unimpressed; it struck her as a place to see and be seen rather than anywhere one might comfortably have a cup of tea and a cake. Miss Geary's establishment was, in Jennet's opinion, far superior in quality. But it was better to have Miss Geary's tea shop be out of the fashionable way. Obscurity suited Jennet.

She found a rag and set to work wiping down the tables and chairs. Obscure the shop might be, but Miss Geary prided herself on her cleanliness, something Jennet agreed with. She continued her cleaning by wiping the counter and then the door knobs. Technically, the shop was open now, but in practice they rarely had customers before noon. Jennet used the time to chat with Miss Geary and the other shop girls, Hannah and Sophy, or just to sit in the back and watch the fire. It was a peaceful existence, if not one that could last forever. She had already determined to move on next spring. She had yet to decide what she intended to move on to.

She returned the rag to the sink in the kitchen and strolled back into the shop proper, looking at the display. Some of the tiny cakes had shifted when Miss Geary set the tray down, and Jennet neatened their order.

The bells over the door jingled. Jennet did not look up. "One moment, please," she said. The customer said nothing. Jennet heard a sharp *tock* as of an object being placed on the wooden counter. "I beg your pardon for the delay," Jennet said, straightening, and caught sight of the object.

It was her father's silver pocket watch.

Jennet snatched it up in both hands and stared at the customer. Falconer regarded her calmly, every bit as haughty and beautiful as she remembered. He looked odd, and it took Jennet a moment to realize he now wore captain's epaulettes. That, more than anything, made him seem a complete stranger, someone she had met in a dream once and never seen again upon waking.

"How did you find me?" she blurted out, taking a step back in momentary fear.

Falconer gestured at the watch. "I found an Extraordinary Seer who used that as a focus to locate you."

Jennet clutched the watch to her chest, feeling as if it had somehow betrayed her. "Just like that?"

Falconer scowled, and the haughty expression faded, leaving him looking more like himself. "No. It turns out to be remarkably difficult to find an Extraordinary Seer who will help a strange man locate a woman to whom he is not related and whose given name he does not know."

Jennet would have been amused at his irritation if she were not so filled with contrary emotions, fear and confusion and a terrible longing. She managed to maintain a neutral expression. She did not want Falconer to believe she welcomed his presence, particularly since she did not know why he was there. "And yet you found one."

"It took most of three months. I finally threw myself on the mercy of a Mrs. Rutledge of London, told her my whole sad story, and she took pity on me." Falconer gestured at the watch again. "I apologize for the delay. I hope you did not worry too much about its loss."

She had made herself stop remembering it months before. "No. Thank you for returning it." She could not understand why he had gone to so much trouble. What sad story? Deep within her heart, a little quiver of hope blossomed, and she crushed it into oblivion. He was not her friend, had never been her friend, and she needed to stop being a fool.

Falconer took a step closer. "I don't—"

"Jennet!"

Jennet, startled, turned hastily to face Miss Geary, who came out from the back room dusting her hands on her apron. "Jennet, I—oh, I *beg* your pardon." Miss Geary's musical voice suddenly swooped from one end of the octave to the other, and her lips curved in a coy smile as she examined Falconer. "If you are with a customer, it can wait."

"No, Miss Geary—that is—" Jennet looked helplessly at Falconer, who had returned to looking haughty.

"I would like tea, if you don't mind," Falconer said.

"Certainly, captain, certainly, we'll just..." Miss Geary grabbed Jennet's arm and tugged her out of sight as Falconer settled down at one of the little tables.

In the back room, Miss Geary fanned herself ostentatiously. "Oh, *my*, he is positively *edible!* Why did you say you were not with a customer, Jennet? He is *precisely* the sort of man we wish to serve here!"

"It isn't like that. That is, he is an old friend." Jennet managed only the slightest pause before *friend*, nothing Miss Geary would take notice of.

Miss Geary's eyes widened. "Jennet! I declare, you have been keeping secrets from me! An old friend who looks like *that*? Jennet, go out there immediately and entertain him!"

Jennet snatched up the teapot and a cup and saucer, belatedly realizing she should have put it all on a tray. By the time this realization struck her, she was setting the tea things on the table in front of Falconer and saying, "I never did find out if you prefer milk first or after it's poured, sir."

Falconer raised an eyebrow. Jennet wished she could sink into the floor. "I prefer neither, actually," Falconer said before she could fumble around correcting herself. In a lower voice, he said, "Then...is your name truly Jennet?"

The way he asked the question angered her, as if he expected her to lie. "Why would it not be?" she shot back.

Both Falconer's eyebrows raised. "I apologize," he said. "I meant only that I know you treasure your privacy, and I could understand you choosing to protect it with a false name. I will not judge you."

Feeling as if he had yanked her right to be angry from beneath her, Jennet swallowed another hasty reply. "It is truly Jennet," she said. "Jennet Graeme."

"Jennet. Ned. I see." Falconer sipped tea and smiled. "This is excellent."

"We do our best," Jennet said, and made her escape.

She nearly ran into Miss Geary when she entered the kitchen, as Miss Geary had clearly been eavesdropping at the door. "Tell me *everything*," Miss Geary said, her voice dropping dramatically. "How do you know him, and why are you not married?"

Her question hit Jennet an almost palpable blow. She took a moment to control herself, and said, hating herself for the necessary lie, "We were acquainted with one another in France. I have not seen him for months. He is uninterested in marrying me."

She realized the impression she had given Miss Geary when the woman's eyes and mouth formed perfect circles, and she said, "But you are in love with him! Oh, Jennet, how perfectly thrilling!"

"No, Miss Geary, please." Jennet drew in a breath. "It is not like that at all, truly it is not. There is nothing between us."

"I *beg* your pardon, Jennet, but that is simply impossible. Not with the way he looked at you." Miss Geary drew herself up to her full five foot one inch height. "And if he is here, it is surely because he cannot bear to be without you one moment longer!"

Jennet wished she could Coerce sense into someone rather than emotion. "He did not look at me in any particular way, Miss Geary."

"That is absurd, Jennet." Miss Geary made a shooing motion. "Go back out there and see if he wishes for refreshments."

Jennet did not believe anyone would like overly sweet confections at barely ten o'clock in the morning. She felt crushed between the Scylla of Miss Geary's romantic assumptions and the Charybdis of Falconer's mysterious arrival. But he was, however unexpectedly, a customer, and she had a duty. So she returned to his table.

She had forgotten she had left the teapot, and Falconer was engaged in pouring himself another cup of tea. He looked perfectly content, as if he might sit there all day drinking tea and watching passersby on the street. Jennet walked to his side, feeling more awkward than she had in her entire life, and said, "Is there anything else I can get you, sir?"

That time, "sir" could justifiably have been a politeness and not a mark of military rank, but Falconer smiled anyway. "You seem rather engaged at the moment," he said. "I would like to speak to you, but perhaps later? When your work here is finished?"

Jennet blanched. She had no desire to speak with Falconer privately, not when so much had passed between them that she wished she could forget. "I don't know," she said, stumbling over her words as if her tongue had swollen to twice its size. "That will be much later—"

"Oh, Jennet, dear!" Miss Geary trilled. Jennet, feeling relieved, hurried behind the counter, but Miss Geary continued in a loud voice, "I quite forgot yesterday, but I have no need of your services today. *So* foolish of me, don't you agree?"

Jennet, stunned, said, "But—"

"Now, dear, don't fret. Tomorrow will be soon enough for work! And now you may go for a walk, or visit a museum, or—there are *so* many things to do in London when one is free! Alone, or with a companion." Miss Geary shot a sly look at Falconer, who did not pretend he was not listening.

"Miss Geary, what of my wages?" Jennet said, feeling desperate.

"Oh, it was my mistake, so naturally I will compensate you! Now, you truly have no excuse. Run along, dear." Miss Geary smiled and made a little shooing motion with both hands. Jennet gave up.

She collected her cape and bonnet and let Falconer hold the tea shop door for her, exactly as if she was a young lady. Which, of course, she was. But walking beside him, even dressed as she was, she could not help remembering all those days on the road to Valenciennes.

They walked without touching one another through the streets of London. Falconer did not offer her his arm, though Jennet believed he likely should have, for the sake of good manners if nothing else. She was just as happy not to be touching him; her emotional state was in turmoil as it was.

She paid no attention to their path, caught in old memories that allowed for nothing so mundane as a planned route. So she was surprised when they ended up in a park, strolling beside couples and nurses chastising children for running too fast. The trees lining the road still clung to most of their leaves, but golden or red or coppery drifts made the trees seem like guardians of an ancient treasure.

"I have something else that belongs to you," Falconer said abruptly. He reached into his coat and withdrew a purse. "I believe it is all there."

Jennet accepted the purse and nearly dropped it when it turned out to be heavier than it appeared. "All of what, sir?" She mentally kicked herself again for her slip, but it was so easy, now that it was just the two of them, to fall into old habits.

"Everything you spent on our behalf in France. I told you I would not permit you to impoverish yourself." Falconer was not looking at her, a fortunate thing given that Jennet was sure she looked like a fish, eyes and mouth wide.

Jennet weighed the purse in one hand again. "This is too much."

"I fear I did not keep careful track. At any rate, it compensates you fairly."

She wanted to argue with him, but the knowledge that gently-born ladies did not wrangle with gentlemen over money in public stilled her tongue. "Thank you," she said, rather stiffly. This seemed a rather definitive way for him to declare he felt nothing for her, and she wished he would leave and never come back.

But he did not walk away. He did not bow and make his farewells. He simply continued to stroll by her side, ignoring the looks passing men and women—mostly women—gave him. Jennet's heart ached with longing and sorrow. "Is this why you came? To return my property?" she asked, hating that her voice shook.

"You disappeared rather thoroughly," Falconer said. He had his head bowed and seemed intent on kicking the few leaves on the pavement. "It was not until Napoleon was discovered after the Battle of Waterloo that I guessed where you had gone."

"Is that what they called it? Where is Waterloo?"

"It is, in fact, a few miles north of where the battle took place, but that is where Lord Wellington composed his official letter explaining the outcome, and that is the name that stuck." Falconer glanced briefly at her, then returned his gaze to his feet. "I would have thought you would want to be aware of the details. Of the outcome of what you did."

Jennet shook her head. "I read about the great victory. About the French surrender, and the gradual and ongoing...awakening, I suppose, of Napoleon's victims. And then I found I wished to stay as far away from war as I could get."

"I see. At any rate, there are many official stories about what happened to Napoleon. The currently accepted one is that he received a blow to the head that crippled his Coercion. Only a few of us know differently. Myself, and the Scorcher company who swore to having escorted you across the battlefield, and those who heard their testimony at court-martial—they were acquitted, by the way—and Lord Wellington himself, who proved remarkably open-minded about the matter. Though with Napoleon incapacitated, the true story became significantly more believable."

Jennet had no idea where he intended this line of conversation to go. "And?"

"And, nothing, I suppose. Your secret is safe. Those who know either believe there is no point spreading the truth, or feel you are due some consideration for a tremendous service to mankind."

"And which of those are you?" Jennet burst out. "No, do not say. You must have believed you owed me something, so you restored my father's watch and repaid my money, and for that, I am grateful. But surely we can have nothing left to say to one another. You know what I am. You know what I have done. I hardly deserve your forgiveness when I cannot forgive myself."

Falconer stopped walking. "And I cannot forgive myself for how you left us," he said, his voice low and intense. "I was stunned, of course, to realize what talent you had, and yes, I believed the worst of you, but I should never have assumed my initial reaction should be the end of it. You saved me—saved all of us—outside Troyes, and that alone should have made me consider the matter anew."

Jennet took a step sideways, out of the path of another pedestrian. "You were right," she said, her throat aching. "I Coerced all of you. I made Fosse and Sadler and Whitteney and Corwin like me so they would not look too closely at Ned Graeme. I made you all frightened so you would not be Coerced by Napoleon. I might have Coerced *you* a thousand different ways. Why do you care about the details?"

Falconer raised his head so his hazel eyes met hers. "Because I love you," he said, "and I would forgive you anything for the sake of that love."

Jennet's mouth fell open. "Impossible."

Falconer raised one eyebrow. "And are you so unlovable, then? I assure you I know my own heart."

"Do you?" Jennet said, despairing. "For all you know, I Coerced you to love me. No one who is Coerced ever knows it has happened. You can *never know*, do you understand?"

Falconer shook his head. "I know you did not."

Jennet wished she dared scream, here in this very public park. She had dreamed of hearing him say those words. She had never imagined being forced to tell him they were a lie. "And how is it you, sir, happen to be the only man in the world who knows he has not been Coerced?"

He ignored her bitter sarcasm. "Because you would not have Coerced me to love Ned Graeme."

Jennet, her mouth open to protest again, instead said, "What does that mean?"

Falconer closed his eyes and let out a deep breath. When he opened them again, the misery in his expression stunned Jennet, as if he faced the hangman's noose. "I lied to you," he said. "I have lied to you over and over again. I told you I discovered you were female in Châlons-sur-Marne. That was a lie. I knew you were a woman before we left Soissons."

Jennet's mouth fell open again. "You knew? But how?"

Falconer shook his head. "It doesn't matter. At first, I hoped only to protect you. I made you my servant not because I needed a scribe or a translator, but because I wished to draw you out of the line of march and keep you away from the fighting. But gradually, you captivated me—your quick intelligence, your sense of humor—and before I knew it, I loved you as a man loves a woman. And then, after we fled Napoleon, I kept you close because I could not bear being without you."

"Then, you...that cannot be why you insisted on sharing my tent," Jennet said.

Falconer nodded. "I told myself it was to protect you from sleeping beside men who did not know your secret, as if that made any sense. And then, in Châlons-sur-Marne, I had no real hope that ploy would work. I kissed you because I could not endure going to my death without having once done so."

The memory of those wonderful kisses made Jennet's heart swell. He had meant it, after all. "But you could have told me the truth then."

Falconer lowered his head so he was not looking at her. "At that point, I feared what you would say when you learned the extent of my lies. I knew how it looked, and I was a coward. So I pretended my knowledge dated from that moment, and I continued lying to you. That night in Cambray, after Madame Durand Healed Lady Ashford—she charged us nothing for the Healing because I blackmailed her. We had more than enough money for you to have a room to yourself, and I told you otherwise because I loved sharing a bed with you, being able to speak so frankly in private, listening to you breathe quietly as you slept. I would never have touched you, but that does not make my behavior right. I know it was inexcusable."

"It is impossible," Jennet breathed. "No, *you* are impossible. How dare you abuse my trust so?"

Finally, Falconer met her eyes. "I have never been more ashamed of anything in my life, Graeme. But do you see why I regret treating you so poorly when I learned of your talent? I have lied to you, misled you, used my position to compromise you, and what is a little Coercion beside that?"

Jennet could not look away from his eyes. She had never seen him look so desolate, so despairing, before. She was aware of men and women walking past, staring at them—what a peculiar couple they must make! And yet the passersby might as well be people in a dream.

Falconer shook his head again. "And that is why I know you did not Coerce feelings of love in me," he said. "I loved you long before you could have known it would be possible to make me love you. What I feel for you is real, and I regret not being open with you, where there might have been a chance of you loving me in return. Graeme, I truly apologize for what I have done, and I beg you to believe that however it might appear, I am guilty only of loving the most remarkable woman I have ever known."

His words rang in her ears, dizzying her. She heard herself say, "I thought you were as beautiful as a statue."

Falconer blinked. "I beg your pardon?"

"It was what you said, that you disliked being treated like a thing. I liked to watch you because you are handsome. I apologize."

He smiled, a warm, amused expression. "Men endure that sort of thing from the women they love better than from strangers, Graeme. So, you found me handsome?"

She looked at him sideways. "You know you are as beautiful as the day is long, sir."

Falconer choked back a laugh. He took her hand in his and held it, running his thumb along her knuckles. "I can appear any way I choose. What matters to me is, if you can admire a statue, can you find it in you to love a man? A man who, I might add, has just abased himself before you, opening his heart with no hope that his love will be returned?"

The touch of his hand made her shiver. It was suddenly difficult to meet his eyes. "I did not," she began, swallowed, and tried again. "I told myself I should not love you. That admiring you was safe, because you had no reason to care for me. But it was not your beauty I fell in love with—it was your compassion, and your strength, and how you never abandoned us. And then you kissed me, and from that moment, my heart was yours."

She made herself look at him, afraid despite his words of what she might see. His eyes were wide and astonished, and her fear made her say, "I swear to you I never Coerced you but twice, sir, and then only to make you afraid, never to force you to do what I wished."

Falconer smiled, and took a step closer. "Don't call me 'sir' anymore, Graeme. I cannot keep a straight face when the woman I love might well salute me at any moment."

Jennet giggled and put a hand over her mouth to control her mirth. "It would be highly inappropriate for you to call me by my given name, Captain Falconer, but it is nearly as bad for you to address me like a common soldier."

"I do not believe you could be called a common anything, Miss Graeme." Falconer took her other hand, sending a thrill through her. "May I call you Jennet if I ask for your hand in marriage?"

"What, here, sir? In front of all these people?" Jennet was sure her face might split from smiling so helplessly.

"I care so little for all these people," Falconer said, "that I am inclined to kiss you in front of them, and public decency can go to the devil."

"I could make them indifferent," Jennet said with an impish smile. "Then you might kiss me as much as you like, and no one will care."

"A tempting proposal." Falconer ran his thumb over her knuckles again, so lightly she could barely feel it. "But I daresay we can wait. I know I have memories that make the waiting easier."

He did not kiss her. But the gentle touch of his hand made her feel as if he had.

CHAPTER 36

IN WHICH JENNET'S HAPPY ENDING SURPASSES ANYTHING SHE IMAGINED

They spent the day on a leisurely walk through London, arm in arm. "I had almost given up hope I would ever find you," Falconer told Jennet later that day. "I was never so grateful as when Mrs. Rutledge told me you were here in London, and I need not find a Bounder to convey me all over creation."

"But you cannot have been on leave these many months, Thomas," Jennet replied.

"Only for the last two weeks. Before that, I shamelessly took advantage of the company's Bounder every week, an hour or two at a time, while I was also on company business."

Jennet's heart warmed at this declaration. "What company is that? Not the 3rd, surely."

"The 3rd has been officially disbanded." Falconer sobered, and his smile vanished. "It is considered lost, though some of its former members have returned, having thrown off their Coercion. Captain Lord Adair, unfortunately, is not one of them; he was reported killed in the fighting as the Grande Armée retreated from Waterloo. But Corporal Josephs turned up in Paris three weeks ago, having been captured on his ride there and released after Napoleon's defeat. I have command of the newly re-formed 6th Company, which comprises the remaining men of the 3rd as well as the 5th, which was decimated during the fight in Belgium."

MELISSA MCSHANE

Jennet remembered Appleton, and hoped he was not dead. "There are still many who remain Coerced."

"I had hoped you would know how long it takes for Coercion to end. That knowledge would give hope to so many."

Jennet shook her head. "Until I fought Napoleon, I was not even certain Coercion *could* fade. The best guess I have is that a year is more than long enough, and two weeks far too short. And that it varies by the individual. I hoped...I hoped my Coercion of my companions had ended well before our journey to Valenciennes."

"They assure me they do not care if it has, because they choose to believe their affection for you is natural. All of them are with the 6th, and Sadler has been made sergeant." Falconer squeezed her hand lightly. "I long to be able to return with you."

"And what of Veronique? Simon Appleton has not returned?"

Falconer shook his head. "Mrs. Appleton is with the 6th as well. The others persuaded her to remain, as they feel great affection for her as well. But I fear Private Appleton has met a dire fate. What is left of the 3rd disappeared after Waterloo, and we assume they moved south with others of Napoleon's elite forces. We have had no word of them in three months. Private Whitteney, too, has lost his wife, and remains inconsolable."

Jennet's sadness on Whitteney's behalf warred with her feeling that he was perhaps better off without Marie. "I promised Veronique I would help her find a trade that would permit her to support herself."

"And you will certainly be in a position to do so." Falconer smiled. "I anticipate with great pleasure returning to the Army with Mrs. Falconer by my side."

Jennet eventually steered them both in the direction of Mrs. Frobisher's establishment and ushered him inside. The foyer was empty, and Jennet heard no sign that anyone else was home. "You cannot come up, naturally, and my room is nothing special as it is. But—"

"Even this privacy is enough," Falconer said, and drew Jennet into his arms for a kiss.

She had believed the first kiss was only wonderful because of how danger had heightened all her senses. She knew now that had been a lie, because the feel of his lips against hers once more thrilled through her body, filling her with joy and a deep passion she felt might never be satisfied except by his touch.

Someone gasped. "*Miss Graeme!*"

Jennet disentangled herself from her love's embrace. "Mrs. Frobisher, I beg your forgiveness. This is Captain Falconer, and he and I are to be married. I am afraid my delight rather carried me away. Please excuse my lack of decorum—I assure you it will not happen again."

Mrs. Frobisher's hand covered her mouth, and two spots of color rode high on her cheeks. "Well, I," she began, took a good look at Falconer, and added, "that is, well, Miss Graeme, I was young once, too. I hope you are sensible of Miss Graeme's reputation, captain."

Falconer removed his hat and swept her a perfect bow. "I am, Mrs. Frobisher, and may I offer you my thanks in providing my bride with such admirable shelter?"

Mrs. Frobisher's agitation deepened, and she blushed harder. "Well, of course," she said. "And may *I* congratulate you both on your upcoming nuptials? When is the happy day?"

Jennet and Falconer exchanged looks. There was a light in Falconer's eye Jennet was sure matched hers. "Oh, sometime very soon," she said.

NEITHER JENNET NOR FALCONER HAD A HOME PARISH, AND FALCONER'S leave of absence was nearly up, which gave them very little time for the usual formalities. Jennet, as an Extraordinary, could likely have requested and got a special license, but the nature of her talent made it impossible for her to declare herself publicly. So, in the end, Falconer paid for a very expensive common license, and the two were married quietly five days after their engagement. Jennet had not truly understood the extent of the Falconer family fortune until Falconer told her casually what the license had cost, as if he had been buying apples at the market. It resigned her to the sum of money he had handed her as reimbursement—well, the money belonged to both of them now.

They had no time for a wedding trip, but Jennet had wished only to return to the Army. The 6th was stationed near Paris, in a little town where she and Falconer were billeted with one of the town's most prominent citizens. It was strange to be addressed as Mrs. Falconer, and even stranger to observe the riflemen walking the streets as casually as if they belonged;

she still remembered the tent cities outside Soissons, and needing poor dead Ensign Townsend's permission to enter the city.

The sense of disconnection persisted throughout the first two days, all the way until she walked downstairs one morning and found the drawing room full of green-jacketed soldiers. All of them turned to look at her as she stopped, startled, on the threshold. Then she felt as if she had forgotten how to breathe.

Sadler and Fosse set down the china miniatures they had been examining, knocking several others over that they did not attempt to right. Whitteney, who was looking closely at a portrait of a fat Frenchwoman holding a tiny poodle, now regarded her without a trace of a smile. Corwin's gruff face, clean-shaven for once, still looked as if he might be cast as the villain of a melodrama.

Words failed Jennet. All of Falconer's assurances that these men had forgiven her flew away into the distance. She swallowed. "I know I do not deserve your forgiveness," she said in a small voice, "but I hope you will believe me when I say how much I regret not having trusted you."

No one spoke. Jennet considered fleeing, but her feet were rooted to the floor.

Then Fosse said, completely straight-faced, "And aren't you the prettiest lass I've ever seen, Ned."

Jennet choked on a startled laugh. Smiles appeared on every face, even Corwin's. Sadler stepped forward and clapped a hand on Jennet's shoulder. "We're none of us unfamiliar with uncertainty, lass, and you had a mort o' reasons to fear being found out."

"And you never betrayed us, not in any other way," Whitteney said.

Jennet nodded and blinked wetness from her eyes. "You have always been true friends, always," she said.

"'Tis unfortunate the Army has lost such a soldier as you," Corwin said, "but I don't doubt as how you feel you've traded into a better position."

"And well you should," Sadler said. "You ought know, lass, if you've spent all your nights on end with a man, you ought let him make an honest woman of you."

That set off a roar of laughter, with Jennet laughing hardest of all.

A FEW DAYS LATER, JENNET SAT IN HER HOST'S UPSTAIRS DRAWING ROOM, trying and failing to set a straight seam. She muttered a curse under her breath.

Her companion giggled. "You should not use such language," Veronique said. "They will believe you have been corrupted by all these soldiers."

"So long as they do not believe I *was* a soldier, my reputation is secure," Jennet replied. She tore out her stitches and threaded her needle a fourth time. "I cannot imagine ever needing this skill. I shall pay others to sew for me."

"You were the one who insisted you needed an occupation," Veronique chided her. "And sewing is a useful skill, even for those with great fortunes." Infant William let out a soft cry, and Veronique nudged his rocking-cradle with her toe, soothing him.

"Yes, but I had hoped to find an occupation rather more in keeping with the skills I already possess." Jennet pinned the sleeve to the jacket and once more set her first stitches. "But I have so few that I may exercise in polite company."

"You are not bored, are you?"

Jennet shook her head. "It is not boredom, not precisely, just that..." She laid down her mending, sighing. "I spent so many years being useful, I wish for more of the same. No, not 'of the same,' but I wish to make a difference."

"You have already made more of a difference in the lives of every man and woman in France, I believe you have built up a wealth of spiritual credit." Veronique did not smile as she said this. Jennet knew, when Veronique became still and serious in that way, she was remembering her lost husband.

"I suppose that is one way of looking at it."

The drawing-room door opened. Jennet immediately brightened. "Thomas! Are you here to take me away from my mending?"

Falconer did not smile. "Pray, join me, Jennet, I have something to discuss in private. Forgive me, Mrs. Appleton."

Jennet rose, casting a quick glance at Veronique, whose English was much better now but still not perfect. Veronique looked puzzled but not unhappy at being excluded.

In the hall outside, Falconer took Jennet's arm. "I have need of your talent," he said. "A soldier has returned, and I am not certain he is telling the truth that he is no longer Coerced."

"I am happy to test his emotions," Jennet said, "but surely Veronique, as a Discerner, would be a better choice."

Falconer shook his head. "It is imperative that Mrs. Appleton not be involved. The soldier is Private Appleton."

Jennet's eyes widened. "Then let us go quickly."

Falconer explained the details as they walked down the stairs and out into the town—how Appleton had walked of his own accord into the temporary headquarters and claimed to be, not a deserter, but a victim of Napoleon's Coercion. "But he is not being truly forthcoming, and I dislike how reticent he is. It is possible he is lying, and wishes to find a way to sabotage our company on his Emperor's behalf."

"I can determine if he adores Napoleon easily. Thomas, what of Veronique, if it turns out Simon Appleton is lying?"

Falconer looked even grimmer. "I do not believe we should spare her the knowledge. It will be painful, but how much the worse if she discovers it later from some other source, after believing him merely dead? No, someone will have to tell her."

"You mean *I* will. Never fear, Thomas, I would rather it were I."

The temporary company headquarters was in an abandoned shop that had once belonged to a tailor. Jennet knew only that the man had been killed in the fighting south of Paris, and while she wondered that his heirs had not found a buyer for the business, she had little interest in discovering the truth. Now, as Falconer held the door for her, she marveled at how little of the original shop remained. There was one counter, where Falconer's aide transacted company business, but no bolts of cloth or dressmaker's models. The windows, however, were clean, and clear autumn light shone through them, illuminating the several officers and soldiers within.

Jennet's attention immediately turned to Appleton, who stood alone and unrestrained in the center of the room. He appeared much the worse for wear, a deal thinner than he had been and scruffy with three days' beard growth. His hands twitched ceaselessly, opening and closing in a way that suggested he did not realize they were moving. He looked briefly at Jennet when she entered, but immediately turned his attention on Falconer. "Sir, I have told you everything I can," he said, his voice hoarse and not at all as Jennet remembered it.

"We shall see," Falconer said coldly.

Feeling oddly shy, Jennet examined Appleton's emotions. She had not done anything related to Coercion for months, and it was strange to do so now, and with official sanction, too. His emotions were faint, suppressed by exhaustion, but still distinct. He felt discouragement, which made sense, and distant anger, probably that he had been interrogated unjustly as he saw it, and over all that an aching desire Jennet recognized immediately. She had not expected it, but it was a reassuring sight. Napoleon's peculiar emotion of adoration was absent.

She had not been listening to Falconer's conversation with Appleton while she was preoccupied, and now she drifted back into awareness. "—don't know what more you want from me," Appleton was saying.

"Some assurance that you are not withholding critical information," Falconer replied.

Jennet put a hand on his arm. "Captain, a word?"

She drew Falconer into the farthest corner of the room and whispered in his ear, "He is not Coerced. And I know why he is not being forthcoming. It is not a dangerous secret."

"Then what secret is it?" Falconer asked.

"He longs for his wife," Jennet said, "and I believe he is afraid she is lost to him. My knowledge of Private Appleton is that he is strongly committed to Army regulations, and he believes you will see his desire as unmilitary, possibly making him unfit for duty."

"That is ridiculous."

Jennet smiled fondly at her husband. "Thomas, you and I know that, but Private Appleton knows only that he has never told Veronique he loves her, and he believes he has lost that chance entirely. Love makes us all do ridiculous things, isn't that true, sir?"

Falconer sighed, but he was smiling. "Understood, Graeme. Will you return and prepare Mrs. Appleton for her husband's arrival?"

Jennet ran as fast as her skirts would permit back to the house and pounded up the stairs. "Veronique, you must promise to remain calm," she told the woman, who now held William in her arms, cooing to him.

Veronique's eyes grew wide and startled. "What is amiss?" she said, returning the babe to his cradle.

"Nothing. But, Veronique, Simon has returned."

Veronique's face paled to pure white, and she slumped against the arm of her chair. Jennet cursed herself for not being more sensible. She knelt, chafing Veronique's wrists and speaking quietly to her until she roused. Veronique still looked very pale, and her lips quivered. "I do not know why I fear," she said, "except that it has been so long, and perhaps he wishes to be free of me and the child."

Jennet was certain she should not tell Veronique of the longing she had perceived in Simon Appleton. "You must speak with him, and then you will know."

Veronique nodded. "Should I go to him?"

Jennet heard the front door open, and footsteps on the stairs. "I believe he is coming to you," she said, and stepped away from Veronique just as the drawing-room door swung open and Falconer entered. Appleton was immediately behind him.

Jennet backed away farther, but Veronique and Appleton had eyes only for one another. "Simon," Veronique whispered.

Appleton let out a tremendous sigh. Then he took three steps and sank to his knees before Veronique, taking her hands in his and pressing them to his heart.

Veronique gasped as if she had just discovered a startling secret. "*Simon*," she said again, with all the feeling a once-broken heart could muster, and burst out weeping.

Jennet edged carefully around their reunion and drew Falconer into the hall, shutting the door behind them. "That is a better ending than I ever imagined," she said.

Falconer put his arms around her and lightly kissed her forehead. "You did not weep when I told you I loved you," he murmured. "Perhaps you lack true womanly feeling."

Jennet arched an eyebrow at him. "Perhaps you have forgotten how I *did* respond," she said, and pulled him close for a warm, passionate kiss.

A FEW DAYS LATER, JENNET WATCHED AS THE MEN OF THE 6TH PARADED for inspection. Most of them were veterans, but recruitment had been strong ever since Waterloo, with men gladly volunteering to help destroy the last of the Grande Armée. Jennet personally believed this drive could not last, given that the Grande Armée was falling apart as Napoleon's Coercion failed, but she also could not deny that Napoleon's remaining soldiers fought like demons in defense of what they believed, and ordinary people suffered for it.

So she watched the inspection, idly picking out which were veterans and which were barely able to hold a rifle right ways 'round. At the far end of the field, Sadler barked orders in his best sergeant's voice. Jennet remembered Sergeant Hedley, who had been killed outside Troyes along with Ensign Townsend, and indulged in a moment's regret for all the lives Napoleon was ultimately responsible for taking.

Falconer, standing beside her, offered her his arm. "Would you care to join me, Mrs. Falconer?"

They walked along the lines of soldiers, who stood at varying degrees of attention, reminding Jennet of other inspection parades, other drills. For the first time, she did not miss those days, nor her place among the soldiers. Ned Graeme was gone; Jennet Falconer had a new life before her.

A low whisper startled her out of recollection. "What was that?" she said sharply, forgetting herself.

A soldier she and Falconer had just passed stood immediately more erect, his plump face suddenly shiny with sweat. Jennet was certain he had not intended her to hear *never expect* her *to dirty her hands, not the likes of her.*

Falconer looked as if he had heard the words too, because his jaw was rigid with anger and he was turning on the private with the appearance of someone who intended to rain down hell upon the deserving. Jennet looked more closely at the soldier and said, "Captain?"

"Yes, Mrs. Falconer?" He sounded furious.

"Captain, I do not believe these soldiers have had a proper demonstration of the use of their prized weapon."

Falconer half-turned toward her. Enlightenment was beginning to dawn. "And you suggest such a demonstration?"

"I believe it would be salutary, captain."

Falconer cast a swift glance at the offending soldier, who seemed uncertain of his imminent fate. "Then—be my guest, Mrs. Falconer."

Jennet walked back to the soldier and took the rifle from his unresisting hands. "Powder and shot, please," she said, and removed the pouch without waiting for a response. She gave Falconer her silver pocket watch. "Call time, sir."

Falconer's smile was wicked. Jennet knew hers matched his. "Your target, Mrs. Falconer?"

"Fourth post from the left on the western fence," Jennet said.

Falconer cracked the watch open, waited for a count of four, then said, "Time!"

Jennet had only anticipated him by half a breath. Her hands were already moving of their own accord, raising the powder cartridge to her lips, pouring powder, ramming home the shot. She slotted the ramrod into place and swiveled, pointing the loaded rifle directly at the offending soldier's face. "Duck," she said.

The soldier dropped, terror contorting his features. Jennet fired. A fence bounded the field on that side, two hundred yards away; the rifle ball struck the fourth post on the left with an echoing crack, sending splinters flying. Jennet lowered the rifle as a murmur sounded all along the line.

Falconer closed the watch. "Twenty-three seconds, Mrs. Falconer. You are slipping."

"I apologize for my slowness, sir," Jennet replied.

"I will overlook it this once." Falconer raised his voice. "That is the time you will aim for, gentlemen. A minimum of two shots a minute. Remember what you have seen here today."

Jennet extended the rifle and ammunition pouch to the soldier, who took them like someone in a dream. "Thank you for their loan," she said. Then she stepped closer and leaned in to where she could speak into the soldier's ear. "Never speak ill of another woman, recruit," she whispered. "You cannot know who she used to be."

The soldier's eyes widened again. Jennet smiled pleasantly and walked to where she could take her husband's arm.

"That was daring. And saved that man a flogging," Falconer murmured.

"And now they will all feel the need to prove they are better shots than a woman," Jennet said placidly. "Feel free to thank me at any time."

"I should not thank you for behaving so improperly, but as I find your handling of a rifle *extremely* attractive, you have my profound thanks, for that and for everything else."

The low, provocative tone of his voice made her shiver with delight and the awareness that they would share a room that night. "And I thank you," she said as they left the fields for the town's streets, "for never revealing my secret, even though you might have."

"I fell in love with you so rapidly, I hardly had time."

Jennet laughed at how wry he sounded, as if laughing at himself. "And for not hating me for the other secret."

Falconer guided her along a tree-lined avenue that rose gradually to the top of the hill overlooking the town. "I never hated you. I was devastated, at first, and then angry with you and with myself, but hatred, no. I loved you too much for that."

"You do not appreciate how profoundly deep hatred born from love can be. It is a terrible thing. It breaks my heart to see it."

"Have you ever Coerced anyone out of that state?"

Jennet shook her head. "It is akin to Coercing someone to love, and I swore years ago I would never do that to anyone. So I only observed, and hoped the person would come to his senses. Which he never did." She sighed. "Oh, Thomas. Sometimes I remember what I have seen and what I have done, and I wonder if there really is any hope for a talent like mine."

Falconer stopped and put his hands on her shoulders, gently turning her. "Look there."

Jennet looked. She saw the whole town laid out before her, with Paris an angular shape in the distance. "What am I to see?"

"Napoleon turned aside from Paris to divide the allied armies on the east," Falconer said.

"I know that, Thomas, we were there."

Falconer ignored her mildly sarcastic tone. "He never made it this far. But the reports from his freed generals and Marshals say he intended to return to enslave Paris once he had defeated Wellington. He would have overrun this town and Coerced everyone in it."

Jennet was unexpectedly breathless. "But he did not."

"He did not. Because someone stopped him." Falconer took both her hands in his. "This is your hope, Jennet. Because of you, none of these people will ever know Coercion. They, and France, and possibly even the world will live free because you chose to turn your talent to doing good instead of evil. How many people can claim that kind of victory?"

Jennet looked back over the town. "'And if you seek absolution, you will surely find it,'" she whispered. "Oh, Thomas."

For the first time in ten years, she wept.

THE TALENTS

The Corporeal Talents: Mover, Shaper, Scorcher, Bounder

MOVER (Greek τελεκινεσις): Capable of moving things without physically touching them. While originally this talent was believed to be connected to one's bodily strength, female Movers able to lift far more than their male counterparts have disproven this theory in recent years. Depending on skill, training, and practice, Movers may be able to lift and manipulate multiple objects at once, pick locks, and manipulate anything the human hand can manage. Movers can Move other people so long as they don't resist, and some are capable of Moving an unwilling target if the Mover is strong enough.

An EXTRAORDINARY MOVER, in addition to all these things, is capable of flight. Aside from this, an Extraordinary Mover is not guaranteed to be better skilled or stronger than an ordinary Mover; Helen Garrity, England's highest-rated Mover (at upwards of 12,000 pounds lifting capacity), was an ordinary Mover.

SHAPER (Greek μπιοκινεσις): Capable of manipulating their own bodies. Shapers can alter their own flesh, including healing wounds. Most Shapers use their ability only to make themselves more attractive, though that sort of beauty is always obvious as Shaped. More subtle uses include disguising oneself, and many Shapers have also been spies. It usually takes time for a Shaper to alter herself because Shaping is painful, and the faster one does it, the more painful it is. Under extreme duress, Shapers can alter their bodies rapidly, but this results in great pain and longer-term muscle and joint pain.

Shapers can mend bone, heal cuts or abrasions, repair physical damage to organs as from a knife wound, etc., make hair and nails grow, improve their physical condition (for example, enhance lung efficiency), and change their skin color. They cannot restore lost limbs or organs, cure diseases (though they can repair the physical damage done by disease), change hair or eye color, or regenerate nerves.

An EXTRAORDINARY SHAPER is capable of turning a Shaper's talent on another person with skin-to-skin contact. Extraordinary Shapers are sometimes called Healers as a result. While most Extraordinary Shapers use their talent to help others, there is nothing to stop them from causing injury or even death.

SCORCHER (Greek πιροκινεσις): Capable of igniting fire by the power of thought. The fire is natural and will cause ordinary flammable objects to catch on fire. If there aren't any such objects handy, the fire will burn briefly and then go out. A Scorcher must be able to see the place he or she is starting the fire.

Scorcher talent has four dimensions: power, range, distance, and stamina. Power refers to how large and hot a fire the Scorcher can create; range is how far the Scorcher can fling a fire before it goes out; distance is how far away a Scorcher can ignite a fire; and stamina refers to how often the Scorcher can use his or her power before becoming exhausted.

The hottest ordinary fire any Scorcher has ever created could melt brass (approximately 1700 degrees F). When she gave herself over to the fire, Elinor Pembroke was able to melt iron (over 2200 degrees F).

Scorchers are rare because they manifest by igniting fire unconsciously, in their sleep. About 10-20% of Scorchers survive manifestation.

EXTRAORDINARY SCORCHERS are capable of controlling and mentally extinguishing fires. As their talent develops, Extraordinary Scorchers become immune to fire, and their control over it increases.

BOUNDER (Greek τελεταχύς): Capable of moving from one point to another without passing through the intervening space. Bounders can move themselves anywhere they can see clearly within a certain range that varies according to the Bounder; this is called Skipping. They can also Bound to any location marked with a Bounder symbol, known as a signature. The room must be closed to the outdoors and empty of people and objects. Bounders refer to the "simplicity" of a space, meaning how free of "clutter" (objects, people, etc.) it is. Spaces that are too cluttered are impossible to Bound to, as are outdoor locations, which are full of constant movement. It is possible to keep a Bounder out of somewhere if you alter the place by defacing the Bounding chamber or putting some object or person into it.

An EXTRAORDINARY BOUNDER lacks most of the limitations an ordinary Bounder operates under. An Extraordinary Bounder's range is line of sight, which can allow them to Skip many miles' distance. Extraordinary Bounders do not require Bounding signatures, instead using what they refer to as "essence" to identify a space they Bound to. Essence comprises the essential nature of a space and is impossible to explain to non-Bounders; human beings have an essence which differs from that of a place and allows an Extraordinary Bounder to identify people without seeing them. While Extraordinary Bounders are still incapable of Bounding to an outdoor location, they can Bound to places too cluttered for an ordinary Bounder, as well as ones that contain people.

The Ethereal Talents: Seer, Speaker, Discerner, Coercer

SEER (Greek προφητεία): Capable of seeing a short distance into the future through Dreams. Seers experience lucid Dreams in which they see future events as if they were present as an invisible observer. They may or may not be able to recognize the people or places involved, so Seers tend to be very well informed about people and events and are socially active. Their Dreams are not inevitable and there is no problem with altering the timeline; they see things that are the natural consequence of the current situation/circumstances, and altering those things alters the foreseen event. Just their knowledge of the event is not sufficient to alter it.

No one knows how a Seer's brain produces Dream, only that Dreams come in response to what the Seer meditates on. Seers therefore study current events in depth and read up on things they might be asked to Dream about. Seers have high social status and are very popular, with many of them making a living from Dream commissions.

An EXTRAORDINARY SEER, in addition to Dreaming, is capable of touching an object and perceiving events and people associated with it. These Visions allow them not only to see the past of the person most closely connected to the object, but occasionally to have glimpses of the future. They can also find a Vision linked to what the object's owner is seeing at the moment and "see" through their eyes. Most recently, the Extraordinary Seer Sophia Westlake discovered how to use Visions attached to one object to perceive related objects, leading to the defeat of the Caribbean pirates led by Rhys Evans.

SPEAKER (Greek τελεπάθεια): Capable of communicating by thought with any other Speaker. Speakers can mentally communicate with any Speaker within range of sight. They can also communicate with any Speaker they know well. The definition of "know well" has meaning only to a Speaker, but in general it means someone they have spoken verbally or mentally with on several occasions. A Speaker's circle of Speaker friends is called a reticulum, and a reticulum might contain several hundred members depending on the Speaker. Speakers easily distinguish between the different "voices" of their Speaker friends, though Speaking is not auditory. A Speaker can send images as well as words if she is proficient enough. Speakers cannot Speak to non-Speakers, and they are incapable of reading minds.

An EXTRAORDINARY SPEAKER has all the abilities of an ordinary Speaker, but is also capable of sending thoughts and images into the minds of anyone, Speaker or not. Additionally, an Extraordinary Speaker can Speak to multiple people at a time, though all will receive the same message. Extraordinary Speakers can send a "burst" of noise that startles or wakes the recipient. Rumors that Extraordinary Speakers can read minds are universally denied by Speakers, but the rumors persist.

DISCERNER (Greek ενσυναίσθηση): Able to experience other people's feelings as if they were their own. Discerners require touch to be able to do this (though not skin-to-skin contact), and much of learning to control the skill involves learning to distinguish one's own emotions from those of the other person. Discerners can detect lies, sense motives, read other people's emotional states, and identify Coercers. Discerners are immune to the talent of a Coercer, though they can be overwhelmed by anyone capable of projecting strong emotions.

An EXTRAORDINARY DISCERNER can do all these things without the need for touch. Extraordinary Discerners are always aware of the emotions of those near them, though the range at which they are aware varies according to the Extraordinary Discerner. Nearly three-quarters of all Extraordinary Discerners go mad because of their talent.

COERCER (Greek τελενουναίσθηση): Capable of influencing the emotions of others with a touch. Coercers are viewed with great suspicion, since their ability is a kind of mind control. Those altered are not aware that their mood has been artificially changed and are extremely suggestible while the Coercer is in direct contact with them. By altering someone's emotions, a Coercer can influence their behavior or change his or her attitude toward the Coercer.

Coercers do not feel others' emotions the way Discerners do, but can tell what they are and how they're changing. Many Coercers have sociopathic tendencies as a result. Unlike Discerners, Coercers have to work hard at being able to use their talent, which in its untrained state is erratic. However, Coercers always know when they've altered someone's mood. Coercers do not "broadcast" their emotions, appearing as a blank to Discerners. Because Coercion is viewed with suspicion (for good reason), Coercers keep their ability secret even if they don't use it maliciously.

An EXTRAORDINARY COERCER does not need a physical connection to influence someone's emotions. Extraordinary Coercers are capable of turning their talent on several people at a time, and the most powerful Extraordinary Coercers can control mobs. The most powerful Extraordinary Coercer known to date is Napoleon Bonaparte.

HISTORICAL NOTE

This book is where the Extraordinaries series was always headed. The Battle of Waterloo is one of those moments in time that has captured the imagination of generations of readers, scholars, historians, and authors of fiction. For me, having established that Napoleon's military ability in my universe was aided by his ability to control the emotions and therefore minds of everyone around him meant I needed another Extraordinary Coercer to stop him. Making that Extraordinary Coercer a soldier provided tremendous scope for telling this story.

I took very little license with historical fact that I hadn't already established in previous books, specifically with how the existence of magical talent operates as a kind of leveler of class and gender. The biggest change has to do with Napoleon's strategy and tactics; in real history, he did not have nearly the resources he does here, and the maneuvering of armies that led to the final confrontation in Belgium is completely fictional.

I did plenty of reading on the final battle that ended up being unnecessary, given Jennet's part in that battle and how little of the conflict she sees. More useful was the reading I did on the 95th Rifles. For anyone interested in learning more about the legend and fact surrounding this much-storied army unit, I recommend Mark Urban's *Wellington's Rifles* (the US title) as a fun and readable account. I also drew heavily on Antony Brett-James' *Life in Wellington's Army* and, for more general information on

19th century British military life, *Wellington's Army 1809-1814* by Sir Charles Oman.

I originally envisioned Waterloo as the final volume in the Extraordinaries series, but as the writing progressed, it became clear that in the internal timeline I was going to hit 1815 well before all eight books were finished. Now, with the war over, the final two books will have to deal with the aftermath, as well as the consequences of all those soldiers coming home—and the question of what to do with female Extraordinaries whose horizons were broadened by being expected to do a man's work...

ACKNOWLEDGMENTS

As always, I am grateful for the valiant efforts of first readers Jacob Proffitt and Jana Brown, whose feedback helped me see where the emotional heart of the story was. When my failure to thoroughly research resulted in me gutting the middle of the book, Sherwood Smith generously guided me to see where I'd misstepped and provided valuable insight into the military mind. All remaining mistakes are my own.

ABOUT THE AUTHOR

In addition to the Extraordinaries series, Melissa McShane is the author of many other fantasy novels, including the novels of Tremontane, the first of which is *Servant of the Crown; Spark the Fire,* first in The Dragons of Mother Stone; and *The Book of Secrets,* first book in The Last Oracle series.

She lives in the shelter of the mountains out West with her husband, two children and a niece, and two very needy cats. She wrote reviews and critical essays for many years before turning to fiction, which is much more fun than anyone ought to be allowed to have. You can visit her at her website **www.melissamcshanewrites.com** for more information on other books and upcoming releases.

For news on upcoming releases, bonus material, and other fun stuff, sign up for Melissa's newsletter **here**.

facebook.com/melissamcshanewrites
twitter.com/mmcshanewrites

ALSO BY MELISSA MCSHANE

THE DRAGONS OF MOTHER STONE

Spark the Fire

Faith in Flames

Ember in Shadow

Skies Will Burn

THE EXTRAORDINARIES

Burning Bright

Wondering Sight

Abounding Might

Whispering Twilight

Liberating Fight

Beguiling Birthright

Soaring Flight (forthcoming)

THE NOVELS OF TREMONTANE

Pretender to the Crown

Guardian of the Crown

Champion of the Crown

Ally of the Crown

Stranger to the Crown

Scholar of the Crown

Servant of the Crown

Exile of the Crown

Rider of the Crown

Agent of the Crown

Voyager of the Crown

Tales of the Crown

THE LAST ORACLE

The Book of Secrets

The Book of Peril

The Book of Mayhem

The Book of Lies

The Book of Betrayal

The Book of Havoc

The Book of Harmony

The Book of War

The Book of Destiny

COMPANY OF STRANGERS

Company of Strangers

Stone of Inheritance

Mortal Rites

Shifting Loyalties

Sands of Memory

Call of Wizardry

THE CONVERGENCE TRILOGY

The Summoned Mage

The Wandering Mage

The Unconquered Mage

THE BOOKS OF DALANINE

The Smoke-Scented Girl

The God-Touched Man

Emissary

Warts and All: A Fairy Tale Collection

The View from Castle Always

Printed in Great Britain
by Amazon

78123938R00220